MB
1800-398-0197
meaningful Beauty 59.95
Save10

HOSTILE TERRITORY

LOOK FOR THESE EXCITING WESTERN SERIES FROM BESTSELLING AUTHORS WILLIAM W. JOHNSTONE AND J.A. JOHNSTONE

The Mountain Man
Luke Jensen: Bounty Hunter
Brannigan's Land
The Jensen Brand
Smoke Jensen: The Early Years
Preacher and MacCallister
Fort Misery
The Fighting O'Neils
Perley Gates
MacCoole and Boone
Guns of the Vigilantes
Shotgun Johnny
The Chuckwagon Trail
The Jackals
The Slash and Pecos Westerns
The Texas Moonshiners
Stoneface Finnegan Westerns
Ben Savage: Saloon Ranger
The Buck Trammel Westerns
The Death and Texas Westerns
The Hunter Buchanon Westerns
Will Tanner: U.S. Deputy Marshal
Old Cowboys Never Die
Go West, Young Man

Published by Kensington Publishing Corp.

WILLIAM W. JOHNSTONE
AND J.A. JOHNSTONE

HOSTILE TERRITORY

PINNACLE BOOKS
KENSINGTON PUBLISHING CORP.
www.kensingtonbooks.com

PINNACLE BOOKS are published by

Kensington Publishing Corp.
119 West 40th Street
New York, NY 10018

PUBLISHER'S NOTE: Following the death of William W. Johnstone, the Johnstone family is working with a carefully selected writer to organize and complete Mr. Johnstone's outlines and many unfinished manuscripts to create additional novels in all of his series like The Last Gunfighter, Mountain Man, and Eagles, among others. This novel was inspired by Mr. Johnstone's superb storytelling.

First Printing: July 2023
ISBN-13: 978-0-7860-4987-5
ISBN-13: 978-0-7860-4994-3 (eBook)

10 9 8 7 6 5 4 3 2 1

Printed in the United States of America

CHAPTER 1

MacCallister's Valley, Colorado

"Put your eyes back in your head, boy," Jamie Ian MacCallister said to his teenage son Falcon. "It's not polite to stare at a woman that way."

"Even one as pretty as her?" Falcon responded in an awed tone of voice.

"Even one as pretty as her," Jamie said.

But he could understand why Falcon was so interested in the woman who had just climbed out of the red-and-yellow Concord coach parked in front of the stage station.

She was easy on the eyes. *Mighty* easy on the eyes.

Tall, well-built, with ample curves, strong shoulders, and broad hips, she looked like she could work all day and still give a man all the loving he could handle at night. He could think such things because he was an old married man, Jamie told himself, and was, in fact, hitched to a woman just like that.

Kate was waiting for him out at the ranch, though, so all he could do was think . . . which was fine with him. They'd gotten married when they were both young, and honestly, he had never wanted anyone else.

"Now you're starin' at her, Pa," Falcon said with a mocking tone in his voice.

"No such thing," Jamie said as he turned away and swung a hand at the youngster's head in a light cuffing motion that deliberately missed. "Just naturally curious every time a stranger shows up in these parts."

He did have a proprietary feeling about the valley and this settlement, which was also called MacCallister. He and Kate had been the first white settlers around here. The town and the other ranches in the valley had grown up because Jamie and Kate MacCallister had dared to be pioneers. That daring was in their blood. They came from people who always pushed out into the unknown, ahead of the more cautious ones.

He and Falcon had brought the wagon into town today to pick up some supplies. Jamie put his hand on the strapping blond teenager's shoulder and steered him across the high front porch that also served the store as a loading dock.

Just before they reached the door, though, Jamie looked back over his shoulder and across the street to see that the new arrival had lifted her arms to take a couple of carpetbags from the coach's shotgun guard, who was handing down luggage from the vehicle's roof. The bags appeared to be somewhat heavy, but she handled them without much trouble as she turned away from the coach.

A man who'd been loafing in front of the stage line office, apparently waiting for the coach to roll into town, stepped up to her and spoke. At this distance, Jamie couldn't make out what he said.

Whatever it was, the woman replied and shook her

head. The man said something else. He wore a long duster that had seen better days and a battered old hat and hadn't made the acquaintance of a razor in quite a while. Jamie was just guessing, but he figured the *hombre* wasn't on regular speaking terms with soap and water, either.

The woman said something and tried to step around him. The man moved to block her path and reached for the carpetbags. She jerked back away from him.

Jamie said quietly, "Falcon, you go on in the store and wait for me there."

"Pa—"

"Do what I told you."

Jamie moved toward the steps at the end of the porch without looking back to see if his son was following his orders.

"I said, I'm perfectly capable of handling my own bags, *thank you.*"

Hannah Craigson tried to stay out of the reach of the man who had offered to take her bags. Her nose wrinkled at the smell coming off him. She couldn't control the reaction.

"Now, dadgummit, a purty lady like you hadn't ought to be luggin' heavy bags around in this heat," the man insisted. "Ain't no need for you to act stuck-up. I'm just tryin' to help you. Gimme them carpetbags and I'll take 'em right on down to Miss Annie's—"

"Where?"

A look of surprise appeared on the man's grimy, bearded face. "Why, Miss Annie's. It's the best cathouse in town. I figured that's where a gal who looks as fine as you would be workin'."

He reached for the bags again, and again, Hannah avoided him. But then she set the bags on the ground at her feet and said, "Wait just a moment, sir."

Now the man looked confused and stood there for a couple of seconds with his mouth hanging open before he said, "Huh?"

"You believe that I'm here to work in a house of ill repute?"

"Well, as nice-lookin' as you are, you could make a heap of *dinero*—"

She stepped forward and slapped him, her right hand flashing up to crack solidly against his whiskery cheek and jerk his head to the side. "How *dare* you make such an improper assumption?"

Ever since this man had accosted her, she'd expected the stagecoach's driver or guard or one of the hostlers to come to her assistance. Or even one of the townspeople loitering nearby. However, it appeared she was going to be forced to take matters into her own hands, and to Hannah, once an idea had formed in her mind, it was meant to be put into action.

So she'd slapped him as he so richly deserved.

Now, surely, he would leave her alone.

Instead, his features twisted in sudden anger, and he lunged forward, reaching out with both hands to grab her arms.

"I ain't lettin' no soiled dove haul off and wallop me like that," he said as he jerked her toward him. "Just for that, I reckon you owe me a little somethin'—"

The words broke off in a startled yowl that also ended abruptly as a huge figure loomed up behind the man and clamped both hands around his neck. He let go of her arms as the man who had him by the throat lifted him off his feet. His legs kicked futilely as he hung suspended in midair some six inches off the ground.

Then the giant who had taken hold of her scruffy, odiferous, insulting tormentor turned and flung him away, like a child discarding a no longer cherished doll. The bearded man landed in the street and momentum rolled him over several times before he came to a stop facedown. He tried to lift his head, groaned, and gave up, letting his face sag back down against the hard-packed dirt.

Hannah stared up at her rescuer in awe. His towering height, solid build, and wide shoulders made her think of a tree. He wore canvas trousers, a buckskin shirt, and a wide-brimmed brown hat with a tall crown that was slightly pinched. The butt of a heavy-looking revolver stuck up from the holster on his right hip. A bone handle protruding from a fringed sheath on his left hip told her that he carried a long-bladed knife there.

His face was rugged, deeply tanned, and weathered enough to indicate that he wasn't a young man, despite the almost overpowering air of vitality he gave off. The gray in his mustache and the thick brown hair under his hat told the same story.

He reached up with his left hand, pinched the brim of that hat as he nodded to her, and said in a deep, powerful, yet somehow gentle voice, "My apologies for the rude welcome you've received in our town, ma'am. Or is it miss?"

"It . . . it's miss," Hannah heard herself say. "Miss Han—"

Loud, angry voices interrupted her. They shouted curses that made Hannah's ears start to warm with embarrassment. The big man looked around at the four men who hurried along the street toward them. From the looks of it, they had just emerged from the saloon behind them.

The man who had accosted Hannah found the strength to raise his head again. Weakly, he waved a hand and called, "Get that . . . big hombre . . . fellas!"

The four newcomers, who looked to be cut from the same cloth as their friend, yelled more curses and charged even harder.

Hannah's rescuer started to turn toward them, saying as he did so, "Pardon me, miss. You, uh, might want to step up on the boardwalk out of harm's way . . ."

CHAPTER 2

Jamie wasn't surprised that the varmint who'd been bothering the young woman had friends. Coyotes tended to run in packs, after all.

He didn't recall ever seeing any of the men rushing at him, but that wasn't surprising, either. Drifters passed through the settlement pretty frequently. Most were good folks, but some were hardcases like these, usually on the prod for trouble, especially when they'd been drinking.

Jamie was willing and able to give them all the trouble they wanted.

The first man to reach him snarled and swung a fist at his head. Jamie leaned aside and let the punch fly harmlessly past him. He grabbed the man's extended arm and yanked down hard on it at the same time as he brought his right knee up.

One of the bones in the man's arm broke with a sharp crack as Jamie snapped the arm over his knee. He didn't know which bone had broken, but it didn't really matter.

The man screamed in pain and forgot about wanting to fight.

Jamie gave him a hard shove that sent him staggering back in the way of his friends. Two of them ran into him. One tripped and fell as he tried to recover. The other had to pause to push the fella with the busted wing out of his way.

But that left the fourth man with an unimpeded path of attack. He was big, too. Not as big as Jamie, but larger than most men. Not only that, he was also smart enough to have seen how fast Jamie reacted to the first punch thrown at him. So he didn't rush in but approached more cautiously, hamlike fists raised and moving back and forth a little in front of him.

"You may've busted Grover's arm, mister, but the odds are still three to one," he rasped.

"Come on," Jamie said. "I've got better things to do than listen to you flap your jaw."

That deliberate goading worked, at least well enough to prod the man into launching his attack before he was completely ready. His footwork was clumsy as he bored in and tried to feint with his left.

Jamie didn't bite. Instead, he drove his right fist straight ahead and felt the crunch of cartilage under his knuckles as they slammed into the man's nose. Blood spurted hotly across the back of his hand. The man's head rocked back under the blow.

He didn't go down, though. He swung a right of his own that barely got over Jamie's left arm. It clipped Jamie on the chin, not a solid punch but with enough force behind it to make Jamie take a step to his right.

His attacker lowered a shoulder and bulled into him. Jamie tried to plant his feet, but the man had too much strength and size. Jamie went over backward and crashed to the ground with the man on top of him.

It took a lot to knock Jamie MacCallister down. This was no ordinary bruiser he was facing, he realized. This hombre might actually be dangerous.

The man tried to ram his knee into Jamie's groin. Jamie twisted his hips so he took the blow on his left thigh instead. At the same time, the attacker groped for Jamie's throat with his left hand and hammered a punch into the older man's face with his right. The blow stunned Jamie just enough so that the man was able to clamp fingers around his throat.

The fella squeezed hard and lifted his fist, poised to come crashing down again. Before that punch could fall, Jamie reached up and clapped both hands as hard as he could against the man's ears. The man yelled in pain, and his grip on Jamie's throat loosened. Jamie grabbed the front of his shirt and heaved.

The man flew through the air but throwing him off like that caused Jamie to roll onto his left side. That put his back to the other men, and one of them took advantage of that to land a vicious kick in the small of Jamie's back. Jamie grimaced in pain, his lips pulling back from his teeth. One of the other men closed in from his front, booted foot raised to stomp down at him.

Jamie flung his hands up, caught hold of the boot that was coming toward his face, and rolled again, which threw the would-be stomper off his feet. The man landed hard on his back and lay there gasping with the wind knocked out of him.

The man whose arm Jamie had broken was the only one actually out of the fight. He lay curled in a ball, cradling the injured limb and whimpering. The one with the breath knocked out of him didn't pose a threat at the moment, but he would recover, probably pretty quickly. That still left two men upright and ready to do battle.

Not only that, the first man Jamie had grabbed, the one who had accosted the attractive young woman, had caught his breath by now and scrambled to his feet to join the attack. The three of them rushed at Jamie from different directions.

Even with those odds, he was confident that he would emerge triumphant from this clash. He figured he could take more punishment than they could dish out. But it was going to be a pretty rugged battle.

Then, with an angry shout, an ally suddenly appeared. Falcon tackled one of the men from behind. Although still a teenager, he was already a strapping, brawny youngster, and he picked one of the hard cases who was only a little bigger than him. The impact drove both of them off their feet.

That gave Jamie enough room to take a step back, forcing the other two to alter their angles of attack slightly. Jamie ducked under a punch from the largest of the trio, clubbed his hands together, and lifted them in a tremendous two-handed uppercut that caught the man under the chin. The devastating blow was powerful enough that it lifted him completely off his feet. He went over backward, and his legs kicked high in the air as he landed on his upper back and neck.

If he had come down slightly differently, the landing probably would have broken his neck. As it was, he lay there with his arms and legs twitching, so Jamie figured his spine hadn't snapped.

Jamie was only vaguely aware of that because he still had his hands full with the other man, who happened to be the long-bearded hombre who had started the trouble in the first place by accosting the young woman. He got close enough to pepper several punches into Jamie's face, but his scrawny form didn't have enough weight to give the blows any real power. Jamie shrugged them off, grabbed handfuls of the man's grimy shirt, and once again turned to pitch him through the air.

This time his back struck a nearby hitch rail, and his momentum bent him over backward, almost double. His legs went up and over with the duster flapping around them. He landed in a huddled heap and didn't move again.

Jamie turned to see how Falcon was doing against his opponent. Falcon had the man on the ground, straddling his chest, pounding rights and lefts into his face. Blood already covered the man's features, and he wasn't fighting back anymore. Jamie stepped closer, hooked his hands under Falcon's arms, and lifted the youngster up and off the man.

"Fight's over," Jamie said. "That fella's done in. You whipped him." He paused. "And you didn't stay in the store like I told you to."

Falcon twisted out of his father's grip and said, "All right, all right. I'm not goin' after him again. But Pa, you can't honestly just expect me to stand there and watch while five varmints are gangin' up on you."

"What I expect is for you to do what I tell you, at least until you're a man full-grown." Jamie shrugged. "But . . . I reckon I *am* obliged for your help. I could've handled all five of them by myself, but you speeded things up a mite."

Movement in the corner of his eye made him look around. The hard case who'd had the breath knocked out of him was back on his feet, circling wide around Jamie and Falcon.

He wasn't trying to sneak up on them, however. When he saw that Jamie had caught sight of him, he quickly held up both hands, palms out, in a gesture of surrender.

"No more, mister," he said. "Please, no more. I swear, we didn't set out to look for trouble—"

"You could've fooled me," Jamie snapped.

"Teddy there"—the man nodded toward the one had started everything and wound up flipping over a hitch rail—"he ain't the smartest fella when it comes to womenfolks. He just plumb forgets how to think straight whenever he's around a gal who's pretty enough."

Jamie glanced at the newcomer, who still stood beside the stagecoach with her carpetbags at her feet. To be fair, Teddy probably wasn't the only man in these parts who wouldn't be able to think straight with her around.

"Is that your way of apologizing to the lady?"

"Yes, sir!" The hard case snatched his hat off his head, held it over his chest, and looked at the young woman. "Ma'am, I am so, so sorry our friend caused trouble for you. I give you my word we'll ride herd on him from here on out and won't let him come near you, however long you're here. I . . . I hope you'll accept my heartfelt apology."

"What's your name?" the woman asked coolly.

"It's Reynolds, ma'am. Walt Reynolds."

"And your . . . friend there?"

"Teddy Keller, ma'am." Even though she hadn't asked him, he quickly supplied the names of the other three who had pitched into battle against Jamie. "Those other boys are Grover Appleton, Billy Bob Moore, and Ox Tankersley."

"Which one's arm did I break?" Jamie asked out of idle curiosity.

"That'd be Grover, sir."

Jamie reached in his pocket, dug out a five-dollar gold piece, and flipped it to Walt Reynolds, who caught it with deft instinct despite holding his hat.

"Not that he deserves it, but tell him to use that to pay the doc who tends to him," Jamie said. "I'm in the habit of covering any damages I cause, even when I'm pushed into it."

"Grover'll be much obliged, sir, once he stops hurtin' enough to know what happened."

Jamie jerked his head in a curt nod. "All right. Help your friends up, and then all of you get him to the sawbones. Take care *not* to cross my path again."

"Yes, sir." Reynolds clapped his hat on his head again. "I reckon you can count on that."

Jamie's own hat had come off during the fight. Falcon picked it up, knocked the dust off it, and handed it to his father. Jamie didn't put it on yet, but rather held it in front of him as he turned back to the young woman.

"I'm sorry for the rude welcome you got here, miss."

"Are you the local lawman, or perhaps the mayor?" she asked.

Jamie chuckled and shook his head. "No, ma'am. Just a citizen."

She looked around and said pointedly, "None of the other *citizens* seemed moved to come to my assistance."

"Folks tend to mind their own business," Jamie said with a shrug. "But some of them would have stepped in to help you once that fella laid hands on you, I can promise you that. We're not going to stand for things like that around here. I just happened to get there first."

"And I'm glad that you did. I appreciate your help."

"You were about to introduce yourself to me," Jamie reminded her.

"That's right, I was." She smiled slightly, which did a lot to dispel the rather severe expression that had been on her face. "My name is Craigson. Hannah Craigson."

"I'm Falcon," the youngster spoke up, grinning.

Hannah Craigson nodded to him and said, "Thank you, too, Mr. Falcon."

"Oh, it ain't Mr. Falcon. It's Falcon MacCallister." Falcon nodded toward Jamie. "Like my pa here."

"MacCallister?" the young woman repeated as she arched one auburn eyebrow.

"That's right, Miss Craigson," Jamie said with a nod. "I'm Jamie MacCallister."

"Jamie Ian MacCallister?"

"You've heard of me?"

"More than that, Mr. MacCallister." Hannah Craigson's chin lifted and excitement sparkled in her green eyes. "You're the very man I came here to Colorado to find!"

CHAPTER 3

Jamie stood there silently for a moment, with a frown creasing his forehead, as he took in what the young woman had just said. He was pretty sure he had never laid eyes on her before. Once a man saw Hannah Craigson, she would be mighty hard to forget. And he couldn't recall ever meeting anyone named Craigson . . .

Wait, he told himself. Something *was* familiar about that name. He couldn't quite come up with the memory, but maybe he *had* heard it at some time in his life.

"We haven't met before, have we?" he asked.

"No, we haven't, but you were acquainted with my grandfather, Tobias Craigson."

That name was familiar, too, but only vaguely so. Jamie shook his head and said, "I can't quite place him."

"You didn't know each other for very long. It was at the Alamo."

Jamie stiffened and caught his breath. That one word—*Alamo*—was enough to bring vivid memories flooding back into his brain. He had spent a brief period of time at the old Spanish mission in San Antonio de Bexar while it was besieged by the vast army of the Mexican dictator Santa Anna. At that point, Texas had not yet won its independence from Mexico; that would come later in the spring of 1836.

Defending the mission and slowing down Santa Anna's bloody advance through Texas were less than two hundred men, some of them native Texicans but most were valiant fighters who had come from other places to join forces with those battling for freedom. For a short time, Jamie had been one of them, despite being a very young man, until circumstances had led him elsewhere.

The Alamo was where he had made the acquaintance of Tobias Craigson, a rawboned farmer from Missouri who, stirred by reports of what was going on in Texas, had picked up his rifle and gone to fight Santa Anna. Jamie could see the man in his mind's eye now. . . .

All those thoughts flashed through his brain in a couple of heartbeats after Hannah said the name of the place. Jamie pushed the memories back a little as he looked at her and said, "You're Tobias Craigson's granddaughter, you say?"

"That's right. You *do* remember him, don't you, Mr. MacCallister? He spoke highly of you."

Jamie nodded. "Yeah, I remember—" He broke off as he frowned again. "Wait a minute. You said he spoke highly of me? How's that possible? He died at the Alamo, along with Bowie and Crockett and the others. Didn't he?"

Hannah sighed and replied, "Yes, he did. But before that dreadful tragedy happened, he wrote a letter to my grandmother and was able to get it out of there with some of the men who left before the old mission fell. It took a long time, but eventually that letter made its way to her."

Still frowning in thought, Jamie rubbed his chin, feeling the graying stubble scrape against his fingertips. What she said sounded reasonable enough, he thought, but he wanted to know more . . . especially about one particular thing.

"You said you came to Colorado looking for me?"

"That's right."

"And I reckon it has to do with something your grandfather said about me in that letter?" he guessed.

"Yes, it does. We should talk more. If you can direct me to a decent hotel, I'll engage a room, and then perhaps we can sit in the lobby . . ."

Her voice trailed off as Jamie shook his head. He pointed at Hannah's carpetbags and said, "Falcon, get the lady's bags and put 'em in the back of the wagon."

"Sure, Pa." Falcon stepped forward hurriedly.

Hannah held up a hand to stop him. "Mr. MacCallister, this isn't necessary."

"As far as I'm concerned it is, Miss Craigson. If you came all this way to see me, then the least I can do is offer you the hospitality of my ranch house." Jamie smiled slightly. "Believe me, my wife wouldn't be happy with me if I didn't ask you to stay with us."

"You don't even know what I've come here to discuss."

"It doesn't matter. You'll do it as our guest."

Falcon said, "You're wastin' your breath arguin' with him, miss. I know that better than anybody. And like my pa says, my ma will be even more set on being hospitable."

"Well, then . . . I suppose I should say thank you." She nodded. "I accept your kind offer, Mr. MacCallister."

Jamie said again, "Get the bags, son," and this time Hannah didn't stop Falcon from doing so.

Jamie put his hat on and offered Hannah his arm. She took it, and he led her across the street.

"We came to town for supplies, so it'll be just a little bit before we start back out to the ranch," he said. "I hope you don't mind waiting."

"Not at all. In fact, I'm just glad to be out of that stagecoach. It bounced and jolted so much, I swear I thought my teeth might come out of my head!"

Jamie chuckled. "Hate to say it, but that wagon ride you're looking forward to won't be much smoother."

"Perhaps not, but at least we'll be out in the open air. The atmosphere got a bit close in the stagecoach."

Jamie could well imagine that was true. Stagecoaches weren't his favorite means of transportation, either.

As they walked toward the store, he glanced around. He didn't see any sign of the men he and Falcon had fought with a short time earlier. He supposed they had taken their broken-armed compadre to get his injury tended to. And after that, more than likely they would head for one of the saloons to soothe their wounded pride, not to mention their bumps and bruises, with plenty of whiskey.

Jamie didn't care one way or the other what they did . . . as long as they stayed out of his way.

"I ain't never hurt this bad in my life," Grover Appleton moaned. He had to shift his right arm a little as he reached with his left hand for the glass on the table in front of him. It was half full of amber liquid. Grover tossed it back and licked his lips, then set the empty glass on the table and said, "Somebody pour me another."

"We ain't waitin' on you hand and foot just 'cause you got a busted wing," Teddy Keller growled. "You shouldn't've got close enough to that big hombre for him to grab you like that."

Grover scowled and said, "I noticed he was tossin' you around pretty good. Sort of like a rag doll, in fact."

Teddy's lips peeled back from his teeth as he leaned forward to glare across the table at Grover. "The son of a buck took me by surprise, that's all. I never got a chance to put up a real fight, or things'd've been different."

Ox Tankersley laughed, a low, rumbling sound. "From what I've heard, you got in some good licks, Teddy. They just didn't amount to much, that's all, because you ain't much of a brawler."

"Is that so? Well, he sure laid *you* out cold—"

"Why don't you boys quit your wrangling?" Walt Reynolds suggested. He was leaning back in his chair, cradling a glass of whiskey in both hands. He studied the way the light shifted on the fiery liquid as he rolled the glass back and forth slightly. Sounding a little distracted, he went on, "We got whipped good an' proper, that's all. It happens."

"Not by one man it don't," Ox protested.

Billy Bob Moore spoke up, his voice distorted by lips swollen and puffy from the pounding they'd received. He had two black eyes, too. "It weren't just one man. That fella who tackled me helped."

"Yeah, he walloped the stuffin' out of you," Ox said. "And he was just a kid."

"He didn't hit like no kid."

Walt stopped studying the whiskey and drank it instead. He looked around the table at the other four men. They all bore the marks of battle, but Billy Bob and Grover appeared to be in the worst shape.

Grover would win that contest because he had a broken arm. The doctor had set it, splinted it, wrapped it up, and given Grover a sling in which to keep his arm so it would stay still and heal. The break was a clean one, according to the doc, a few inches below the elbow. If Grover took care of it properly, he stood a good chance of regaining full use of the arm. He wouldn't be fighting or drawing a gun for a couple of months, though. He wasn't even supposed to ride for a least a week.

The five saddle tramps sat at a round table in a rear alcove in the saloon. The mostly full bottle of whiskey in the center of the table was the second bottle they'd ordered since coming in here. They might go through a couple more before night fell. They needed the booze to dull the pain of their injuries, especially Grover and Billy Bob.

Walt wasn't as big a drinker as the others, though, so he was in no hurry to refill his glass. He picked up the bottle anyway and spilled a few inches into Grover's glass. He wouldn't begrudge his friend whatever comfort he could get from the Who-Hit-John.

"The question now," Teddy mused, "is what're we gonna do about it?"

"Do about what?" Walt asked.

"What do you reckon I'm talkin' about?" Teddy demanded. "We got to settle the score with that big son of a gun!"

"And that other fella," Billy Bob added, mumbling through his swollen lips.

Walt said, "The other fella is the big one's son. And the big one is Jamie MacCallister. I asked around about 'em, to find out who they are."

Ox shook his head. "Can't be MacCallister. MacCallister's dead. Heard tell he got gunned, somewhere down along the Mexican border."

"No, it was up in the Rockies fightin' the Blackfeet, but he's dead, all right," Grover said. "I heard it from a fella who knew a fella who knew another fella who saw him get shot full o' arrows."

Walt said, "You may have heard those things, but the

hombres who told you didn't know what they were talkin' about. This town is *named* MacCallister. The whole valley's called MacCallister's Valley, on account of he settled it. Don't you think folks who live here would know who he is?"

"Well, I reckon that makes sense," Ox admitted grudgingly.

"I don't care if he's Jamie MacCallister," Teddy said. "I don't care if he's blasted Kit Carson! He's still got to pay for what he done to us, and for stickin' his nose in our business!"

"He didn't stick his nose in anybody's business but yours," Walt said, "and it wasn't very smart business, at that. And after that, *we're* the ones who jumped *him*. He and the boy were just fightin' back, defendin' themselves."

"Of course you jumped him. What else were you gonna do when he attacked me like that? We're pards, ain't we? Been ridin' together for nigh on to a year, haven't we?"

Teddy was right about that. They weren't exactly friends, but gents who rode the dark trails together had to stick up for each other because most of the time, the rest of the whole blamed world was dead set against them. That was how it seemed, anyway, Walt reflected.

"So what do you think we should do?" he asked Teddy.

"Get even, of course. Settle the score."

"By givin' MacCallister a whippin'?"

"I was thinkin' more like by givin' him a dozen or so pieces of hot lead."

"An ambush?"

Teddy leaned forward and pointed a bony finger across the table. "Now don't you start goin' on about how you don't like the idea of bushwhackin' folks, Walt. You've made that mighty plain."

"I don't mind breakin' the law when it's necessary," Walt said stiffly. "But I don't hold with gunnin' folks down in cold blood."

"Neither do I," Ox rumbled. "If I'm gonna settle a score with somebody, I want to do it up close, where I can look right in the varmint's eye when I'm doin' it!"

To punctuate his statement, Ox smacked his hamlike right fist into his massive left paw and ground it back and forth.

"All right, all right," Teddy said in an exasperated tone as he grabbed the neck of the whiskey bottle and refilled his glass. "We won't ambush him. But Jamie MacCallister's still got to pay for what he done." He looked at Walt. "You happen to find out where he lives while you were doin' your askin' around?"

"Matter of fact, I did. He has a ranch not too far from here. Big spread."

"Think you can find it?"

Walt shrugged. "Pretty sure I can."

"Then it's your job to keep an eye on him," Teddy said. "And when the right time comes . . . we'll make Jamie MacCallister wish he'd never crossed our trails."

Walt nodded slowly, thinking that MacCallister probably felt that way about them already . . . but for totally different reasons than what Teddy meant.

CHAPTER 4

Falcon had placed Hannah Craigson's bags in the back of the wagon and then taken it upon himself to start loading the supplies that the store's clerks had gathered for them. Jamie helped Hannah up onto the seat and then joined in the loading himself. It didn't take long to get it done.

"Climb in the back," Jamie told Falcon when they were finished.

"We might be able to make room for him up here on the seat," Hannah said.

Jamie waved away the offer. "No, there's plenty of room for the boy back there." He tried not to grin at the disappointed look on his son's face. Falcon would have enjoyed being crowded up against their comely visitor, no doubt about it, but being that close to Hannah Craigson likely would give him ideas he didn't need to be having yet.

Jamie, of course, was immune to such things, him being

an old married man and all. In fact, he told himself that very thing—sternly—as he stepped up onto the seat and took hold of the reins attached to the team of four draft horses.

As they headed out of town, Hannah said, "Should we go ahead and talk about what brought me here, Mr. MacCallister?"

"If you don't mind, I'd rather wait on that until we get out to the ranch. That way my wife can hear what it's about, too, and we won't have to go over it again."

"Is it that important that your wife know about it?"

"Yes, ma'am, it is," Jamie said. "Kate and I have been pulling in double-harness for a long, long time, and she's the smartest person I know. If what brought you here is something that requires any thought, I want her in on it from the start."

"How do you know it's anything that important?"

"I don't," Jamie said, "but a wagon's not really a good place to have a conversation."

Hannah lifted a hand to the hat that perched on her auburn curls as the wagon jolted over a rough place in the road.

"Still better than a stagecoach, though!"

Jamie laughed. "You've got fresh air and a view, all right."

And quite a view it was, too, with snowcapped mountains bordering the lush reaches of MacCallister's Valley on both sides. This was beautiful country, the loveliest and most spectacular Jamie had ever seen, and Kate agreed with him. That was why they had chosen to make their home in what was then a mostly untamed wilderness. They had wandered quite a bit after meeting while both were captives of the Shawnee, back on what had been the frontier in those days, and as soon as they laid eyes on this valley, they knew where they were meant to be, at last.

Less than an hour later, the wagon turned onto a trail that branched off from the main road, passing under an arched entrance made from heavy logs as it did so. A big letter *M* was burned into one of the logs over the trail.

The air was thick with the sharp but appealing fragrance of pines as Jamie followed the winding trail through stands of trees and open pastures. Horses and cattle grazed in those pastures. Anyone who knew anything about ranching could tell that this was a fine spread.

The wagon rattled over a sturdy bridge built of thick beams that spanned a swift, bubbling creek. Another bend in the trail brought them in sight of the ranch headquarters, dominated by the sprawling log ranch house surrounded by corrals, barns, a bunkhouse, and other outbuildings. The structures sat on a broad, partially cleared bench of land, behind which rose the heavily wooded, steep-sided slope of an impressive peak.

"That's it," Jamie said. "Home."

For a moment, Hannah seemed to have trouble finding her voice. Finally, she said, "It's magnificent. I can't imagine anyone actually living in a place like this. There's nothing like it back in St. Louis."

"That's why I've never been particularly fond of cities," Jamie said. "Nothing in any of them I've ever seen can compare to this."

From behind them, Falcon put in, "I still want to see some big cities, one of these days."

"One of these days, I reckon you probably will," Jamie said.

And those days might not be too far in the future, Jamie mused. The wanderlust was already strong in his youngest son. He knew that because he recognized the signs, having seen them in his older children. Falcon was the baby out of nine children and the only one left at home.

Going back even farther, Jamie saw in Falcon the same restlessness that had gripped him as a young man. Of course, the grim realities of life had demanded that Jamie grow up in a hurry, but he still knew what that urge to wander felt like.

For now, he would be glad to keep Falcon as close to him and Kate as he could, for as long as they could.

And he was a fine one to be thinking such things, he scolded himself, since even at his age, he was still prone to taking off for the tall and uncut whenever adventure called him. Seemed like life had a habit of dangling invitations in front of him that he had a hard time refusing.

He glanced over suddenly at Hannah Craigson as that thought crossed his mind. Was that why she was here? To reveal something that would send him off on another twisting, dangerous trail?

They would find out soon enough, Jamie told himself as he pulled the wagon to a stop in front of the ranch house and saw Kate waiting for them on the front porch.

He knew Kate's still-keen eyes would have spotted Hannah by now, and although Kate had never been the jealous sort, he was sure she would be curious why some strange, beautiful, auburn-haired young woman was sitting on the wagon seat next to him. She wouldn't be mad or anything, but she'd want some answers.

So did Jamie, so he set the wagon's brake lever, wrapped the reins around it, and stepped down quickly, circling the wagon so he could help Hannah down from the seat.

He wasn't fast enough to get in front of Falcon, though, who had vaulted over the vehicle's sideboards and was there already, reaching up with both hands to assist the visitor as she climbed down.

"There you go, Miss Craigson," he said when she had

both feet on the ground. "I'll get your bags and take 'em on in the house."

"Thank you, Falcon," she told him.

"Oh, it was my pleasure," he said, and Jamie thought, *I'll just bet it was.*

Kate was already coming down the porch steps to greet them. "Hello, Jamie," she called. "I didn't know we were going to have company. Who's this?"

Jamie didn't answer immediately. Instead, he took a second, as he always did when he'd been away from her even for a little while, to look at the woman he'd spent most of his life with. Kate MacCallister was every bit as lovely as Hannah, although her beauty was a more mature one that mixed in plenty of character and experience. Pale blond hair fell around her shoulders and down her back. She put it up sometimes, but Jamie loved it best when she wore it loose like that. It reminded him of when they had first met, all those years ago.

Years that had rested a lot lighter on her than they had on him, he had to admit. She looked almost young enough to have been one of their daughters.

Jamie cleared his throat and said, "Kate, this is Miss Hannah Craigson. She's visiting the valley from St. Louis. She came in on the stagecoach while Falcon and I were in town."

Falcon was passing by with the carpetbags, heading for the porch. He said over his shoulder, "She's here to see Pa. And there was a fight!"

Kate arched an eyebrow at both of those bits of information. She looked from Jamie to Falcon and back to her husband again.

"The two of you do look a little rumpled," she said. "And I'm very glad to meet you, Miss Craigson. Won't you please come in?"

"Thank you, Mrs. MacCallister," Hannah replied. Her tone was cool, but only ever so slightly, as Kate's had been. Two women sizing each other up, Jamie thought. A natural reaction for females. But he knew better than to say as much, since more than likely it would get him a frosty look from Hannah and a wallop on the arm from Kate.

Instead, he followed the two ladies up the steps to the porch. Falcon had already disappeared inside the house with the carpetbags. Kate called after him, "Put Miss Craigson's bags in the spare room on the east end of the house."

"Yes, ma'am," his reply floated back.

"That room gets the morning sun over the mountains," Kate said to Hannah. "It's lovely."

"It sounds like it." Hannah smiled. "Everything about this country is beautiful." She paused. "Well . . . almost everything."

Jamie said, "If you're talking about those saddle tramps back in town, you're right about that. Nothing beautiful about them."

Kate looked over her shoulder at him as they went into the house. "What happened?"

"Some fella took it into his head to get forward with Miss Craigson when she got off the stage."

"At first he claimed he just wanted to carry my bags for me," Hannah said, "but when I told him that wasn't necessary, he became more insistent . . . and more insulting. I was forced to strike him when his comments became absolutely crude."

"And then he laid hands on Miss Craigson," Jamie added.

"And he's still alive?" Kate asked.

Jamie shrugged. "Was the last time I saw him."

"You must have been feeling particularly merciful today."

"Blood all over the street's bad for business," Jamie explained. "I don't like to cause trouble for the folks in town."

Hannah said, "Then that ruffian's friends attacked Mr. MacCallister. It was quite unfair."

"How many of them were there?" Kate asked her.

"Four!"

"They were outnumbered, all right." Kate looked at Jamie. "I suppose Falcon had to pitch in?"

"He didn't have to, but he did it anyway."

Kate tried to look stern, but a smile tugged at her lips. "I'm not surprised. Let's go in the parlor and sit down. Would you like some tea, Miss Craigson? There's a kettle on the stove already."

"In that case," Hannah said, "I'd love a cup. Thank you."

"I'll be right back," Kate said. "Please, make yourself at home."

They had been talking in the foyer. While Kate went down a hall toward the kitchen, Jamie hung his hat on a hook on the wall and then ushered Hannah into the comfortably furnished parlor.

"You have a lovely home," Hannah said as she looked around the room.

"That's Kate's doing, not mine. She's always been able to make anywhere she happened to be feel like home, even when it was just a little log cabin in the East Texas woods."

"That would have been when Texas was still part of Mexico? Before the revolution and . . . the Alamo?"

"Yes, ma'am." Jamie gestured for her to have a seat on a well-upholstered divan, then sank into an armchair across from her.

Kate came back carrying a tray with three cups on it. Two of the cups were dainty china and had tea in them.

The third cup was heavier and was filled with strong black coffee.

"I figured you might need something a little stronger since you've been brawling," Kate said as she handed the coffee cup to Jamie.

"Obliged," he replied, nodding. "It really wasn't that much of a fight, though. Nasty while it lasted, but that wasn't long." He sipped the strong black brew and smiled appreciatively. "But I'll never turn down a cup of your coffee."

Kate sat at the other end of the divan from Hannah. Both women sampled the tea, then Kate said, "Now, what is it that brings you to Colorado, Miss Craigson?"

"As your son mentioned, I came to see Mr. MacCallister."

That was a pretty straightforward answer, and Jamie noted that it made Kate's lips tighten just slightly. But her tone was still friendly as she said, "Please go on."

"Your husband and my grandfather were friends when they were both defenders of the Alamo during that notorious siege."

"Oh." Kate looked and sounded a little surprised. "That was a terrible time for Texas."

"But it ended well," Jamie said. "Those folks won their freedom and eventually got to become part of the United States." His broad shoulders rose and fell. "Time'll tell whether or not they might've been better off sticking with being the Republic of Texas."

He thought about what Hannah had said. He wouldn't have gone so far as to claim that he and Tobias Craigson were friends. Acquaintances, that was about as far as he would go. They had played some cards together, and talked some during long, tense nights when they'd been standing watch on the parapets inside the adobe wall that surrounded the mission and its outbuildings.

On those nights, they'd been able to look out into the darkness and see the vast sweep of hundreds of cooking fires from the Mexican Army encampment. Those fires had been visible proof of the overwhelming odds against the men holed up at the old mission.

Beyond the Mexican Army's lines lay the lights of San Antonio de Bexar. The Texicans and their oppressors had done battle over the town before and might well do so again before the struggle was over. At the time, everything was uncertain, even whether a fella would live to see the sun come up the next morning.

Jamie recalled looking at the campfires of Santa Anna's horde and then turning his head to peer back in the other direction, at the Texas prairie rolling away in unrelieved darkness. It was almost like they were at the edge of the world, he had thought, about to be pushed off into a bottomless abyss.

But even though he couldn't see them, he knew others were out there . . . settlers who just wanted to be left alone but were forced to flee from tyranny . . . fighters waiting for their chance to make a stand, being rounded up into an army of sorts by Sam Houston . . . uncounted men and women willing to risk everything they had for freedom . . .

And the men gathered here in the Alamo were the last line of defense between Santa Anna's bloodthirsty mob and those who would one day be called *Texans*.

It had been quite a time, he thought. Yes, sir, quite a time. But now almost twenty years gone.

Kate said to Hannah, "I take it your grandfather wasn't one of those who made it out of the Alamo . . . before it fell?"

"No, he wasn't. He was there for all of it . . . Colonel Travis's line in the sand, the victory or death letter, the final assault by Santa Anna's troops . . ." Hannah looked over at Jamie. "I'm glad you were able to leave before all of that, Mr. MacCallister."

"Folks came and went quite a bit at first," Jamie said with a shrug, "before the Mexicans surrounded the place and cut it off. If I'd known what was going to happen, I might have stayed." He looked at Kate. "But I reckon fate worked out the best for me, too. Sad the same can't be said for all the men who died there that morning in March."

Hannah's chin lifted a little as she said, "They died for a cause they believed in."

"They did, indeed," Jamie agreed.

Kate said, "So you came here to meet Jamie, just because he knew your grandfather?"

Hannah shook her head. "No. I have a letter he wrote to my grandmother while he was at the Alamo. I have it here, along with another document he sent . . ."

She reached into the reticule she'd carried ever since getting off the stagecoach. Jamie frowned slightly and sat up a little straighter. She had mentioned that letter of her grandfather's, but she hadn't explained that she had it with her.

And what was that other document?

She took two sheets of folded paper from her bag. Time had tanned the pages and faded the ink, but from where he was, Jamie could tell that the writing on the top sheet was still dark enough to be legible as Hannah unfolded it and spread it out on her lap.

"He mentions several men in the letter, Mr. MacCallister, and you're one of them," she went on. "Although he speaks highly of all of you, his best friend inside the mission seems to have been Colonel Bowie."

Jamie nodded. “Jim Bowie provoked strong reactions from the fellas who knew him. Some didn’t care for him at all, but most seemed to like and admire him. I know I did. And he and his brother sure designed a fine knife.”

His hand moved, seemingly of its own volition, to the bone handle of the blade sheathed on his left hip. He had carried a Bowie knife for years.

“After Colonel Bowie was injured and confined to his bed in a room in the chapel, Grandfather spent a great deal of time talking with him. They made plans for what they would do after the siege was over. The colonel invited my grandfather to take part in a business venture with him.”

Jamie nodded. By that time, all the men inside the Alamo must have known just how unlikely it was that any of them would make it out of there alive. But talking about those overwhelming odds wouldn’t have done any good. Men who were in a situation such as that, men who were almost certainly doomed, were more likely to pass the time as if they didn’t believe such a terrible fate would come to pass. Talking about future plans was as good a way as any to accomplish that.

“Colonel Bowie even drew up some papers regarding the venture,” Hannah went on. “Including a map that my grandfather made a copy of and smuggled out along with this letter.”

She held up the other sheet of much-creased paper. Jamie saw the lines and markings on it, although he couldn’t make out the details from across the room.

As he looked at the map Hannah displayed, more memories stirred inside him. Not memories of the Alamo and the desperate siege this time, but rather of stories he had heard since then.

Or rather, seemingly endless variations of the same story . . .

"It seems, according to what Colonel Bowie told my grandfather, that as a younger man, he had discovered an old Spanish mine, operated with slave labor from the Indians, during the time when Texas was still part of the Mexican colony owned by Spain."

Yep, Jamie thought, she was headed in exactly the same direction as he'd expected when she started brandishing that so-called map.

"The mine was full of a fabulously valuable lode of silver and gold, and Colonel Bowie was able to transport most of it away from there. The mine itself would be worth a great deal, but just what the colonel took away amounted to an incredible fortune. Bowie didn't reveal the location of the mine, only the fact that it was somewhere on the San Saba River, but he told my grandfather where he had hidden the cache." Hannah's hand shook a little as she lifted the map. "And this . . . this will lead whoever has it straight to that fortune." She swallowed hard and looked at Jamie. "What do you say to that, Mr. MacCallister?"

Jamie set his coffee cup aside on a small table next to the armchair and leaned forward, clasping his hands together between his knees. He looked solemnly at Hannah, who was watching him intently, and said in as gentle a voice as he could manage, "I'm sorry, Miss Craigson, but that's the biggest passel of lies I've ever heard."

CHAPTER 5

"Jamie!" Kate practically gasped, obviously shocked at her husband's rudeness to their guest.

Jamie held up a hand to forestall anything else from her for the moment. Hannah looked pretty surprised, too, and more than a little hurt.

"I meant no offense by that," he went on, "and I probably stated it badly—"

"I'd say that you did," Kate told him.

"But I just wanted to make it clear that you shouldn't get your hopes up about this," he went on to Hannah. "Folks have been talking about Bowie's treasure and the lost mine of the San Saba since almost right after the Alamo fell. I don't know exactly how long it took for the rumors to get started, but I know I started hearing them within a few months after the battle."

Hannah lifted the letter and the map and said, "Are you telling me that this is common knowledge? That someone has already found Colonel Bowie's hidden treasure?"

She looked and sounded like she was on the verge of emotional devastation.

Jamie shook his head. "Nobody's found the cache, as far as I know, probably because it doesn't exist."

"But Colonel Bowie *told* my grandfather about it!"

"Colonel Bowie spun a yarn to pass the time while he and the rest of that bunch in the Alamo were waiting for Santa Anna to make his move."

Hannah's jaw firmed with determination. "You can't possibly know that."

"No, I don't suppose I can," Jamie allowed. "Not for sure. But like I said, I've heard the rumor dozens of times since then, so he must've told the story to others besides your grandfather. There are almost always some differences, too, which isn't surprising because the colonel was probably using laudanum to help him with the pain from his injured leg. One of the most common claims is that the gold and silver were buried either inside the Alamo or somewhere around it. But treasure hunters have dug holes all over the area for almost twenty years now, and nobody's found a thing other than some old busted guns and bayonets from the Mexican rifles. Don't you think that if it was there, somebody would have come across it by now?"

"But it's *not* there," Hannah said. She waved the map. "It's here, at the location drawn on this map."

"There have been plenty of so-called genuine Jim Bowie maps floating around, too," Jamie told her. "Some of them are supposed to show where the treasure's hidden, and some show the location of the lost mine. But again, people have been searching for two decades and have never found either of those things."

Hannah stared across the parlor at him for a long moment and then began slowly shaking her head.

"I had no idea," she said, her voice hollow with disappointment now. "Living in St. Louis, I . . . I didn't know any of these things were going on, out here on the frontier. I was only a small child when my grandmother received this letter from my grandfather. I grew up with it being regarded as a cherished family heirloom. I wasn't even allowed to read it until . . . until about six months ago."

"What happened then, dear?" Kate asked. Hannah seemed to have won her sympathy.

"My grandmother sent for me," Hannah explained. "She . . . she knew she didn't have long to live. She gave me the letter and the map and told me to study them. She said that my grandfather had wanted her to have the gold and silver, but she'd always been too timid to do anything about it. She didn't know how she would have even gone about hunting for it. But there was a man mentioned in the letter who she thought *might* know how to go about it."

"Me?" Jamie guessed as his eyebrows rose.

"That's right. You're a well-known frontiersman, Mr. MacCallister. Even my grandmother had read about you. She suggested that you might be willing to help me carry out my grandfather's wishes and retrieve the treasure."

Jamie and Kate exchanged a glance. Hannah's story was pretty absurd, Jamie thought, but her voice had the ring of truth. Hannah clearly believed the letter and the map were authentic, even though he was convinced they were pure hokum.

Kate asked, "Why didn't your grandmother give the letter and the map to your mother? Why skip a generation?"

"My grandmother and my mother never got along well," Hannah said. "It's really as simple as that. But my grandmother said that I . . . that I have some of the same daring that led my grandfather to go to Texas and help fight for its freedom. I'd like to believe that's true."

That was the problem, Jamie mused. Hannah *wanted* to believe.

And he had to admit to a certain amount of curiosity himself. He said, "Do you mind if I take a look at those papers?"

"Of course not. I can't ask you to help me without allowing you to study them, too. Just handle them carefully." She smiled. "They're rather fragile."

Jamie stood up and crossed to the divan to take the two documents from her hand. While he was doing that, Kate asked, "Did your grandmother pass away?"

"Yes, just a week or so after she gave me the letter and the map. As I said, she knew her time was short."

Jamie scanned the letter, which was written in small, cramped script to get as many words onto one sheet of paper as possible. It professed Tobias Craigson's love for his wife, Mildred, and apologized for going off to get himself killed fighting a horde of Mexicans. It mentioned several of the famous men who were there—Bowie, Travis, Colonel David Crockett from Tennessee—as well as some of the others, such as Jamie, who hadn't possessed such notoriety. Craigson referred to Jamie as a brave, smart lad and expressed satisfaction that he had gotten out of the Alamo while he still had the chance. Jamie would amount to something one of these days, Craigson declared.

Then there was a brief paragraph about the gold and silver and how he and Colonel Bowie were going to work that mine on the San Saba River once the war was over . . . but if they didn't survive, he wanted his family to have the treasure, and Bowie was agreeable to that, which was why he revealed the location of the cache's hiding place. It all *seemed* reasonable enough.

Jamie had no way of knowing whether Tobias Craigson

actually had written this missive, but presumably Craigson's wife would have known his script. Jamie felt his forehead creasing in a frown as he asked himself why Craigson would have written such a thing if it wasn't true?

But there had been so many stories similar to this, and none of them had ever turned out to be factual. What were the odds that this one was?

Jamie slipped the letter behind the map and studied the markings on the paper. He recognized the rough shape of the Texas coastline and the lines drawn down at an angle from the upper left corner of the map to meet it that represented various rivers flowing southeastward to the Gulf of Mexico. He oriented himself more with some crosshatched lines that had the word *Bexar* printed beside them. San Antonio de Bexar, site of the Alamo. The line to the north of it would be the Colorado River, and then still farther north, the Brazos.

The letter *B* printed just above the line seemed to confirm that, as did the course of the river itself, winding northwestward and eventually splitting into several smaller branches that were also drawn on the map.

Seven fingers of the Brazos. Jamie recalled hearing that phrase from Texans. He knew what he was looking at.

And it convinced him more than ever that this map was a lie.

Between two of those branches of the river lay the letter *X*, gone over several times to make it darker. He turned the paper so that Hannah could see it, and as she leaned forward, he pointed to the *X* and said, "This mark here, this is where the treasure's supposed to be hidden?"

"It is," Hannah said with a faint smile. "The letter says that's what the mark indicates."

Jamie shook his head. "Well, it just can't be. This spot is right exactly in the middle of Comancheria!"

Hannah looked up at him blankly. "What in the world is that? That area is still part of Texas, isn't it?"

"Comanches," Kate breathed.

Jamie said, "It may be part of Texas as far as legal boundaries and lines on maps are concerned, but that doesn't mean Texas has any say over what happens there." He traced the river with his fingertip as Hannah watched. "This is the Brazos River. It used to be the end of civilization in Texas. I've heard tell that there's an army fort farther west now, and a few settlers here and there, but for the most part, it's still wild, untamed country. The folks who really own it are the Comanches."

"You're talking about Indians," Hannah said. "I think I've heard of the Comanches. Aren't they supposed to be extremely hostile?"

"Yes, ma'am, the Comanches can be downright savage when they want to be. They're also some of the best warriors there have ever been, and nobody can ride a horse and fight from its back any better than a Comanche." Jamie tapped the map. "Beyond the Brazos River is Comancheria . . . Comanche land. There's no chance Jim Bowie ever hid any gold and silver out there. He'd have been mighty lucky just to ride in and out of that region with his hide intact and his hair still on his head."

"Jamie . . ." Kate said with a slight warning tone in her voice.

"I'm sorry for being so plainspoken, Miss Craigson, but I want you to understand just how impossible it is that this map is right. Now, maybe Colonel Bowie really did tell your grandfather the treasure was there. I don't have any way of knowing about that. I'm not saying old Tobias was lying because he may have sincerely believed every word of what he wrote. I'm just saying the story can't be true."

She looked up at him with equal measures of hope and

despair warring in her green eyes and said, "But what if it *is* true?"

"Like I told you, people have been searching for years—"

"But not there," Hannah said, pointing to the map in Jamie's hand.

Jamie shrugged. "No, more than likely not. I can't say for certain that no white man's ever been foolish enough to venture up the Brazos to look for treasure that probably doesn't exist, but I never heard of anybody doing it." He thought about it for a moment, then continued, "Anyway, unless they had a map like this one, nobody would even think about the possibility of gold and silver being cached out there."

"And *that* is the only map. So the gold and silver could have been there all along, and no one would even know about it. They'd have no reason to search for it."

She was determined, Jamie had to give her that. "It doesn't matter," he said. "That country is swarming with warriors who like nothing better than killing any white folks they happen to come across. No amount of money is worth a man's life."

Hannah's chin jutted out defiantly. "I mean no offense, Mr. MacCallister, but that sounds like something that would be said by a man who already has plenty of money."

Jamie started to scowl, but he realized she was right. Not only was the ranch very successful and lucrative, but he had found mining claims himself that paid off richly. He would never hurt for money, although he still lived in a humble fashion, uninterested in the usual trappings of wealth. The risks of going after a fortune might look a lot different to him than they would to someone who had always struggled to get along.

Even so, he thought that whatever she was leading up to was a bad idea, so maybe it was time to pin that down.

"Just what is it you want me to do, Miss Craigson?"

"I suspect that you've figured that out already, Mr. MacCallister." She stood up and held out her hand. "If I could have my map?"

Jamie gave it to her. Part of him wanted to stride over to the fireplace and chunk it in there to put an end to this foolishness, but he didn't have the right to do that.

Hannah held up the papers and said, "This map will lead us right to the treasure. I'm certain of it."

Jamie started to shake his head. "I'm not going . . . Wait a minute. Did you say *us?*"

"That's right. Colonel Bowie wanted my grandfather to have the gold and silver, and my grandfather wanted my grandmother to have it. And *she* wanted me to have it, or else she never would have given me this letter and map." Hannah folded the documents and replaced them in her reticule, then looked at Jamie and said, "I'm going after that treasure, Mr. MacCallister, and I was hoping that you'd come with me . . . but one way or another, I'm going."

CHAPTER 6

"Hoorah!" Falcon exclaimed from the doorway between the parlor and the foyer. "A treasure hunt!"

Kate gave him a stern look. "Have you been eavesdropping out there all along, young man?"

"I put Miss Craigson's bags in her room like you told me to, Ma, and then unloaded all those supplies, but you didn't say anything about what to do after that." Falcon turned to Jamie. "Come on, Pa, we have to help her find that treasure."

"*We* don't have to do anything," Jamie said, "and you can head on out to the barn and get started on your chores."

"But Pa—"

"You heard me."

Falcon didn't look happy about it, but he went. As he left, though, he said over his shoulder, "I'll be a man full-growed one of these days, and then I'll do what I want."

When he was gone, Kate sighed and said, "He's right, you know, Jamie, and that's exactly what worries me."

"He'll be all right," Jamie said. "He's just a mite headstrong, like a young colt." He turned back to Hannah Craigson, who still stood there regarding him intently. "As for you, Miss Craigson—"

"Hear me out, please," she said.

She was a guest in their home, Jamie thought, so he supposed hospitality demanded that he honor her request . . . even though what she had in mind was just about the most crazy notion he had ever heard.

He nodded and said, "All right. Please, sit back down. I'll listen to what you have to say . . . but no promises beyond that."

She smiled. "Thank you. I really didn't mean to sound rude."

They all resumed their seats, and Hannah went on, "I was afraid from looking at the map that it might lead into unexplored territory—"

"That's putting it mildly," Jamie said, then shook his head. "Sorry. I shouldn't have interrupted you."

"You know a great deal more about this sort of thing than I do. I don't mind admitting that. That's why I was hoping . . . no, praying . . . that you'd be willing to help me."

"By taking you into the middle of those Comanche-infested badlands?"

"I wasn't thinking that we'd go alone."

That statement intrigued Jamie enough that he said, "Go on."

Hannah rested a hand on the reticule in her lap and said, "The map is pretty straightforward and clear about where the cache is located. I thought that if a well-armed group of men went straight there, recovered the gold and silver, and came straight back out, they might have a chance to make it. They might not even encounter any Indians."

Jamie shook his head. "Not likely. The Comanches

would probably know we were there as soon as the horses set foot in what they consider their domain. They likely have scouts out roaming around all the time."

"That's why I said the group would be well-armed, and I would also want to make certain they were all men experienced in this sort of thing."

"Indian fighters, you mean."

"Yes."

Jamie rubbed his chin as he thought. "And you'd pay these men by promising them a share of the cache, I reckon?"

"That's what I had in mind, yes."

"They'd need supplies, ammunition, things like that. Can you pay to outfit them?"

Hannah drew in a deep breath. "Actually, no, I can't."

"And that's where I come in," Jamie said, nodding.

"You would, of course, recoup whatever money you put into the expedition, plus a generous share of whatever we recover, once we return to civilization."

"There you go saying *we* again. What in the world makes you think it would be a good idea for you to go along on a trip like this?"

"I'm not turning over the map," Hannah said. "If I did that, there would be nothing stopping the men from taking the gold and silver and disappearing with it."

"You're talking about a group of fifteen or twenty hard-nosed hombres," Jamie pointed out. "There's nothing you could do to stop them from, well, doing whatever they wanted to."

And not just where the treasure—if it existed—was concerned. He hoped she understood that without him having to say it.

"I know. That's also where you come in, Mr. MacCallister. My hope is that you can recruit a group of individuals who will be at least somewhat honorable and trustworthy, and that you can assure they remain so during the journey."

Jamie looked across the parlor at her for a moment, then nodded.

"So, you want me to round up these men, ride herd on them while we travel into the heart of Comancheria, get you and them back out safely, and pay for the whole thing, to boot. Is that about the size of it?"

Kate, who had been listening intently, said, "Don't be rude to our guest, Jamie."

"I'm not trying to be rude. Just want to make sure that I understand."

Kate turned to Hannah and said, "It really *is* a great deal to ask, Miss Craigson."

Hannah sighed. "I know that. But I'm somewhat desperate. I need the money that gold and silver will be worth, even splitting it up into a number of shares."

"Why?" Jamie asked bluntly.

Her chin lifted again, a reaction Jamie had already come to recognize as a sign of her stubbornness.

"That is a personal and private matter, Mr. MacCallister. I must ask you to honor my request to keep it private. I can assure you, however, that my reasons are both valid and important . . . not to mention possessing a certain degree of urgency."

"And if I say no?"

Hannah swallowed hard but didn't back down. "I shall simply have to find someone else to take up the gauntlet."

"I'm not sure where you'd do that. Not somebody you could trust, anyway."

"That's why I've come all the way here to Colorado. As far as I can tell, all the other men Grandfather mentioned in his letter are dead."

"Yeah," Jamie said, "none of them made it out of the Alamo."

She shrugged. "But abandoning the idea simply isn't possible." She drew in a deep breath. "If I have to go by myself—"

"Now you're just being foolish," Kate said. "I don't wish to be rude, Miss Craigson, but you'd never survive such an attempt on your own."

"You wouldn't even come close," Jamie added.

Hannah looked back and forth between them and said, "But what do you do when you have no other choice?"

The bleak finality of her tone told Jamie that no amount of argument would persuade her to give up on the notion. He frowned, scraped a fingernail along his jaw, and said, "Let me think about it."

Hannah's eyes lit up. "You mean—"

"I mean let me think about it," Jamie said.

"In the meantime," Kate said, "you'll stay with us, of course." She smiled. "It'll be good to have some company for a few days."

"Not too long," Hannah said. "I can't delay if I'm going after that treasure."

"You said it yourself. If that map is right, then the only ones who know the cache is there are right here in this room," Jamie pointed out. "Well, and Falcon, too, I suppose. So it doesn't seem to me like there's any big hurry in going after it. Unless those reasons you mentioned earlier have some bearing on that."

Hannah frowned but shook her head and replied, "I suppose you're right. There's no hurry."

She didn't sound completely sincere about that, Jamie thought. There was more to this story than she was letting on, he decided.

And blast it, that just intrigued him that much more.

* * *

Falcon was happy to have Miss Craigson staying at the ranch, of course. Like any teenage boy, he enjoyed being around beautiful women. After his mother gave him a few stern looks, however, he stopped gazing at Hannah with such open admiration. His face still lit up with a big smile every time she spoke to him, though, or even acknowledged his existence in any way.

That night in their bedroom, as Kate brushed out her long blond hair, she said to Jamie, "Are you seriously considering going up the Brazos to look for that treasure?"

The unspoken implication of such a question from some women would be, *Have you completely lost your mind?* When Kate asked something like that, however, it was simply a question. She wanted to know what Jamie was considering.

"I'm afraid if I don't, she'll find somebody else who will," he replied. "Or who'll agree to it but then try to swindle her or worse."

"Or worse," Kate repeated meaningfully.

"Yeah. Most fellas on the frontier, even the most low-down skunks you can find, won't harm a respectable woman. And they'd die to protect her, too. But if you round up a bunch big enough and tough enough to head out into some place as untamed as Comancheria . . . well, there's a chance that some of them won't be trustworthy."

"Unless you're the one picking the men and keeping them in line."

Jamie shrugged in agreement. "That might be a big job, even for me."

"That was why I was thinking you might need some help."

A speculative look appeared in Jamie's eyes. "You know,

that hadn't occurred to me," he mused. "But come to think of it, this *does* sound like something he might be interested in."

"Do you have any idea where he is?"

"Not really. But I know a heap of places he might be, and I could put the word out. There's a good chance a message would get to him."

"That might affect the decision you have to make."

"Yeah, it might," he allowed.

Kate set the brush on her dressing table and turned on the stool where she sat to face Jamie. "There's something else we need to think about. If you do go, you know that Falcon's going to want to go with you."

Jamie nodded. "Yeah, that thought crossed my mind."

"You can't take him," Kate said. "I know he thinks he's old enough to go off adventuring with you, and heaven help us, he's probably getting close to that age . . . but not yet, Jamie. Not yet."

He smiled, went over to her, and rested a hand on her shoulder.

"Don't worry," he told her. "I feel the same way. That boy needs to stay home." He shook his head. "But he's not gonna like it."

"He doesn't have to like it," Kate said with a fierce note in her voice. "He's staying here, even if I have to hog-tie him."

Jamie chuckled. "And that might be what it takes to keep him here, too."

Kate drew in a deep breath and said, "We're talking as if you've already made up your mind to go."

"I haven't," Jamie said. "But I'd be lying if I claimed I wasn't considering it."

"It sounds like it would be quite an adventure . . . and quite dangerous, too." She laughed, but it was a slightly wistful sound. "Not that such a thing ever stopped you before."

Jamie put both hands on her shoulders then and looked down into her eyes. "If you're ready for me to stop galloping around all over the place and getting into trouble, all you have to do is tell me," he said. "I can stay right here and never budge off this ranch again, and that'll be fine."

She reached up with her right hand and rubbed his left arm. "That's not true and you know it," she said. "And I'd never stand in the way of you doing whatever you think is the right thing, Jamie. You know that, too."

"I sure do," he replied. He leaned down and kissed her, letting his lips linger on her for a long moment. When he straightened, he said, "I reckon I'll sleep on it."

"You can do other things in bed besides sleep, you know."

A grin stretched across his leathery face. "You're making it more difficult to think about traipsing off across Texas to probably run into a horde of bloodthirsty Comanches."

"Well, then," Kate said, "you'll just have to think about it later."

CHAPTER 7

At breakfast the next morning, Jamie looked along the big table in the kitchen at Hannah and said, "I've been pondering your proposition, Miss Craigson."

"Do I dare allow myself to hope, Mr. MacCallister?"

"That depends on what you're hoping for, I reckon. I'm leaning toward taking you up on it—"

Her eyes lit up. "That's wonderful—"

Jamie held up a hand, palm out, to stop her. "Hold on, I'm not finished. There are a couple of conditions we have to talk about before I agree."

"I'm prepared to negotiate." Her tone hardened slightly. "But I can give up only so much of the treasure."

Once again, Jamie got the distinct impression that there were things going on here she wasn't telling him. He didn't like that, and the feeling was almost enough to make him flatly refuse. But instead he said, "Those conditions aren't about the gold and silver. I don't care about that. If we find it . . . and that's a mighty big *if* . . . I reckon I'd take enough to cover what I've put into the trip, but I don't care about making a profit."

She gave him a puzzled frown. "What else can there be to negotiate?"

"You," Jamie said bluntly. "You're not going."

Her eyes widened. "Oh, but I am! I told you, Mr. MacCallister, I'm simply not going to turn over the letter and the map to anyone. Not even you."

"If you trust me enough to take you into the wilderness and bring you back out, you've got to trust me enough to come back to you."

"You intend to leave me here, then?" she asked, jutting her chin at him.

"I didn't say that. The settlement closest to where that map says the treasure lies is a place called Fort Worth. That's probably where we'd need to outfit the expedition. There'll be a hotel or boardinghouse or some place you can stay, so that once we come back out, it won't take long to reach you."

"You'd leave me in some squalid little frontier hamlet? Do you think I'd actually be safer there than riding with you and the other men?"

"I don't know much about Fort Worth," Jamie admitted. "But would you be safer there than way up the Brazos in Comanche country? Yes, ma'am, you would be. I can guarantee you that. In fact, I can guarantee that *no* place in Texas is going to be less safe than where that map says the cache is."

Hannah frowned at him for a moment longer, then sighed. "I'm starting to think I shouldn't have let you look at it. One glance was probably all it took for a man like you to know exactly where the treasure is hidden."

Jamie shrugged and said, "I could find the spot, more

than likely, or at least come close to it, but I'd do better with the map. I give you my word it would be safe with me."

Kate said, "My husband doesn't give his word lightly, Miss Craigson. If Jamie says it, you can believe it."

"I know that. My grandfather wouldn't have spoken so highly of him if that weren't the case. It's just that this is so important . . ." She thought for a long moment, then said, "You won't go unless I agree to remain behind and wait for you in Fort Worth?"

"That's right, miss."

"All right. I suppose if that's the only way I can enlist your help, I shall have to agree. You said you had two conditions—"

Before she could continue, Falcon came into the room with his hat pushed to the back of his head. When he saw Hannah, he snatched the headgear off and held it in front of his chest.

"Oh . . . ah . . . good mornin', Miss Craigson," he said. "I, uh, hope you slept well last night."

"I slept fine, thank you, young Mr. MacCallister," Hannah told him. Her smile made a bright red flush begin creeping up Falcon's face.

Falcon turned to Jamie and said, "I got the chores done, Pa."

Jamie nodded. "Good." Even though Jamie had a crew of hands who took care of most of the work around the ranch, Falcon had regular tasks assigned to him, too. By the time he was of age, he would know everything there was to know about running a spread such as this. He would be ready to take over.

But whenever Jamie thought about that day, an uncomfortable feeling stirred inside him and made him believe it would never come. Falcon would never run the ranch because he was just too blasted fiddle-footed to stay still long enough to do that. Whatever it was that made men want to put down roots, Falcon had been standing behind the door when the good Lord passed out that quality.

That was a concern for another day. Today, Jamie went on, "Sit down and eat your breakfast before it gets cold." He gestured at Falcon's place at the table, where a tall stack of flapjacks awaited him on one plate. Another plate piled high with bacon and eggs was beside it, as well as a cup of coffee. Falcon pulled out his chair, sat down, and dug into the meal with enthusiasm.

Even the presence of a pretty girl at the table couldn't put a dent in a teenage boy's appetite.

Hannah began, "As you were saying, Mr. MacCallister, your other condition for agreeing to go—"

"Pa, you're goin' after that treasure?" Falcon exclaimed. Without waiting for an answer, he went on, "You can take me with you!"

"Shush," Kate told him. "Eat your breakfast. If your father decides to help Miss Craigson, you won't be accompanying him. You have too much to do here, not to mention I haven't given up on your education."

"Aw, Ma, you've already shoveled as much book learnin' in my head as it'll hold."

"That's not true. Your brain can always expand to hold more."

"Well, it feels like it's fit to bust out already," Falcon muttered.

Jamie said, "I know you want to go off on an adventure, son, but not this time. It's too dangerous."

"Then you *are* goin'," Falcon said. "I knew it."

"Don't get ahead of yourself. Maybe I am and maybe I'm not." Jamie looked at Hannah. "That all depends."

"Depends on what?" she asked tightly. "What else is it you want from me, Mr. MacCallister?"

"That's just it. This other thing isn't really up to you, Miss Craigson. I'm not going unless I can convince a friend of mine to come along and give me a hand."

Hannah said, "That shouldn't be a problem. I plan to leave the recruitment of the other men in the party to you. Whoever this other individual is, simply offer him a share of the treasure."

Jamie leaned back in his chair and grinned. "Gold and silver won't be enough to get him to come along, plus there's the matter of finding him. But I'll tell you flat out, Miss Craigson . . . I'm not going into Comancheria unless Preacher comes with me."

CHAPTER 8

Hannah was in too big a hurry to wait around the MacCallister ranch for too long, so in the letter Jamie sent to St. Louis in hopes of contacting Preacher, he asked the old mountain man to meet them in Fort Worth. That way he and Hannah could go ahead and start for Texas. He could still call the whole thing off if Preacher wasn't able to rendezvous with them or if something else went wrong.

Also, by leaving now, he would remove temptation from Falcon, who was still upset about not being allowed to come along. The sooner they were away from the ranch, the sooner the boy would get over being left behind.

Jamie wasn't worried about Falcon trying to sneak off and follow them. He knew Kate would make sure that didn't happen.

A couple of days later, Jamie drove the wagon toward the settlement with Hannah on the seat beside him. One of the ranch hands rode behind them. He would take the wagon back to the spread once Jamie and Hannah had caught the southbound coach.

"I've been looking at the map in your office, Mr. MacCallister," Hannah said. "The one that shows all the western states and territories?"

Jamie nodded, quite familiar with the map that hung on the wall there. "What about it?"

"We're almost as close to our destination here as we will be once we're in Fort Worth," she said. "It would mean coming at it from the directly opposite direction, but why can't we mount our expedition here and do that?"

"Because that's not the route that's marked on the map," Jamie explained. "Bowie didn't go that way . . . if he went at all."

"You won't give up the idea that it's all just a fanciful hope, will you?"

"I reckon I'll have to see that gold and silver with my own eyes to be convinced," he admitted. "But to get back to what I was saying . . . Texas is a mighty big place, especially once you get out beyond the part that's been settled. If we rode down from this direction, we'd be liable to get lost, and we might wander around for weeks without a clue of where we are . . . or until we die of thirst or the Comanches get us. This job's going to be dangerous enough at its best. No point in stacking the odds against us even higher."

"Even if it means taking a roundabout route and wasting a great deal of time?"

Jamie shrugged. "Time's something we have plenty of to burn. Like we talked about, if the treasure's there, nobody else knows about it, and there's almost no chance of anybody just stumbling over it. If it's been hidden safely for the past twenty years, it'll stay hidden for another couple of months."

"You can't be sure of that."

"I'm as sure as I need to be," Jamie said. "Anyway, I'm not leaving Fort Worth without Preacher, and there's no telling how long it'll be before he shows up, if he does at all."

"This fellow Preacher must be quite an amazing individual, the way you talk about him."

Jamie grinned. "You could say that. He's been out on the frontier for more than forty years, ever since he was barely more than a boy."

"Then he must be an old man by now!"

"Preacher's got the years on him, all right, and he's traveled plenty of miles, too. But there's something about him that keeps him young. To look at him, you wouldn't think he was much older than me, if any." Jamie chuckled. "I joked with him once and told him that some Indian shaman must have given him a magic potion to keep him from getting old. He didn't deny it."

"So he has a great deal of experience with the Indians?"

"As much as any man alive," Jamie stated flatly. "I'm talking about experience fighting them, but he knows more about getting along with them, too. He probably has more Indian friends than he does white."

Hannah shuddered. "I can't imagine being friends with savages."

"Sometimes, savagery is just a matter of what you're used to," Jamie said. "I promise you, white folks do things that make Indians shake their heads and wonder what in the world is wrong with us."

"Perhaps. But I still say I wouldn't be friends with them."

"Well, you don't have to worry about that. Where you'll be staying, there in Fort Worth, there won't be many Indians around and the ones who are won't be hostile. You shouldn't have to have anything to do with them. And where the rest of us are going . . . I don't figure the Comanches will want to be friends with us any more than we want to be friends with them."

"I still wish you'd allow me to accompany you."

Jamie wasn't going to argue about that, so he didn't say anything. He just flapped the reins and kept the horses hitched to the wagon moving toward town.

Getting to Fort Worth from MacCallister's Valley wouldn't be the easiest thing in the world. The stagecoach line, which Jamie had helped found and finance, ran south to Santa Fe, where it connected with the Butterfield line that went east to Missouri. Jamie and Hannah wouldn't have to take it all the way to St. Louis. They would leave it in Arkansas and travel on to Fort Worth by wagon or buggy.

Jamie would have made the trip on horseback if it was just him, but he knew Hannah wouldn't be able to stand up to the rigors of such a journey.

After a while, Hannah said, "I do appreciate your help, Mr. MacCallister, but at the same time, I *am* sorry for taking you away from your family like this."

"I reckon if Kate's not used to it by now, she never will be," Jamie said. "I've always had a bad habit of wandering around and getting into trouble." He paused. "And if we're going to be traveling together, you might as well call me Jamie."

Hannah looked surprised. "That would be disrespectful, wouldn't it? I mean . . . you're so much older . . . I mean . . ."

That brought a laugh from Jamie. "Yeah, I'm old enough to be your pa, that's true. Maybe it would be best if we left things like they are. I'm Mr. MacCallister, and you're Miss Craigson."

"Fine." She looked off for a second and then back to him.

"Although, if we were going to be traveling companions long enough for us to reach Colonel Bowie's treasure . . ."

"You don't give up easy, do you, Miss Craigson?"

"No, Mr. MacCallister, I do not. And that's something I'm sure you'll learn about me."

Jamie figured he had a pretty good idea already.

"They got bags in the back of that wagon, Teddy," Billy Bob Moore said. "Where do you reckon they're goin'?"

"How in blazes should I know?" Teddy Keller replied. The five saddle tramps had reined in at the top of a hill to watch as the wagon with Jamie MacCallister and the Craigson woman rolled toward the settlement.

Walt Reynolds rested his hands on his saddle and leaned forward. "Looks to me like they're going on a trip somewhere. We'll just have to give up that idea of yours about getting even with MacCallister, Teddy."

"Like blazes we will!" Keller exclaimed. It was at his insistence that the five men had ridden out toward MacCallister's ranch today. Keller wanted to scout the place and start trying to figure out the best way for them to get their revenge.

Now it looked as if fate might steal that chance from them, no matter how determined Keller was, and to be honest, Walt Reynolds was all right with that. Tangling with Jamie MacCallister once was more than enough as far as he was concerned.

Teddy was going to be stubborn about it, though, just like he always was. He turned his horse and called over his shoulder, "Come on!"

Grover Appleton, his broken arm in the black silk sling, turned to Reynolds and whined, "Walt, do we have to?"

Loyalty to a pard was important, despite a man's personal feelings. Reynolds lifted his reins and said, "We ride with Teddy. Don't you want to get even with MacCallister for busting your arm?"

Appleton sighed and said, "I reckon so." He didn't sound completely sincere, though.

But he nudged his horse into movement as he and Reynolds followed Keller, along with Billy Bob Moore and Ox Tankersley . . . and all five of them followed Jamie MacCallister and the beautiful auburn-haired young woman.

CHAPTER 9

Hannah didn't like traveling on the stagecoach. Jamie knew that, and he didn't blame her. He wasn't overly fond of it as a method of travel, either. But it was the fastest way for them to get where they were going. Several long days followed, days spent rocking back and forth on the hard bench seat and breathing the dust kicked up by the team's hooves, which inevitably made its way into the coach despite the oilcloth curtains over the windows. The atmosphere inside the coach was made even more unpleasant by the company of assorted traveling salesmen, who brought with them lingering aromas of cheap tobacco and liquor and unwashed flesh.

Hannah bore up well under the hardship, though. Jamie could tell she was determined not to let anything stand in the way between her and that treasure she believed in so fervently.

They disembarked from the coach at a small town in Arkansas, where Jamie bought a wagon, a team of mules, and a couple of decent-looking saddle mounts. He would need better horses for riding up the Brazos into the Comanche domain, but he figured he could find those in Fort Worth.

"This is much better," Hannah commented as they drove southwest through a corner of Indian Territory. She looked around warily as she went on, "But how much danger are we in from the savages here?"

"Not much," Jamie replied. "Hardly any, in fact."

Hannah looked confused. "But this is Indian Territory, isn't it? I heard you call it that more than once."

Jamie chuckled and said, "Different Indians. The ones who live here are sometimes known as the Five Civilized Tribes. The government moved them over here from the southeastern states about seventeen years ago." A solemn look appeared on his face. "Some of us thought that wasn't really fair to them, but even though those politicians up in Washington are supposed to work for the people, they're not really in the habit of listening to what we have to say. So they rounded up those mostly peaceful Indians and forced them to come over here."

"Mostly peaceful?" Hannah repeated.

Jamie laughed again. "There was a time when some of them weren't. The Creeks and the Seminoles put up good fights against the army and the settlers. Those days are behind them now. The tribe that lives here in this area we're passing through, the Cherokee, are about as civilized as any white folks you'll find. More civilized than some, to be honest. They live in regular houses and farm their land, and from what I hear, they have towns that look like any regular settlement, with businesses and schools. You don't have to worry about them."

"I'll take your word for it, I suppose. But I'm going to keep my eyes open anyway."

"Nothing wrong with that," Jamie told her as he flicked the reins at the mules' rumps.

They saw some of those Cherokee farmers working in their fields over the next few days. Sometimes the men had women and children toiling alongside them. Nearly always, they waved at the travelers in the wagon passing by on the road. Hannah acknowledged that she was beginning to understand when Jamie referred to them as a civilized tribe.

"To be honest, there's not much law in these parts," he said. "So there are white outlaws who like to hide out here. It's not likely we'll run into any of them, but if we do, they'll be a bigger threat than the Cherokees."

"Should I be carrying a gun?"

"No, if there's any shooting to be done, I'll take care of it," Jamie said.

That conversation planted a seed in his mind, though. Maybe it *would* be a good idea for Hannah to be armed. Even though Fort Worth was a good-sized settlement now, from what he'd heard, trouble was never too far away anywhere on the frontier. The more Jamie thought about it, the more he was convinced that she needed to know how to protect herself.

That evening while they were camped at the base of a small hill, next to a little creek, Jamie found a couple of broken tree branches, paced off about twenty feet, and stuck the branches upright in the ground. Hannah wasn't paying attention to what he was doing, so she was surprised when he walked back to her, pulled the Colt from the holster on his hip, and held it out to her, butt first.

"Here," he said. "Time you got a little shooting practice."

"What?" Her brows arched dramatically over her green eyes. "You want me to shoot that gun?"

"That's right. Use those branches I stuck in the ground for targets." He pointed at them.

Hannah looked leery of the idea. "I don't think I'll be any good with a gun, Mr. MacCallister. Especially not that enormous weapon you carry."

"The Walker's a heavy gun, that's true. I don't have anything lighter weight, but we can get you something in Fort Worth. I'm not expecting you to be any good with it, but I'd like to see what you can do."

"I . . . I've never fired a gun before." An idea occurred to her and perked up her interest. "Does this mean you're thinking about letting me come along on the expedition after all?"

"Not hardly," Jamie answered. "But out here, it's a good idea for most folks to be armed and to know how to shoot. Trouble can crop up when and where you least expect it, and you need to be able to protect yourself."

"That makes sense, I suppose." Hannah sighed and reached out to take the Walker from him. The gun sagged toward the ground and she exclaimed, "Oh, my, it's heavy!"

"That's why I said we'd get you something smaller in Fort Worth. Something that's more your size. But I know you can handle this, if you just give it a try."

She tightened her two-handed grip on the Colt. "All right. Shoot at those two branches, you said?"

"That's right. Start by pointing the gun at them."

Letting out an unladylike grunt with the effort, Hannah raised the Colt and aimed at the branch on the left. The barrel wavered quite a bit. After a moment, she pulled the trigger. Nothing happened.

"What's wrong?" she asked.

"You didn't cock it."

"Well, you could have told me I have to do that first!"

"Yeah, I reckon I could have. Cock it first. Use your thumb and pull the hammer back until it locks into place."

Hannah had to use both thumbs to ear back the hammer. She thrust the gun out in front of her as far as her arms would reach and took aim again.

"Take a deep breath," Jamie told her. "That'll steady you a little. Hold it, aim, and squeeze the trigger."

"I'll try," Hannah said. She drew in a breath, and as she held it, the Colt's barrel did stop jumping around quite as much. Jamie saw her finger tighten on the trigger.

The gun boomed. The recoil kicked the weapon up and back, right out of her hands, as she loosed a wordless, shocked exclamation. Jamie was standing behind her, ready to reach up and grab the Colt before it dropped to the ground. She stumbled back against him and probably would have fallen if she hadn't caught herself on his solid form.

The two branches stood there, untouched.

"Merciful heavens!" she cried. The loud voice she used told Jamie that the Colt's roar had partially deafened her. "That was awful!"

"Yeah, you didn't hit either one of those branches," he said, raising his own voice so she could hear him. "Didn't even come close."

"That's not what I'm talking about! How . . . how can you shoot such a monstrous thing and hit any target?"

"Practice," Jamie said. He moved her to the side, pointed the Colt at the branches, and thumbed off four shots as quickly as he could. Hannah cried out and clapped her hands over her ears, but she watched in amazement as, one after the other, the .44 caliber balls clipped a few more inches off the right-hand branch. When the gun fell silent, the branch was only half as long as when Jamie had started firing.

Hannah lowered her hands and said, "I never saw such a thing."

"Well, I've been handling shooting irons for a long time," Jamie said. "Want to try again?"

"I'll never be that good."

"No, you won't, not with a gun this size. But with something that's more suited to you, you might find that you have a knack for it. Or maybe not. Won't know until you try."

Hannah stood there frowning in thought for a moment before abruptly nodding.

"Yes, I'll try again," she declared. "Like you said, Mr. MacCallister, this would be a good thing for me to know."

"Yes, ma'am, Miss Craigson, it sure would," Jamie said as he began reloading.

Half a mile away, Walt Reynolds lifted his head as he heard the gunshots and their echoes rolling over the hills of southeastern Indian Territory.

He wasn't the only one who noticed the shots. Teddy Keller had been dozing under a tree, legs stretched out in front of him and hat tipped forward over his eyes. He sat up sharply, pushed his hat back, and then stood up.

"Sounds like a war breakin' out," he said.

The shots had stopped. "Sounds more like target practice to me," Reynolds said. He had been rubbing down his horse after the day's hard ride. A few yards away, Ox Tankersley and Billy Bob Moore were building a fire. Grover Appleton was sitting on a log and feeling sorry for himself, as usual. Keller had kept the group moving at a fast pace for days now, and all the riding made Grover's arm hurt like blazes. He liked to complain that it was never going to heal up unless he got a chance to rest—and he was probably right about that, Reynolds knew.

Keller said, "You think MacCallister's teachin' that gal to shoot?"

Ox grunted. "No gal ever squeezed off four rounds from a Walker Colt like that."

"No, but that first shot could have been hers," Reynolds said. "Then MacCallister fired the others to, I don't know, show her how it's done."

Keller raked his fingers through his long beard and said, "Maybe."

Another single shot sounded.

"And that's the girl again," Reynolds said.

"That makes sense, Teddy," Billy Bob put in.

"Yeah, I reckon." Keller scowled. "I ain't worried about no girl, though. MacCallister's the one we got to deal with if we're gonna settle the score."

"Just when do you plan on doin' that?" Ox asked. "We've been trailin' them for almost a week now, and we haven't made a move yet."

"The time ain't been right yet," Keller said, his expression darkening even more. "I'll let you know when it is."

Tankersley grunted and went back to arranging the wood he and Moore had gathered for the fire. Like the others, he had learned that it didn't pay to argue too much with Keller, who had a short fuse and a fast gun hand.

Reynolds scraped fingers over his beard-stubbled jaw and said, "If they keep goin' in the same direction, they'll be in Texas in a day or two, Teddy."

"So?"

"There are more towns in Texas than here in Indian Territory. Dallas, Fort Worth, places like that. If you're bound and determined to jump MacCallister, it might be easier to do it when there isn't a bunch of other people around."

Keller sneered and said, "You just leave the thinkin' to me, Walt. I've been doin' most of it for us for a good long time now, and we've done pretty well for ourselves, ain't we?"

If you called barely scraping by and having to run for their lives from posses now and then doing pretty well, then he supposed they were, Reynolds thought.

But if Teddy wanted to wait to make their move against MacCallister, that was fine with him. He wouldn't care if they *never* got around to "evening the score." Vengeance didn't mean much to Walt Reynolds, who preferred getting along with folks when he could. Teddy was the one who'd been so dead set on following MacCallister and dragged the other four along with him. Reynolds hadn't argued because when you got right down to it, one place was just about as good as another and they didn't have anything better to do.

"We'll deal with MacCallister when I say we deal with MacCallister," Keller went on with his usual bluster.

"Sounds good to me, Teddy," Reynolds said.

And if they hadn't done anything by the time they reached Fort Worth—assuming that's where MacCallister and the girl were headed—then that might be a good place to take off on his own. Nothing said he had to ride with Keller and this bunch the rest of his borned days.

The more Walt Reynolds thought about that possibility, the better *it* sounded to him, too.

CHAPTER 10

For the next few evenings, after they had made camp, Hannah practiced more with Jamie's Colt. That first time, she had never managed to hit either of the sticks, or even come close to them. But she got somewhat accustomed to the sound and the way the gun kicked when she fired it.

The evening after that, she came closer to the mark, hitting the ground not far from one of the branches Jamie stuck in the dirt. The evening after that, when he found a big knot on a tree she could use as a target, she actually hit what she was shooting at a couple of times. That improvement surprised and pleased her, and she stopped complaining about being forced to practice.

"It's not so bad, once you get used to it," she told Jamie as he was reloading once their session was over.

"Colt makes a pocket revolver in .31 caliber," he told her. "It's considerably lighter than this one, and I reckon you could handle it better. They make a .36 Navy, too, but

I think you might be better suited for the .31. It's not as accurate, or so I've heard, but it'll do just fine for close work, which is how you'd be most likely to need it."

Hannah swallowed hard and asked, "For shooting a man, you mean?"

Jamie had been talking about the guns without really considering the fact that he was speaking to a woman. Although he had known plenty of women who were tough-minded and capable of fighting, Kate foremost among them, there was a reason they were sometimes called the gentler sex.

"There are more varmints out here than just the two-legged kind," he told her. "Rattlesnakes and coyotes, for example."

"I wouldn't think I'd want to get very close to them."

"Well, no," he acknowledged. "But if we can find one of those pocket revolvers for you and you get some practice with it, I'm betting you'll be able to hit something from twenty feet away."

"Especially if it's man-sized," she persisted.

Jamie shrugged. "Better to be able to do it and not need to than need to and not be able to."

"That makes perfect sense, I suppose. When will we reach Texas?"

"We've been in Texas all day today," he said with a smile. "That river we crossed early this morning was the Red. That's the border between Texas and Indian Territory in this part of the world. We ought to make Fort Worth in another few days."

She returned the smile. He heard excitement in her voice as she said, "And then we can start preparing for the journey."

"And then we wait to see if Preacher shows up," Jamie corrected her. "Although it won't hurt to make a few preparations while we're at it, I suppose. If I know that old mountain man as well as I think I do, he won't pass up the chance for another adventure!"

Preacher's hands streaked for the two Colt Dragoon revolvers holstered at his hips. He heard a rifle boom and felt the wind rip of a ball next to his left ear as he twisted in the saddle and raised the guns to open fire on the brush at the side of the trail. The rangy gray stallion stood stock-still beneath him. Horse was used to the sound of gunfire and the sharp tang of burned powder—and the coppery smell of freshly spilled blood, as well.

The Dragoons roared and bucked in Preacher's strong hands. He alternated fire, left and right, shooting as fast as he could ear back the hammers. The .44 caliber balls tore through the brush like a deadly hailstorm. The heavy report of another rifle sounded. Preacher didn't know where the ball went, but it didn't strike him or Horse, and that was all he cared about.

Preacher fired eight shots, four from each gun, and then held his fire as the brush began to wave around as someone thrashed around in it. He raised the right-hand revolver again when a man burst out into the open, but he didn't squeeze the trigger. The man's hands were empty. He stumbled back and forth as he pressed his left hand to the holes in his chest that welled blood. Crimson streams leaked between his fingers. His eyes rolled wildly in their sockets, and then he pitched forward onto his face. After a couple of spasms, he lay still.

Preacher knew that hombre was either dead or the next thing to it. He kept the right-hand gun pointed in that general direction, anyway, while the Colt in his left hand remained trained at the screen of brush. No movement or sound came from there.

After a few minutes, Preacher swung his right leg over Horse's back and dropped to the ground. Holding the Dragoons ready, he moved to the fallen man, hooked a boot toe under his shoulder, and rolled him onto his back. Glassy, wide-open eyes stared sightlessly up at the blue Texas sky.

A groan came from the brush.

Preacher swung around sharply and leveled both guns. He didn't hear anything else. The brush didn't move. The old mountain man stalked forward and used the long barrel of the Colt in his left hand to part the branches.

A man lay there on his side, curled up in a ball with both arms clenched across his middle. When Preacher saw that, he shook his head. The varmint was gutshot, and that was a mighty miserable way to die.

But there was just a chance that he was shamming, trying to draw Preacher in and make another try for him. In case that was true, Preacher aimed one of the Dragoons at him and said, "If you can hear me, mister, better speak up or I'll go ahead and put a ball in your brain to make sure of you."

The man jerked at the sound of the voice. He lifted his head slightly and gasped, "D-don't shoot, mister! I . . . I'm hurt bad."

"I reckon you are, all right," Preacher said. He pushed through the brush. The branches caught at his clothes, but the buckskin shirt and canvas trousers were tough and sturdy. Preacher moved around until he could see the wounded man's face.

A frown creased the mountain man's forehead. The fella he had shot was young, probably no more than twenty years old. Preacher could see now that his shirt was sodden with blood. The youngster wasn't shamming. He was dying, all right.

Preacher had gotten a good look at the dead man's face when he rolled him onto his back. He saw a resemblance between the two attackers, although the first man was considerably older.

"Was the other one who tried to bushwhack me your pa?"

"My . . . my brother Jed. Is . . . is he all right?"

"I'm afraid not, son. He didn't give me no choice but to kill him. Just like what's fixin' to happen to you."

"I . . . I'm going to . . . die?"

"Shot in the guts the way you are, I don't see no way to avoid it. Didn't do it like that a-purpose." Preacher shrugged. "I'd just as soon drilled you through the head. Got it over a heap quicker and easier."

The youngster moaned and sobbed. "I . . . I'm sorry! You gotta . . . help me."

"Not a blamed thing in the world I can do for you, unless you want me to finish you off."

For a long moment, the youth didn't say anything. Preacher thought he might have crossed the divide. But then he whispered, "Do it."

"Tell me somethin' first," Preacher said, his voice flat and hard. "Are you and your brother the ones who've been followin' me since the Red River?"

"Y-yeah. We were camped . . . by the river . . . saw you ford and ride on . . . Jed said we could . . . rob you. Said you . . . must be rich . . . on account of . . . you were trailin' a pack horse."

"So you got ahead of me and set up your little ambush."

"Honest, mister, we . . . we weren't gonna . . . hurt you. Jed said . . . we'd just get the drop on you . . . make you give us . . . your horses and gear . . . Jed didn't shoot . . . until you reached for those guns . . . How . . . how did you know . . ."

"My horse's ears twitched and told me somebody was lurkin' in that brush," Preacher explained. "I might've held my fire if your brother hadn't taken that shot at me. Once he started the ball, though, wasn't nothin' left to do but dance."

The wounded man took a couple of wheezing breaths and said, "Lord, it . . . it hurts . . ."

Preacher's voice wasn't quite as harsh as he asked, "What's your name, son?"

"Si . . . Silas . . ."

"Close your eyes, Silas," Preacher said as he raised the right-hand Colt.

He didn't have to pull the trigger. The rattling breath that came from the youngster's throat told him that Silas was dead. So did the limp way the arms fell away from the bloody middle.

Shaking his head in disgust, Preacher emerged from the brush. Movement overhead caught his eye. He looked up to see a couple of buzzards circling lazily on the wind currents high above. They had spotted the dead man lying out in the open. They would descend soon enough, once Preacher was gone.

And he was in no mood to bury men who had tried to kill him, so nature would have its bounty today.

He pouched one of the irons, reloaded the other, and then repeated the process. He was finishing up with the second gun when he saw a big, wolflike cur bounding down a hill on the other side of the trail.

"I wondered where in blazes you'd got off to," Preacher greeted the cur, who was known only as Dog. "You're supposed to be scoutin' the trail ahead of me, but instead you went gallivantin' off chasin' rabbits or prairie dogs, didn't you?"

Dog sat down in the trail, cocked his head to the side, and gazed up at Preacher.

"Oh, all right, don't worry about it," the old mountain man said with a wave of his hand. "I reckon even you can't be everywhere at once. And I can't blame a critter for followin' his instincts. Next time you hear shootin', though, you come to see what it's about right then, instead of takin' your time."

Dog stood up, trotted over, and licked Preacher's hand. He grunted and scratched the cur's head between the ears.

"Come on," he said. "We still got to get to Fort Worth and find out what it is that Jamie wants."

CHAPTER 11

Preacher had been in St. Louis when Jamie's message arrived. Jamie had sent it to Preacher's favorite tavern in the riverfront city, where he knew the proprietor would spread the word by way of all the mountain man's friends who passed through.

But good fortune meant that hadn't been necessary. Preacher got the message directly and had set out for Fort Worth as Jamie requested, as soon as he had picked up some supplies.

It had taken two weeks to angle across Arkansas and then through Indian Territory, and that was pushing the animals at a pretty stout pace, but now that he had crossed the Red River into Texas, he ought to reach Fort Worth in another couple of days. He wondered why Jamie MacCallister wanted to meet him in that settlement on the Trinity River.

Jamie's message had said only that he was involved in something that he believed Preacher might find interesting.

That meant some sort of trouble. Preacher was certain of that.

He and Jamie had met more than twenty years earlier, when Jamie wasn't much more than a kid and a far cry from the famous frontiersman he was now. In recent years, circumstances had brought the two of them together for several adventures. More than once, they had escaped death by the skin of their teeth.

But they *had* escaped, and to men such as Preacher and Jamie, risking their lives to do the right thing came as second nature. If Jamie thought something was worthwhile, Preacher knew it was highly likely that he would, too.

So he was certainly curious what Jamie was up to now.

He was thinking about that as he rode south and already had forgotten about the two brothers and their ill-advised attempt to waylay him. He didn't look back to see that the number of buzzards swooping around the sky had grown larger.

Around the middle of the day, two days later, Preacher rode into Fort Worth. Half a dozen years earlier, there hadn't been anything here on the rugged bluffs overlooking the meandering course of one of the Trinity's branches. Preacher knew that because he had ridden along those bluffs several times when this was still wild country.

Then the US Army had established a fort here, part of an effort to protect the settlers from Indian depredations.

As usual, a civilian settlement had grown up around the military post, and when the soldiers had abandoned the place a year or so earlier to move even farther west, the settlers had moved right in and taken over the empty buildings.

One of them had been converted into a hotel, Preacher saw from the sign that now hung over the entrance, which read *DAGGETT'S HOTEL*. Looked like it might have been a stable, originally. The smell of horse manure probably lingered in there, but anybody who wanted a place to stay in Fort Worth with a roof over their heads might not have any other options.

Beyond that was a long building that Preacher figured had been a barracks, originally. Now several wagons were parked in front of it and the sign on the front of the awning above the entrance read *DAGGETT & LEONARD, GENERAL MERCHANDISE*. Preacher wondered idly if it was the same Daggett, or if there was more than one of them in Fort Worth.

When the army vacated the fort, the blacksmith shop had simply been taken over by a civilian in the same line of work. Some of the other quarters now housed a lawyer's office, a doctor's practice, and a barber shop and bath house. A couple of good-sized buildings on the settlement's outskirts appeared to be warehouses of some sort. Around the business area were scattered several dozen residences, some of them log cabins, others built of crudely cut and planed lumber. Roofs were mostly wooden shingles.

There was nothing fancy about Fort Worth, but folks on the frontier didn't have the time or inclination for fanciness. They wanted places that provided shelter and commerce, and in that respect, Fort Worth appeared to be a thriving community.

Preacher figured the hotel was the place to start looking for Jamie. He swung down from the saddle, looped Horse's reins around a hitchrack in front of the former stable, and told Dog, "Stay."

The big cur sat. He wouldn't let anybody mess with Horse—although anyone foolish enough to try to steal the stallion would soon find that he'd bitten off a bigger chunk of trouble than he could handle.

Preacher had just started toward the hotel's entrance when he heard gunshots coming from behind the place. He stopped and frowned, thinking that trouble was breaking out. His hands drifted instinctively toward the butts of the Colts on his hips.

But then, as the gun fell silent, several whoops of appreciation sounded. That didn't seem like a normal reaction to a gun battle. He wondered what in blazes was going on back there.

One way to find out, he told himself. He adjusted the gun belt holding the two holstered Dragoons and walked around the building.

A small grove of post oak trees stood about fifty yards behind the hotel. Somebody had fastened a paper target onto one of the tree trunks. A group of people stood maybe thirty feet from the trees. A man walked up to the oak with the target nailed on it and pulled the paper loose.

Preacher had already recognized the man's tall, powerful frame. When the man turned around to return to the group of onlookers, Preacher saw the craggy face of his old friend, Jamie MacCallister. Jamie grinned as he held up the target and called, "Even better this time, Miss Craigson."

Preacher grunted in surprise as he realized from Jamie's words that a woman was in the bunch. He couldn't see her, just men in an assortment of garb: buckskins, homespun work shirts, and canvas trousers, supplemented by what appeared to be parts of cast-off army uniforms.

The crowd parted a little as Preacher strode up behind them. Through the gap, he caught a glimpse of a young woman with reddish-brown hair. Jamie handed her the target. Preacher was close enough now to see that all the bullet holes were fairly close around the center. Not perfect shooting, by any means, but not bad. Especially for a woman, if she was the one who had done it.

And it appeared that she was because she had a Colt pocket revolver in her right hand as it hung at her side. She studied the paper target Jamie had given her, which she held in her left hand, and said, "You were right, Mr. MacCallister. It does appear that I have a certain knack for shooting."

"You just needed a gun more suited to you," Jamie told her.

Jamie hadn't seen him yet, Preacher realized. He lowered his voice to a deeper pitch and rumbled over the soft hum of conversation in the group, "Better not listen to that old varmint, ma'am. He don't know a thing about shootin'."

The young woman turned her head to look in his direction and said, "I beg your pardon?"

Jamie glared and said, "If you've got an opinion, mister, why don't you step up and state it?"

The crowd parted more. Most folks tried to get out of the way of a stern look from Jamie MacCallister. They sure didn't want to be in his path if he stalked toward them.

Preacher stayed where he was, though, a big grin on his face as he raised his head more so that the brim of his hat no longer obscured his weather-beaten features.

"Preacher!" Jamie said. A couple of long-legged steps carried him past the young woman and up to the old mountain man as he extended his hand. Preacher gripped it hard, and then the two of them started pounding each other on the back with their free hands. Those blows would have knocked down a lot of men, but Preacher and Jamie barely seemed to feel them.

When Jamie let go of Preacher's hand and stepped back, he said, "I've been hoping you'd show up. You must've made good time. Miss Craigson and I have only been here in Fort Worth for a few days."

"Happened to be in St. Louis when your letter got there," Preacher explained. "So the message didn't have to go gallivantin' all over the frontier lookin' for me."

"A stroke of luck, all right," Jamie said with a nod. He added, "Now, what's this about calling me an old varmint? You're older than I am!"

"And I always will be, so respect your elders. Anyways, I was just joshin' you." Preacher took his hat off and nodded to the young woman. "Since it don't look like Jamie's gonna introduce us—"

"Blast it, I just didn't think of it yet," Jamie interrupted. "Miss Craigson, this old pelican is none other than Preacher, the fella I've been telling you about. Preacher, meet Miss Hannah Craigson."

"It's an honor and a pleasure, ma'am," Preacher told her.

"I've heard a great deal about you, Mr. Preacher," Hannah said. "I'm honored to meet such a famous frontiersman."

"No mister about it. Just Preacher."

"Are you a . . . minister of the gospel?" She sounded as if she found that difficult to believe as she looked at Preacher with his rough clothing, beard-stubbled face, and two guns on his hips.

"No, ma'am, not hardly. The way I got the name is—"

"You can tell Miss Craigson that story later," Jamie broke in. "I've heard it so many times I know it by heart. Some of these fellas probably do, too."

A few nods and mutters of agreement came from the assembled onlookers. The story of how Preacher got his name was well known on the frontier.

"Well, fine," Preacher said a little testily. "Does Kate know you're travelin' with such a comely young lady?"

"She knows."

Preacher went on, "You're riskin' your reputation, Miss Craigson, by associatin' with this here reprobate."

"I'm doing more than associating with him," Hannah said.

Preacher raised his bushy, graying eyebrows.

"We're business partners," Hannah continued.

"We can talk about that later," Jamie said—a little hastily, Preacher thought, as if Jamie didn't want to discuss whatever had brought them to Fort Worth. "Right now, I reckon we've been out in this hot sun long enough. Let's go in the hotel. We need to get you a room, Preacher."

"Am I gonna be stayin'?"

"I think there's a good chance of that."

Jamie's comments whetted Preacher's interest that much more. As the crowd broke up, the two frontiersmen walked around the hotel to the front with Hannah Craigson between them.

They went inside. The floors were dirt, adding to Preacher's hunch that this building had started out as the army stable. But considerable work had been done to make it nicer. The lobby had wallpaper with a floral pattern on the walls, some comfortable chairs were placed around, and a registration desk was set up on one side of the room. A central hallway with doors on both sides led toward the back. Preacher figured the dividers between some of the stalls had been knocked out and others had been extended to the ceiling to form rooms. A set of stairs appeared to indicate that the hayloft had even been turned into a second floor.

Preacher sniffed and detected just the faintest lingering odor of mingled straw and manure, but really, it wasn't too bad. Almost pleasant to anybody who'd spent much time around animals.

A well-dressed, burly man with thinning hair and a neatly trimmed mustache stood behind the desk with his hands resting on its surface. Jamie went up to him and said, "Mr. Daggett, this is my friend we've been waiting on. He'll need a room, too. Preacher, meet E.M. Daggett."

"Daggett, eh?" Preacher said as he shook hands with the hotel man. "Same one as owns the general store I saw?"

Daggett chuckled. "No, that's my brother Henry. Running this hotel is enough for me right now, although I'll admit I *do* have plans for the future." He turned the registration book around and pushed an inkwell and pen toward Preacher. "If you'll just sign in, sir."

Preacher scrawled his name. Daggett didn't ask for a Mister or a second name, which was a relief. He said, "I've been holding Room Six for you. It's just beyond Rooms Four and Five, where Mr. MacCallister and Miss Craigson are staying."

Preacher glanced at Jamie. "Pretty sure I was gonna turn up, were you?"

"I never knew you to pass up a chance for something interesting," Jamie said.

"You sound pretty sure I'll find it interestin', too."

Jamie nodded toward the hallway and suggested, "Why don't we go find out?"

CHAPTER 12

As they were about to leave the hotel lobby, Daggett said from behind the desk, "If you have any gear outside, sir, you might want to go ahead and bring it in. Since the army left, there's no real authority in Fort Worth, and while I don't think anybody would try to help himself to your things—"

"Anybody foolish enough to do that would plumb regret it," Preacher said.

Jamie smiled. "Dog?"

"Dog," Preacher said.

Jamie nodded to the hotel man and said, "Don't worry, Mr. Daggett. Preacher's gear is safe."

He led the way down the hall to Room Five.

"This is where Miss Craigson is staying," he explained as he opened the door.

Preacher looked at the young woman and said, "I'm still a mite worried about your reputation, ma'am, bein' in a hotel room with two men who ain't your kinfolks."

"Please don't worry about that, Preacher." She patted the pocket on her dress where she had placed the small revolver. "I can defend my honor any time I need to."

"She can, too," Jamie said. "We practiced some, out on the trail while we were coming here, and Miss Craigson got to where she could squeeze off a few rounds from this old Walker of mine and at least come close to the target most of the time. She took to that little .31 right away and is even better with it."

"I saw," Preacher said, nodding in approval.

The room was spartanly furnished with a bed, a single ladder-back chair with a wicker seat, and a small rug on the hard-packed dirt floor. The single window, cut in what had been the stable wall, had an oilcloth shade over it that let in some light.

Hannah sat on the bed. Jamie offered Preacher the chair, but the mountain man said, "I've been in the saddle all day. Feels good to stand up for a spell."

"All right, then," Jamie said. He took off his hat and hung it on one of the bedposts, then turned the chair around and straddled it with his crossed arms resting on the back. "I reckon you want to know what this is about."

"That's why I rode all the way down here."

"Treasure," Jamie said. "Gold and silver. Jim Bowie's cache that he took out of the lost San Saba Mine."

Preacher stared at his old friend in the gloomy shadows for a long moment . . . then burst out in a laugh.

The sound echoed in the room, then died away. Preacher looked back and forth between Jamie and Hannah. He couldn't read anything on his old friend's face, but the young woman looked somewhat offended.

She sounded touchy, too, when she said, "You may find it amusing, sir, but I assure you, it's the truth."

"You really think you know where Jim Bowie's treasure is hid?"

"I'm certain of it," she said.

Preacher looked back at Jamie. "And you're goin' after it?"

Jamie's broad shoulders rose and fell in a shrug. "Thinking about it," he said. "But I've been waiting until you got here before I make up my mind for sure."

"And why's that?" Preacher asked, his eyes narrowing in suspicion now.

Jamie nodded toward Hannah and said, "Because of where the map Miss Craigson has in her possession says that the cache is hidden."

"Where might *that* be?"

"Up between a couple of the Seven Fingers of the Brazos."

Preacher drew in a sharp breath. "Why . . . why, that's . . ."

"Right in the middle of Comancheria," Jamie said. "Yeah, I know."

For a long moment, Preacher didn't respond. When he finally did, he said, "I reckon you'd best tell me the whole thing."

It took a while for Jamie and Hannah to do that. Preacher listened attentively to the story, asking a question now and then. Hannah got out the map and the letter and let him look at them, although she did so with some reluctance.

"I hope you men are trustworthy," she said. "I'm placing all my faith in you that you won't betray me."

"You don't have to worry about that," Jamie assured her.

Preacher gave the papers back to her and said, "If all I wanted was gold and silver, I already know a heap of places in the mountains where I could find it. Shoot, I knew there was gold out yonder in California a long time before James Marshall came across it in that creek at Sutter's Mill. Didn't flap my jaws about it, though, 'cause I knowed what'd happen if I did." He nodded solemnly. "I was right, too. All them forty-niners dang near ruined the whole place."

"I don't know if most folks in California would share that opinion, Preacher," Jamie said dryly. "But I understand what you mean."

The old mountain man nodded. "Most don't, these days. They figure so-called civilization's a *good* thing." He sounded as if he could barely comprehend that notion. Turning back to Hannah, he went on, "I reckon Jamie told you that all those stories about lost mines and Jim Bowie's treasure are just a bunch of, uh . . . well . . ."

"He told me they were lies," Hannah said.

Preacher looked at Jamie. "And yet here you are, at the jumpin' off place for a trip to Comancheria."

"Yeah, I know. But what if it's true?"

Preacher frowned. "No offense to the young lady's grandpappy, but I don't see how it could be. Not even Jim Bowie his own self could've taken a bunch of gold and silver up the Brazos and hid it. The Comanch' would've lifted his hair, sure enough, and he never would've been at the Alamo to start with."

"Maybe . . ."

"Lord help us, she's won you over!" Preacher burst out. "You've done got the gold fever. Never thought I'd see Jamie MacCallister come down with a case o' that."

"I don't have gold fever," Jamie said. "You know me better than that, Preacher. But if Colonel Bowie actually did manage to make it up the Brazos and back, then whatever he hid is probably still there. If a man could find it, that would be quite an adventure . . . and quite a story to tell, too."

Preacher scratched at his jaw as he frowned in thought. "Yeah," he said slowly. "That ain't a thing many white men have done."

"And it would be a help to Miss Craigson here, too, not to mention proving that her grandfather was telling the truth."

"It ain't a matter of whether ol' Tobias was tellin' the truth. He was just repeatin' in that letter what Jim Bowie told him. Now, Bowie wasn't one to spin some wild yarn just for the sake of tellin' a tall tale, like Davy Crockett was. Generally, you could count on what Bowie said to be true. But he was hurt and usin' laudanum and whiskey to dull the pain, so there ain't no way of bein' sure he even knew what he was sayin'."

Hannah said, "Strong drink makes some men *more* likely to tell the truth, doesn't it?"

"She has a point there," Jamie said.

Preacher paced back and forth, although he couldn't go very far before having to turn around each time because the room was small. After a minute, he stopped and looked at Jamie.

"You've made up your mind to go, haven't you?"

"If you'll go with me, I have."

"You want me to ride up the Brazos with you, right into the heart of Comanche country, where there'll be hundreds, maybe even thousands, of them devils who'd like nothin' better than to kill us both?"

"That's about the size of it," Jamie said, nodding.

"Well, shoot!" Preacher exclaimed. "Why in blazes didn't you just say so, right from the start? Of course, I'll go. Sounds like a heap of excitement . . . and there ain't nothin' I like better than excitement!"

CHAPTER 13

The five saddle tramps sat around a table in a tavern not far from Daggett's Hotel, idly passing around a bottle of whiskey. The raw stuff in the unlabeled bottle tasted like home brew to Walt Reynolds. He hoped whoever had cooked it up hadn't dumped in too many rattlesnake heads for flavoring.

They had ridden into Fort Worth several days earlier on the trail of Jamie MacCallister and the Craigson woman. Teddy Keller still insisted that the time wasn't right for them to seek revenge on MacCallister.

By now, Walt Reynolds was convinced that the time would *never* be right.

Keller had blustered about how he was going to settle the score with MacCallister, and now his pride wouldn't allow him to abandon the idea even though he clearly didn't want to go through with it. They had ridden all this way for nothing. But they hadn't had anything better to do, Reynolds reminded himself.

The problem was that they were running mighty low on funds. They would have to do something soon to come up with some money.

That probably meant holding up a store somewhere and then making a run for the tall and uncut. Reynolds didn't care much for the idea, but what else could they do?

The tavern was a windowless log building. The door stood wide open, letting in a breeze that blew from the west off the river. Gaps between the logs created a draft, which provided some welcome coolness.

Something suddenly blocked the light from the door. The man who loomed in the entrance was so big and broad shouldered that he blocked the breeze, too. Keller looked up from the glass of whiskey he'd been staring at. Reynolds saw the anger on Keller's face and knew he was about to yell at the newcomer to get out of the door.

"Take it easy, Teddy," Reynolds said in a quick, quiet voice. "That fella's as big as a mountain. You don't want to get on his bad side."

"I ain't afraid of him," Keller said. A sneer twisted his lips.

"You don't have to be afraid of him to be smart. He probably weighs twice as much as you."

"Not twice as much as me," Ox Tankersley rumbled.

"No, I reckon not," Reynolds said. "We still don't need to go around begging for trouble."

Keller snapped, "Who put you in charge, Walt?"

"Nobody. I'm just saying, that's all."

Billy Bob Moore said, "Walt's right. Anyway, the fella's moving."

It was true. After pausing for a moment, the huge stranger stepped on into the tavern. The crown of his brown felt hat almost brushed the low ceiling as he went to the bar, which was a crude affair made from planks laid over the tops of barrels.

The bartender, a heavyset, bald man in a dirty canvas apron, said, “Howdy, Otis. You want your usual?”

“Reckon I do,” the newcomer replied in a deep, gravelly voice. Long, shaggy black hair stuck out from under his hat, and a tangled black beard jutted from his chin and cheeks to hang over the upper part of his chest. He carried a holstered revolver and had a tomahawk stuck through a loop in a piece of rope tied around his waist. He looked like a man to whom killing would come as natural as breathing, Walt Reynolds thought.

Instead of one of the unlabeled bottles, the bartender took a jug off a shelf and slid it across the planks to the man he called Otis. Using his teeth, Otis pulled the cork from the jug and then spat it to the side. He tipped the jug up, letting it rest on his forearm, and wrapped his whiskery lips around the neck.

Over at the table, the five men could hear the liquid in the jug gurgling as it ran out. Otis’s beard jumped up and down a little each time he swallowed.

Grover Appleton let out a curse in a low, awed voice. “Is he gonna drink the whole thing?”

“Starting to look like it,” Reynolds said.

Long moments went by as Otis continued drinking. Finally, he lowered the jug, thumping it on the bar, and dragged the back of his other hand across his mouth. A huge belch came from him. He dug a coin from a pocket and rattled it on the bar.

“You got more of that prime stuff comin’?” he asked.

“Sure do,” the bartender replied. He looked a little nervous, as if he were conversing across the planks with a bear.

"You better." Otis turned away, and as he did so, his gaze fell on the table where the five saddle tramps sat. Eyes set deep in pits of gristle narrowed suspiciously. "Who in blazes are you?"

Keller couldn't sit still for that. He bounded to his feet and snarled, "What business is it of yours?"

"I'm makin' it my business."

Reynolds had to clamp his jaw shut to suppress a gasp of surprise. He had barely seen Otis's hand move, but the big Colt was out in the blink of an eye, gripped rock solid in the big man's fist as he pointed it at Teddy Keller. Otis hadn't just taken Keller by surprise. He was faster on the draw. Faster than all of them.

Keller was a reckless hothead, but he wasn't a complete fool. He said, "Take it easy, mister. I didn't mean no insult. My name's Keller, Teddy Keller. These boys are pards of mine." He waved a hand at the others and supplied their names.

"What are you doin' in Fort Worth?"

"Just driftin', that's all. Just driftin'."

Keller didn't mention anything about Jamie MacCallister, Reynolds noted, which was good. No need to complicate a tense situation even more than it already was.

"Well, stay outta my way." Otis lowered the hammer on the Colt and slid the iron back into leather. He stalked toward the door, his boots thudding heavily on the puncheon floor, and went back out into the afternoon light.

Over behind the bar, the tavern's proprietor blew out a relieved breath. "You boys is mighty lucky," he called to Reynolds and the others. "I ain't never seen Otis Lynch in such a good mood. Must've been that jug of whiskey that smoothed out his rough edges for a minute."

"That was a *good* mood?" Reynolds asked.

"Oh, yeah. I've seen him jerk a fella's arm plumb outta

its socket and break another hombre's back, just to blow off a little steam. When he's really worked up, ain't no tellin' how much damage he can do."

"Local badman, is he?" Keller said.

"The worst we got in these parts. No tellin' how many men he's killed. He can't go over to Dallas no more. They got some law over there these days, and if they was to get their hands on Otis, they'd string him up, sure as blazes. Or they'd try to, anyway. He might just lay waste to the whole town. I wouldn't put it past him."

Keller snorted in contempt. "Fellas like that are full of hot air. You let it out, and they don't amount to nothin'. He'd better hope he keeps outta *my* way. Caught me off guard, is what he done. He ever draws on me again, I'll let daylight through him, you can count on that."

The bartender made a face. "I surely do wish you wouldn't talk like that, friend. It might get back to Otis somehow, and then he'd be liable to take out some of his mad on me and my place."

"You can be scared of him if you want. I got better things to do." Keller fished out a coin and dropped it on the table. "Come on, boys. We don't have to stay here."

That was true enough, Reynolds thought as he pushed himself to his feet. They could go somewhere else . . .

But it would have to be somewhere that didn't require any money because the way Reynolds had it figured, that gold piece Keller had just tossed down so heedlessly was the last of their funds.

They were broke.

CHAPTER 14

"How many men do you think we'll need for an expedition like this?" Jamie asked as he and Preacher sat on stumps in the shade of some post oak trees.

From where they were, they could see down the bluffs to the curving course of the Trinity River. A half mile or so to the west, another fork of the Trinity flowed, and beyond it were rolling hills that seemed to stretch endlessly into the distance.

Preacher was whittling on a piece of wood. He pursed his lips in thought and then said, "An expedition to go hundreds of miles up the Brazos into Comanche-infested badlands? Oh, I reckon we could get by with . . . let's say, a thousand or so. And maybe a couple dozen cannons while we're at it." He grinned. "We ought to be able to come up with all that here in Fort Worth, don't you reckon?"

Jamie laughed. "I was thinking more along the lines of twenty men, well-armed, with plenty of ammunition, and maybe a dozen pack horses. Plus a bigger wagon."

"Wagon's liable to slow us down some."

"Yeah, but depending on how much gold and silver we find, we may need the wagon to carry it all back here."

Preacher squinted at his old friend. "You really figure there's a chance we'll find that cache? That it really exists?"

"When Miss Craigson first told me about it, I wouldn't have bet a nickel there was anything to the story, let alone a new hat. Like you, I've heard too many windies about Bowie's treasure."

Jamie thumbed back his hat and peered off into the distance as he went on, "But the more I thought about it, the more curious I got. If anybody actually *could* venture up there into Comanche country and make it back out with his hair on his head and his hide in one piece, it'd be Jim Bowie. Before he fell off that wall at the Alamo and hurt his leg, he was one of the saltiest hombres I've ever known."

Preacher didn't look up from his whittling as he said, "And I reckon when you come right down to it, if somebody *did* have a mess of gold and silver he wanted to hide, you couldn't hardly come up with a safer place to stash it. As far as anybody else findin' it, I mean." He chuckled. "Ain't nothin' *safe* about that country beyond the Brazos."

Jamie nodded in agreement and resumed what he'd been talking about.

"The wagon and the pack horses won't be any trouble. I've already talked to a fella who owns a wagon yard and livery stable at the edge of town. Nice hombre, name of Patterson. He has a wagon that'll do for what we need it to, and he can round up a team and some pack horses. I've got my eye on a few good saddle mounts, too. Where we're going, you sure don't want to run out of good horseflesh, happen you should need it."

"Amen to that," Preacher said.

"The problem may be coming up with enough good men. There are plenty of fighters around here. Fort Worth's got a reputation as a tough town, and it's well deserved, from what I've seen. They have to be men we can trust, though. Men who can stand up to the temptation of gold."

"The gal's gonna promise 'em a share, ain't she?"

"That's the plan . . . but some men are liable to ask themselves, why settle for a share when you can have the whole thing?"

"They'd be fools to pull a double cross," Preacher said flatly. "However many men we take with us, we'll all want to stick together out there in the middle of Comancheria. Nobody's gonna try anything until we're well on the way back to civilization. That's when you'll have to keep an eye out for trouble. Assumin', of course, that we make it that far . . . and that there's any gold and silver to bring back."

"That's a big mess of assumptions, isn't it?"

"Yep," Preacher agreed. He nodded toward the hotel, which was about fifty yards away. "Yonder comes the girl."

"Miss Craigson?" Jamie turned to look.

Hannah was walking toward them, wearing a plain long-sleeved white shirt and a long brown skirt. Despite the simple garb, she looked lovely with her auburn curls loose around her head and draped over her shoulders. When she saw Jamie and Preacher watching her, she smiled and raised a hand in greeting.

Preacher suddenly stiffened and drew in a sharp breath. "Jamie," he said, "what in blazes is that thing followin' her? Is that a bear?"

"That's no bear," Jamie said. "That's a man . . . and it looks like he's got his eye set on Miss Craigson."

The huge stranger, whose face was almost completely obscured by his thatch of hair, thick, prominent beard, and wide-brimmed, battered hat, strode determinedly after Hannah, who didn't seem to have noticed him following her.

She must have realized something was wrong, though, when Jamie and Preacher abruptly stood up and turned toward her as she approached them. That made her hesitate and turn her head to glance back over her shoulder . . .

She broke stride as she saw the hairy behemoth coming after her. With an evil leer on his face, barely visible under the thicket of his beard, he lunged toward her, reaching out with a long-fingered hand the size of a ham.

Hannah screamed, whirled around, and dashed for her life.

Her quick reaction saved her. The man's fingers brushed the collar of her shirt but failed to get a grip on it. Then she was out of his reach.

Jamie and Preacher ran to meet her as she hurried toward them. They drew their guns as she went between them. The huge man came to an abrupt halt as he found himself staring down the barrels of two Dragoon Colts and a Walker.

That was a lot of firepower.

"Hold it right there, mister," Jamie rasped. "You don't need to be chasing after that lady."

"She's pretty," the man responded. "Wanted a better look at her." He sneered. "I wasn't gonna hurt her. Maybe just love on her a mite. Like she was a fluffy little rabbit."

The man's voice was as rough as ten miles of bad road. Hearing the way he spoke and seeing the way he looked, Jamie thought for a second that he might be simpleminded. But then he believed he spotted keen intelligence in the man's dark, deep-set eyes.

"She ain't a rabbit, and she don't need no attention from the likes of you," Preacher snapped. "Why don't you just go on about your business, mister?"

"Don't shoot me." The man held up his big paws and started to back away. "I don't want no trouble."

"Then go on and leave the lady alone. Don't come around and bother her again," Jamie said.

"Sure, sure." The big man slowly lowered his hands and turned to shuffle away, back toward the hotel. Jamie didn't trust him the least little bit, so he didn't holster his Colt until the man had gone out of sight around a building. Preacher waited until then to pouch his irons, too.

The two men turned to find Hannah waiting not too far away, near the stumps where they had been sitting earlier. She had an anxious look on her face and was still breathing a little hard from her mad dash to escape the giant.

"Thank you," she said. "I . . . I probably shouldn't have been so frightened. It's just that I've never seen a man so large and threatening looking."

Preacher chuckled and said, "Yeah, that ol' varmint was even bigger than you, Jamie, and I wouldn't have said that was even possible. Seemed like he was dumb as a rock, though."

"I wouldn't count on that," Jamie said. "I got the feeling that maybe he was just putting on a show by acting that way. Like he was just playing with us, the way a cat does with a mouse."

"This mouse has got some mighty big teeth." Preacher tapped the holstered Colts on his hips. "If he tries to bother you again, Miss Craigson, he'll sure find out fast enough."

"Thank you," Hannah said. "But surely he'll leave me alone, now that he knows I have two such gallant protectors."

"Might be a good idea if one of us stuck closer to you for

a while," Jamie mused. "Just in case he comes back around. We probably haven't been careful enough. Fort Worth's not the kind of a place where a young woman needs to be walking around by herself."

"How long do you think we'll be here?"

"Preacher and I were just talking about that. It all depends on how long it takes us to find enough men willing to go along on what's bound to be a dangerous journey. It could be several weeks before we're ready to go."

Hannah sighed. "I'll admit, I'm eager to get started. But I've put myself in your hands, Mr. MacCallister, and I suppose we'll proceed as you think best."

"I'll do what I can to hurry things along, Miss Craigson, but for an undertaking like this, you want to be sure you're prepared as well as you can be."

"Absolutely!" She smiled. "If there's anything I can do to help, please tell me. For now, I believe I'll go back to the hotel."

"I'll walk with you," Preacher said. "Just to make sure nobody bothers you."

Hannah nodded and started toward Daggett's. Preacher lingered just for a moment to say quietly to Jamie, "I don't know if you noticed or not, but she's talkin' again like she's comin' with us."

"I noticed," Jamie said. "The problem is, after what just happened . . . I'm not sure but what she's right. She might be safer with us."

Preacher frowned. "You're crazy! Safer in the middle of a bunch of Comanches?"

"I didn't like the looks of that big fella. I don't think he's through causing trouble for us."

"If he tries, he'll sure be sorry."

Jamie nodded, but at the same time, he hoped it wouldn't be the other way around.

CHAPTER 15

There was no dining room in Daggett's Hotel, but a café was nearby and Jamie, Preacher, and Hannah took most of their meals there. Like everywhere else in Fort Worth, it wasn't fancy. Instead of round tables where the diners sat, two long tables with benches alongside them filled the room. The bill of fare was either stew or steak and beans, depending on what the proprietor felt like. The man's wife baked mighty tasty pies, though, and that brought in most of the business.

The three of them were there that evening, enjoying dishes of apple pie following their bowls of stew, when three roughly dressed men approached where they were sitting. Jamie and Preacher tensed, but the men took off their hats and smiled as if to say that they meant no harm.

"Mr. MacCallister?" one of them said.

"I am," Jamie replied. He saw a resemblance between the men now and figured they might be brothers. All three were in their twenties, he judged.

"I'm Pete Barnes," the spokesman said. "These here are my brothers Gil and Nate. We heard that you were lookin' to hire some men for a trip."

"That's right."

"We're outta work, to be honest, Mr. MacCallister, and we'd plumb admire to sign on with you."

Preacher said, "You don't want to know where you'd be goin'?"

"Does the job pay?"

"Only a little up front," Jamie said. "You'd get most of your share when we get back."

He had agreed to provide a small amount of wages, knowing that he might have to do so in order to recruit enough men.

Pete Barnes had picked up on something Jamie said, though. He licked his lips and repeated, "Our share? Does that mean you don't know for sure how much money we're talkin' about?"

"That's right. I wouldn't hire a man under false pretenses. There's liable to be some danger involved, and we don't know what the payoff will be."

Pete exchanged glances with his brothers, then said, "But there *will* be a payoff?"

"If we make it back," Jamie said, nodding. He had already decided that if Jim Bowie's treasure proved to be nonexistent, he would still make sure any man who survived got paid something, anyway. He wasn't comfortable for men risking their lives for nothing.

Pete Barnes rubbed his chin and grimaced. "You got to admit, Mr. MacCallister, that don't make the job sound all that appealin'," he said.

"Just being honest with you, men. Like I said, I won't sign a man on unless he knows what he's getting into."

"There's nothin' else you can tell us?"

Jamie looked at Preacher. They had discussed this very matter at length. They didn't want to spill too much information. If word got around that they were going after Jim Bowie's lost treasure, more men might venture up the Brazos on their own, men who couldn't be trusted, who would complicate their mission and quite possibly make the danger even worse.

"I'm sorry," Jamie said. "I can't tell you where we're going until we're on the trail. But I won't lie about the possible danger and not knowing how much it's going to be worth to you."

Preacher said, "Before we talk more about this, do you boys have horses and guns?"

"Guns, yeah," Pete said. "We had to sell our horses."

Gil Barnes spoke up for the first time. "Kept our saddles, though. We wouldn't sell those."

That was a point in their favor, Jamie thought. Circumstances might force a man to sell his horse, but if he was worth his salt, he hung on to his saddle.

"Rifles or pistols?" Preacher asked.

"Rifles," Pete said.

"Can you handle 'em?"

"We growed up over in East Texas, knockin' squirrels outta the trees so the family could eat. We can shoot." Pete looked at his brothers. "All three of us."

"You say you're short of funds?" Jamie asked.

"Didn't exactly say so," Pete allowed, "but as a matter of fact, we are."

Jamie took a coin from his pocket and handed it to the man. "Get yourselves something to eat, so Preacher and I can talk about it. When you're done, you can come back over here, and we'll let you know."

"Obliged to you, sir," Pete said, nodding. The other two brothers nodded their thanks, as well, and then all three of them moved to the front of the room to get their food. Carrying bowls of stew, they took seats at the far end of the other table, where they sat with some other men who were eating.

"They seem all right," Hannah said quietly when the brothers were out of earshot.

"Don't know how well they'll stand up to the trip, or to Indian fightin'," Preacher said. "But they strike me as honest, hardworkin' boys."

Jamie nodded. "I thought so, too. And there has to be a certain amount of trust involved, on both sides. I'm leaning toward hiring them."

"I think that's a good idea," Hannah said. She frowned and added, "I just realized . . . we're recruiting men to risk their lives, with no real promise of a reward at the end."

"That's sort of the way all of life is, ain't it?" Preacher drawled. "Ain't no guarantees for any of us. And I don't reckon I'd want one, even if I could get it." He grinned. "That'd sort of take the fun out of it, wouldn't it?"

"It would, for a fact," Jamie agreed, even though he had decided that the men who went with them would get something out of the deal . . . if they made it back.

As for himself, though, risk was one of the things that gave life its spice.

Hannah looked back and forth between them and said, "You men seem to have a rather unusual idea of fun."

"Now you're gettin' the idea, ma'am," Preacher told her.

A while later, after cleaning up the meals they bought with Jamie's money, the Barnes brothers came back over. Pete said, "While we were eatin', we talked to some fellas sittin' up at the end of that other table."

"I noticed that," Jamie said.

"They want to sign on, too?" Preacher asked.

Pete shook his head. "I wouldn't know about that. They were tellin' us that you fellas had a run-in with Otis Lynch."

"Great big fella?" Preacher said. "Bushy black beard and a bad attitude?"

"That's him, all right," Pete said. "If you're on Lynch's bad side, we ain't sure we want to throw in with you."

"He has a bad reputation around here, does he?" Jamie asked.

"The worst. He's an outlaw and a troublemaker. Rumored to have killed no tellin' how many men."

Hannah shuddered. "And that . . . that's who was chasing me? I was terrified of him."

"And with good reason, ma'am," Pete said, nodding.

"But when he talked, he sounded almost like a little child."

Nate Barnes tapped a finger against the side of his head and said, "That's because there's somethin' ain't right up here for him, ma'am. Sometimes he talks one way, and sometimes he talks another."

His brother Gil added, "Folks say there's half a dozen different hombres livin' inside Otis Lynch's head . . . and all of 'em are plumb evil."

"I don't know about that," Preacher said, "but the one we saw today was annoyin' enough. I'm not in the habit of goin' around bein' scared of folks, though, even the crazy ones."

"We don't have any business with Lynch," Jamie said. "As long as he leaves the lady alone, we'll leave him alone. And we'll be leaving Fort Worth before too long, I hope. He'll forget about us and go bother somebody else."

"That's a good thing to hope for," Pete said. He and his brothers exchanged looks. Gil and Nate nodded. Pete went on, "I reckon you can consider us ready to go, Mr. MacCallister. You need us to sign something?" He added proudly, "We can all read and write . . . a little."

Jamie shook his head. "This isn't the army, boys. If you say you're coming along, we'll take you at your word." He took out a five-dollar gold piece and handed it to Pete. "Since we don't know yet when we're leaving, this'll help you get by until then."

"We're mighty obliged to you, Mr. MacCallister," Pete said. His brothers echoed the sentiment.

Preacher said, "If you know any other fellas you think would be good for us to talk to, send 'em along."

"We sure will."

The Barnes brothers went on their way. When they were gone, Hannah said, "That's a good start, isn't it? We have three men for the journey now."

"Any start's a good one, I suppose, because you've got to start somewhere," Jamie said. "How good those fellas will turn out to be, and how long it'll take to find the others we need, well, we'll just have to wait and see about that."

CHAPTER 16

If Otis Lynch was still around Fort Worth, he stayed out of Jamie and Preacher's way for the next week. Neither man laid eyes on him. Despite that, one of them stayed close to Hannah at all times, trading off on the duty.

It was a busy time, as they rounded up the wagon, mule team, horses, and supplies for the trip, as well as talking to men who were interested in coming along even though the details of the journey were vague. Jamie had figured they would find plenty of tough, fiddle-footed hombres in Fort Worth, and that proved to be the case.

Even so, by the end of that week, they had only fourteen men lined up to accompany them, including the Barnes brothers. All the other preparations were made, but Jamie wanted at least twenty men for the group. Fourteen just struck him as not enough for the dangers they might be facing.

But then again, even though Preacher had been joking when they talked about it, in a way the old mountain man was right; a thousand men and a battery of cannon wouldn't have been too much for what they were planning to do.

A group of a couple of dozen could move a lot faster, though, and speed and stealth might well prove to be the keys to their survival.

They would wait a little while longer, Jamie and Preacher decided, but if they didn't find anybody else, they might have to set out with that smaller number.

Walt Reynolds knew he risked angering Keller, but as they sat in the tavern, passing around a bottle they had bought with some money Ox Tankersley had earned by mucking out a stable, Reynolds said to Keller, "You know, Teddy, I'm thinking it's time we moved along."

"From Fort Worth, you mean?" Keller snapped.

"That's right."

Keller shook his head. "Can't do that. We ain't settled things with that varmint MacCallister yet."

Ox said, "We're *never* gonna settle things with MacCallister, and you know it, Teddy. We followed you down here because you was all hot and bothered about gettin' revenge on him for bustin' us up the way he done, but he's been walkin' around town, bold as brass, for more than a week now and we haven't done a blasted thing. I agree with Walt. It's time to just forget about it and move on."

Keller glared across the table. "You think so, do you? Well, you don't make the decisions around here, Ox. I do. And I say MacCallister's got to pay—"

"Then you make him pay," Reynolds said. He pushed back his chair. "I'm finished. No law says we've all got to ride together, so I reckon I'll be heading out in the morning."

"Yeah? And just where in blazes do you think you're goin'?"

Reynolds shook his head. "I don't know. Away from here. Figure maybe I'll head south. I hear there's an ocean down there, or a gulf, anyway, next to where Texas and Mexico come together. Maybe I'll take a look at it."

Keller put his hands flat on the table and started to push himself to his feet. "You ain't goin' nowhere until I say you can leave—" he started.

Reynolds was ready to bolt to his feet and reach for his gun if Keller wanted to push it that far. He didn't know if he could beat Teddy to the draw, but maybe it was time they found out.

That was when Otis Lynch swaggered through the tavern's door with six men behind him. They were smaller than him—just about everybody in Fort Worth was smaller than Otis Lynch—but they looked almost as rough and mean.

Lynch's piggish gaze traveled around the room and came to rest on the table where Reynolds, Keller, Ox, Grover Appleton, and Billy Bob Moore sat. Moore's cuts and bruises had healed, and Appleton's arm wasn't in the sling anymore, although he still handled it mighty gingerly whenever he had to use it.

Since Reynolds was already halfway out of his chair, he straightened the rest of the way. So did Keller.

Lynch must have taken that as a sign of defiance because his bearded face twisted in a snarl, and he stomped across the room toward the table.

The rest of the tavern's customers headed for the door as fast as they could, not wanting any part of whatever might be about to happen. The nervous-looking bartender glanced around as if he couldn't decide whether to follow them or just hunker down behind the bar. He stayed where he was, evidently unwilling to abandon his business.

"You!" Lynch said to Keller as he pointed with a long, thick finger. "I thought I told you to get out of Fort Worth."

Keller was half drunk, and mad enough at the potential mutiny among his riding pards that he shot back, "That ain't the way I remember it, you big hairy ape. Anyway, nobody puts the run on me!" He sneered and added, "Not like the way MacCallister did on you, from what I hear."

Reynolds bit back a groan of dismay. That was the wrong thing to say to Otis Lynch, but Keller was too full of his own bile to realize it.

He got the idea pretty quickly, though, when Lynch let out a bellow of rage and lunged at Keller, his massive hands outstretched to grab and crush and break bones.

He didn't lay those hands on Keller because Ox Tankersley moved fast for a man of his bulk and got in the way first, stepping between Keller and Lynch and using his momentum to launch a right fist that crashed into Lynch's jaw with a sound like an ax hitting a solid stump. A powerful blow like that should have put any man on his back.

Lynch didn't even seem to notice it. Still roaring, he swung a backhand that connected solidly with Ox and knocked him sideways on the table, sending the partially empty whiskey bottle flying. The table's legs gave way under Ox's weight and collapsed. He landed hard on the floor in the middle of the wreckage.

Dealing with Ox had slowed Lynch down enough that Reynolds was able to grab Keller's arm and yell, "There's too many of 'em, Teddy! Let's get out of here!"

Danger must have sobered Keller, at least a little. He allowed Reynolds to pull him away from the table. There was a narrow angle through which they could make a dash for the door and maybe escape—but that would mean abandoning Ox.

Ox wasn't out of the fight, though, despite the wallop he'd gotten from Otis Lynch. He surged up partially from the floor, grabbed Lynch around the knees, and heaved.

Lynch had stood up to the punch Ox had given him, but he was caught off-balance this time. With a startled yell and windmilling arms, he went over backward, right into his companions crowding up behind him. For a second, they were all tangled up with each other. A couple of the other men lost their footing and fell, too, adding to the confusion.

"Go!" Reynolds called to the others. "Run!"

They dashed for the door while Lynch and his companions kept getting in each other's way. Reynolds heard heavy footsteps pounding behind him and knew that Ox had made it back to his feet and was fleeing, as well.

The five men spilled out into the early evening. Shadows had begun to gather over Fort Worth. A faint red line along the western horizon was the last vestige of the sun.

They stumbled to a halt a short distance from the tavern. Keller panted, "I don't like runnin' from a fight!"

"Neither do I, Teddy," Reynolds told him, "but they outnumber us to start with and that fella Lynch is like four or five men all by himself. Let's hunt a place to hole up—"

"Too late," Grover Appleton said in a voice that trembled with fear. "They ain't givin' up. Here they come now!"

CHAPTER 17

With Hannah walking between them, Jamie and Preacher were on their way back to the hotel from the café where they had eaten dinner. It was a pleasant evening, but a sense of restlessness gripped Jamie. The time had come to get on with this adventure if they were going to, and he knew it.

"I was thinking that tomorrow morning—" he began.

Before he could finish, Hannah exclaimed, "Philip!" and hurried toward the hotel ahead of the two men, who exchanged a puzzled glance in the gathering gloom.

"Who in blazes is Philip?" Preacher asked.

"That hombre, I reckon," Jamie replied as he nodded toward a man who had just pulled up at one of the hitchracks and dismounted. He turned to face Hannah with a big smile on his face and held out his arms. She rushed into his embrace, and he hugged her tightly.

Preacher looked over at Jamie and said, "Yeah, I reckon you're right, but that don't tell us who he is."

"No, it doesn't, and I don't have any idea," Jamie replied, "but Miss Craigson seems to know him."

"Appears you're right about that," Preacher said dryly as they watched Hannah lift her face so that the stranger could kiss her. "Either that, or she just guessed his name's Philip and she gets acquainted mighty easy."

Jamie chuckled and shook his head. "We'd better go see what this is all about."

Their long legs carried them quickly to Hannah and the stranger. The man looked over Hannah's shoulder and saw them coming, even though he was still kissing her. He broke the kiss and straightened. She saw where he was looking and half turned toward Jamie and Preacher.

"Don't worry, Philip," she said. "I know they can look very intimidating, but these are my friends. I already mentioned Mr. MacCallister in my letter, and this other gentleman is known as Preacher."

"A gentleman is somethin' I ain't been accused of bein' very often," Preacher said.

The stranger smiled and said, "If Hannah vouches for you, sir, that's more than good enough for me." He stepped away from her and extended his hand. "I'm Philip Saunders. Hannah and I are betrothed."

Preacher's bushy eyebrows went up as he clasped the man's hand. "The two of you are gettin' hitched?"

"That's right." Philip Saunders turned to Jamie and shook hands with him, too. "It's an honor to meet you, Mr. MacCallister. I know that Hannah's grandfather spoke highly of you, and so did she in her recent letter."

Jamie looked at Hannah and asked, "What letter was that?"

"I sent one to Philip before we left Colorado," she explained. "At the same time you sent your letter to Preacher. They probably reached St. Louis almost simultaneously."

"It took me a while to get here, however," Saunders said.

"You rode horseback all the way?" Jamie asked.

"That's right. I hoped I would reach Fort Worth before the three of you departed."

Hannah took hold of his left arm with both of hers and said, "Let's go in the hotel. I'm sure there's a room available."

"What about my horse?"

"I'll tend to him," Preacher volunteered. "I can take him down to the livery stable and make sure that he's took good care of."

"Thank you," Saunders said. "I'm pretty tired after a long day in the saddle, so I really do appreciate that."

"And I'll go see to it that Mr. Daggett finds a room for you," Jamie said.

Being helpful wasn't his only motivation, however. He wanted to get a better look at this Philip Saunders, supposedly Hannah's fiancé . . . but also somebody Jamie had never even heard of until just now.

He wondered why Hannah hadn't said anything about him.

After Saunders untied a small carpetbag that was lashed behind the saddle, Preacher led the horse toward the livery stable while Jamie went inside the hotel with the two young people. Once they were in the light from several lanterns hung up in the lobby, he saw that Saunders was a few years older than Hannah but still in his twenties, more than likely. He was tall and well-built, with sleek dark hair and clean-shaven except for thick side whiskers. He wore a soft-crowned brown hat and a darker brown frock coat and trousers over a white shirt and dark cravat. The clothes had been expensive at one time and were still perfectly respectable, but they were beginning to show tiny signs of wear in places.

E.M. Daggett greeted them from behind the counter. Hannah said, "Mr. Daggett, this is Mr. Philip Saunders, my fiancé. He's newly arrived in Fort Worth and needs somewhere to stay."

"Well, sir, you've come to the right place," Daggett said. He shook hands with Saunders and had him sign the registration book. "I'll have to put you in Room Twelve. I'm sorry I don't have anything closer to Miss Craigson."

"That's quite all right," Saunders assured him. "Since we're not yet married, it's only proper that the young lady and I maintain a respectable distance."

They hadn't been doing that a few minutes earlier, kissing out there in the middle of the street, Jamie thought, but they hadn't seen each other in a good long while so he supposed such a reaction was understandable.

"We just ate supper," Hannah told Saunders. "I wish you'd gotten here earlier, Philip, so you could have joined us."

"That's all right," he said. "I had some jerky that I bought at a place back up the road earlier today. What I'd really like to do is hear more about this exciting journey we're going to be taking."

"Hold on a minute," Jamie said with a glance at Daggett. The fact that he and Preacher were recruiting men for an expedition of some sort was common knowledge in Fort Worth, but they had taken pains not to reveal where they were going or what they were after. He didn't know if Hannah had supplied those details for Saunders, but if they were engaged to be married, it was quite possible the young man knew what was going on. Jamie didn't want him spilling it in front of Daggett, who might spread the news. "You need more than some jerky. Let's go back over to the café, and you can have a bowl of the best stew this side of St. Louis. It's on me."

"Why, that's awfully kind of you, Mr. MacCallister," Saunders said. "And it does sound good. Let me put this bag away . . ."

"I can put it in your room for you, sir," Daggett offered. "It'll be safe there, I assure you."

"Very well." Saunders handed over the carpetbag and then he and Hannah and Jamie left the hotel to stroll toward the café.

Jamie spotted Preacher headed toward them, having taken Saunders's horse to the livery. The old mountain man was still about fifty yards away and had just raised a hand in greeting when several men suddenly burst out the door of a building between them. They acted like the Devil himself was after them . . .

And maybe he was because just as one of the fleeing men yelled something, more men erupted from the doorway, led by none other than the towering, unmistakable figure of Otis Lynch.

CHAPTER 18

The men trailing right behind Lynch seemed to be cut from the same ugly cloth he was. In the poor light, Jamie couldn't tell much about the men they were pursuing. Those hombres stopped and hesitated, as if unsure whether to keep running or stand and fight.

If they fought, they weren't likely to win, Jamie knew. Not only were they outnumbered, but only one of them had any real size to him, and even he wouldn't be a match for Otis Lynch.

Jamie wasn't the only one who had recognized the outlaw. Hannah exclaimed, "It's that monster, Lynch! What's he going to do now?"

"Those fellas are in for some trouble, I reckon," Jamie said.

"You have to help them!"

Jamie frowned. He wasn't in the habit of sticking his nose into other people's problems . . . but at the same time, he didn't take kindly to seeing anybody ganged up on. His first instinct in any fight was to help the folks who were outnumbered. He had to be careful about that because sometimes the bunch that was outnumbered was actually in the wrong.

He didn't see how that could be true now, though, with Otis Lynch involved. Anybody Lynch was after had to deserve some help, Jamie decided.

Those thoughts flashed through his mind in a heartbeat, just long enough for Philip Saunders to react to Hannah's plea. He exclaimed, "I'll put a stop to this!" and charged forward.

At the same time, Jamie heard an angry yell from a voice that he recognized as Preacher's. The old mountain man had spotted Lynch, too, and wanted to get in on the ruckus himself.

That left Jamie no choice. Besides, with him and Preacher and Saunders pitching in, the two sides would be just about even.

"Get back to the hotel and stay there!" he barked at Hannah, and then he plunged ahead into what had turned, in the blink of an eye, into a wild melee in the middle of the street.

The biggest member of the first bunch met Lynch head on. They came together with a huge crash and started whaling away at each other. Lynch was several inches taller than his opponent and probably thirty or forty pounds heavier, but the other man was broad shouldered and barrel-chested and packed plenty of muscle of his own. Once he got his feet set, he was able to stand toe-to-toe with Lynch and trade punches.

That standoff couldn't last very long, though. Lynch's

sheer size and strength would overwhelm the other man, probably in a matter of moments.

While that battle was going on, several other violent clashes spread through the street. Fists flew back and forth and slammed into flesh and bone. Men yelled angry curses and grunted with pain and effort. One man from the first bunch ran back and forth crazily, evidently trying to avoid the fight, but an unshaven bruiser from the other group chased him, reaching out in an attempt to grab him.

He got Jamie instead of his intended victim, coming to an abrupt halt as the big frontiersman stepped between them. The attacker snarled an obscenity and swung a roundhouse punch at Jamie's head. Jamie leaned back to let the fist pass in front of his face. He raised his right hand, and while the other man was a little off-balance from that missed punch, he brought the side of that hand down against the man's neck, right where it joined the shoulder. The man stiffened, nerves numbed from the blow. He wasn't able to make even a token effort to block the left hook that Jamie sent whistling toward his jaw.

The powerful punch landed cleanly and knocked the man to his left. His feet came off the ground, and he landed in a limp sprawl that signified he was out cold and no longer part of the fight.

A few yards away, Preacher had rushed in from the other direction and tackled one of the attackers. They both landed hard and rolled over a couple of times in the street, raising a small cloud of dust with their exertions. The man wound up on top of Preacher and drove his knees into the old mountain man's chest, pinning him to the ground as he hammered punches into Preacher's face.

That advantage didn't last long. Preacher flung his right leg up, hooked it in front of the man's chest and throat, and scissored him off. Preacher had learned to wrestle against young Indian warriors while wintering with some of the friendly tribes, back in his early days in the mountains, and nobody was better at grappling than them.

Preacher rolled and pounced on the man, slugging him twice in the face. Preacher had been able to withstand the punishment he had received, but his opponent couldn't say the same. The man's head jerked to the side under Preacher's fist, then lolled loosely back the other way. He was unconscious.

While Preacher was busy with that, one of the other men came up behind him, drew a knife from a sheath at his waist, and lunged forward as he raised the blade high to bring it down into Preacher's back.

The treacherous stroke never fell. Jamie spotted what was about to happen and drew his Colt with blinding speed, but his bullet wasn't necessary. A large, gray, hairy shape hurtled through the early evening shadows and slammed into the knife wielder. Sharp teeth and powerful jaws clamped onto the man's upraised arm. He screamed as he fell with Dog on top of him. The big cur had either followed Preacher from the livery stable or been attracted by the sounds of a fight.

And to Dog, it would have seemed completely natural that if a fight was going on, Preacher would be exactly in the middle of it!

The rest of the men in the group that had been chased out of the building had paired off against the others from the second bunch, and they were all flailing and punching, biting and kicking. They seemed evenly matched.

The battle between Lynch and the other big fella ended suddenly when Lynch threw a roundhouse punch that the other man was a little too slow to block. The blow landed on the man's jaw and lifted him off his feet. He flew through the air and landed with his face skidding in the dirt.

Somehow, Philip Saunders found himself in front of Lynch. He stepped in and peppered the giant's face with punches. Jamie saw that and admired the young man's grit, but he knew grit wasn't going to do Saunders any good in this situation. He wasn't sure anything would do any good against Lynch, unless maybe it was a sledgehammer.

Saunders's fists might as well have been gnats for all the effect they had. Growling like the bear he resembled, Lynch reached out and grabbed Saunders by the arms, just below the shoulders. He lifted Saunders off the ground and shook him. Saunders's head jerked back and forth crazily.

"Philip!" Hannah cried in alarm.

Preacher was back on his feet. He glanced at Jamie, and they exchanged a nod. If they both tackled Lynch at the same time, they might have a chance against him.

They could have pulled their Colts and shot him, of course—Jamie would have shot that man with the knife to save Preacher's life—but neither of them cottoned to the idea of gunning a man down in what had, until now, been a bare-knuckles brawl.

The end came unexpectedly. Dog, leaving his previous prey a bloody, whimpering, huddled shape on the ground, turned to Lynch and grabbed the man's trouser leg in his teeth. As the big cur pulled on the cloth, Lynch looked down, saw him, and bellowed, "Get that critter away from me!"

With a spasmodic reaction, he flung Philip Saunders backward. Saunders might have been hurt badly if Jamie hadn't been there to catch him.

Roaring insanely, Lynch kicked his leg and tried to dislodge Dog. Dog hung on stubbornly, though, even as Lynch hopped and scuttled away. The man waved his arms and yelled. A note of hysteria came into his voice.

A lot of men were unreasonably scared of dogs, Jamie knew, even to the point of panicking if one was around. To be attacked by a dog might drive such a man out of his mind. Lynch appeared to be almost there.

Jamie pushed Saunders aside and strode forward quickly. Preacher was right beside him. Both men drew their guns and held the irons ready. Jamie had no doubt that if Lynch tried to hurt Dog, Preacher would kill him, no matter what the consequences.

"Better call him off," Jamie said.

"Yeah, I was just thinkin' the same thing," Preacher replied. "Dog! Back!"

Dog shook his head one last time, ripping out a piece of Lynch's trousers. He backed away holding the scrap in his clenched teeth and continued growling at the big man.

With the intent to commit canine murder shining brightly in his eyes, Lynch clawed at the holstered gun on his hip. His surprising swiftness on the draw didn't do him any good this time. Jamie and Preacher already had their Colts drawn and leveled. Lynch saw that and froze with his fingers just about to wrap themselves around the butt of his gun.

Glowering darkly, he spread those fingers wider and slowly raised his hand away from the weapon. "Don't shoot," he said.

"I'm mighty tempted to blow a hole in you anyway, mister," Preacher said. "As troublesome as you are, I figure it'd be justified just on gen'ral principles."

Knowing Preacher had Lynch covered, Jamie glanced around and saw that the battle was over. A couple of

Lynch's companions were still on the ground, groggy and only half conscious, but they were being helped up by their friends. The same was true of the men Lynch and the others had attacked. A couple of them were lifting the man Lynch had knocked out to his feet. His head hung forward over his chest, showing that he hadn't fully regained consciousness yet.

Off to one side, Hannah stood with Philip Saunders. His hat had come off when Lynch was shaking him. He'd picked it up and stood there brushing the dirt off it as Hannah worriedly grasped his left arm with both hands.

Lynch sneered at Preacher and said, "You wouldn't shoot a man in cold blood."

"I wouldn't be too sure about that," Preacher told him. "And speakin' of cold blood, I'd shoot a snake and never bat an eye. That pretty much feels like what I'm lookin' at right now."

Jamie rasped, "You men get on out of here. This is twice we've laid eyes on you, Lynch. Don't let there be a third time. We'll *start* with shooting if there is."

Lynch looked like he wanted to say something in response to that, but he continued glaring silently and after a moment, with a sour twist of his mouth under the bushy whiskers, he turned away.

"Come on," he yelled at his friends. "I need a drink."

Casting unfriendly glances back over their shoulders, the men shuffled away and disappeared into the building they had come from, which Jamie assumed was a tavern.

He was about to holster his gun when a voice with a note of defiant challenge in it said, "MacCallister? Is that you?"

Maybe it would be a good idea not to pouch the iron just yet, Jamie thought. He looked at the man who had spoken and found him vaguely familiar. The man was tall and had a beard that hung down over his chest, like Otis Lynch, but unlike the massive Lynch, he was rail thin.

"Do I know you, mister?" Jamie asked.

"You sure as blazes do," the man snapped as he stepped forward. His hand quivered over the butt of his gun from his eagerness to draw.

The sight of the Colt gripped rock steady in Jamie's hand stopped him, as did one of the other men who stepped up beside him and grasped his arm.

"Back off, Teddy," this man said. "They helped us. That lunatic Lynch and his pards might've killed us all."

The man called Teddy shook off his friend's hand. "That don't change what happened back in Colorado."

Jamie drew in a sharp breath and said, "Now I recognize you, mister." He looked at the others. "I know all of you." A grim smile tugged at his lips as he asked one of them, "How's that busted arm?"

"It hurt all the way down here," the man whined.

"Well, I probably acted a little hasty-like, but it wouldn't have happened if you hombres hadn't started the fight." Jamie moved his gaze back to the skinny, bearded man. "And it sure wouldn't have happened if you hadn't bothered Miss Craigson the way you did."

"Here, now, what's all this?" Philip Saunders asked with an angry frown.

"I'll explain it to you later, Philip," Hannah told him.

Still looking intently at the five men, Jamie said, "Did you follow us down here to Texas with the idea of getting even?"

"You reckon you don't deserve it for what you done?" the bearded man shot back at him.

"Defending a lady, as well as myself?" Jamie grunted. "Mister, I'll do that any day of the week. Twice on Sundays." He drew in a breath. "Now, if you've got your heart set on more trouble—"

"We don't, Mr. MacCallister." That was the one who'd held Teddy back. "We've put that behind us. We're not looking to cause any problems for anybody." He turned to look at the others. "Isn't that right, fellas?"

One of the men nodded without hesitation. The one whose arm Jamie had broken looked sullen and muttered something under his breath before saying, "Yeah, I'd just as soon not have no more trouble. When you get right down to it, I reckon it *was* our fault."

That left the big man, the first to take on Otis Lynch. He still looked a little groggy as he shook his head and then scrubbed a big hand across his face.

"I never was all that interested in comin' down here to this place," he rumbled. "I never lost nothin' in Texas."

With a furious glare on his face, Teddy backed away, saying bitterly, "Fine! All y'all can give up on settin' things right if you want to. But not me, blast it! Not me!"

He turned, bent to grab his fallen hat off the ground, and stalked off into the gathering night.

The young man who had stepped up as the spokesman for the group said, "Don't mind him, Mr. MacCallister. He'll get over being mad after a spell."

"I don't care if he gets over it or not," Jamie said, "as long as he stays out of our way."

"He will," the young man said. He stuck out his hand. "My name's Walt Reynolds, by the way. Thank you and your friends for pitching in to help us. That hombre Lynch is next thing to a monster, and he's pixilated to boot, I'm thinking."

"You'd be right about that," Jamie said. He didn't hesitate in clasping the young man's hand. Anybody who wanted to let the past be the past and start fresh deserved that chance, as far as Jamie was concerned. "Good to meet you again, Reynolds. In better circumstances this time."

"Better, yeah . . . but not by much, I reckon," Reynolds said. "Maybe the third time'll be the charm."

CHAPTER 19

As the four men drifted off in the same direction as their friend Teddy had gone, Jamie and Preacher finally holstered their guns and turned to Hannah and Saunders.

"That was a pretty brave thing, going up against Lynch like that," Jamie said to Saunders.

"Maybe not the smartest thing you ever did, though," Preacher added.

"I consider myself somewhat capable in an altercation," Saunders said, "but I've never encountered anyone like that. It felt as if I were punching a wall. I don't know what would have happened if that dog hadn't come along. I must admit, he's a, uh, pretty frightening-looking creature."

Preacher grinned and reached down to scratch between Dog's ears. The big cur had come up beside him and sat down.

"He don't like to miss out on any of the fun, that's for sure. But you don't have to worry about him as long as we're on the same side."

"I certainly don't intend to be on the wrong side of either of you!" Saunders declared.

"Come on, let's get you that bowl of stew we were after before that little ruckus interrupted us," Jamie said.

They went into the café, with Preacher telling Dog to stand guard outside. It wasn't likely that Lynch and his friends would come back and try to start more trouble, but Dog would give them plenty of warning if that happened.

The evening rush was over and only a few people were in the café. Jamie, Preacher, Hannah, and Saunders sat at the far end of one of the long tables, as usual. A solid wall was behind them, and Jamie and Preacher both liked being able to see anybody who came into the place.

Saunders ate some of the stew and declared it as good as advertised. Then he said, "I take it this wasn't your first encounter with that behemoth."

"You mean Lynch?" Jamie said. "Yeah, we've tangled with him before."

Hannah said, "He acted quite aggressively toward me one day, but Preacher and Jamie soon put a stop to that."

Saunders frowned at the two men. "Perhaps you should've gone ahead and shot him."

"Yeah," Preacher said, "we might have cause to regret that we didn't."

"Well, it's good that we're all leaving Fort Worth soon, then. Once we've started on the journey, we shouldn't have to worry about this fellow Lynch anymore."

Jamie and Preacher exchanged a look, then Jamie said, "You know where it is we're going?"

"Of course. We're going to look for Colonel—"

Jamie held up a hand to stop him. He said to Hannah, "You told him about those papers you have?"

"Certainly," she said. "Philip and I are engaged to be married. He knows everything that I know."

She might have mentioned that before now, Jamie thought, but he supposed it wouldn't help anything to bring that up. Instead, he nodded and said to Saunders, "Then you ought to have a pretty good idea what a dangerous trip this is going to be."

"I'm aware that there's an element of risk involved, but with everything that's at stake, you can't expect Hannah not to go along. Her entire future . . . *our* entire future . . . is riding on this."

Preacher's eyes narrowed as he said, "If I was in love with a gal, I don't reckon I'd want her riskin' her life unnecessarily no matter what the stakes were."

Hannah laughed. "You don't know how many times Philip made that same argument to me before I ever set out for Colorado. Eventually he came to realize that I was right."

"You mean you wore him down," Preacher said.

Saunders said, "I'm still not fond of the idea, but remember, none of us would be setting out on this journey if it weren't for Hannah. She's at the very center of the whole thing." He shrugged. "At any rate, I intend to make sure that she's safe. You gentlemen will be the leaders of the expedition and in charge of everything else, but my sole concern and responsibility will be Hannah's safety and well-being."

"So you see," she said, "I'll have my own personal bodyguard. Everything will be fine."

Jamie wasn't convinced of that—not for a second. He figured that Hannah and Saunders both were underestimating just how perilous this trip up the Brazos might turn out to be. They had never dealt with Indians before. Jamie had, and Preacher had even more experience than he did.

Saunders used a biscuit to wipe up the last of the stew clinging to the sides of his bowl, and after he had eaten it, he said, "Besides, after everything that's happened, you can't believe that it would be safe to leave Hannah here in Fort Worth by herself."

A frown creased Jamie's forehead. That very thought had been troubling him. This frontier settlement was a rough place, full of rough men. E.M. Daggett seemed like a solid businessman, and under different circumstances, Jamie might have trusted him to look after Hannah while they were gone.

But then Otis Lynch had reared his ugly head, and even though Jamie and Preacher had faced him down twice, Jamie wasn't convinced that would be enough to make Lynch leave them alone in the future.

If Lynch found out that Hannah was still here in Fort Worth with no real protector, that would be asking for trouble, indeed. And Philip Saunders would be no match for Lynch, even if they could persuade the young man to stay behind.

It was beginning to look like they were between a rock and a hard place.

And the situation might be about to get worse. Preacher said quietly, "Look who just came in."

Jamie raised his gaze to the café's entrance and saw four men. He recognized them as Walt Reynolds and the other three who had battled Otis Lynch and his friends. Reynolds spotted them sitting at the far end of the table and started toward them with his companions trailing him.

"They don't look like they're hunting for trouble," Jamie said.

"Yeah, but they've got a grudge against you, don't they?" Preacher asked.

Jamie shrugged. "Like I told you, we tangled before, but that was a while back. Reynolds claimed that was all over."

"Some fellas never give up a grudge. They like to hang on to it while it festers."

Jamie knew that was true. He noted, as well, that the one called Teddy, the man who had started the ruckus back home by accosting Hannah, wasn't with these men. He hadn't come looking to be a friend.

Jamie got to his feet and moved to put Hannah and Saunders behind him. Preacher did likewise. Standing shoulder to shoulder, they were a very formidable obstacle. And Dog was right outside, where a call from Preacher would bring him swiftly to join them. The big cur had allowed these men to pass because they had been fighting on the same side as Preacher and Jamie a short time earlier.

Reynolds came to a stop a few feet away. The other three men halted behind him. He nodded and said, "Mr. MacCallister."

"What can we do for you?" Jamie asked.

"The boys and I have been talking, and we're hoping there's something we can do for you."

"I can't think of what it would be," Jamie said bluntly.

"Well, we heard talk that you're going to be leaving town on some sort of trip. Some folks even called it an expedition."

"That's our business."

"Sure, but we were told you've been looking to hire some men to go with you."

"Already did," Jamie said. He wasn't sure he liked the way this conversation was going.

"You don't have enough, though, do you?"

Preacher said, "After the trouble you caused Jamie up in Colorado, do you really reckon we'd trust you enough to hire you to come with us?"

"Why not?" Reynolds asked. "We were in the wrong,

the first time we ran into Mr. MacCallister, and we don't mind admitting it. We don't mind apologizing for it, either."

Jamie said, "You don't owe me any apologies."

Reynolds appeared to understand what he meant. The young man took off his hat, held it in front of him, and raked his long blond hair back from his face with the other hand. He leaned to the side so he could look past Jamie and said, "Miss Craigson, on behalf of me and the other fellas, I want to apologize for everything that happened up in Colorado. That trouble was all our fault, and it wouldn't have happened if, uh, we hadn't been drinking quite a bit . . ."

"It wouldn't have happened if your friend hadn't been a total boor," Hannah said tartly.

"Yes, ma'am, that's true as well, and I apologize for what Teddy did, too."

"What's his full name?" Jamie asked.

"Teddy Keller, sir."

"Where is he?"

Reynolds hesitated, then said, "I don't rightly know. Teddy and the rest of us, well, we've parted company, sir."

"But you let him lead you down here to Texas because he was holding a grudge against me, and probably against Miss Craigson, too."

"We kind of got in the habit of letting Teddy do the thinking for us," Reynolds admitted. "We've been riding together for a while, and you know how that is. One fella starts making the decisions, and the others go along with him, for a while, anyway."

"And you're saying that's over now?"

"Yes, sir. Even before the trouble broke out tonight, we'd already told Teddy that we weren't going to have anything more to do with trying to settle any scores—"

"Why'd Lynch and his mob come after you?" Preacher broke in.

The biggest member of the trio with Reynolds spoke up for the first time. "Because he's plumb loco! It's like he just goes around lookin' for people to get mad at and fight with."

Jamie nodded. "Seems to be about the size of it, all right."

"That's another thing," Reynolds said. "Lynch and his friends could have killed us. At the very least, they'd have busted us up pretty bad. Ox here"—he jerked a thumb over his shoulder at the big man—"he's the only one of us who's really any good at brawling."

"And I'm no match for that fella Lynch," Ox said. "Even though I sure don't like to admit it."

"So we figure we owe you," Reynolds went on. "That's another reason we'd like to sign on with you. We'd like to help you with whatever it is you're setting out to do, to pay you back for that . . . the right way this time."

Jamie gave them a skeptical look, then turned his attention to the man whose arm he had broken and said, "How about you? Do you feel the same way, mister? Want to let bygones be bygones, even though I busted your arm?"

The man scowled and said, "I ain't gonna lie to you, MacCallister. I cussed you many a time while my arm was healin' up. Every time it hurt, I cussed you . . . and it hurt a lot." He shrugged. "But it ain't too bad now, and like Walt said, we started that ball. I don't reckon I'll ever count you as a pard, but I don't want no more trouble with you, neither. My name's Grover Appleton, by the way."

"Billy Bob Moore," one of the men introduced himself.

"And I'm Ox Tankersley," the big man rumbled.

Jamie regarded the four of them for a moment, then asked, "Any of you wanted by the law?"

"No, sir," Reynolds replied.

"Is that because you're not outlaws, or because you've never been caught at it?"

Reynolds drew in a breath and said, "Well, sir, it's true that we haven't always, uh, walked the straight and narrow, but I swear to you that the law in Texas doesn't want us. You won't be bringing down any legal trouble on your head by hiring us to go with you."

Preacher said, "Well, if that ain't a strong recommendation, then I reckon I never heard one."

Surprisingly, the old mountain man's blistering sarcasm made a flush creep into Reynolds's face. "A fella can try to turn away from his old ways and follow a new path. Doesn't it say that somewhere in the Good Book? Seems like I've heard it."

"It does," Jamie agreed. "It's just a question of whether we believe that's what you're really trying to do."

"Meaning no disrespect . . . but there's only one way to find out, isn't there?"

He had a point there. Jamie turned to look at Preacher, who shrugged and said, "You know these hombres better than I do. I'll leave it up to you, Jamie."

"Miss Craigson?"

She smiled and said, "I've put my faith in you from the start, Mr. MacCallister. I trust your judgment."

"And I just got here," Saunders said, "so I wouldn't venture to interfere."

Not that Jamie would have paid much attention if he had.

Since it was up to him, he turned back to Reynolds and the other three and studied them intently for a long moment before saying, "We'll be leaving in the morning."

"That's fine with us," Reynolds said. He looked back at the others, who nodded their agreement. "It's not like we have anywhere else we have to be."

"Don't you want to know where you're going?" Jamie asked.

"Just point us in the right direction. That'll be fine."

Preacher asked, "You got plenty of guns and ammunition?"

"Plenty of guns. We're a mite low on ammunition, though."

Jamie said, "Stock up, if the general store's still open. If it's not, do that first thing in the morning." He held out a coin. "You can use this to pay for it."

Reynolds nodded and took the gold piece. "We're obliged to you, Mr. MacCallister, not just for staking us like this . . . but for trusting us, too. I reckon we're part of the bunch now?"

"You are," Jamie said. "And if you ever give me a reason to regret it, I'll make sure to kill you myself."

CHAPTER 20

Before they parted to go to their rooms at the hotel, Hannah cornered Jamie and said, "Have you made up your mind, Mr. MacCallister? Are you going to allow me to come along on this journey?"

"You've said all along that you're going whether I like it or not," Jamie pointed out.

"Yes, but for all practical purposes, how could I enforce that? You could always simply refuse to go if I insisted."

"I'm not backing out now," Jamie declared. He smiled. "For one thing, you've gotten me curious. Even though it's farfetched, I want to know if Jim Bowie's treasure is really out there where you say it is."

"You haven't answered my question."

"I *don't* like it," Jamie said. "I don't like it one little bit. But leaving you here in Fort Worth with Otis Lynch around is just asking for trouble. I'm not saying he's as dangerous as the Comanches, but we're going to do our best to avoid them. Here in town, I don't reckon you could avoid Lynch."

"And he frightens me. Terrifies me, to be honest. I think he's a madman."

Jamie nodded. "You're not far wrong. And because of that . . . yeah, you're coming along with us, at least part of the way."

"Part of the way?" she repeated, clearly surprised. "What do you mean by that?"

"Fort Worth's not the real jumping off point when it comes to civilization here in Texas. That would be Fort Belknap, an army post about a hundred miles northwest of here. We'll have to wait until we get there and have a look at the place, but it might be a good idea for you to stay there while the rest of us move on."

Her lips thinned. She said, "I don't care for that idea, Mr. MacCallister. But I won't argue with you about it . . . right now."

"Fair enough," Jamie told her. "Better turn in and try to get a good night's sleep. You'll need to be rested up once we start out in the morning."

Philip Saunders had gone into his room already, and so had Preacher. Jamie and Hannah were alone in the dirt-floored hallway. With a look on her face that said she was giving in to impulse, she put a hand on Jamie's arm, came up on her toes, and stretched upward to brush her lips against his grizzled cheek.

"Thank you, Mr. MacCallister," she said. "No matter what happens at Fort Belknap . . . and beyond . . . thank you for bringing me this far."

Jamie cleared his throat, pinched the wide brim of his hat, and nodded. "Good night, Miss Craigson."

"Good night, Mr. MacCallister." Still smiling, she went in her room and closed the door behind her.

Jamie shook his head slowly. He didn't know what was going to happen at Fort Belknap, either . . . but he wasn't going to bet a hat that that redheaded gal wouldn't get her way in the end.

He and Preacher were up well before dawn the next morning. They rode to Patterson's Wagon Yard on the edge of town to pick up the wagon, the team, and the pack horses and extra saddle mounts, then brought everything back to the hotel, where E.M. Daggett had been storing their supplies. The Barnes brothers showed up a couple of minutes later, yawning because of the early hour, and Jamie put them to work loading the supplies into the wagon and onto the pack horses.

Some of Fort Worth's citizens who were stirring early took note of the activity and wandered over to observe with interest. Jamie knew quite a few rumors about this expedition were floating around town, although he and Preacher had succeeded in keeping the details of it a secret, at least as far as he was aware.

More of the men who had signed on showed up as the sky lightened in the east. Jamie had warned them that they would be leaving at first light, which he had known all along was a little too optimistic. But they would be rolling by sunup, he promised himself.

The four men who had signed on after the brawl the previous night were some of the last to arrive. Jamie had wondered if they had thought better of joining the expedition, which he figured had been Walt Reynolds's idea. But they walked up in front of Daggett's Hotel leading horses. Jamie didn't know where they had spent the night and didn't care.

Reynolds was the only one who really looked awake, but he nodded and said, "Morning, Mr. MacCallister."

"Morning," Jamie returned with a nod. "Did you manage to stock up on ammunition like I told you?"

"Yes, sir, the store was still open yesterday evening, so we got plenty of rounds for our Colts and powder and shot for our rifles. Where we're going, I figure we'll need it."

That caught Jamie's interest. Maybe more details of the journey had spread than he'd hoped. "What do you mean, where we're going?"

"Well, word is that we'll be heading west. Where, exactly, in that direction, I don't know, but some folks have started saying that Fort Worth is where the West begins because there was a treaty with the Indians that said they'd stay west of a line that went through here on the map. So it's not what you'd call tame anywhere that way."

Reynolds waved a hand toward the nearby Trinity River.

Whether he actually knew more than he was saying or not, Jamie couldn't tell. But for now he nodded and said, "You're right. That's the way we're headed. You boys want to change your minds?"

"Nope."

"We said we'd go," Ox Tankersley added. "We'll go." Billy Bob Moore and Grover Appleton nodded.

"Any sign of your other friend?" Jamie asked.

"Teddy?" Reynolds sighed and shook his head. "No, he probably got drunk and is holed up somewhere sleeping it off. After that falling-out we had, though, he won't want anything more to do with us. Kind of a shame. He's a good hombre, when he's not on the prod."

From what Jamie had seen of him, Teddy Keller was always on the prod. But that wouldn't be his problem anymore once they had left Fort Worth.

Everyone was there except Hannah Craigson and Philip Saunders. Jamie was about to go into the hotel to check on them when they both emerged from the building into the gray dawn. Saunders still looked half asleep, but Hannah was wide awake and eager.

"Is everything ready, Mr. MacCallister?" she asked.

"Yes, ma'am, it is," he told her. "All I have to do is give the order for everybody to mount up. After you climb up on the wagon seat, of course. Pete Barnes is going to handle the team today, if that's all right with you."

"Of course. Whatever you think best."

"I'll ride right beside the wagon, dear," Saunders said. "So I won't be far away if you need anything."

"Thank you, Philip." Hannah looked at Jamie and nodded. "I'm ready."

Saunders helped her onto the seat. Pete Barnes climbed up beside her and unwrapped the team's lines from the brake lever. He smiled and nodded pleasantly to Hannah.

Preacher had saddled one of the extra horses for Saunders. He handed the reins to the young man and said, "Since you've ridden that other horse all the way down here to Texas, you need to give it a rest. Patterson tells me this is a good saddle mount, not prone to skittishness and with plenty of sand."

"Thank you. I'm a good rider, so I should be able to handle this one just fine."

"Uh-huh," Preacher said, nodding. Saunders didn't lack for confidence. But he swung up into the saddle with a lithe ease, so maybe he actually was a good rider.

On a trip like this, it wouldn't take long to find out.

Jamie and Preacher mounted up, as well. Jamie rode along the line of men, checking to see if everyone looked to be ready. He paused and spoke to a few of them.

When he passed Walt Reynolds, the young saddle tramp

said, "Thanks again for giving us this chance, Mr. MacCallister."

"Just don't let me down," Jamie warned.

"No, sir. We sure won't."

Satisfied that they were ready to go, Jamie headed back to the front of the line. The sun hadn't quite popped over the eastern horizon yet. They hadn't left by first light, but he was pleased anyway. He raised himself in his stirrups, lifted his hat over his head, and waved it forward.

"Move out!"

CHAPTER 21

A few days earlier, Jamie and Preacher had scouted out the best way to cross the Trinity. The bluffs were too steep for the wagon to descend here at the settlement, so they had to travel a mile or so southwest before dropping down to a level spot where the river could be forded over a rocky bottom. Then they jogged back north a short distance to ford the river's other fork.

Beyond the Trinity were post oak–dotted hills that rolled westward in long, gentle swells, easy traveling for the most part, at least starting out.

A while back, Jamie and Preacher had joined forces to guide a wagon train along the Oregon Trail. With only one wagon and a group of horsemen on this journey, Jamie expected to make much better time.

The miles fell behind them. There was yet another fork of the Trinity up ahead of them somewhere, Jamie knew, and he wasn't sure how much trouble it would be to find a place to ford it, but they would deal with that when the time came.

He and Preacher took the lead most of the time, with Dog venturing ahead of them. The wagon came next, with some of the men flanking it on both sides while the rest of the group followed with the pack horses and extra saddle mounts.

Preacher rode with his rifle across the saddle in front of him, ready for use if he needed it. He said, "From what I've heard, it's been a few years since the Comanche or any other Injuns raided this far east, but I reckon it won't hurt nothin' to keep our eyes open. You know as well as I do that Injuns are notional critters. You can't never tell what they might do."

"We might run into outlaws, too," Jamie commented. "We'll stay alert, and we'll post guards at night."

Preacher squinted over at him. "You figure there's any chance that fella Lynch will come after us?"

"I don't know him well enough to say, but I don't think we can rule it out."

The old mountain man nodded. "Yeah, I feel the same way. Well, if he shows up, we'll give him the ol' hot lead welcome. I figure he won't be the only varmint gettin' one o' those 'fore this trip is over."

Jamie nodded and said, "I'm afraid you're probably right about that."

From time to time, he dropped back to see how Hannah was doing on the wagon. She always had a cheerful smile for him and assured him she was fine.

Philip Saunders was beginning to look a little tired and pained by the middle of the day, however. Despite his claims of being a good rider, he probably wasn't accustomed to such a brisk pace. But he didn't complain, and he stayed close to the wagon, as he had promised Hannah he'd do.

They reached the next river crossing in midafternoon. They had already forded a few small creeks without any problems. Jamie and Preacher rode up and down the river looking for a good place to ford and located one about half a mile south of their current location. Once they were across the stream, they continued angling northwestward.

They had passed a few farmhouses during the day, log cabins with stone chimneys at one end and garden patches and cultivated fields around them. Most were built in the dogtrot style, with two rooms sharing a common roof but separated by an open space in between.

"You just can't keep those farmers out, can you?" Preacher commented when they passed one of those cabins. "Even when it ain't safe, they'll risk their own hides and those of their family, too, just to plow up the ground."

"It's natural for a man to want a piece of land for his own," Jamie said. "Some place where he can feel like he's building something that nobody can take away from him."

"Nobody except a bunch of Injuns that want his hair." Preacher shrugged. "But I never listened much to anybody who tried to tell me what I ought to do, so I reckon I can't blame these folks for not listenin', either."

The terrain became more rugged as they pushed on. Some of the ridges were too steep and rocky for the wagon, but luckily there were broad valleys winding between them. Late in the afternoon, they came to an actual trail, evidence that wagons had come through here before. Those vehicles probably belonged to more settlers.

Jamie and Preacher told Pete Barnes to continue following the trail and rode ahead to see where it led. They came to a winding creek that had a plank bridge over it. Someone had put up a sign, a flattened chunk of wood that had the words *ASH CREEK* burned into it.

"Some durned farmer put that sign up, I'd bet a hat on that," Preacher said.

"More than likely, but we can thank him for building that bridge. It'll make it easier for the wagon to cross the creek. Those banks are pretty steep."

"Aw, we would've found a place to ford it." Preacher shrugged. "But I reckon if we don't have to, that's even better."

A short distance past the creek, the two frontiersmen reined in. Jamie said, "That looks like a trading post up ahead. I didn't expect to find anything like that on this side of the Trinity, short of Fort Belknap."

"Sign up yonder next to the trail says *MOORESVILLE*," Preacher pointed out. "I don't know who decided that one tradin' post deserves a name like a town does, but it appears that's what they call the place."

Jamie chuckled. "I expect the man who owns the trading post is named Moore. Let's go find out."

They rode on with Dog trotting beside them. As they approached the store, they saw a wagon parked in front of it, with a team of two mules hitched to the vehicle. A man emerged from the sturdy log building and started to climb onto the wagon, but he stopped and stood there with his hand on the seat as he watched Jamie and Preacher riding toward him.

He was a burly, barrel-chested man in a dark suit and hat, with white hair and a bristling mustache. As the two newcomers reined in, he greeted them with a nod and said, "Howdy, boys. What brings you to our little community?"

"You've got a community here besides this tradin' post?" Preacher asked.

"Yes, indeed. There are at least half a dozen families of

settlers in the area. We have a school, a gristmill, and two doctors, including myself. I'm Dr. J.G. Reynolds."

"Reynolds," Jamie repeated. "We have a young fella by that name traveling with us. His first name is Walt."

"No relation, as far as I know," Dr. Reynolds said with a shake of his head.

"Where are all those other things you mentioned?" Preacher asked.

"Back along Ash Creek," Reynolds replied with a wave of his hand toward the winding stream. "We're going to have us a nice little town here, one of these days."

"I wouldn't doubt it," Jamie said. "We've got a wagon and a good-sized group of riders coming up behind us. Will it be any problem if we camp for the night on the banks of the creek?"

"None at all, as far as I can see. We're friendly folks, here in Mooresville."

Jamie nodded toward the trading post. "Fella name of Moore owns the business, I take it?"

Reynolds chuckled. "Indeed, he does. When people began moving here, they called the area Elizabeth Town at first, but Moore persuaded us to change the name. Seeing as how he provides most of our supplies and other goods . . ."

"Yeah, that makes sense."

"Don't you worry about Injuns?" Preacher asked.

"Of course. The Kiowa and the Comanche have been known to raid in this area, so we remain alert at all times." Reynolds reached into the back of the wagon and picked up a shotgun. "And we're always armed, as well. But so far, we've had no trouble, and we pray that continues."

"So do we, Doctor," Jamie said.

"I don't believe you fellows have mentioned your names."

"I'm Jamie MacCallister. This is my friend Preacher."

"A minister of the gospel?" Reynolds asked with interest. "There's been talk about starting a church in the area. I'd be willing to let the congregation use the school building I put up."

"Sorry, Doctor," the old mountain man said. "I ain't that kind of a preacher."

Reynolds frowned in puzzlement. "But what other kind *is* there?"

"Don't ask him that," Jamie advised. "He's liable to tell you." He turned his horse. "We'll ride back and lead the rest of our bunch in."

"Very well." Reynolds lifted a hand in farewell. "So long, gentlemen, and again, welcome!"

CHAPTER 22

The group camped that night in a grassy meadow with the creek on one side of it. Ash, cottonwood, and pecan trees grew along the stream, and thick groves of oak surrounded the meadow on the other three sides.

"This is very pleasant," Hannah commented as she sat on a fallen tree beside the fire with Jamie, Preacher, and Philip Saunders.

"Don't expect it to stay like this," Jamie warned her. "The country won't be bad for the first week or so, but the farther north and west we go, the worse it'll get."

"Will there be mountains?" Saunders asked.

Jamie shook his head. "No. Some fairly rugged hills and ridges here and there, but no real mountains. But it'll be hot and dry, with some deep gullies. We might have to go miles out of our way at times to get around them. It won't be like crossing the Rockies, but it won't be enjoyable, either."

Preacher grunted and added, "And that ain't even figurin' on what the Comanch' might do. They can make things *real* unpleasant."

Hannah looked a little shaken by the conversation, but her voice was strong as she said, "Then I suppose we really ought to be enjoying the journey while we can."

"Yes, ma'am," Jamie said. "Because it's liable to just get worse from here on out."

Otis Lynch and his friends were in a different tavern in Fort Worth tonight, but it was the same sort of squalid place they usually frequented. They slouched in rickety chairs at a roughhewn table in the back, shoving a couple of jugs of whiskey around as they took turns drinking. Several sported bruises from the ruckus the night before, and they winced from sore muscles whenever they reached for one of the jugs.

Lynch wasn't saying anything, just scowling darkly at the table with his head lowered so that his beard pressed against his chest. Nobody else spoke much, fearful of setting him off. Lynch's moods were unpredictable, at best, and no one wanted to be around him when he exploded, even his so-called friends.

Despite that caution, one of the men gathered his courage and spoke up when he saw a familiar figure shuffle into the tavern. He said, "Otis, look who just come in."

Lynch raised his head to glare toward the entrance. He saw the tall, skinny, bearded man who had just come in looking around the smoky, dimly lantern-lit room. A rumble like a distant avalanche came from deep within Otis Lynch's chest as he recognized the man he had clashed with twice before.

"What's he doin' here?" another man at the table muttered. "Is he plumb crazy?"

Evidently that was the case because the newcomer spotted Lynch and the other men and strode toward them. His thumbs were hooked in his gun belt, and his gait had an unmistakable arrogance to it.

Lynch rose to his feet, towering over the table and the other men. His hand moved toward the gun on his hip, but the stranger held up a hand, palm out, as he came to a stop and said, "I ain't lookin' for trouble."

"Well, you found it," Lynch said, "and this time you don't have MacCallister and Preacher to help you."

The giant didn't sound simpleminded now, or insane with rage, either. His voice was cold and controlled and filled with menace. Clearly, whatever demons were normally roaming around inside his head, he had them reined in at the moment.

"I never wanted any help from them," the stranger said. "Especially MacCallister. I hate that big son of a gun just as much as you do, Lynch. I came all the way down here from Colorado just to get even with him." A bitter note came into his voice as he went on, "But my so-called friends ran out on me. Even worse, they up and threw in with MacCallister his own self!"

Lynch frowned, although the way his shaggy hair fell in front of his forehead, it was hard to tell. "What in blazes are you talking about?"

"MacCallister and that old codger Preacher are takin' some sort of expedition out west. The fellas I've been ridin' with joined up with them."

"How do you know that?"

"I ran into one of them late last night. The others had already turned in. Grover told me about it. Said he didn't know what MacCallister and Preacher are after, but rumor is that it's somethin' valuable."

"Out west of here? In Indian country?"

The other man's narrow shoulders rose and fell. "I'm just tellin' you what I heard. Figured you might be interested, seein' as how you've got a grudge against MacCallister, too."

"So you're saying that the two of us should join forces and go after MacCallister?" Lynch threw his head back and bellowed in laughter. "That's the craziest thing I've ever heard!"

The other man's face tightened with anger, but his voice remained calm as he said, "There's an old sayin' . . . the enemy of my enemy is my friend. I know we've had a couple of run-ins, Lynch, but I'd be willin' to forget all about 'em if it meant settlin' the score with Jamie MacCallister. How about it?"

"You don't have anybody else to help you, and you can't do it alone. That's what you mean."

"That's true, I reckon. But it don't change what either one of us wants, and that's for MacCallister to get what's comin' to him, along with anybody else who's sidin' him."

"Including your old pards?"

"Includin' them, if it comes to that," the man said, his voice as hard as flint. "They turned on me, and they might as well be dead to me now."

"And I reckon you'll be expecting a share in whatever it is that MacCallister is going after?"

"That seems only fair, don't it, since I brought the idea to you?"

The other men around the table looked as if they expected Lynch to erupt in violence at any second, but instead the big man chuckled.

"I reckon you've got a deal, mister," he said. "What's your name, anyway?"

"Teddy Keller."

Lynch stepped closer and thrust out his hand. "All right,

Keller. Here's to seeing that Jamie MacCallister gets what's coming to him . . . and that we get whatever he's going after."

The huge paw all but swallowed Keller's hand, but he shook and nodded.

Lynch grinned, thinking that he could always kill Keller later, after getting all the use out of him that he could.

And, he reminded himself, more than likely Keller was thinking the same thing about him . . .

CHAPTER 23

Following directions he'd gotten from the storekeeper Moore, Walt Reynolds rode across Ash Creek that evening and followed some wagon ruts up a gentle hill and along a winding path to the home of J.G. Reynolds. Nearby was the gristmill the settler operated, along with the picket-style building used for a school.

The older man's residence was a frame structure built of lumber rather than logs, probably one of the first such in this area. The walls had been whitewashed so that they gleamed in the moonlight. A couple of dogs barked to announce Walt's arrival, and the commotion drew Reynolds out of his house. Lamplight spilled through the open door and revealed that he was carrying a shotgun.

"What can I do for you, young fella?" Reynolds asked, keeping the shotgun's twin barrels pointing in Walt's general direction as the visitor drew up in the long, slanting rectangle of light coming from the doorway.

Walt didn't dismount, since he hadn't been invited to do so. He smiled, nodded, and said, "You'd be Dr. Reynolds?"

"John Giles Reynolds, that's right." The man's broad shoulders rose and fell slightly. "I have some medical training, but I don't really practice anymore. The gristmill takes up most of my time. If you need medical assistance, you'll have to ride over and see my friend Dr. Steward. He lives in the old Rumsfeldt cabin—"

Walt held up a hand to stop the older man. "No, sir, I don't need a sawbones, and it's you I came to see. My name's Reynolds, too. Walter John Reynolds, but most folks call me Walt."

"Are you claiming to be kin?"

"No, sir, just didn't want to miss the opportunity to say hello to another Reynolds."

"Well, in that case . . . light down from that saddle and come up here on the porch. You're too late for supper, but I'd be pleased to talk for a spell."

"That sounds good to me, sir." Walt swung down from the saddle. Reynolds set the shotgun aside and waved the young man into one of several rocking chairs on the porch.

They talked for an hour as the last of the evening light faded from the sky. As they traded information about their families, they realized that they weren't related, or if they were, it was so distantly that the link couldn't be traced.

"Where are you folks headed?" Reynolds asked. "Plan on settling west of here?"

"No, sir, I don't think so," Walt replied. "It sounds a mite odd, but I don't really know where we're headed. Me and my friends and some other fellas hired on to ride with Mr. MacCallister and Preacher, and I get the sense that *they're* working for the young lady who's traveling with us—"

"Wait a minute. There's a young woman with your group?"

Reynolds had left the trading post before the rest of the party arrived, so he hadn't seen Hannah Craigson.

"Yes, sir. Her and the fella she's betrothed to. They're looking for something, but I don't know what it is or where we'll find it."

"But you're heading west."

"Yes, sir."

Reynolds frowned in the gathering darkness and said, "Young man, I don't know how familiar you are with Texas—"

"Not much. This is my first time here."

"Well, I can tell you this much. The farther west you go, the more dangerous it'll be. Why, some people said that my friends and I were crazy to settle anywhere west of Fort Worth. They claimed we'd be scalped before the first year was out." Reynolds shook his head. "So far it hasn't happened, of course, and as more people come in, I believe the Indians will become even less likely to raid in this area. But I could be wrong, and believe me, I think about that every single day."

"Mr. MacCallister and Preacher seem to know what they're doing."

"After I met them this afternoon and thought about it for a while later, I believe I've heard of MacCallister. He's supposed to be a good man, so I suppose it's not unreasonable for you to have faith in him. I'm sure that fellow Preacher is the same sort, from the look of him. But even so, you need to keep your eyes open, son. Be alert for trouble at all times."

"I sort of am, anyway, just out of habit."

Reynolds eyed him intently. "Ridden some dark trails, have you?"

"Well . . ."

Reynolds held up a hand and said, "Never mind. None of my business. I just don't want to see another Reynolds come to a bad end, whether we're blood kin or not. There's still the family name to consider, you know."

"Yes, sir. I'll do my dead-level best not to dishonor it."

As he made that pledge, Walt realized, somewhat to his surprise, that he meant it. He had done plenty of things in his life to bring dishonor on his name. Looking back on those days now, he was ashamed of himself. He had gone along with whatever schemes Teddy Keller had come up with, just because it was easier, and hadn't worried too much about whether they were legal. He'd always been more of a follower than a leader.

He was still following, he told himself, but now it was Jamie MacCallister and Preacher leading the way, and they were much different from Teddy Keller. He might be riding into danger with them, but at least he was siding with honest men for a change.

From here on out, maybe he'd be an honest man, too.

As Walt shook hands with J.G. Reynolds and got ready to leave, the older man said, "Good luck to you, son. I fear that you're going to need fortune smiling on you, wherever it is you're going!"

"Yes, sir, more than likely. And I'll take all the good luck we can get, I promise you that!"

As Jamie had told them, the terrain gradually became rougher as the miles unrolled and the travelers followed a course that took them several degrees north of due west. For the most part, it was still easy country—broad, generally level benches that rose like giant stair steps separated by a series of ridges that were gentle enough the wagon could handle them. Those benches were so wide that sometimes the wagon and riders couldn't get all the way across one in a day.

By the time they had covered fifty miles from Fort Worth, they had stopped seeing isolated farms and ranches, and they didn't come across any settlements beyond Mooresville. They were too far from civilization now. No man would risk bringing his family out here.

But with the army extending its line of forts farther westward, including Fort Belknap, the post they were headed for, that would change, Jamie knew. More and more settlers would come, and eventually, this land would be tamed.

Preacher would insist that wasn't a good thing. A lot of the time, Jamie would have agreed with him, although he had more of a tolerance for civilization than the old mountain man did.

"This is beautiful country," Hannah commented one day when Jamie happened to be riding alongside the wagon. Philip Saunders had gone on ahead and taken the point with Preacher for a change. "It reminds me of places I've seen back in Missouri. This is good farming land, isn't it?"

"Yes, ma'am," Jamie replied. "Plenty of water, a long growing season . . . A man could raise some decent crops here, no doubt about it. It would make good grazing land for cattle, too."

"I'm surprised no one has put such good land to use."

Jamie smiled. "They have. The Wichita Indians hunt all through here. There are a lot of deer in these woods. Maybe even a few buffalo, although you're a lot more likely to find them farther west."

Hannah looked at him with concern in her eyes as she asked, "You mean there are Indians in this area? I thought we hadn't gone far enough yet to worry about them."

"Anywhere west of Fort Worth is far enough to worry about Comanche and Kiowa raiding parties. We could run into something like that any time. The Wichita are peaceful for the most part, although they've been known to get riled up. Wouldn't surprise me if they've been keeping an eye on us for several days now."

Hannah looked around hurriedly. "You mean they could be watching us right now?"

"It's possible. Might be a lookout or two on top of some of these wooded hills where we'd never spot them. But as long as they can tell that we're just passing through, I don't think we'll have any trouble with them."

"I don't see how you can be so casual about it," Hannah said with a sigh and a shake of her head. "Just the thought that savages may be watching us right now makes my skin crawl."

"You might want to get used to that," Jamie told her bluntly. "Because where we're going, it'll likely be a lot worse before it gets any better."

Not surprisingly, Hannah didn't look the least bit comforted by that.

Jamie didn't say anything else about it, but if he'd wanted to tell her the whole truth, he'd have to admit that he'd been plagued by a bit of an uneasy feeling, too. His skin wasn't crawling or anything like that, but the last couple of days, some instinct had begun stirring inside him. It wasn't a warning, specifically—rather, more of a sensation that not all was right with the world. That trouble might be on their trail . . .

Jamie figured that when they were camped that evening, he ought to ask Preacher if the old mountain man had been feeling the same thing.

* * *

A little more than a mile back, Otis Lynch rode at the head of eight men, including Teddy Keller. The ninth member of the party, who rode a short distance ahead, was an old-timer who went by the sole name of Tuscarora because he was a half-breed who claimed the heritage of that eastern tribe.

Lynch didn't know if he actually was part Tuscarora or plain old Cherokee or some other tribe, and he didn't care, either. What mattered was that Tuscarora was a fine tracker, even though he had only one good eye. The left one was milky and useless. It was easy to see why from the knife scar that ran at an angle, slanting down from his forehead onto his leathery cheek, its path lying directly across that eye.

Tuscarora was a mean son of a gun, too, which made him even more valuable to a man like Otis Lynch.

But it was his tracking ability that allowed Lynch and his companions to remain well back of the group they were following. MacCallister and Preacher didn't appear to be trying to hide their trail. Lynch figured they didn't believe anyone would be wild enough to follow them into Comanche territory.

Lynch was more than crazy enough and didn't mind admitting that to himself. He knew the others believed him to be crazy in the head, and they were right now and then, but most of the time Lynch was crazy like a fox. He just carried on sometimes like he wasn't right in the head. That made folks underestimate him, which they would never do because of his size but might because they considered him feeble-minded.

That was what he told himself, anyway.

The riders were moving through a stretch of woods with Tuscarora out in front, as usual, when Keller urged his horse alongside Lynch's and asked, "How much longer are we gonna follow this bunch before we jump them?"

Lynch turned his head slowly to glare over at Keller. "Are you tellin' me what to do, Teddy? Givin' me orders?"

"No, I'm not," Keller declared without hesitation. "You know better than that, Otis."

Lynch had figured out that Keller was dumb as a rock, but he wasn't a complete fool. Keller was also fairly fast with his gun and had a vicious streak a mile wide, which made *him* valuable to Lynch, too.

"I just thought that if we're gonna jump them, kill MacCallister, Preacher, and the others and then carry that woman off with us, we might want to go ahead and do it pretty soon," Keller went on. "Fort Worth's a far piece back now, and this is wild country."

"Scared of the Comanche, are you?"

"You're dang right I'm scared of the Comanches! I may not have ever been in this part of the country before, but I've heard plenty of stories about those red devils and what they do to white men. I'd just as soon not cross paths with them. If it was up to me, I'd go ahead and ambush that bunch, kill the men and grab the woman, take all the supplies and any money they got, and light a shuck back to somewhere safer!"

"I thought all you cared about was settling the score with MacCallister."

"I do want to kill MacCallister, but I'd like to keep my hair while I'm doin' it. And I'd like to get back to Fort Worth and spend some of my share of the loot from this job."

In the back of Lynch's head, a harsh voice whispered insistently, *He's saying you're stupid. This idiot thinks he's smarter than you are. You're not going to let him get away with that, are you, Otis?*

Lynch drew in a deep breath. Prodded by that voice, the urge to draw his gun and blast Teddy Keller out of the saddle welled up inside him. He longed to see the look of surprise on Keller's dull-witted face in the split second after a bullet exploded through his brain.

Maybe someday, but not today. He could still make use of Keller, so he ignored the goading voice and pushed the murderous impulse away.

Besides, sound traveled out here. A shot just now might be heard by those he was trailing. No point in warning them that someone was behind them.

Sounding a lot more jovial than he felt, Lynch said, "You're in luck, Teddy. I happen to agree with you."

"You do?" Keller sounded surprised, but not nearly as surprised as he would have been if Lynch had shot him.

"Yeah. Tonight I'm going to send Tuscarora ahead to do some scouting and see if he can find us a good place to lay a trap for that bunch. When he does, we'll circle around and get ahead of them. Another day or two and you'll get your wish, Teddy." Lynch smiled. "We'll be sure and save Jamie MacCallister just for you, so you can be the one to kill him."

"Well, uh . . . you don't have to do that," Keller said. "I mean, if somebody else gets a good chance to put a bullet in that big son of a—"

"No, no," Lynch said heartily as he reached over to give Keller a friendly slap on the back, which almost knocked the stick-thin man out of the saddle. "Jamie MacCallister is all yours, Teddy, and I'm looking forward to watching you kill him."

CHAPTER 24

Two more days brought the group in sight of a steep, rocky bluff that stretched as far in both directions as Jamie and Preacher could see. The two men reined in to study it.

"The wagon ain't gonna be able to get up that," Preacher said after a moment.

"It's still a couple of miles away," Jamie said. "It might look different when we get closer to it. There could be a trail we can't see from here."

Preacher rasped fingertips over his beard-stubbled chin and frowned in thought. "How far do you reckon we are from Fort Belknap?"

"I figure we'll get there day after tomorrow."

"You think the girl could ride horseback that far?"

"Maybe," Jamie said. "Are you suggesting we leave the wagon here?"

"Might not have any choice, if we want to keep goin'."

"We're liable to need the wagon to carry out all that gold and silver we're going to find."

Preacher laughed. "You really think there's anything to that wild story, Jamie? You believe we're gonna find Bowie's treasure?"

Jamie had to chuckle, too. He said, "I don't know, but if I didn't think there was a chance, I'm not sure I would have come this far. Don't you feel the same way?"

"Shoot, I just came along for the fun of it."

"If you think maybe having to fight the whole Comanche nation is fun."

"Well, it wouldn't be borin', I'll say that much for it." Preacher lifted Horse's reins. "Why don't I ride on ahead and have a look-see while you hold the rest of the bunch here? You're right, there might be a trail up to the top of that bluff somewhere along the way. If we're gonna have to swing north or south, might as well angle in the right direction back here."

"That makes sense," Jamie agreed. He squinted at the sky. "It's late enough in the day that we'll go ahead and make camp when the others catch up."

"Sounds good. I'll come back and find you somewhere around here." Preacher nudged Horse into motion and called, "Come on, Dog."

The big cur bounded ahead eagerly as Jamie turned his mount back in the other direction, toward the wagon and the rest of the group.

It didn't take long before Preacher was able to look around and no longer see Jamie or any other sign of humanity. As far as he could tell, he might have been the only man in a hundred miles or more.

And that felt good, too. Preacher considered Jamie MacCallister to be his best friend, and he was always glad to join Jamie in one of the adventures that cropped up from time to time, but he enjoyed being out on his own with just Dog and Horse, too. Ever since leaving home and heading west as a boy, he had spent more time alone than with other people. Considerably more time, in fact. He didn't mind being around folks, but he was perfectly happy with his own company.

That bluff had sort of a dark and brooding look about it, he thought as he rode closer. He knew that on top of it would be more rolling terrain like that through which he traveled now. The grass might be a little sparser, the trees fewer and farther between, the brush lower and scrubbier. But the changes would be gradual, not dramatic.

He wondered, as he sometimes did, at the mighty forces that had shaped the world in the ancient past. Maybe where he was riding had all been an ocean, he thought, and the top of that bluff had been the shore of a much different Texas, full of different kinds of people and plants and animals than what the world knew now.

Or maybe not. He had no way of knowing.

But he did know that he suddenly spied a dark slash on the face of the bluff that might mark a trail, and he pointed Horse toward it so he could take a closer look.

Sometime in the distant past, part of the bluff's rimrock had split off and slid down to crash and burst into dozens of boulders that littered the ground along the slope's base.

Unlike the far western reaches of Texas where rain was a rare occurrence and water was a precious commodity, plenty of thunderstorms moved through this region, accompanied by tornados and hail, especially during the spring. With each drenching downpour, more water sluiced through the crease in the bluff that the rockfall had left. That cascading water, over the centuries, washed away more dirt and carried off gravel and even some small boulders, and gradually the elements carved a rough path that led to the top of the bluff. It was steep and rough, but a wagon with a good strong team could make it. Men on horseback wouldn't have much trouble, although they might have to swing down and lead their mounts part of the way.

At the top of that cleft, nine men crouched behind boulders and waited. Tuscarora held a spyglass to his one good eye and watched the rider approaching the bottom of the trail.

"Looks like an older man," he said. "He's got some gray in his hair and mustache, and I can tell by the color of his face that he's spent most of his life outside. His skin looks like old saddle leather."

"Is he wearin' a brace of Colts?" Otis Lynch asked.

"He is." Tuscarora smiled, which didn't make his lean, evil face any prettier. "And he has a wolf with him."

"It ain't a wolf. Might be part wolf, I suppose. But he calls the critter Dog." Lynch nodded. "That's Preacher, all right. What about MacCallister and the rest of the bunch?"

Tuscarora lowered the spyglass and shook his head. "No. Just the one man and the . . . dog."

"He's scoutin'," Teddy Keller said. "MacCallister sent him out ahead of the others to find a trail to the top of this bluff."

"Seems likely," Lynch agreed. "And we know this is the only trail for miles in either direction."

That was what made it a perfect spot for an ambush. Lynch had known that as soon as Tuscarora described it to him. He had wasted no time in ordering the men to swing wide around their quarry and push their horses to a faster pace in order to get ahead of MacCallister's group. They had reached the bluff, climbed up that steep trail, and barely gotten themselves situated at the top before Tuscarora's keen eye spotted Preacher approaching.

They had cut it close, but they were here in time to finish this, to deliver much-deserved vengeance on Jamie MacCallister and Preacher . . . and, not coincidentally, to seize whatever loot they could, including a beautiful, auburn-haired young woman.

Lynch had been thinking about something else, too. Keller had it in mind that they would cut and run back to Fort Worth as soon as they had wiped out their enemies, but Lynch wasn't sure that was the best idea. MacCallister, Preacher, and the others were heading west, into hostile territory, for some reason, and it had to be a compelling one to make them willing to run that risk. Lynch wanted to find out exactly what it was they were after. He figured he could make the young woman tell him.

And once he knew, maybe he'd decide to go after whatever it was, too.

Tuscarora said, "We have a problem, Otis."

That brought Lynch out of his greed-stoked reverie. "What problem?"

Tuscarora nodded in Preacher's direction. "He's liable to ride all the way up here, to make sure the trail is good enough for the wagon to make it to the top. But this late in the day, I expect the others will camp and not attempt the climb until in the morning."

"So?" Keller said. "We just wait until mornin' to kill 'em all."

"But that man, the one you call Preacher, will see us when he rides up here and gallop back to warn the others."

Lynch frowned. "Then we'd better pull back and find some place to get out of sight."

"Where?" Tuscarora waved a hand at the landscape behind them.

Lynch turned and looked. His frown deepened. He hadn't thought about it until now, but the half-breed was right—there was no place to hide. A grassy flat stretched for a mile or more. The few bushes growing here and there weren't big enough to conceal a man, let alone a horse. A hill with some trees on it rose in the distance, but Lynch wasn't sure they could reach it before Preacher made it to the top of the trail. Even if they did, they'd have to gallop their horses to do so, and Preacher would hear the pounding hoofbeats.

Tuscarora seized the initiative. He pointed down the cleft and said, "He hasn't started up yet. I can reach one of those boulders and hide there before he spots me. The rest of you pull back where he can't see you until he rides past where I am. I'll jump him and kill him, so he can't go back and warn the others."

Keller said, "But when he don't come back, MacCallister will know somethin's wrong. He'll come lookin' for Preacher."

"Then we kill him, too," Tuscarora said. "Those two are the most formidable members of the party, aren't they? The others will have to come up this trail sooner or later, with Preacher and MacCallister or without them, or else turn back."

Lynch raked his fingers through his tangled beard and made a swift decision. He didn't like anybody else coming up with plans or giving orders, but he knew what had to be done.

"Tuscarora's right," he said. "There's really nothing else we can do. The rest of you fall back." He nodded to Tuscarora. "Go ahead and kill the old pelican."

"My pleasure," Tuscarora replied with a smile.

CHAPTER 25

Preacher reined in when he was still a hundred yards from the beginning of the trail that led to the top of the bluff. He studied the ground intently, but only for a few seconds before he kneed Horse forward again.

That few seconds had been enough for him to see what he needed to see. Horses had come through here not long ago. Shod horses, which meant they weren't Indian ponies.

An army patrol, maybe? According to Jamie, they weren't far from Fort Belknap. So it was certainly possible that a group of dragoons could have ridden along here.

But other possibilities existed, too, Preacher knew, and they were more threatening. For a split second, he had considered turning around, right then and there, and riding back to the others to let Jamie know they might be headed into trouble. They could try to find some other route.

That might mean going hundreds of miles out of their way, and the detour might be for nothing. He needed to know more, Preacher had decided. To the old mountain man, thought was equal to action, so he rode to the base of the trail and started up it.

"Dog, stay with me," he said quietly to the big cur. If any threat was lurking up there, Dog would flush it out, maybe before Preacher was ready. Whatever was waiting for them, they would meet it together.

Meanwhile, part of Preacher's attention was focused on the trail itself, evaluating it to see if he thought the wagon could use it. He decided that was likely. The mules were sturdy, powerful animals, and sure-footed enough to handle the rough surface. Some or all of the supplies might have to be unloaded to lighten the wagon, taken up by horse or carried by men instead, and then reloaded at the top, but they could do that if they had to.

A few boulders sat along at the sides of the trail, having rolled down from the top in some ancient cataclysm before grinding to a stop here and there. They could wreak havoc if any of them started rolling again, but Preacher thought that was pretty unlikely. They looked like they'd been sitting right where they were for hundreds of years.

Preacher's eyes narrowed. Those boulders also made good hiding places . . .

He rode past several of them with nothing happening, though. Then, abruptly, Dog growled, a low rumble deep in his throat, and stiffened in alarm as he swung his head to the left.

Preacher heard the faint scrape of boot leather on rock from the same direction and twisted in the saddle to face that way. He drew his right-hand Colt with blinding speed and brought the revolver up and around as his thumb looped over the hammer and eared it back. From the corner of his eye, Preacher saw a man leaping toward him from the top of the boulder.

The Dragoon roared and bucked in Preacher's hand. He

thought the shot struck the attacker, but the man's momentum carried him on anyway and he crashed into Preacher, driving the old mountain man out of the saddle.

The jarring impact with the hard ground jolted the air out of Preacher's lungs and he felt the shock all through his body. The man who'd jumped him might be wounded, but he still had plenty of fight in him. He rammed a knee into Preacher's midsection, which made it even harder for the old mountain man to get his breath back.

But the next instant, a large, hairy, gray-and-brown shape flew through the air and knocked the man off Preacher. Fangs flashed, and loud snarls echoed back from the cleft's walls. In situations such as these, Dog didn't wait for a command. He just went after whatever varmint was trying to hurt Preacher.

Most men, when Dog bared his teeth, screamed in terror of the big cur and flailed around, trying wildly to fight him off. This hombre was more self-possessed than that. As he rolled over and Dog lunged at him, ready to rip out his throat, he thrust up his left arm and caught Dog under the muzzle with his forearm, forcing the cur's head up and causing the snapping jaws to miss their target.

As if he were in a fight with a human, the man hammered a punch into Dog's ribs. The blow knocked Dog off-balance. The man grabbed the thick fur on both sides of the animal's neck and heaved him to the left.

The man rolled the other way and came up on hands and knees. By now Preacher had caught his breath and made it back to one knee. He had dropped the Colt he held when the man tackled him off Horse's back, but the other revolver was still holstered on his left hip. He drew it before the attacker could even hope to cross the ten feet between them.

Preacher intended to make the man his prisoner and

force him to answer some questions. He saw instantly that the varmint wasn't hurt bad. A bloodstain showed on the upper left sleeve of his homespun shirt. Preacher's quickly aimed shot had just creased him.

But before Preacher could say anything, a rifle cracked somewhere above him. He felt as much as heard the wind rip of the ball going past his cheek. Another shot blasted, kicking up gravel and dust no more than a foot from him. He fell back on his rump, twisted, and triggered twice in the direction of the powder smoke he spotted at the top of the trail.

The man who'd jumped him had friends . . . and they were gunning for him.

Dog yelped as more shots roared. Fearing that his trail partner was wounded, Preacher surged to his feet. The attacker was up, too, and running toward the top. More bullets hummed around Preacher as he shouted, "Dog, go!"

The big cur took off, heading down the slope. If one of those shots had hit him, evidently it hadn't done much damage because Dog was running low and fast.

The fight and the gunfire hadn't spooked Horse. The rangy gray stallion was used to trouble. He stood still as Preacher vaulted back into the saddle. Preacher fired twice more toward the rim, figuring he wouldn't hit anything but might be able to make the bushwhackers duck for a second. He whirled Horse and dug his heels into the stallion's flanks.

The shooting continued, but Preacher and his companions were moving fast. Shooting downhill like that made it hard to get the range, especially with moving targets. The barrage fell short of Preacher, Horse, and Dog as they reached the bottom of the trail and headed out onto the more level terrain.

A bitter taste filled the old mountain man's mouth. Running from a fight didn't sit well with him. Never had, never would.

But he'd known he was badly outnumbered, and he hadn't lived so long by being foolhardy, either. Not only that, he also had to consider the fact that Jamie and the others had been following him, and he needed to warn them before they rode into trouble, too.

Jamie's instincts had been right, Preacher thought. Somebody *had* been dogging their trail, and Otis Lynch was the prime candidate. Lynch, or whoever it was, had gotten around them somehow and set a trap, but Preacher had sprung it early.

Now, more than likely, if Lynch was as loco as Preacher believed he was, he and his companions would come after them, abandoning the idea of an ambush and attacking them head on. That was the only move Lynch had left, other than abandoning his quest for vengeance.

Preacher didn't think the bearded giant would do that. So he headed back in the direction of Jamie and the rest of the bunch as fast as Horse could carry him.

Lynch had hold of Teddy Keller's shoulders and shook the man so hard it seemed like Keller's head might snap right off his shoulders. He roared curses and shouted, "Why'd you start shooting? Why?"

Keller was already half stunned because Lynch had backhanded him a moment earlier, staggering him and making him drop his rifle. Now, being shaken like this, he couldn't form an answer, couldn't do anything but jerk back and forth in Lynch's brutal grasp.

"Otis, don't kill him!" Tuscarora was out of breath from

his desperate dash back up the trail. He leaned over, rested his hands on his thighs, and panted and wheezed for a moment before saying, "We need him! We need every gun we've got."

Lynch's bearded features twisted with disgust. He flung the half-senseless Keller away from him like a rag doll. Keller sprawled on the ground and lay there breathing hard.

Lynch turned to Tuscarora and said, "You're right. We're going after them. That's all we can do now."

Tuscarora was starting to recover from his exertions. He straightened and said, "I figured that's the way you'd see it, Otis." He hesitated. "Sorry the plan didn't work out."

"Not your fault," Lynch snapped. "That dog warned him, and he's quick as a snake."

"And Keller probably saved my life when he took that shot and distracted Preacher," the half-breed went on. "I can't complain too much about that."

Behind Lynch, Keller had begun to get his wits about him again. He pushed himself up on his left hand and, glaring hate at Lynch's back, clawed at the gun on his hip with his right hand.

Nobody had time to call a warning to Lynch . . . or the need to. Lynch whirled, his gun flashing into his hand as he did so, and he had the revolver leveled at Keller before the gaunt man had cleared leather.

"Next time you try to draw on me, you're a dead man," Lynch rasped. "But like Tuscarora says, we need every man, so I'm not going to kill you . . . this time." Without holstering the gun, he bellowed at the others, "Mount up!"

"They'll know we're comin'," one of the men pointed out.

"You want to go back to Fort Worth empty-handed?"

None of them wanted that. They hurried to their horses and began swinging up into the saddles.

Keller let his gun sag back into leather. He clambered awkwardly to his feet and said, "One of these days, Lynch."

"I reckon you're right," Lynch said, "but not today." His voice rose to an angry shout. "Today I kill MacCallister and Preacher!"

CHAPTER 26

With Preacher scouting ahead, Pete Barnes had joined Jamie at the head of the group. His brother Gil was driving the wagon today. Gil was so awkward and tongue-tied around women—especially young, pretty ones—that having Hannah beside him on the seat had had him blushing furiously all day, Pete told Jamie.

"But I figure that's good for him," Pete went on. "I mean, if he's ever gonna get hitched, he'll have to be able to say *something* to a woman."

"When the right one comes along, he won't have quite as much trouble talking to her," Jamie said.

"You really think so, Mr. MacCallister?"

"If a woman's the right one, you'll be easier around her right from the start. You might still be nervous . . . probably will be . . . but it's different. That's one way you know you've found somebody special."

Pete chuckled. "You sound like you're speakin' from experience."

"Oh, I am," Jamie said, thinking of Kate. "I sure—"

He stopped what he was saying, reined in, and sat up straighter in the saddle as the sounds of distant gunfire came to his ears.

Pete heard the shots, too, and exclaimed, "What in blazes is that?"

"Sounds like a battle, somewhere over there around that bluff," Jamie answered grimly.

"Where Preacher went, you mean?"

"That's right." Jamie turned and looked back at the wagon and the rest of the riders, who were about a hundred yards behind him and Pete Barnes. He took his hat off and waved it back and forth above his head, the signal for them to stop where they were.

As he clapped his hat back on his head, Jamie looked around and spotted a small hill with some rocks and trees on it, about a quarter of a mile to the north.

He pointed at the hill and told Pete, "Ride back to the others and tell them to get over yonder and take cover until we find out what's going on. Your brother can drive the wagon around to the other side of the hill, and then he can help Miss Craigson up there with the rest of you."

"You think Indians are gonna attack us?"

"Right now, I don't know. But whoever's doing that shooting, I don't trust that they have our best interests at heart. I'm going to see if I can find Preacher. Now move!"

Pete jerked his head in a nod and kicked his horse into a run. Jamie went the other way, toward the bluff where Preacher had been scouting for a trail.

As Jamie rode hard, the shooting trailed off and then stopped. That wasn't necessarily a good thing. It might mean that the target was dead.

And Jamie instinctively knew that the target had been Preacher.

At the same time, the old mountain man had demonstrated again and again in his life that he had an uncanny, almost supernatural knack for survival. Jamie would never believe Preacher was dead unless he saw the body with his own eyes, and even then, he might be a little doubtful.

So he wasn't the least bit surprised when he spotted a familiar figure galloping toward him on a big gray stallion with a wolflike cur bounding along behind, trying to keep up. Jamie reined in and drew his rifle from its saddle sheath, then peered intently at the landscape beyond Preacher, searching for any sign of pursuit.

He didn't see any, but that didn't mean nobody was back there. They might not have come in sight yet.

Jamie was still watching the terrain when Preacher pounded up on Horse a couple of minutes later. Preacher drew the stallion to a halt. Horse was breathing a little harder than usual from the hard run but didn't seem overly winded.

"You hurt?" Jamie asked.

Preacher shook his head. "Nope. I ain't so sure about Dog, though."

He threw a leg over the saddle and dropped hurriedly to the ground, calling the big cur over to him. Preacher knelt to examine him.

"His head's bloody," Jamie said.

"Yeah, but as far as I can see, ain't nothin' wrong with him except a bullet clipped the tip of his ear. When a dog's ear gets nicked, it bleeds like a stuck pig."

Jamie nodded. "He was running like he wasn't really hurt."

"Yeah, I reckon he'll be all right." Preacher straightened. "There's a trail up that bluff, Jamie, but somebody was waitin' in it to ambush me. And there were more varmints lurkin' at the top. They're the ones who started burnin' powder at me when I got the drop on their pard."

"Did you recognize him?"

"He might've been one of the bunch who was with Lynch back in Fort Worth. I ain't sure. But I'd bet a hat it's Lynch and his friends, anyway."

Jamie nodded. "That's the only thing that makes sense. Did they come after you?"

"They hadn't, last time I looked. I reckon it's pretty likely they will, though. They lost the chance to surprise us, so now all they can do is hit us out in the open."

"You don't know how many of them there are?"

Preacher shook his head. "Never got a good look. I lit a shuck outta there to let you know there's trouble ahead."

Jamie nodded toward the bluff and said, "I reckon it's on the way now."

Preacher turned to look and saw the dust cloud rising into the late afternoon sky. "Yeah, that'd be them, all right," he said.

"I told Pete Barnes to take Miss Craigson and the others and fort up on top of a hill about half a mile back. We'd better join them."

Preacher mounted up quickly, and the two men rode back the way they had come.

Jamie was glad to see that the wagon and the other riders were out of sight when he and Preacher reached the spot where he'd left the rest of the group. They swung to the north, toward the wooded hill. It wasn't very tall, but it would give them a slight advantage, anyway, if they were attacked. It was always easier to defend higher ground.

They rode around to the far side of the hill. The wagon was there, and so were the horses, the extra saddle mounts, and the pack animals. Three mounted men were holding the group of livestock together. One of the riders was Nate Barnes.

He waved at Jamie and called, "Pete and Gil and everybody else are up on the hill like you said, Mr. MacCallister."

Jamie nodded and dismounted. He and Preacher turned their horses over to Nate, then, taking their rifles with them, they headed for the hilltop.

Men stood behind trees and knelt behind rocks, holding rifles ready for trouble. Hannah Craigson and Philip Saunders were sitting on the ground behind a cluster of small boulders. At the sight of Jamie, Hannah said, "Mr. MacCallister, are we about to be attacked?"

"Can't say for sure yet, but more than likely," Jamie told her.

"Indians?" Saunders asked. His face was pale and drawn. He had acquitted himself fairly well and demonstrated some courage in that brawl back in Fort Worth, but evidently the idea of fighting Indians was more frightening to him.

"No. Otis Lynch and his friends."

"Otis Lynch?" Hannah repeated. "That . . . that giant lunatic?"

"One and the same," Preacher said. "I didn't lay eyes on him, but I don't have any doubt he's behind this."

"Then we probably outnumber them," Saunders said. "And at least they're not savages."

"A white man's bullet'll kill you just as dead as a Comanche arrow."

Saunders swallowed hard. There was no arguing with Preacher's logic.

"Just keep your heads down, and you'll both be all right," Jamie told them. "When Lynch sees that we have a good defensive position and realizes that he's outnumbered, he might just give up and go home."

"Do you really think Lynch will do that?" Hannah asked.

"Well, not really," Jamie said with a faint smile. "You can't count on a man like him doing the reasonable thing."

"You sure can't," Preacher said, "because here he comes now, and he's got his whole bunch with him!"

CHAPTER 27

Walt Reynolds was on one knee behind a slab of rock with his rifle resting on the stone as he peered out across the open ground in front of the hill. He had been in a number of fights before, so he wasn't particularly scared, but any time you swapped lead with other men, you ran the risk of not coming through the battle. Walt was able to push that thought to the back of his head but couldn't banish it altogether.

Not far away, Grover Appleton knelt behind another rock. "What are they doin'?" he asked with a slight whine creeping into his voice. "They got to know there's more of us than there is of them."

"I don't reckon that fella Lynch really cares about that," Walt said. "He's just mad and wants to hurt somebody, especially Mr. MacCallister and Preacher. He's crazy, that's all."

"He ain't the only one," Billy Bob Moore said from behind the tree where he had taken cover. "Look who's ridin' with him!"

"Where?" Walt asked with a frown.

"To the left of Lynch, two or three men over!"

The way the attackers were bunched up, it was difficult to pick out individual figures, but Walt squinted at the distant riders and after a moment saw the one Moore was talking about. The man's hat brim was pushed up because of the wind, and that same wind caught the long, sandy brown beard and whipped it back over his shoulder.

Teddy!

Walt Reynolds caught his breath and his heart slugged in his chest. That was Teddy Keller riding with Lynch and the others. No doubt about it.

After their falling-out, Walt didn't consider Keller a friend anymore, but even so, they had ridden together for quite a while. He had been closer to Keller than to any of the other men. They had faced danger together, even though that danger had usually been of Keller's making because he'd gotten them mixed up in some robbery that hadn't gone exactly as planned.

That sort of thing created a bond between men. They had run from the law together, fought side by side as they traded shots with posses.

How could Walt line his rifle's sights on Teddy Keller now and pull the trigger?

At the same time, remembering how things had ended between them, he had a hunch that if the situation were reversed, Keller wouldn't hesitate. He'd shoot and never lose a second of sleep over it.

"That's Teddy!" Grover Appleton cried. "What're we gonna do?"

Walt steeled himself. He said, "Teddy made the choice to throw in with Lynch. We fight, that's what we do!"

Jamie and Preacher lifted their rifles. Both men were armed with revolvers, and some of the other members of the group carried repeating Colts of various models. All the rifles were single-shot breechloaders or muzzle-loaders, though, some of which had been used in the Mexican War a few years earlier before being sold off by the army. Someday soon there would be repeating rifles, Jamie had thought more than once, and that would change things on the frontier even more than Colonel Sam Colt's invention had.

For now, they would fight a shot at a time. Jamie raised his rifle to his shoulder and was ready to draw a bead on Lynch just as soon as the attackers came a little closer.

Instead, the men galloping toward the hill suddenly spread out, splitting up so that some went east while the others went west.

"They ain't gonna attack head on," Preacher said as he observed the same thing. "They're gonna circle us and stay just at the edge of rifle range, like the Comanch' and the other horse Injuns do. They'll keep us pinned up here and try to wear us down by pickin' us off one by one."

"They can't do that if we pick them off instead," Jamie said. He nestled his cheek against the smooth, polished wood of his rifle's stock and peered over the sights. He was strong enough that he didn't need anything on which to rest the heavy barrel. It was rock steady as he lined up his shot, leading one of the men. He couldn't see Lynch anymore.

Just before he squeezed the trigger, he bellowed, "Open fire!" The rifle boomed and kicked hard against his shoulder. Smoke gushed from the barrel and made it hard to see for a second. Jamie squinted through it and spotted the man who'd been his target. He scowled as he saw that the man was still mounted. If Jamie had hit him, it hadn't been enough to knock him out of the saddle.

The rider vanished around the side of the hill.

Gunshots filled the air now. A cloud of powder smoke began to form over the hilltop. More shots blasted from the attackers. It sounded like a small-scale war had broken out, which, Jamie supposed, it had.

"They're goin' after the horses!" Preacher yelled.

That was a smart move on Lynch's part. Stampede the horses and they really would be stuck up here on this hill. Plus, the three men holding the livestock made good targets and killing them would whittle down the odds some.

"Pete! Gil!" Jamie shouted at the two Barnes brothers, knowing that Nate was down there with the horses and they would want to go to his aid. "Go help your brother!" He glanced around and called the names of the first two men he saw. "Reynolds! Tankersley! Come with me!"

Pete and Gil had already started down the slope. Jamie, Reynolds, and Tankersley weren't far behind them. Preacher remained atop the hill to direct the rest of the battle and continue trying to pick off some of the attackers. Jamie hadn't seen any of Lynch's bunch go down yet. They were moving so fast that it was hard to draw a bead on them.

Three of the attackers had split off and charged the men tending to the horses. They were close enough to use revolvers. Shots slammed out. Nate Barnes and his two companions met fire with fire, putting themselves between the attackers and the animals and shooting back at them. The air was thick with smoke and flying lead.

Jamie stopped before he reached the bottom of the hill

and slid a fresh cartridge into the breech of the Sharps he carried. He raised it to his shoulder, aimed, and fired over the heads of the defenders.

One of the attackers flew backward out of his saddle with his arms flung wide. The heavy caliber round had punched a hole through him and killed him instantly.

One of the defenders was down, too, Jamie saw, but in the dust and powder smoke, he couldn't tell who it was. He drew his big Colt and opened fire with it. Reynolds and Tankersley had joined the fight, adding their shots to the ones coming from the two men on horseback.

Another of Lynch's men suddenly dropped his gun and doubled over in the saddle. He dropped the reins, too, and when his mount began to jump around, he pitched to the side and landed on the ground in a limp sprawl, either dead or close to it.

The third man wasn't willing to continue the attack alone. He peeled off, throwing a couple more shots back at the defenders as he did so. Then he started to race away, leaning low over his horse's neck.

That might have been enough to allow him to make a getaway, if Jamie hadn't been there on the hillside. Jamie holstered the Colt, reloaded the rifle, and raised it again. Peering over the sights, he saw the man twist around in the saddle to look back over his shoulder.

Jamie squeezed the trigger.

Even at this distance, he saw the red ruin that the fleeing man's face turned into as the bullet struck it. The round went on and hit the horse in the neck. The luckless animal's forelegs collapsed and it pinwheeled forward, throwing the man Jamie had just shot and rolling over him. The hombre never felt that crushing impact, though, since he was already dead from being shot in the head.

Grimly, Jamie reloaded. Now he saw that it was Nate

Barnes who had fallen to the vicious gunfire of the attackers. Nate lay motionless on the ground with his brothers kneeling on either side of him.

"Jamie!" Preacher called from the hilltop. "They're regroupin' in front! Looks like they're comin' straight at us after all!"

The circling technique hadn't worked, so now Lynch was going to try a frontal attack. Considering the odds, Jamie figured that attempt was doomed to failure, but Lynch and his men might inflict some damage anyway. He wanted to keep casualties to a minimum.

"Stay here in case any of them try to double back around on this side," he told Reynolds and Tankersley. He didn't wait for their nods of acknowledgment. He turned and his long legs carried him up the slope again. By the time he reached the top, he'd reloaded the rifle.

"There are only six of the varmints left," Preacher said as Jamie joined him. "Lynch is plumb crazy as a loon if he thinks he can beat us."

"You've seen the man," Jamie said. "Plumb crazy is a pretty good description of him."

Preacher grunted in agreement.

Quickly, Jamie checked on Hannah and Saunders. They were both unhurt. The rocks behind which they had taken shelter had protected them from the storm of lead that swept across the hilltop.

"I should lend a hand," Saunders said as he touched the butt of the revolver on his hip.

"Stay there and look after Miss Craigson," Jamie told him. "I don't reckon there's much chance any of those men will make it to the top, but if they do, it'll be up to you to make sure she doesn't get hurt."

For a second, Saunders looked like he wanted to argue, but then he put his arm around Hannah's shoulders and nodded. "All right. You can count on me, Mr. MacCallister."

Jamie didn't know if that was true or not, but if things went badly, he supposed they would find out.

Lynch had done some damage already, he saw as he looked around the hilltop. One man was dead, and a couple more were wounded and sporting bloodstained bandages.

Preacher said, "Take a look out there, Jamie. Ain't one of those fellas with Lynch the one who was with Reynolds and the others back in Fort Worth?"

"The ones who followed Miss Craigson and me from Colorado?" The idea surprised Jamie, but when he looked where Preacher indicated, he saw that the old mountain man was right. Even at this distance, he recognized the skinny, bearded Teddy Keller.

"I thought him and Lynch was enemies," Preacher said.

"I reckon they must've made up," Jamie said dryly. "Or else they threw in together because they both hate me."

"You ought to try bein' more friendly. Spread light and joy in the world, like me." Preacher grinned.

"Yeah, I'll do that," Jamie said, "but after we deal with Lynch because here they come now."

The half dozen men charged toward the hill, firing as they came. They were spread out in a line so they wouldn't interfere with each other's shooting. Clouds of powder smoke streamed behind them.

"Open fire!" Jamie called.

The volley that rang out from the hilltop knocked one of the men from his saddle. Lynch, Keller, and the other three came on, triggering as they galloped toward the hill. They reached the bottom of the slope and started up.

Grover Appleton cried out, bolted to his feet, and reeled back as he dropped his gun and clapped both hands to his bloody head. That exposed him even more to the attackers' fire. His body jerked as bullets punched through it. Spinning slowly, he collapsed.

"Grover!" Billy Bob Moore yelled in shock and fury. He started to dart out from behind the tree where he had taken cover, but Preacher reached him first and clamped a hand around his arm.

"Nothin' you can do for him now," Preacher said. "Settle the score by killin' those varmints who drilled him."

Grimacing, Moore followed Preacher's advice and fired at the men charging up the slope.

Preacher filled his hands with the Dragoons and opened up with both of them, firing left and right, left and right in a long peal of rolling gun thunder. Jamie had his Walker blasting now, too. Another of Lynch's men, riddled with bullets, toppled off his horse. A third man had his horse go down under him. He stumbled up and continued the assault on foot, but he had gone only a couple of steps when slugs tore through his body and tossed it back down the slope.

Otis Lynch wheeled his horse and pounded back down the hill in full retreat. Teddy Keller and the remaining man followed him. Jamie triggered the last two shots in his Colt after them, and Preacher emptied his revolvers.

Lynch, Keller, and the other man kept going. Their mounts picked up speed as they reached level ground.

Preacher reached for his rifle, which he had leaned against a tree. "I can still get Lynch," he said as he raised the weapon to his shoulder.

He aimed and fired, then grated a curse as Lynch's horse swerved slightly and dirt exploded from the ground where Preacher's bullet struck.

"Pure dumb luck!" the old mountain man exclaimed. Hurriedly, he began reloading.

"Might as well forget it," Jamie said. "They're out of range already."

Preacher glared, but he finished sliding another cartridge in the rifle's breech at a more deliberate pace.

"Reckon you're right," he said. "I hope lettin' those varmints get away don't come back to haunt us."

"So do I. But if Lynch has any sense, he won't stop running until he gets back to Fort Worth."

The problem was that, as both of them knew, Otis Lynch had no sense . . .

CHAPTER 28

Three members of the group had died in the battle: Nate Barnes, Grover Appleton, and a man named Reuben Miller, who had kept to himself and said very little to anybody during the journey thus far.

Jamie picked out several men for a burial detail that dug three graves at the base of the hill, since this was as good a place as any to lay them to rest. They could have taken the bodies on to Fort Belknap, but Jamie didn't see any point in that.

Once the dead men had been wrapped in blankets, gently lowered into the graves, and the dirt replaced and mounded above them, the rest of the company gathered next to them to pay final respects.

The sun had disappeared below the western horizon a short time earlier, leaving luminescent streamers of purple, cobalt, and golden light slanting across the Texas sky.

A faint breeze drifted across the landscape, carrying with it the evening songs of birds nested in the trees along the bluff, the cheerful sound a counterpoint to the sorrow that gripped the group. Yet there was something faintly mournful to the birdsong, as well, as the creatures commemorated the end of another day.

As the leader of the group, Jamie took his hat off and said in a loud, clear voice, "I didn't know any of these three fellows very well, but I'd ridden with them long enough to know that they were good men. I fought side by side with them. They lost their lives battling to protect others from harm. They died as honorable men, and that's the way they'll be remembered." He looked around. "Would anyone else like to say a few words?"

Pete and Gil Barnes had shed some tears earlier for their brother, but they were grim faced and dry-eyed now. Pete clasped his hat to his chest, over his heart, and said, "Nate never got much attention, seein' as how I'm the oldest and Gil's the baby and he was the middle one, but I never heard him say a word of complaint about that. Hardly ever saw him without a smile on his face, too. Gil and me, we're sure gonna miss him, and I hope we see him again someday when it's our turn to cross the divide, the good Lord willin'."

Hannah reached over and squeezed his arm. "I'm sure you will, Mr. Barnes."

Pete swallowed hard and said, "Thank you, ma'am."

Walt Reynolds cleared his throat. "I'll say a word for Grover," he declared. "To tell the truth, even though we rode together for a good spell, I don't really know where he came from or anything about his life when he was younger. But he was a good trail partner who never shirked his share of whatever work had to be done." Reynolds smiled a little. "Now, he might complain about having to do it, mind you . . . but he'd get the job done."

"Did he ever get over his grudge against me for breaking his arm?" Jamie asked.

Reynolds shook his head, still smiling. "No, sir, I don't reckon he did. He'd have been mad at you from now on, I expect. But when he agreed to sign on and ride with you, that was all it took to make him put that grudge aside. He was ready and willin' to back any play you made. Willing to back it with his life." The young man nodded toward the mound of freshly turned earth on the left. "And I reckon he proved that."

"I'd say he did," Jamie agreed. "I'm sorry for your loss."

No one had known Reuben Miller well enough to say any words over his grave. That was sad, but nothing could be done about it.

No one wanted to make camp here next to the fresh graves, so while there was still some light in the sky, the men mounted up, Hannah climbed onto the wagon, and they all pushed on toward the bluff, finding a place near the bottom of the trail to spend the night.

The dead men from Lynch's bunch were left where they had fallen, which was another good reason to move on. That way the buzzards and the coyotes wouldn't have to worry about any interruptions as they feasted.

Later, after a bleak supper, Walt Reynolds came over to Jamie and Preacher and asked to talk to them for a minute.

"Teddy Keller was riding with Lynch," he said. "I spotted him before Ox and I went back down the hill to help defend the horses."

Jamie nodded and said, "Yes, we saw him, too. It was quite a surprise."

Preacher added, "We never figured he'd throw in with Lynch, the way they was tryin' to kill each other back in Fort Worth."

Reynolds shook his head. "You mentioned poor Grover holding a grudge, Mr. MacCallister," he said. "When it came to grudges, he ran a mighty poor second to Teddy. Teddy would throw in with the Devil himself to get back at you, sir."

"I reckon he just about did," Preacher said.

Jamie asked, "Why didn't he try to get even before? You and your friends followed Miss Craigson and me all the way to Texas. Surely there was a chance to make a move against us before we got to Fort Worth."

Reynolds nodded slowly and said, "I've given some thought to that. Best thing I can figure is that he didn't really have much faith in us backing his play. Teddy's not the most decisive fella you'll ever meet, either. He gets mad and swears he's going to do something, then later he wonders if he really ought to go through with it. But I guess he figured that by teaming up with Lynch, he couldn't lose."

"He was plenty wrong about that," Preacher said.

"Yes, sir, he was." Reynolds paused. "He got away, though, didn't he? That's what I heard from Billy Bob. He said that Teddy rode off with Lynch and the only other one from their bunch who survived."

"That's right," Jamie said. "Do you think he'll try again?"

"I don't see how, if there are only three of them left. But as long as Teddy's alive, I wouldn't feel completely safe, either."

Preacher said, "Son, where we're goin', nobody's gonna be safe for a long time."

The next morning, following Preacher's suggestion, they unloaded the wagon to lighten the load for the mules. Pete Barnes, who had handled the team more than anyone else, took hold of the harness and led the animals up the steep trail. They made it with no trouble, and once all the supplies had been carried up, they were placed back in the wagon.

The terrain on top of the bluff was even flatter than it had been down below. While the men were leading their saddle mounts up the trail, Jamie and Preacher stood near the rim and looked back the way they had come.

The bluff didn't seem very tall, but they had a surprisingly good view from up here and could see at least fifteen or twenty miles, until the landscape turned hazy and indistinct in the distance.

"I done some thinkin' the other day," Preacher mused. He waved a hand to indicate the countryside falling away before them. "What if all that used to be an ocean, and this here bluff used to be the shore?"

Jamie smiled. "This part of Texas is a little on the dry side to have been an ocean, Preacher."

"I ain't talkin' about any time recent-like," the old mountain man insisted. "I mean years ago. Lots of years ago. Hundreds. Maybe even thousands."

"An ocean and a shore," Jamie repeated.

"That's right. Just study on it a minute. You'll see what I mean."

Jamie peered off into the misty distance and slowly began to nod.

"Maybe," he said. "I don't reckon we'll ever know for sure, though. The Comanche might be able to tell us. Indians like stories about what happened in the before times. But it's not likely that we'll have a chance to talk to them about it."

"No, I expect not. But I've spent a lot of my life in lonely, far-off places, Jamie, you know that. And sometimes . . ." Preacher hesitated, then shook his head. "No, you'll think I'm off my nut, too."

"Not hardly. You're the most hardheaded but also the most levelheaded hombre I know. What is it, Preacher?"

Quietly, the old mountain man said, "Sometimes, I seem to see and hear things that ain't . . . well, that ain't there. Great big critters the likes o' which ain't around no more. Men like the Injuns, but *not* like 'em, at the same time." He swept his hand toward the view from the bluff. "Things swimmin' in that ocean that ain't in any ocean, anywhere in the world, these days."

"You see these things with your eyes?"

Preacher shook his head. "No, not really. It's more . . . memories. Memories of things I never saw and never did, but they're there in my head, anyway." He made a disgusted sound. "I should've kept my fool mouth shut. Now you'll think I'm crazy for sure."

"No, I don't," Jamie said. "You forget, I've spent a lot of time in the high lonesome, myself. A man out on his own like that, he sometimes senses things, connections with the world around him, that other folks never get quiet and alone enough to recognize. And I know this—wherever you are, somebody always came before. And somebody will always come after, and our time here . . . well, it's never long enough, but it's what we have and it's up to us to do what we can with it. Other than that . . ." His broad shoulders rose and fell. "Somebody else can figure it out. It's not our worry."

"No, it ain't," Preacher agreed. He clapped a hand on Jamie's shoulder and added, "Come on, let's head for Fort Belknap. Them Comanch' are waitin' for us, up on the Seven Fingers of the Brazos. They just don't know it yet."

CHAPTER 29

Fort Belknap, unlike most forts back east and some of the ones out here on the frontier, didn't have tall stockade walls made from logs enclosing it. In this region, where the climate was dry a lot of the year and vegetation became sparser the farther west you went, it would have been difficult to find trees that were big enough to furnish suitable logs.

Instead, for protection the fort relied on buildings sturdily constructed of stone, thick wooden beams, and adobe. Comanche arrows wouldn't penetrate those walls, and most bullets wouldn't, either.

Jamie heard a bugle blowing as they approached the fort later that day. One of the lookouts must have spotted them and was announcing their arrival, blatting out an off-key warning on a no doubt battered bugle.

Preacher chuckled and said, "Sounds like that boy needs some lessons, the way he's got that horn caterwaulin'."

"It's getting the job done," Jamie said. "Looks like the troops are assembling."

Just in case the unknown visitors represented a threat of some sort, uniformed figures carrying rifles hurried out of buildings and hastily assembled on the parade ground that formed the fort's centerpiece. Around that broad, open space were close to a dozen buildings.

The headquarters building, the commanding officer's quarters, the other officers' quarters, the barracks, the kitchen and mess hall, the infirmary, the armory, the sutler's store, the blacksmith shop, the stable, and several storage sheds were all arranged to form a neat rectangle. An American flag hung limp on a flagpole at one end of the parade ground. Not much wind was moving this afternoon.

A few other buildings were scattered on the prairie outside the fort itself. One of them would be a civilian trading post, Jamie supposed, and another was bound to be a saloon and brothel. Civilization, such as it was out here, always followed the army. Anywhere there were soldiers, whiskey, gambling, and women of dubious virtue were in high demand.

A short distance west of the post stood half a dozen Indian lodges with blanket-draped figures sitting cross-legged in front of them. Dogs and kids ran around, barking and yelling.

Philip Saunders urged his horse alongside Jamie and Preacher and asked with obvious concern, "Are those savages camped here?"

"They're friendly," Jamie said. "They won't bother us."

"Blanket Injuns," Preacher added. "You'll find 'em hangin' around most forts. They've given up fightin' and just want to live in peace, takin' whatever handouts the army decides to give 'em."

The old mountain man frowned in disapproval as he spoke.

Saunders noted Preacher's expression and said, "You don't think it's good that some of the Indians want to be peaceful instead of fighting?"

"Bein' peaceful's one thing. Givin' up the way you and your people have always lived and becomin' beggars . . . Well, I ain't sure peace is worth it."

"You'd rather they were out slaughtering white settlers?"

"No, I'd rather they were out killin' buffalo and hadn't never laid eyes on white folks, if you want the truth," Preacher said. "I've heard folks from back east blatherin' about how peaceful the Injuns are when they're left alone. Ain't a word of truth in that. Nobody's ever been better at killin' Injuns than other Injuns. Us white fellas are puredee pikers when it comes to that. Some tribes have just about wiped out all the other tribes around 'em, or else driven 'em off. The Comanch' are like that. There used to be Apaches around this part of Texas, until the Comanch' come in and shoved 'em hundreds of miles west o' here. And if you knew how stubborn and ornery most Apaches are, you'd realize what that says about the Comanches."

"So you're saying they *are* savages, but we should just leave them alone to kill each other."

"No, that ain't what I'm sayin'." Preacher shook his head. "I don't reckon a fella like you can understand, Philip, without livin' out here for ten or fifteen or even twenty years. And then you still might not."

"Let's just say you don't have to worry about those Indians camped outside the fort," Jamie told Saunders. "They're harmless. Harmless enough, anyway. They might still decide to cause a ruckus now and then, but it takes a lot to stir them up."

The young man nodded. "I'll go back and assure Hannah that she has nothing to worry about, then. She saw those lodges and was concerned."

Based on how Saunders had acted during the battle the day before, when he thought they might be under attack from Indians, Jamie figured he was probably more worried than Hannah was. She had continued to practice nearly every day with that Colt pocket revolver, and he thought that more than likely, she would be cool under fire.

But Jamie didn't comment on that as Saunders turned his horse to ride back to the wagon.

A couple of riders, one of them carrying a guidon on a short staff, left the fort and rode toward the newcomers. Preacher said, "Yonder comes a shavetail lieutenant to ask us who we are and what in blazes we're doin' here, I'll betcha."

They reined in and waited for the soldiers to reach them. Jamie saw that one of them was a young lieutenant, just as Preacher predicted. The officer had blond hair and a friendly, sunburned face under his tall hat with its strap fastened tightly under his chin. He brought his horse to a stop about fifteen feet from Jamie and Preacher. The stocky, dark-haired trooper carrying the guidon halted a few feet behind the lieutenant.

"Good day to you, gentlemen," the young man said. "Do you have business at Fort Belknap?"

"We're headed west," Jamie said. "Thought we'd stop here, maybe rest our horses and mules for a day or two before pushing on."

"West?" the lieutenant repeated. "But that territory is controlled by the hostiles, sir. The fort is the, ah, last outpost of civilized Texas."

Jamie nodded. "We're aware of that, son."

The lieutenant stiffened a little at Jamie's informal tone.

"That's Lieutenant Woodard, sir. Lieutenant Hobart Woodard. May I inquire as to your names?"

"MacCallister," Jamie said. "This is Preacher. Who's your commanding officer?"

"That would be Captain Glennister, sir."

"Stephen Glennister?"

Lieutenant Woodard's pale eyebrows rose in surprise. "That's right."

Jamie looked over at Preacher and said, "I knew him a while back when he was still a lieutenant. That was when I was doing a little scouting for the army."

"Stroke of luck," Preacher said.

"I'll take any I can get." Jamie faced the lieutenant again and went on, "If you would, ride back and tell the captain that Jamie Ian MacCallister is out here, accompanying a party that wants to camp near the fort for a short time. I reckon he'll tell you that's fine."

"No offense, Mr. MacCallister, but I'll need to hear that from Captain Glennister himself."

Jamie nodded. "Well, then, go ahead and ask him."

Woodard still looked a little indecisive. Finally, he glanced at the trooper and said, "Remain here and keep an eye on these people, Private Guthrie."

"Yes, sir, Lieutenant."

Woodard turned his mount and loped toward the fort.

By now, the wagon and the other riders had come up and stopped about fifty yards behind Jamie and Preacher. They sat there waiting.

Less than five minutes later, Lieutenant Woodard returned, accompanied by an older officer. The man rode up next to Jamie and extended his hand.

"Jamie, it's good to see you again!" the captain greeted him with a smile. "I never expected you to show up here at Fort Belknap."

"I didn't have any idea that the commanding officer would turn out to be an old friend, either," Jamie said as he clasped Glennister's hand. He nodded to his companion. "This is Preacher."

Glennister's eyes widened. "Preacher," he repeated. "I've heard of you, sir. It's an honor to meet you."

"Pleased to meet you as well, Cap'n," Preacher said as they shook hands, too.

"Lieutenant Woodard tells me that the party you're leading is headed west." Glennister frowned. "That can't be true, can it?"

"I reckon it is," Jamie said. "We'd like to lay over here for a day or two and rest our animals before we move on, though, if that's all right."

"Of course, of course. You're more than welcome. You can tell your people to come on in and make camp wherever they'd like. And I hope you'll join me in my quarters for supper . . . and an explanation of what this is all about."

"I think that can be arranged," Jamie said.

Jamie and Preacher had the men set up camp on the east side of the fort, away from the Indian lodges, which belonged to a local band of Wichitas.

"Pete, you're in charge," Jamie told Pete Barnes. "I know you're still mourning your brother, but you're the steadiest man I've got."

"I appreciate you saying that, Mr. MacCallister. And to tell you the truth, I don't mind havin' something to keep my mind off of what happened to poor Nate."

"Then your job is to keep everybody from bothering those Indians. They're not looking for any trouble, and I don't want us stirring up any."

Pete nodded and said, "I've already heard some of the

boys wondering about getting a drink. One of those places outside the fort is supposed to be a saloon."

"As long as they stay out of trouble, that's fine. We likely won't be here more than a couple of nights, though, so anybody who plans to stay drunk until then had better be prepared to travel with a hangover the day after tomorrow. I'm not leaving anybody behind, and I sure as blazes won't be waiting around for them to feel better."

Pete grinned. "I'll pass that along, too, Mr. MacCallister, don't you worry."

With that taken care of, Jamie went to see Hannah Craigson. Some of the men had set up the tent she used, and she was gathering a few things from her belongings in the wagon to take inside with her.

"Miss Craigson, Captain Glennister, the commanding officer here, has invited Preacher and me to have supper with him, and I don't think he'll forgive me if I fail to bring you along. Besides, he wants to know why we're here, and I think the whole thing can be explained better if you're there."

Hannah pushed her fingers through her hair, let out an exasperated sigh, and said, "My goodness, I'm not in any kind of shape to have supper with an army officer. After traveling all this way, I must look an absolute fright!"

Jamie grinned. "You'll be the prettiest sight the captain has seen since coming out here, and that would be true even if we weren't in the middle of nowhere."

"You think he's going to ask questions about why we're here?"

"Yes, ma'am, and as the commanding officer, I reckon he's got the right to know about any civilians passing through country he's responsible for."

"Can we . . ." Hannah hesitated. "Can we trust him?"

"Yes, ma'am, I believe so. He's an old friend of mine.

And he's devoted to the army. He's not going to desert his command and rush off to go treasure hunting."

"Well, in that case, I suppose I can accompany you. If Philip comes along, too, of course."

It would have been all right with Jamie to leave Saunders out of this, but he wasn't surprised that Hannah wanted him along. He nodded and said, "I'm sure that'll be all right."

"You *will* give me a chance to make myself presentable first, won't you?"

"Go right ahead," Jamie told her, thinking that from the way he had seen some of the soldiers staring lustfully at Hannah already, if she made herself look any better, they might well be asking for trouble.

CHAPTER 30

Captain Glennister was married, but his wife was back in Little Rock, Arkansas, where their families lived and where they had been childhood sweethearts. He explained that to the four guests who joined him for supper in his quarters.

"It's hard being separated for so long, of course," the captain commented, "but I wouldn't bring her out here where it's so dangerous."

"Isn't it safe here at the fort?" Philip Saunders asked. Jamie wasn't surprised that Saunders would be the one to bring that up. The man certainly was nervous about Indians. Of course, Jamie couldn't really blame him for feeling that way . . .

"As safe as you'll find anywhere west of Fort Worth," Glennister replied. "It's unlikely the Comanches would ever attack the fort, but the possibility can't be ruled out completely. Not to mention, there's the problem of getting here in the first place." Glennister looked along the table where the five of them were seated and said to Jamie at the far end, "You're lucky you didn't run into any of Spotted Dog's raiding parties on your way here."

"Spotted Dog?" Hannah repeated. She was sitting at Jamie's right, with Saunders between her and Captain Glennister. Preacher was across the table from her. They had finished their meals, but they were lingering over cups of coffee as they talked.

"One of the Comanche war chiefs," Glennister said. "He's led raiding parties nearly all the way to Fort Worth in the past. They go around us . . ." The captain spread his hands. "The forts that the army has established out here are supposed to form a defensive line that keeps the Comanches to the west, but with scores of miles between them . . . well, it's like building a dam with holes in it and expecting it to keep water out. My troops carry out regular patrols, but they can't be everywhere at once."

"And Injuns bent on raidin' are usually pretty good at bein' where the folks tryin' to stop 'em ain't," Preacher commented.

"Exactly."

Jamie said, "We didn't see hide nor hair of any Indians until we got here. This fella Spotted Dog must be sticking close to home these days."

"Possibly. But he won't stay home if you provoke him by intruding into what he considers his territory."

"Our intention isn't to provoke him," Jamie said, "but we're not going to let him stop us from going where we need to, either."

Glennister took a sip of his coffee and set the cup on the saucer in front of him. "You're civilians, so I don't suppose I can demand an answer, but even so I'd like to know just where it is you're going."

"We're going to follow the Brazos up to the Seven Fingers country."

Glennister leaned back in his chair and widened his eyes at that blunt statement. For a moment, he didn't seem to know what to say.

Then he declared, "That's insane." He sat forward again and went on forcefully, "That land belongs to Spotted Dog, Red Horse, Iron Jacket, Buffalo Hump, Carne Muerte, and the other Comanche chiefs."

"Legally, it's part of Texas and belongs to the United States, as of nine years ago."

"Yes, of course, but Spotted Dog and the others don't see it that way. To them, it's Comancheria, and they'll be mortally offended if you dare to go in there."

"We plan on making a fast trip. We won't waste any time or go looking for trouble."

"Looking for trouble is exactly what you'll be doing." Glennister sighed. "I hope you have a good reason for this lunacy you propose, anyway."

Hannah spoke up for the first time in a while, though she had chatted amiably throughout dinner with the captain. Now she said, "We have an excellent reason, sir. A fortune in gold and silver."

"A mine?" Glennister guessed. "I've never heard any rumors about there being any mines up in that country."

"Not a mine," Jamie said. "We're after Jim Bowie's treasure."

"Jim Bowie . . . Wait, are you talking about the so-called lost treasure of the Alamo?"

"That's one of the legends. It wasn't buried at the Alamo, though."

"No, it stands to reason that if it had been, it would have been found by now with so many people looking for it." Glennister frowned. "Are you saying that Bowie hid it somewhere up on the Brazos? I never heard anything about him going up there."

Preacher said, "I reckon if he'd set out to hide a bunch of gold and silver, he wouldn't be likely to tell folks what he was doin' or where he was goin'."

Glennister thought about that and admitted, "I suppose that makes sense. But still, the whole idea is very hard to believe."

Hannah said, "Perhaps I should show you the letter and the map I have, Captain."

"Are you sure that's a good idea, dear?" Saunders asked.

"You can trust the captain," Jamie said. "I'll vouch for him."

"Mr. MacCallister's word is good enough for me." Hannah opened the reticule she had brought with her to supper and took out the folded pieces of paper. She handed them to Glennister, who unfolded them and spread them on the table to study them.

After a few minutes, the captain said, "I can see why you'd want to believe this, Miss Craigson. This letter was written by your . . . grandfather, is that correct?"

"That's right."

"Naturally, you'd want to think that he was telling the truth. And quite possibly he was, as far as he knew it. Colonel Bowie could have told him that the gold and silver were hidden somewhere up the Brazos in Comanche territory. But that just seems so unlikely." Glennister looked at Jamie. "Do you believe this?"

"I don't know," Jamie replied honestly. "It seems like something Bowie might have done. And whether it's there or not, Miss Craigson's bound and determined to go see for herself."

"And once you knew that, you couldn't allow her to travel up there unaccompanied," Glennister said.

"It didn't seem like a good idea," Jamie said dryly.

Glennister looked at Preacher. "What do you think?"

The old mountain man grinned. "I think ridin' right into the heart o' Comancheria and then ridin' back out again'd be great sport, whether the treasure's there or not."

"You have an odd idea of sport, sir."

"Ain't the first time I've been accused of that."

"Well, as you probably know, the Brazos River runs no more than half a mile west of here." Glennister tapped a finger on the map, which was still spread out on the table in front of him. "You should be able to follow this without any trouble. All you have to do is follow the river and then take note of which way you need to go each time you come to a fork."

"We can find where we're going," Jamie said with confidence.

"But by the time you're five miles upriver from here, the Comanches will know you're there. They'll try to stop you."

"Maybe, maybe not. We're a large, well-armed bunch. They might think twice about trying to jump us. It might not be worth the price they'd have to pay if they did."

Preacher added, "Not only that, but Injuns are mighty curious folks, too. They'd probably want to know where we're headed, and they might just keep an eye on us to find out."

The captain shrugged and said, "I suppose that's true. I'd hate to bet my life on it, though . . . which is exactly what you'll be doing." His voice hardened with disapproval as he went on, "You'll be risking Miss Craigson's life, too, you know."

"I know," Jamie said. "That's why I hoped I could leave her here with you, Captain."

Hannah's eyes widened. "Mr. MacCallister, no!" she exclaimed. "You promised—"

"Not exactly," Jamie said. "I told you that you could come along when we left Fort Worth, but I never said how far you could go."

"You certainly implied you'd take me all the way to the treasure!"

"You heard the captain. It's mighty dangerous where we're going."

Hannah turned sharply to Glennister. "You send army patrols up the river, don't you?"

"I do," he said, "but that's what we're here for. That's our job."

"Are those patrols any larger or better armed than our party is?"

"Well, no, not from what I saw of your group."

"Do the Indians leave them alone?"

"We've had a few skirmishes with the hostiles, but there haven't been any major battles."

"Then it's like Mr. MacCallister suggested. There's a chance the savages will leave us alone, too."

"No way of knowing that for sure," Jamie pointed out. "It's just a chance, and a pretty slim one, to be honest."

Saunders said, "Perhaps you *should* stay here, Hannah. After all, I'll be going along on the expedition to represent your interests."

That surprised Jamie. As frightened as Saunders was of the Indians, he'd expected the young man to urge Hannah to go along with Jamie's idea and then suggest that *he* remain here at Fort Belknap, too. But evidently Saunders intended to see the mission through to its end, whatever that might be.

"You'd be more than welcome, Miss Craigson," Glennister said. "I'd be honored to have you as my guest. Granted, the accommodations are fairly primitive, especially for a longer stay, and there are very few, ah, respectable ladies here at the fort to provide suitable company for you. Two sergeants' wives, in fact, are the only ones—"

"Thank you, Captain," Hannah broke in coolly. "But I don't need suitable company because I won't be staying. I intend to go with Mr. MacCallister, just as we arranged before we ever left Colorado."

Jamie might have argued more with her, but at that moment, someone knocked urgently on the door of the captain's quarters.

"What is it?" Glennister called.

A corporal rushed in, sketched a hasty salute, and said, "Sorry for the interruption, sir, but the sergeant of the guard asked me to fetch you."

"Is there a problem?" Glennister asked.

Saunders added, "Is the fort under attack?"

The corporal ignored the civilian's question and told his commanding officer, "Trouble at Kimbell's Saloon, sir. Some of the troops and those men who rode in this afternoon . . . well, sir, they're trying to kill each other!"

CHAPTER 31

Walt Reynolds, Ox Tankersley, and Billy Bob Moore sat at a table with a bucket of beer in front of them. They had dipped tin cups into the beer and now raised them as Reynolds said, "Here's to Grover. May he rest in peace."

Moore said, "To Grover," and Tankersley just grunted in acknowledgment of their friend.

After they'd all downed some of the beer, Moore added, "He was a whiny little pain in the rear end most of the time, but he wasn't a bad fella overall."

It wasn't exactly a glowing tribute, Reynolds thought, but it was the best that Grover was likely to get. All three men were thinking that it could just as easily have been one of them who'd been laid to rest out there in the middle of nowhere.

They drank in silence for a few minutes, then Ox Tankersley asked, "Do you reckon we ought to go on with this bunch, Walt, or should we slip off and let 'em ride on without us?"

"Why would we do that?" Reynolds said.

"Well, Grover's dead and so are those other two hombres. From here on out, it's liable to just get more dangerous."

"We knew there'd be some risk when we took the job," Reynolds pointed out.

Ox's broad shoulders rose and fell. "Yeah, but there's no law sayin' we can't change our minds."

"Where would we go?" Moore asked. "Would we head back to Fort Worth? It wouldn't make sense to go any other direction by ourselves. We're already right on the edge of Comanche country."

"Three men alone wouldn't stand a chance," Reynolds said flatly. "I'm not sure we could even make it back to Fort Worth by ourselves. I think we're stuck with Mr. MacCallister's bunch." He paused, then added, "Anyway, I said I'd go with him, and I like to keep my word."

"No need to get huffy about it," Tankersley said. "I just brought up the possibility. Never said that's what I wanted to do."

"Fine." Reynolds reached toward the bucket with his empty cup to dip up some more beer.

Before he could do so, loud, angry shouts came from the other side of the room. The saloon was a large, low-ceilinged place with hard-packed dirt floors, a scattering of mismatched and roughhewn tables and chairs, and a bar made from planks laid across barrels. The air was smoky from pipes and lanterns, and the unmistakable blend of stale beer and human sweat hung in the atmosphere as well. Reynolds turned his head to look at a table where some of the men from Mr. MacCallister's bunch had been playing cards with several troopers from the fort.

Now they were all on their feet, yelling at each other. Accusations of cheating flew back and forth. Reynolds had no idea if there was any truth to those charges, but it didn't matter. Both sides believed they had been taken advantage of, so the confrontation's outcome was inevitable.

One of the soldiers, a burly sergeant with a bristling red mustache, leaped onto the table, planted a big, booted foot in the middle of it, and crashed into one of the other men with a diving tackle that sent both of them to the floor. The sergeant landed on top of his victim and hammered punches into his face.

That was like striking a spark in a thicket of dried brush. More shouted curses rose like exploding flame and the two groups charged each other, coming together in a welter of flying fists.

Reynolds started to his feet, thinking that he and his companions ought to get out of there before they were drawn into the ruckus. He began, "We'd better—"

It was too late to avoid the trouble. A couple of troopers from a nearby table leaped to their feet and charged. One of them grabbed Reynolds's shoulder and jerked him around. The man's fist slammed into Reynolds's jaw and flung him back onto the table where he and his friends had been sitting. His shoulder hit the bucket of beer and knocked it over into Ox Tankersley's lap.

Roaring furiously because he'd had beer dumped on him, as well as seeing his friend punched viciously like that, Tankersley surged to his feet and stepped around the table to sink his fist wrist-deep into the midsection of the man who'd hit Reynolds.

The blow caused the soldier to double over, gagging. His companion grabbed up a chair and brought it down across Tankersley's back with enough force to shatter the chair into kindling. The blow made Ox stumble forward and go to one knee.

Reynolds had wanted to avoid trouble; that was why he'd been about to suggest that they leave the saloon. Since that was no longer possible, he wasn't going to stand by and do nothing while a friend of his was attacked. He rolled off the table where he had fallen, took a quick step, yelled, "Hey!" and when the man who had just busted the chair over Ox's back turned his head, Reynolds broke the man's nose with a right cross that landed in the middle of his face.

The man fell backward and dropped the one broken chair leg he was still holding. Reynolds caught the chair leg before it hit the floor and whipped it across the anger-twisted face of another trooper charging him. That soldier went down, too.

But then three or four of them swarmed around Reynolds, grabbing his arms and immobilizing him so he couldn't fight back as fists sledged into him. He went down as that irresistible force swept over him, and he knew as he fell that he might not ever get back up again.

The crazed troopers might just stomp him to death.

Jamie and Preacher knew from what the excited corporal had said that some of their men were in the middle of the brawl. That came as no surprise, but the realization of it made Jamie briefly think that maybe he should have declared the saloon off-limits to his party.

Not that that would have done any good, he told himself as he and Preacher charged across the fort's parade ground. Once the men had realized they could get a drink there, not to mention a game of cards and maybe even a woman, they would have found a way to go, no matter what orders he had given.

Captain Glennister headed for the saloon with them. Hannah and Saunders remained behind at the captain's quarters, although they stepped out onto the porch to watch Jamie, Preacher, and Glennister cross the parade ground in a hurry.

They heard the sounds of battle coming through the building's open door before they got there. Angry shouts and the crash of breaking furniture told an unmistakable story.

"They're bustin' the place up, all right," Preacher said.

"I'll have my men who are involved thrown in the guardhouse!" Glennister fumed.

"It might not be their fault," Jamie pointed out. "That's no band of angels we've got traveling with us."

"Even so, my men know how I feel about them fighting with civilians," the captain snapped.

As Jamie and his companions reached the saloon, a figure came stumbling out. Jamie recognized Pete Barnes. Blood ran from Pete's nose, and he had a bloody cut on his forehead as well.

"What's going on in there?" Jamie asked him.

"A bunch of fellas have gone crazy," Pete said. "It started as an argument over cards, and then all the soldiers and all of our boys started whalin' away on each other, even the ones who weren't mixed up in the fuss to start with."

Jamie nodded. That was just the sort of answer he'd expected. Saloon brawls were like wildfires—once they started, they spread rapidly and senselessly.

"Anybody killed?" Preacher asked. "They usin' guns or knives?"

Pete shook his head. "Not yet. Just fists and busted chairs and table legs."

"Maybe we can put a stop to it before somebody gets their head stove in," Jamie said. "Come on!"

He stepped past Pete Barnes and went through the door first, followed by Preacher and Captain Glennister. Jamie saw instantly that it wouldn't do any good for him to order the men to stop fighting. They were so caught up in the heat of battle that they wouldn't pay any attention to him. Any orders that Glennister might shout would be just as futile.

Instead, Jamie waded in, starting with one of his men and a uniformed private who were trading punches. Jamie grabbed each man by the collar and flung them in opposite directions, away from each other. He did the same with a couple of combatants who were wrestling and trying to gouge each other's eyes out.

The men involved in the fights he broke up that way reeled into other fighters. Their legs got tangled and they fell, winding up in masses of flailing arms and legs on the hard-packed dirt floor.

Preacher pitched in, too, using his fists to separate the fighters. Captain Glennister stood just inside the door and watched in awe as the two frontiersmen carved a path across the room toward the bar, leaving piles of moaning, half-stunned men behind them.

Several times, soldiers managed to avoid being tossed aside and tried to throw punches at Jamie's head. He avoided those wild blows with ease and snapped short but devastating punches in return. Men's heads rocked back violently from those collisions with Jamie's rock-hard fists. Knees buckled and the unlucky recipients folded up and ended in heaps on the floor, too.

Jamie reached the bar just as Ox Tankersley stumbled up alongside him. The man's face was smeared with blood and already swelling from the punishment he had absorbed. His eyes rolled in their sockets as he struggled to hang on to consciousness. One of the soldiers loomed behind him and raised a mallet-like fist, poised to come crashing down on the back of Ox's head.

That brutal blow began to fall, but it stopped short after traveling only a few inches. Jamie's left hand wrapped around the trooper's wrist. The soldier grimaced and strained so hard that muscles stood out in his neck like cables under the tanned skin. Jamie peered into the man's craggy face. A bristling red mustache dominated the trooper's features.

The sergeant abandoned his attack on Tankersley and twisted to ram a punch at Jamie's belly with his left fist. Jamie avoided it and brought his right around in a looping blow that smashed into the man's jaw. With Jamie's considerable strength behind it, the impact slewed the sergeant's head to the side. When Jamie let go of his wrist, the trooper crumpled to the floor, out cold.

The next second, a gunshot blast, deafeningly loud in the low-ceilinged room, caused a stunned silence to drop over the whole place.

CHAPTER 32

Powder smoke still curled from the muzzle of the Colt Dragoon that Captain Stephen Glennister lowered after firing the shot into the ceiling.

"Ten-hut!" he barked. *"Now!"*

Most of the troopers in the saloon were in no shape to snap to attention. They were either unconscious or lying on the floor, moaning. A few were able to stand up stiff and straight. They looked like they were worried that Glennister might dispense with a firing squad and just shoot them himself.

Instead, Glennister holstered the Colt, stalked a few more steps into the room, and ordered in a loud, clear voice, "You men who are still on your feet, get those others up and out of here. Return to your quarters. This saloon is off-limits for the next week!"

A few of the soldiers started to groan in dismay, but as the captain glared at them, they stifled that reaction and started trying to follow his orders. Battered, bruised, and bloody troopers were helped to their feet. They stumbled out of the saloon.

A handful couldn't be roused from their stupor, including the mustachioed sergeant Jamie had knocked out with one punch. He and the others still unconscious were dragged from the building by their friends.

Eventually, no one was left in the place except Jamie, Preacher, and the men from their party, along with Captain Glennister and the nervous-looking proprietor of the saloon.

"I know this isn't your fault, Kimbell," Glennister said to the man. "I regret the revenue you'll lose over the next week."

The saloonkeeper spread his hands. "I ain't gonna interfere or complain about your orders, Cap'n. I'm just grateful you let me stay in business here. I'll go along with whatever you want."

Jamie said to Glennister, "If you'd like, we'll leave in the morning instead of laying over for a couple of nights."

The captain shook his head. "That's not necessary. Who started this fracas, Kimbell?"

The saloon man rubbed his angular jaw and said, "Well . . . I'd say it was pretty much mutual, Cap'n. Both sides was yellin' at each other over a card game, and I couldn't tell you exactly who got a burr under his saddle first."

Glennister thought about it and nodded. "We'll let it go at that, then," he said. "You can punish your men however you'd like, Jamie, but you don't have to leave early on our account."

"I appreciate that," Jamie said. "The least we can do is make sure our boys keep their distance from yours. We don't want this starting up again."

"No, we do not," Glennister agreed. Surprisingly, a faint

smile tugged at the corners of his mouth as he went on, "However, a good fight now and then takes the edge off the men, especially when they spend their days in a tense situation such as knowing that the hostiles could attack the fort at any moment, unlikely though that may be."

Preacher said, "You're right, Cap'n. Fellas got to blow off steam."

"One thing I'm curious about," Jamie said. "Who's that big redheaded sergeant I walloped?"

"Sergeant McKittredge?" Glennister's lips tightened, and he shook his head. "I don't mind saying that he's a bit of a troublemaker. It wouldn't surprise me a bit to find out that he was responsible for what happened here. He's a decent soldier, but he's obstinate, has a mean streak, and drinks too much. You should steer clear of him, Jamie, just to make sure there's no further trouble with him."

"That's what I figure on doing," Jamie said with a nod. "I'm not afraid of him, but I don't particularly want to have to kill him and rob you of a noncommissioned officer."

"Yes, that would be for the best," Glennister agreed. "Now, I suppose we should go back to my quarters and make sure Miss Craigson and Mr. Saunders are all right."

Sergeant Angus McKittredge came up off the bunk bellowing curses and fighting. He didn't know where he was or what was going on at first, but he knew he wanted to lash out and hurt somebody. Wanted to smash his fists into somebody's face and feel blood spurt and bone break under them.

An arm wrapped around his neck from behind and hauled him back. A man's voice said harshly in his ear, "Stop it, Angus! Stop it, you big dumb ape!"

McKittredge jerked his head back and forth but couldn't

dislodge the other man's grip. He went still, and after a minute, Corporal Fred Herndon went on, "If I let go of you, are you gonna settle down? We're back in quarters, and there's nobody here to fight."

"All right, all right," McKittredge growled. "Turn loose, blast your hide."

Herndon let go and stepped back. He was a rawboned man with curly brown hair, leaner than McKittredge but still powerfully built.

McKittredge scrubbed a hand over his rugged face and winced as pain shot through his slab of a jaw.

"What in blazes happened?"

"You got walloped by Jamie MacCallister, that's what happened," Herndon said. "Knocked you out cold with one punch." The corporal chuckled. "I wouldn't have believed it if I hadn't seen it with my own eyes."

For a second, McKittredge was angry and would have gone after Herndon for that comment, but he reined in his temper. Herndon, like McKittredge himself, was a bad man to have for an enemy.

McKittredge looked around the room, which was dimly lit by a single lantern on a table near the door. The men who had been involved in the brawl were lying in their bunks, some snoring, some groaning from the pain of the battering they had taken.

"MacCallister's the one who hit me, you said?"

"That's right. You should be honored, Angus. It's not everybody who can say he was knocked out by such a famous frontiersman."

McKittredge growled a few obscenities about Jamie MacCallister, his heritage, and his activities.

"If you're finished," Herndon said when McKittredge's rant trailed off, "come outside. We need to talk." He glanced around. "Where there aren't so many to overhear."

Despite the throbbing pain in his jaw and head, McKittredge's curiosity was aroused by Herndon's words. The two of them had been mixed up in several profitable schemes together during their years together in the army. Herndon's tone of voice indicated that something potentially lucrative might be in the offing.

McKittredge cursed more as he hauled himself to his feet and followed Herndon out of the barracks. Herndon led him to the end of the building, where the shadows cast by the moon and stars were the thickest.

"Bert, are you still here?" Herndon called softly.

"Right here," Private Bertram Attaway said as he stepped closer to the two big noncoms. "How are you doin' there, Sarge?"

Attaway had been born and raised in London and had immigrated to the States about ten years earlier. He still had his British accent. McKittredge, as a Scotsman—albeit one born in Kentucky—had no use for the English to start with. Attaway's small stature and sharp-featured face reminded McKittredge of a rat, and that was a pretty good description of the private.

McKittredge didn't answer Attaway's question. Instead, he said to Herndon, "What's he doing here?"

"Bert came across something interesting earlier today," Herndon said. "He was over by the captain's quarters while Glennister was having supper with those visitors, and he overheard something through the window."

"I did, indeed," Attaway said with a note of pride in his voice. "They was talkin' about a treasure, Sarge. A real treasure of gold and silver!"

"You're mad," McKittredge said. "There's no treasure out here. There's *nothing* out here except heat and dust and savages."

"No, I swear it! Talkin' about Jim Bowie, they was, you know, the fella what was killed at the Alamo."

"I know who Jim Bowie was." McKittredge looked at Herndon. "I'm surprised you fell for whatever wild story this little weasel is peddling."

"Just listen to him, Angus. That's all I'm asking."

McKittredge listened, and despite what he expected, he found himself growing interested in the tale Attaway was spinning. It sounded too farfetched to believe, and he was about to declare as much when Attaway said, "If you think I'm lyin', Sarge, I seen it. I seen the proof of what they were sayin'."

"What proof?"

"The letter and the map that redheaded girl has. I seen 'em with me own eyes. When the trouble at the saloon started and they all stepped out for a bit, I climbed in the window and had a gander. The girl had left 'em on the table, and I got a good long look at them."

"Yeah? Why didn't you steal them, then? That's probably why you were there in the first place, wasn't it? Looking for something to steal?"

"If I'd nicked 'em, the girl would've noticed that they were gone, and the cap'n would've knowed that somebody was there." Attaway scuffed his feet on the dusty ground. "When things go missin' around here, the cap'n's got hisself a bad habit of thinkin' I had somethin' to do with it."

"Because you usually do, you scurvy little thief!"

"Take it easy, Angus," Herndon said. "Bert did the right thing by leaving those papers there. The captain won't suspect that we know anything about the treasure, and neither will Jamie MacCallister."

"Don't tell me you believe that wild story!"

Herndon shrugged in the shadows and said, "It could be true. The girl believes it, and MacCallister and Preacher are convinced enough that they came all the way out here to look for it. If it really *is* true, something like that would be worth going after, wouldn't it?"

"I suppose so, but what good does that do us?"

"I got a mighty good memory," Attaway said, tapping a finger against the side of his head. "All I've got to do is look at somethin' for a minute or so, an' I can remember it from then on. I know where they're goin', Sarge. I can see that map in me head, plain as day."

"And we've already been talking about how maybe it's time for us to say goodbye to the army, Angus," Herndon said. "You know there are others here at the fort who agree with us."

McKittredge frowned. "Are you saying we ought to desert and go after MacCallister's bunch? Follow them and see whether they find that gold and silver?"

"And if they do," Herndon said, "then we'll step in and make it ours . . . along with that girl."

"Whattaya say, Sarge, whattaya say?" Attaway prodded.

The image of Jamie MacCallister filled McKittredge's mind. A white-hot fury blazed in his chest as he thought about how MacCallister had knocked him out. That was a disgrace he couldn't allow to go unavenged.

"I say we start thinking about how we're gonna do this," McKittredge replied.

CHAPTER 33

Jamie gathered his men in the center of their camp early the next morning. Preacher had been happy to go around rousting them out of their bedrolls. Some of the men weren't pleased about being disturbed because they were hungover and hurting from the fight the night before, but any complaints they attempted to make were silenced quickly when Dog snarled and bared his teeth at them.

Once they were assembled, moaning and cursing under their breath, wearing miserable, hangdog expressions, Jamie stood before the group and said, "I'm not going to dish out any punishment for that brawl last night, but for the rest of the time we're here at Fort Belknap, I want all of you to stay away from those soldiers. Captain Glennister has closed down the saloon for the time being, too, so you won't have any need to go over there."

That last statement was a bit of a stretch. Glennister had made the saloon off-limits to his troopers for a week, but he hadn't actually ordered the proprietor to close. However, Jamie figured it would be a good idea to keep his men away from the place, too.

No one argued with the decision. They probably felt too sick to do so.

Jamie thumbed his hat back and his tone was friendlier as he continued, "I'll admit, I'm a mite curious about what started the ruckus. Somebody said it was over a game of cards?"

One of the men, Hank Tompkins by name, cleared his throat and said, "I was part of that game, Mr. MacCallister. It was friendly enough, I reckon, until this big sergeant lost a few hands in a row and wasn't happy about it."

"What did he do?" Jamie asked.

"He started makin' comments about how there was somethin' funny goin' on, and we all knew he was sayin' that we were cheatin'. We let it pass for a while and hoped he'd calm down, but he didn't. When he lost again, he came right out and accused us of cheatin'." Tompkins shook his head. "I'm sorry, but we couldn't just let that go."

"I understand," Jamie said. "This sergeant, you say he was a big fella?"

"Yeah, with red hair and a mustache that stuck out on both sides."

Jamie nodded. "I know the man you're talking about."

"You should," Walt Reynolds said. "You walloped the tar out of him, Mr. MacCallister. I saw it."

Jamie frowned at Reynolds. "You look almost like you got trampled by a herd of cattle, Walt."

"Kind of feel like it, too." Reynolds's face was puffy, swollen, and covered with purple-and-blue bruises. "Some of those troopers had me down and were stomping and kicking me pretty good. I reckon I'd have been a goner if you and Preacher hadn't come along and hauled them off of me."

Preacher chuckled. "We did that? To tell you the truth, boy, there was so much goin' on, I never even noticed rescuin' you."

"I'm grateful to you either way, sir. You saved my life. As soon as I got a chance, I crawled under a table and sort of hid out there until the fight was over."

Ox Tankersley spoke up. "Walt told me that sergeant was about to bash my head in when you stopped him, Mr. MacCallister. I don't really remember because by then, I was too addlepated to know what was goin' on. So I'm obliged to you, too."

"I'm just glad Preacher and I got there in time," Jamie told him. He looked around at the whole group. "All right. Rest up today. Lick your wounds. And don't start any trouble with those soldiers. There might come a time when we need their help, and we wouldn't want them standing around trying to figure out whether or not to give it to us."

That comment put thoughtful looks on the faces of some of the men as Jamie and Preacher walked off.

They strolled toward Hannah's tent with Dog ambling along beside them. Preacher said quietly, "I've been thinkin' about what we ought to do about that gal, Jamie."

"You mean Miss Craigson?" Jamie laughed and shook his head. "Of course, you do. She's the only woman in these parts other than a couple of soiled doves, and we don't have anything to do with them. So what is it you mean, Preacher?"

"I ain't so sure we ought to leave her here, like you talked to Cap'n Glennister about," Preacher said bluntly.

Jamie paused in his walking, and the old mountain man did likewise. Jamie said, "You think we ought to take her into the heart of Comancheria?"

"Well, that ain't exactly a good solution, neither, but I don't rightly trust that she'd be safe here."

"Stephen Glennister's a good man and a fine officer."

Preacher nodded. "I ain't doubtin' that. But he can't be ever'where at once, and some of them soldiers don't seem too trustworthy to me."

Jamie raked a thumbnail along his jawline and frowned in thought. "Like that big sergeant who started the fight last night? McKittredge?"

"Yeah. We decided not to leave the gal in Fort Worth because of Otis Lynch. From what I've seen of him, that hombre McKittredge is cut from the same cloth."

"He hasn't bothered Miss Craigson," Jamie replied with a shake of his head. "He hasn't acted like he's even noticed her."

"Oh, he's noticed her, all right. I'd bet a hat all those soldier boys have. The question is, what's McKittredge likely to do once we're gone? You really think that young fella Saunders could protect her from the likes of him?"

"Glennister would have him shot if he tried anything," Jamie said.

"More'n likely. But that might be too late to help Miss Hannah." Preacher shrugged. "Reckon it boils down to me havin' a hunch that keepin' her close to us is the best way to keep her safe."

"You might have a point there, and I certainly trust your instincts," Jamie allowed. "Not only that, I've worried that if we force her to stay here, she might try to follow us after we've left. She knows we'll be following the river, so it wouldn't be much trouble to trail us."

"I sure wouldn't put it past her. She's pretty muleheaded for a gal."

Jamie chuckled. "Women can be just as stubborn as men. More so most of the time, I reckon. They have a way of not letting their menfolk know what's actually going on." He grew serious again. "It's just hard to swallow the idea of taking a woman up the Brazos with us."

"Seems crazier than an outhouse rat, just on the face of it, you're right about that, but you're plannin' on gettin' back here safe, aren't you?"

"I wouldn't start a job if I didn't think I could carry it through successfully."

"Nope, me neither. And when you come right down to it . . . she's got a stake in lookin' for that treasure, too."

Jamie couldn't argue with that. He nodded and said, "Let's go talk to her."

When they reached the tent, Hannah had already emerged from it, looking far fresher and prettier than she had any right to, considering the primitive surroundings. Philip Saunders was with her. He usually spread his bedroll under the wagon at night, close by in case anyone tried to bother Hannah.

"Good morning, Mr. MacCallister. Good morning, Preacher," she greeted them. A frown creased her forehead. "I saw you talking to the men. Is there more trouble?"

"No, ma'am," Jamie told her. "Just laying down the law to them so there won't be any more problems while we're here. They understand they're to stay away from the saloon and steer clear of the soldiers, too."

Saunders asked, "Are we staying here until tomorrow the way you planned?"

"That's right."

Saunders smiled. "Good. I can use another day's rest, to be honest. All that riding is more than I'm used to."

Preacher said, "Just what is it you do, son? I don't believe I've ever heard you say."

"Oh, I've been involved in several enterprises. Nothing at the moment because I wanted to help Hannah with this quest to find Colonel Bowie's treasure. Nothing I've done ever required a great deal of horseback riding, though."

"You get used to it," Jamie said. "For now, though, we can all use some rest before we start on this last stretch of the journey."

"I believe I'll find some shade, then," Hannah said. "Thankfully, there are a few trees in this region, even if they aren't very large ones."

"And I'll keep an eye on things," Saunders added.

Jamie and Preacher both nodded their approval of the plan and walked off. When they were out of earshot of the young couple, Preacher glanced back over his shoulder and then said to Jamie, "I reckon you noticed that ol' Philip didn't answer me when I asked him about what he does for a livin'."

"Yeah, I did," Jamie said. "He was downright slippery about it, wasn't he?"

Preacher rubbed his chin. "Somethin' else I've noticed about the fella. He's got mighty soft, pale hands. They look like he's never done a lick of physical work in his life. I've seen other fellas who had hands like that. All of 'em spent most of their time in saloons and taverns, sittin' at a table dealin' pasteboards."

"Gamblers, you mean."

"Yep."

"There are honest gamblers," Jamie said. "Even if you're right about Saunders, that doesn't mean there's any reason to be suspicious of him."

"Maybe the fellas you're talkin' about deal honest games, but I never saw a gambler yet who wasn't out to feather his own nest, first and foremost."

"You're probably right about that, too," Jamie nodded. "We'll keep an eye on Saunders. Shoot, we were already doing that because of the way he showed up out of the blue, back in Fort Worth. Hannah seems to trust him completely, though."

"She wouldn't be the first gal to be taken in by some handsome, sweet-talkin' hombre. I wouldn't be as leery of him if he didn't know about that so-called cache of gold and silver we're goin' after. I'd like to know whether he decided to come with Hannah before or after he found out about that."

"Well, before this trip is over," Jamie said, "maybe we'll have enough evidence to figure out the answer to that."

CHAPTER 34

Although the soldiers and the members of Jamie's party eyed each other warily that day, it was always from a distance and no more trouble erupted.

During the day, Jamie noticed Sergeant McKittredge watching him several times. The glare on the big, rusty-haired noncom's face was enough to tell Jamie that the man harbored a grudge against him, but McKittredge didn't try to start anything.

They would be gone the next day, Jamie told himself, and after that, they wouldn't have to worry about McKittredge anymore.

Despite being grateful for the opportunity to rest, Hannah must have gotten bored. That afternoon, while Philip Saunders dozed with his back propped against a tree trunk and his hat tipped down over his eyes, Hannah stood up and walked toward the fort.

Walt Reynolds, who was doing some mending on his horse's harness, saw what she was doing and frowned in concern. He didn't figure Mr. MacCallister would want her wandering around by herself, so he put the harness aside and ambled after her. Not following her, exactly, because he didn't want to frighten her, but heading in the same general direction.

Reynolds was still sore from the battering he had taken in the fight the night before, but with the resilience of youth, he was starting to feel better already. He knew the bruises and scratches made him look pretty bad, though.

To his surprise, Hannah walked past the fort rather than going to any of the buildings. She went toward the Indian lodges on the far side of the post. Mr. MacCallister had said those were peaceful Indians. Wichitas instead of Comanches. Maybe Miss Craigson wanted a closer look at them, Reynolds thought. Since she was from back east somewhere, she'd probably never seen any Indians close up.

He was convinced that Mr. MacCallister would like this even less than Hannah going to the fort. He started walking a little faster. If he caught up to her, he might be able to persuade her to return to the camp.

He had hung back too far, though, Reynolds saw. As he hurried toward her, Hannah reached the lodges. Several of the Indians who had been sitting in front of the dwellings stood up and clustered around her, talking rapidly and holding out their hands.

They were begging, Reynolds realized. And Hannah was starting to look flustered, maybe even a little scared. Right about now, she probably wished she had stayed away from the lodges.

He needed to get her out of there before things got any worse. He was about to call out to her, as much to let the Indians know he was coming as to reassure her, when he heard rapid footsteps behind him.

Reynolds stopped and looked around, saw Philip Saunders running toward him. Well, not toward *him*, but toward Hannah and the Wichitas. Saunders's eyes were wide and a little crazed.

Worse still, he had drawn his gun and brandished it in front of him.

"Get away from her!" he shouted at the Indians. "Leave her alone, you filthy savages!"

"They're not trying to hurt her," Reynolds said as he raised a hand in an instinctive gesture, trying to get Saunders to slow down. The Wichitas were being annoying and might be scaring Hannah, but they weren't actually threatening her.

Saunders didn't seem to hear what Reynolds said. He came to an abrupt stop nearby and leveled the gun, sighting along its barrel as he was obviously about to open fire on the Indians.

Reynolds didn't think about what he was doing. He acted on instinct, leaping at Saunders and bringing his arm up so that it hit Saunders's forearm and knocked it skyward as the revolver blasted. The bullet went high in the air, a long way over the heads of Hannah and the Indians where it couldn't do any harm.

Hannah cried out in surprise at the sound of the shot. The Indians scurried away from her and ducked into their lodges, not wanting anything to do with the crazy white man who had just pulled the trigger.

"What have you done?" Saunders yelled at Reynolds. "I'm trying to save her!"

He slashed at Reynold's head with the pistol.

Reynolds ducked and tried to back off, holding both hands out in front of him defensively.

"Take it easy, mister," he urged. "Miss Craigson's all right—"

Snarling, Saunders pointed the gun at him. Caught up in

rage and maybe fear, the hombre was about to shoot him. In that split second, Reynolds knew he had only two choices.

He could claw his own gun from its holster and try to shoot Saunders first—

Or he could do what he did, diving at Saunders's legs as the revolver roared and the bullet plucked Reynolds's hat right off his head, luckily not ventilating his skull at the same time.

Reynolds rammed his shoulder into Saunders's thighs and hung on. The impact drove Saunders off his feet. He went over backward and landed hard enough that the gun was jolted out of his hand. When Reynolds looked up and saw that, he hoped it would put an end to this unfortunate incident, but Saunders was crazed and not ready to quit fighting. He bucked and twisted and broke loose from Reynolds's grip, then aimed a kick at the young saddle tramp's face.

Reynolds jerked his head aside. The heel of Saunders's boot caught him on the left shoulder with enough force to make that arm go numb for a moment. Reynolds grimaced in pain and rolled away, still hoping that the other man would get control of himself.

Instead, Saunders scrambled up on hands and knees and came after him, throwing himself on top of Reynolds and pounding at him with his fists.

Reynolds hadn't wanted trouble, but there was only so much he could take. With an angry growl of his own, he fought back, shooting his right fist upward in a punch that landed under Saunders's chin and rocked his head back.

That broke off Saunders's furious attack and gave Reynolds time to bring a looping left up and around. It crashed into the side of Saunders's head and knocked him off. Again, Reynolds rolled the other way to put some space between them. When he came to his feet, he saw that Saunders was getting up, too.

"Philip, stop it! Please stop fighting!"

Reynolds heard that plea from Hannah Craigson only vaguely over the pounding of blood in his head. Saunders didn't seem to hear it at all. He charged Reynolds with both arms pistoning back and forth in a flurry of blows.

Reynolds was already so beat up, he didn't figure a few more punches would make any difference. So he stood his ground and slugged back at Saunders, clubbing blows that stood the other man up straight and made him step back.

Reynolds bored in. Saunders's frenzied attack had been effective, but only for a moment. Reynolds hit him with a swift combination of punches to the body and head. Saunders's knees began to buckle.

Before Reynolds could finish him off, powerful arms encircled him from behind and lifted him off his feet almost as easily as if he'd been a child's toy. He felt himself whirled around, away from Saunders, and then thrown to the ground. He landed hard enough to knock the wind out of him, but he recovered quickly and started to push himself up on his hands and knees.

"Stay down," a harsh, familiar voice ordered.

Panting for breath, Reynolds raised his head and looked over his shoulder. Jamie MacCallister stood over him, looming as big and imposing as a mountain from this angle. A part of Reynolds's brain had known immediately that it was Jamie who grabbed him. Nobody else in the group would be able to manhandle him like that.

A few yards away, Preacher had hold of Philip Saunders. Reynolds wasn't sure if Preacher was holding the man back—or holding him up. Saunders looked like he was only partially conscious.

Reynolds felt a brief surge of satisfaction, knowing that he had whipped the Easterner.

Then Hannah moved up alongside Saunders and began fussing over him, clearly worried about him, and any satisfaction Reynolds felt went away in a hurry.

"Help Saunders back to the wagon," Jamie told Preacher. He held out a hand toward Reynolds. "You just stay where you are."

"Don't worry, Mr. MacCallister," Reynolds said. He raked back the hair that had fallen in his face. "I've had enough." He paused, then added, "I'd had enough before the blasted ruckus started. But I didn't figure he ought to be shooting at those Indians."

Jamie frowned at that. He didn't say anything else as Preacher led Philip Saunders back toward their camp. Hannah hurried along beside them, clutching Saunders's arm to help him.

Once they had disappeared behind one of the fort's buildings, Jamie stepped closer to Reynolds and extended a hand. Reynolds reached up and clasped it. Jamie hauled the young man to his feet effortlessly.

"You say Saunders took a shot at the Wichitas?" he asked. "That's what started this?"

"Well . . . he tried to shoot at them. I knocked his arm up so the bullet didn't come anywhere near them, and he only got the one round off." Reynolds nodded toward the lodges, where the Indians were starting to poke their heads out again and look around curiously. "They ought to be all right, all of them."

"What were the three of you doing over here?"

Reynolds hated to make it sound like he was blaming Hannah, but the facts of the matter were what they were. "Miss Craigson came over here to take a look around, I guess. She must've wanted to see some Indians close up. I saw where she was headed and followed her."

Jamie grunted. "What business of it was yours?"

"Well, none, I reckon. I was just kind of . . . keeping an eye on her. I didn't think she'd be in any danger, but I didn't figure it would hurt to be sure."

"What happened then?"

"When she got here, the Indians sort of swarmed her. They looked like they were begging for a handout of some sort."

Jamie scowled. "They've gotten too many handouts already. That's why they're willing to just sit here beside the fort and wait for the next one, instead of going out and hunting like their ancestors did." He shrugged. "But I don't think they would have hurt her."

"I don't think so, either, but they scared her, sure enough. I could tell that. I was about to step in and try to get her away from them, peaceful-like, when Saunders ran up, yelling and waving a gun around. I could tell he was about to shoot, and I was afraid he might hit Miss Craigson . . . or start a war with the Indians . . . so I stopped him."

Jamie thought in silence for a long moment, then nodded.

"You did the right thing," he told Reynolds. "I reckon when you did that, Saunders went loco and came after you instead?"

"He was already crazed when he came running up," Reynolds declared. "I could see the panic in his eyes."

"He's deathly afraid of Indians, seems like."

"Then why in the world is he coming with us right into the heart of Comanche country?"

"He wants to help Miss Craigson get what she's after, or at least so he claims."

"You don't believe him?"

"That's not your worry, Reynolds," Jamie said sharply. His tone eased as he added, "But I'm obliged to you for stepping in. Things could've gotten ugly if Saunders had gunned down one of those Wichitas. They may be a shadow of what they once were, not all that long ago, but I still wouldn't want to get them riled up."

"No, sir." Reynolds picked up his hat from the ground where it had fallen during the ruckus and slapped it against his thigh to knock some of the dust off of it. "What do you want me to do now?"

"Keep your distance from Saunders. Once we're away from here, he may come to his senses, but he's liable to hold a grudge against you, anyway."

"Yes, sir. I can do that." Reynolds put his hat on. "That fella's a lucky man. I mean, he was the one who lost his head and nearly caused a big problem, but it was him Miss Craigson was carrying on over when they walked off."

Jamie's eyes narrowed. "Don't you go getting any ideas in your head, Walt. Where we're going, we're liable to have enough trouble without some sort of rivalry over a girl."

"No, sir, no rivalry," Reynolds declared.

As they walked back toward the camp, though, he found himself wondering if that was completely true.

CHAPTER 35

Nothing else happened that day, for which Jamie and Preacher were grateful. Hannah tended to the bumps, bruises, and scratches Saunders had suffered in the brief fight, and then he crawled into her tent to rest and recuperate. Hannah sat under the tree nearby with a look on her face that made the men avoid her.

That evening, though, as she, Jamie, and Preacher were walking toward Captain Glennister's quarters to have supper with him again, she said quietly, "I apologize, Mr. MacCallister."

"What for, ma'am?"

"Causing all that trouble with the Indians this afternoon. I didn't think it would be a problem if I walked over there and had a better look at them. You said that they're harmless."

"Most of the time, they are," Jamie said.

"But any Injun can be a threat under the right circumstances," Preacher put in. He chuckled and added, "Of course, I reckon that's true for all men, no matter what color they are. Might be some purple fellas somewhere, for all I know, and if they're attacked unfairly or backed into a corner, they'll fight."

Hannah smiled. "I don't believe there are any purple people. At least I've never heard of any."

"Well, you never know."

Jamie said, "I understand you didn't mean any harm, Miss Craigson, but from here on out especially, you don't need to be wandering off from the rest of the group. You'll want to stay close at all times."

She stopped short and looked at him. "Wait a minute. Does this mean you're going to let me come along the rest of the way?"

Jamie glanced at Preacher, who just looked back at him impassively, as if to say that this was Jamie's decision to make.

"That's right," he told Hannah. "I'm not all that fond of the idea. I should have made you go home to start with. But since you're out here in the wilds of Texas, I reckon it's better if you stay with us."

Smiling, she threw her arms around his neck and hugged him as she said, "Thank you, Jamie!"

He patted her awkwardly on the back with one big paw and said, "Better wait until we actually get back safely to be thanking me. I may be taking you right into more trouble than any of us can handle."

"I'm not sure there's any trouble you *can't* handle," she said as she let go of him and stepped back.

"I'd just as soon not find out." He offered her his arm and nodded toward the commanding officer's quarters. "We'd better go on to supper. I expect Captain Glennister's waiting for us."

Glennister was, and as he greeted them, he asked,

"Where's Mr. Saunders this evening? I heard there was some trouble earlier. I hope he's all right."

"He's fine, Captain," Hannah assured him. "Just a little . . . under the weather."

"Ah," Glennister said as he cocked an eyebrow. "That can happen to a man, all right. I hope he feels better in the morning."

"So do I," Jamie said, "because we're leaving, one way or another."

Jamie and Preacher were up well before dawn the next morning, waking the members of their party and telling them to get ready to travel. A little grumbling went on because some of the men were still stiff and sore from the brawl in the saloon a couple of nights earlier, but there weren't any serious complaints, and the men went about their preparations efficiently enough.

When Philip Saunders crawled out of his bedroll underneath the wagon, he raked his fingers through disheveled dark hair and said, "I want to apologize, Mr. MacCallister, for that altercation I caused yesterday afternoon. I don't know what came over me."

"It seems to me that you're mighty afraid of Indians, Saunders," Jamie said. "Is there a reason for that? Some of them give you trouble in the past?"

Saunders shook his head. "No, I never even saw any of them in the little town back in Ohio where I grew up. Some of the old men who lived there had spent time out on the frontier when they were younger, though, and I heard the stories they told about scalping and other forms of mutilation. Perhaps I was just too much of an impressionable youth. I'm sure all of those bloody stories were just made up. Tall tales to frighten children."

Preacher was standing nearby, close enough to overhear the conversation. He laughed and said, "I wouldn't be too sure about those yarns bein' made up. I've seen some things that'd plumb curl your hair! If the Injuns left you any, that is."

"There are plenty of good reasons to be afraid of some Indians," Jamie said. "Just keep an eye on Preacher and me and follow our lead. We'll let you know if it's time to be worried."

Saunders nodded and said solemnly, "I'll try to remember that, Mr. MacCallister."

Hannah emerged from her nearby tent, fully dressed and looking ready and eager to set out on the last leg of the journey. She came over to join Jamie, Preacher, and Saunders and said, "Good morning. Thank you again, Mr. MacCallister, for agreeing to take me along the rest of the way."

"Wait a minute," Saunders said with a frown. "I thought the plan was for you to remain here at Fort Belknap, Hannah, while I and the others retrieve Colonel Bowie's treasure."

"That was the plan," Jamie said, "but I changed my mind. Miss Craigson's coming with us. I figure we can do a better job of keeping her safe than anybody else."

"But there are savages where we're going." Saunders glanced in the direction of the Indian lodges on the other side of the fort. "Actual savages."

"That's right. So we're going to have to keep our eyes open all the time, and everyone will need to follow the orders that Preacher and I give, without question."

"That's the best chance we've all got of gettin' out of there alive," the old mountain man put in.

Hannah rested a hand on Saunders's arm and said, "It'll be all right, Philip. I'm thrilled with the chance to finish the expedition. And when we come back with Colonel Bowie's treasure, everything will be fine."

"Of course, it will," Saunders said, but Jamie thought he didn't sound completely convinced.

By the time the eastern horizon glowed orange with the approach of sunrise, the wagon team was hitched up, the pack horses were loaded, the riding mounts were saddled, and everyone had washed down their breakfast with several cups of strong, black coffee. Jamie and Preacher walked around checking on everything and were satisfied that the group was ready to go.

Pete Barnes held the reins on the driver's seat next to Hannah. Philip Saunders moved his horse alongside the wagon on the right so that Hannah was closest to him.

But Jamie noticed that Walt Reynolds nudged his mount up on the vehicle's other side. Reynolds nodded to Pete, then leaned forward to look past the driver as he pinched the brim of his hat and said, "Mornin', Miss Craigson. I trust that you're well?"

"Why, yes, I am, Mr. Reynolds," she replied. "Thank you for asking."

"Yes'm. I'm glad to hear you're all right after that little incident yesterday."

"With the Indians, you mean? I was more surprised than I was frightened, but yet, it was rather disturbing in a way." She glanced toward Saunders, who sat his saddle sullenly on her other side, but she didn't say anything else.

"I hope the day goes well," Reynolds said, then he pulled his horse around and moved back to join the other men.

Jamie rode over beside him and said in a quiet voice, "I thought I told you I didn't want any romantic complications on this trip."

"No romance, no complications, Mr. MacCallister," the young saddle tramp replied. "I was just making sure the young lady was all right after getting spooked by those Indians yesterday."

"Sure, you were," Jamie said dryly. "I'll be keeping an eye on you, Reynolds. Don't make me sorry I agreed to bring you along."

"No, sir."

Jamie grunted and rode back to the front of the group to join Preacher, who sat there on Horse, the two of them waiting with Dog by their side. The big cur let out a low, eager growl. He was ready to be on the trail again.

So was Jamie, but before he could signal for the day's travel to begin, Captain Glennister walked out of the predawn gloom and held up a hand, then shaking hands with Jamie and Preacher.

"I came out to wish you good luck," the commanding officer said. "Where you're going, I'm afraid you're going to need it. Plenty of it, in fact."

"We'll take all we can get," Preacher drawled. "Luck works a lot better, though, if you've got a keen eye and a shootin' iron with a full wheel." He grinned. "Happen to have two of those, my own self."

"So long, Captain," Jamie said. "We'll be back this way, by and by."

"I'll look forward to seeing you," Glennister said.

He didn't sound all that confident it would ever happen.

As a sergeant, Angus McKittredge was seldom on duty at this hour of the morning. The men who stood guard duty were young privates. They and the cooks were the only ones up and about well before the sun came up.

McKittredge made it a point to wake early this morning,

however, so he could leave the barracks along with Corporal Fred Herndon and Private Bert Attaway and move through the shadows to the edge of the post.

From there, they watched as the members of MacCallister's expedition prepared to depart. McKittredge growled quietly, animal-like, at the sight of MacCallister walking around the camp, looming big and powerful against the light of the cookfire.

"You've got a powerful hate for that hombre, don't you, Angus?" Herndon asked.

"Yeah. I reckon I'd have to think about desertin' just to go after him and settle the score, even if there wasn't any treasure involved." McKittredge relaxed and chuckled. "But the idea of grabbin' that treasure makes it easier, I'll grant you that."

He didn't let himself think about the fact that the treasure might not exist. He was tired of the army and would be glad to get shed of it. Some men were cut out for the military life, and to be honest, he had done all right for himself in it so far, but enough was enough.

He was ready to be free again.

They caught sight of the redheaded young woman. Hannah Craigson, that was her name, McKittredge recalled. As if reading his mind, Herndon said, "You know, there are places where a gal that pretty would bring a mighty high price. That could be a nice bonus for us."

Attaway snickered. "Not to mention the sport we could have with her along the way."

"Let's not get ahead of ourselves," McKittredge said, acting as the voice of caution for once in his life. "We'll have to get away from here first." He scratched his blunt chin and reached a decision. "Tonight. We'll leave tonight. So if we're going to round up some men to come with us, we need to do it today."

"Let me handle that," Herndon said. "I can think of half a dozen fellas who hate the army and would be happy to come with us."

"Don't say anything to anybody you don't trust," McKittredge warned. "If anybody goes runnin' to the captain, it'll ruin everything."

"Don't worry, Angus, I'll be careful. None of the men I'm going to approach would give us away to Glennister. There wouldn't be any profit in it for them."

McKittredge nodded. He had to put his faith in Herndon, who had come up with the idea of deserting in the first place. If anything went wrong, he mused, he could blame it all on Herndon and claim that he'd played along just to trap the corporal.

But nothing would go wrong, McKittredge told himself. Pretty soon they would be away from the stifling routine and orders and all the drudgery of life on an army post, riding as free men across the plains on a ruthless quest for gold, silver, and a beautiful young woman.

In their way might be not only Jamie MacCallister, the old mountain man Preacher, and the rest of that ragtag bunch, but also the Comanches, as well, who typically responded in bloody fashion whenever anyone intruded on what they considered their territory.

McKittredge didn't care.

Whoever got in his way—MacCallister, Preacher, or a bunch of filthy savages—he'd kill them all to get what he wanted.

CHAPTER 36

The Brazos River twisted and turned, snakelike, across the Texas prairie not far west of Fort Belknap. It followed a generally northwest to southeast course over a broad bed between shallow, tree-dotted banks. When it rained enough to flood, the stream had carved out that riverbed, but during dry stretches, which was most of the time, slow-moving water covered only part of the bed, leaving many visible sandbars and some treacherous areas of quicksand.

"It ain't as impressive as the Missouri or the Mississippi, is it?" Preacher asked as he and Jamie rode along the bank with the rest of the party strung out behind them. The Brazos was to their left, the blue-green water moving along placidly.

"It gets bigger the closer it gets to the Gulf Coast," Jamie said. "It's a good-sized stream down there. But no, it's not a patch on some of the rivers we've seen, old friend."

"Audie told me about one they got down in South America called the Amazon. Wouldn't mind seein' that one of these days." Preacher grinned. "He says they got Injuns called headhunters, too, who'll chop a fella's head off and shrink it down some way until it ain't no bigger'n an apple. You ever hear of such a thing?"

"Can't say as I have, but if Audie says it's true, you can believe him." Preacher's old friend Audie was a very learned man who had given up the life of a professor at one of the universities back east to head west and become a mountain man. "He knows more about more things than anybody I've ever run into."

"If that ain't the gospel, I don't know what is." Preacher turned his head from side to side, studying the landscape all around them. "You gettin' any funny feelin's yet?"

"Like the feeling of being watched? No, can't say as I have."

"Me, neither. Must not be any Comanch' around."

"We haven't gone but a few miles from the fort," Jamie pointed out.

"You reckon that war chief the cap'n talked about . . . What was his name, Spotted Dog? . . . You reckon he don't send scouts to watch the fort and those soldier boys never see 'em?"

"I'm sure that happens. But not even the Comanches can be everywhere at once, all the time."

Preacher grunted. "I wouldn't put it past 'em. Them shamans, their medicine men, got ways of seein' things far off that not even an eagle can see. They may not know we're here yet, but it's only a matter of time until they do."

"You're right," Jamie said, "and then it'll all boil down to them deciding what they want to do about it."

* * *

The farther northwest they followed the Brazos, the more the terrain leveled out. Vegetation became sparser, and the only place the dominant color was green was along the riverbanks. The rest of the landscape was brown and tan and gray, streaked with the dark red of clay banks and sandstone outcroppings.

It was easy traveling, and since all they had to do was follow the river, there was no chance of them getting lost. Jamie told Pete Barnes to keep the wagon moving at a good pace. The riders kept up easily. From time to time, they stopped to rest the animals.

By late afternoon, Jamie estimated that they had covered twenty miles from Fort Belknap. He called a halt and told the men to make camp.

Preacher ambled over and said quietly, "After it gets good an' dark and folks are settled down, I thought Dog and I might slip off for a spell and do a little scoutin'."

"I think that's a good idea," Jamie told the old mountain man. "You can make sure there's nothing troublesome waiting ahead of us."

"Yep. The hair on the back o' my neck is still nice and peaceful-like, but I don't expect that to last." Preacher nodded slightly to his right. "Here comes Saunders."

Jamie looked over to see Philip Saunders approaching them. The young man came to a stop and said, "You're going to continue posting guards every night, aren't you, Mr. MacCallister?"

"Well, considering where we are, it'd be a pretty foolish thing not to, don't you think?" Jamie replied.

"I certainly do. In fact, if I was in charge, I believe I'd *double* the guards."

"You would, would you?" Preacher drawled.

Saunders nodded, evidently missing the note of irony in the older man's voice. "That's right."

Jamie said, "Well, it just so happens that's exactly what I figure on doing, Saunders."

"Good." Saunders stood up straighter. "I want to volunteer."

"To stand guard, you mean?"

"You haven't called on me to do that so far. I just wanted to let you know that I'm willing to do my share."

"I appreciate that," Jamie said. "I'll keep it in mind when I'm figuring out the assignments."

"Thank you." Saunders started to turn away, then paused. "I feel like I let the group down by some of my actions in the past, Mr. MacCallister. And that means I've let Hannah down as well. I don't want that. I don't want her seeing me as some sort of . . . weak link."

He didn't wait for them to respond but walked back across the camp instead.

"That boy's jealous of the attention Reynolds has started payin' to Miss Craigson," Preacher said. "I saw Reynolds talkin' to her a couple of times today."

"So did I," Jamie said, "even though I warned him not to stir up any more trouble."

"When a young fella sets his sights on a gal, he don't always pay much attention to warnings."

"I know." Jamie chuckled. "Sometimes I consider myself lucky that it feels like I've been married since before I was born. Sure has made life a heap simpler in some ways."

"You gonna let him take a turn standin' guard?"

"I will," Jamie said, "but I'll make sure he's paired up with somebody who has a lot more experience. Somebody we can count on until we know what Saunders is capable of."

"Somebody like you, maybe?"

"Could be," Jamie allowed. He smiled. "It won't be Walt Reynolds, that's for sure."

* * *

Back at Fort Belknap that evening, a big, vague shape moved through the shadows along the wall of the stable. Angus McKittredge reached the double doors, one of which was partially open, and slipped through the narrow gap into even deeper darkness.

"Fred?" McKittredge whispered. "Are you here?"

"Right here, Angus," Corporal Fred Herndon replied. "Close that door behind you."

For an instant, McKittredge bristled at the idea a corporal was giving him, a sergeant, an order like that. But if things went as planned tonight, there wouldn't be any more sergeants or corporals. They would all be free men, bound no longer by ranks and regulations.

With that thought in his mind, McKittredge eased the door closed. As soon as what little starlight filtered through the opening was cut off, a match scratched to life and Herndon held the flickering flame to the wick of a lantern in his other hand. It caught, sending a weak yellow glow out in a ragged circle. In that light, McKittredge saw the group of men gathered in the stable.

He did a quick head count. Eight men, nine including himself. All the others were privates except for Herndon and another corporal named Farley. McKittredge knew all of them. Troublemakers and malcontents . . . but tough and ruthless at the same time.

Just the sort of men he wanted on his side if he was going to venture into Comancheria.

"Everybody knows why they're here?" he asked Herndon.

"Yeah. And they're ready to go. We're all ready to leave the army behind for good."

McKittredge had gotten that impression already from the fact that the men had packs with them, no doubt full of personal belongings and supplies to take with them when they deserted.

Corporal Farley spoke up, saying, "What's the story here, Sarge? Where are we going? Herndon wouldn't tell us anything except that we're leaving."

"Are we heading for Fort Worth?" another man asked.

McKittredge shook his head. "We're not going east," he told them. "There's nothing back that way for us except trouble. That's where they'll start looking for us. We're heading west instead. Northwest, actually, along the Brazos."

"Along the—" Farley started to exclaim, then broke off in astonishment. "That's right into Comanche country!"

"That's right. With his troops already depleted, do you really think the cap'n's gonna risk any of the men he has left coming after us?"

"Whether the captain chases us or not won't matter if the Comanches get us," a man said. "Those redskins are murdering devils!"

Profane mutters of agreement came from the other men.

McKittredge let that reaction run its course, then said, "I know it's dangerous out there, but there's an even better reason we're going that way. You know that bunch of civilians that was just here is headed west."

"They're crazy, too," a man said.

McKittredge shook his head. "They're after treasure. Gold and silver, boys. The treasure Jim Bowie took out of his lost mine and hid up there where nobody would ever find it without a map . . . and they've got a map."

The men all stared at him in the dim light, expressions of confusion and disbelief etched on their rugged faces. McKittredge looked at Attaway and went on, "Tell them about it, Bert."

Eagerly, the rat-faced little Englishman explained about the conversation he had overheard and the map and letter he had seen in the captain's quarters. When he was finished, one of the men cursed bitterly and said, "There's no such thing as Bowie's treasure. That's just an old legend. You've brought us here on a fool's errand, McKittredge!"

"That girl believes the treasure's there, and there must be something to it or else MacCallister and Preacher wouldn't be going along with it," McKittredge insisted. "You know the reputations those two have. They're not fools. I may want revenge on MacCallister for knocking me out like he did, but he wouldn't be going up the Brazos if he didn't think he was going to find something worthwhile."

"But they could still be wrong," one of the would-be deserters argued, "and then we'd be riskin' our lives for nothin'."

"You're risking your lives every time you ride out on a patrol, aren't you? And for a lot less than you stand to gain if that treasure story turns out to be true!"

McKittredge's words were a powerful argument. Being posted at Fort Belknap was already a hard, grinding, and dangerous existence. Deserting and following MacCallister's expedition at least held the potential for something much greater.

McKittredge sensed that they were coming around to accepting the idea. To convince them even more, he said, "Having MacCallister's bunch ahead of us will serve another purpose, too. They'll be like a lightning rod. If there's any trouble with the Comanches, they'll attract it, not us!"

Several of the men nodded in agreement, but one said stubbornly, "That don't make sense, Sarge. MacCallister's got more men. Ain't it more likely the hostiles will attack us, since the odds would be better for them?"

"If that happens, we'll throw in with MacCallister,"

Herndon said. Evidently, he had considered this very possibility. "We can tell him that the captain sent us after them to keep an eye on them and help in case of trouble. MacCallister wouldn't be able to prove it's not true."

"Well, then, why don't we just catch up and join them in the first place?"

"Because we want to take them by surprise if we can," McKittredge said, trying not to explode with anger. "That way, once they've done the work of finding the treasure, we can jump them and wipe them out before they know what's going on."

That drew more nods and mutters of agreement. McKittredge continued, "Look, we can hash it all out along the way. What's important now is that we don't let the others get too far ahead of us. That's why we need to leave tonight. Bert knows the way, from looking at that map, so that's not really an issue, but time is. We want to be a long way from the fort when we take that gold and silver away from them."

"And the girl," Herndon said. "Don't forget the girl."

Judging by the way the eyes of some of the men shone lustfully in the lantern light at the mention of Hannah Craigson, McKittredge knew that none of them were likely to forget the girl. He was about to assure them that she figured in their plans, too, when one of the stable doors creaked behind him. A surprised voice asked, "What's going on in here?"

CHAPTER 37

McKittredge whirled around to see one of the sentries who patrolled the fort at night, a young private who stared with wide eyes at the group assembled in the stable.

"I saw a light through a crack around the door," the trooper went on as he came several steps into the cavernous building. "What are you fellas doing in here? There's not supposed to be anybody in here at this time of night—"

When the door opened, Bert Attaway had faded back quickly to one side, out of the circle of light cast by the lantern. The sentry never noticed him, had no idea of the danger lurking behind him until Attaway suddenly stepped up and drove a knife into the young soldier's back. Attaway struck with expert skill, wielding the blade so that it went cleanly between two ribs and penetrated the heart.

The trooper gasped and arched his spine. He dropped his rifle, which thankfully didn't go off. His eyes widened in shock and pain, but within seconds, that response faded and a lifeless glaze replaced it.

Attaway pulled the knife out. The blade was the only thing holding up the dead soldier. Without it, the luckless youngster collapsed.

Fred Herndon was moving even before the sentry hit the ground. He shoved the stable door closed and said in an urgent whisper, "Somebody blow out that lantern!"

Earlier, he had hung the lantern on a nail driven into one of the posts that supported the barn's roof. A man stepped over to it and leaned close to blow out the flame. Utter darkness fell over the inside of the stable.

"I shouldn't have risked the light," Herndon said, adding a curse directed at either himself or fate—or both. "I know the guards' routine and didn't think anybody would be coming along where it would be too visible. Blast it all! What a stroke of bad luck."

"Wot'll we do with him now?" Attaway asked.

"Take him with us," McKittredge answered without an instant's hesitation.

"What?" one of the men exclaimed in the darkness. "We have to carry a dead man around with us?"

"Only until we get far enough away from the fort to find a good place to bury him," McKittredge said. "When he turns up missing, the captain and everyone else will believe that he deserted along with us."

"How does that help us?"

"Like I said, Glennister's not likely to come after us. It would mean leaving the fort too unprotected. But if he thought we were murderers as well as deserters, he might feel like he couldn't afford to just let us get away. He'd be too likely to get in trouble with his superiors over that."

Herndon said, "That makes sense, Angus. We'll need to steal an extra horse to make it look right."

"Nothing wrong with having an extra horse. We need to take several, in fact. Now, is everybody with us? You're willing to follow MacCallister's bunch and try to grab that gold and silver? I want to hear each of you say it."

In the thick gloom, the men responded one by one until all of them had declared their intention to go along with the plan. When he was satisfied, McKittredge ordered them to get the horses ready to move out.

He wanted to be a long way from Fort Belknap by morning . . . dead man and all.

As he had told Jamie, Preacher waited until night had fallen before leaving the camp. He and Dog departed so quietly and unobtrusively, slipping off into the shadows with hardly a sound, that he doubted if anyone other than Jamie would even notice he was gone, unless they had some reason to look for him.

It felt good to be padding along in the darkness with only the big cur beside him. Preacher liked people well enough, and he could spend many comfortable hours around kindred souls such as Jamie and his friends Audie and Nighthawk, but so much of his life had been spent in a solitary existence, just him and Horse and Dog alone in the wilderness, far away from anyone else. Any time he was around more than a handful of folks for very long, Preacher started feeling a mite crowded.

The moon hadn't risen yet, but the untold multitude of stars floating in the vast Texas sky provided plenty of light for the old mountain man's keen eyes to see where he was going. The night was so quiet he could hear the faint chuckle of the Brazos as it flowed to his left.

Dog growled suddenly, and Preacher stopped in his tracks. They stood there motionless while a thick shape writhed across the ground in front of them and disappeared under a bush. A buzzing sound told Preacher that the snake had coiled and was shaking the rattle on the end of its tail in warning.

Don't worry, old son, he thought. *We'll steer clear of you.*

He and Dog moved on, leaving the rattler behind them.

Preacher was carrying his rifle and had both Colt Dragoons holstered on his hips, but he didn't want to use any of the guns. The sound of shots would travel a long way out here, especially on a quiet night like this. He didn't expect to run into any Comanches, but even if he did, he wanted to avoid trouble. If he saw them first, they'd never see him. Indians weren't the only ones who could practice stealth.

He had trotted alongside the river for a couple of miles when he stopped again and lifted his head to sniff the air. Dog halted and sniffed, as well, and then let out a low whine.

"Yeah, I smell it," Preacher said quietly. "Smoke. Ain't strong. Might be from a campfire that's burned down to embers. Let's go find out."

They resumed their course. Several hundred more yards fell behind them. Then Preacher put a hand on Dog's neck and dropped to one knee beside the big cur. Both of them peered intently across the river.

Trees clustered on the far bank of the Brazos. Preacher made out some large shapes under those trees. Indian ponies. They weren't moving except to lift a head or twitch an ear now and then.

A few yards away, more shapes lay on the ground. Those would be the owners of those ponies, Preacher mused. Four or five of them, which wasn't big enough to be a raiding party. These Comanch' were out hunting for game, not trouble.

He didn't spot any sentries. The Indians probably hadn't

posted any. They would consider themselves absolutely safe, here in territory that they controlled.

For a moment, Preacher pondered what he should do next. As a young man, when he was waging his seemingly never-ending war against his mortal enemies, the Blackfeet, on a number of occasions he had slipped into a sleeping Blackfoot camp and slit the throats of half a dozen warriors without ever waking anyone. Then he had departed equally unheard, so that in the morning the other warriors had discovered the bodies of their luckless comrades, slain, as far as they could tell, by a phantom.

They had known who was to blame, though. And that was why, to this day, Blackfoot mothers frightened their children by threatening that Preacher—the Ghost Killer—would get them if they didn't behave.

Now, as Preacher gazed across the Brazos at that Comanche hunting party, he was tempted for a moment to see if he could re-create that grim feat.

Then he shook his head and whispered to Dog, "Nope. Ain't gonna do it. No reason to. If those fellas don't come home, then Spotted Dog'll know that enemies are loose in his land. No need for him to be aware of that any sooner'n necessary."

Dog licked the old mountain man's grizzled cheek.

"Anyway, they're on the other side of the river," Preacher went on. "Maybe they'll stay there for a spell."

He watched the peaceful scene for a short time longer, then stood up and backed away from the stream, putting a little distance between himself and the river before turning to trot back toward the camp where Jamie and the others waited.

Behind him, the Comanche warriors continued to slumber, with no idea just how closely death had stalked them this night.

* * *

Jamie was waiting when Preacher got back to camp.

"Small huntin' party of Injuns about two miles upriver, on the other side," Preacher reported.

"Comanche?"

"Well, I didn't ask 'em, but I don't hardly see what else they could be in these parts. Comanch' have run out just about everybody else."

"That's true," Jamie said, nodding, then he looked sharply at Preacher and added, "You didn't kill them, did you?"

"Nope." Preacher paused and then chuckled. "Thought about it, though."

"Somehow I'm not surprised." Jamie clapped a hand on his old friend's shoulder. "Go get some sleep."

After Preacher had headed off to his bedroll, Jamie stood looking out into the night, thinking. Part of him wished that Preacher had gone ahead and killed the Comanches. That way he wouldn't have to worry about those warriors spotting the expedition the next day.

But he had never believed that they could make it all the way to the location marked on old Tobias Craigson's map without being discovered by the savage inhabitants of this land. The trip was going to require four or five days there, and then four or five days back out. Nobody could spend a week and a half in Comanche territory without the Indians knowing about it.

His hope was that Spotted Dog and any other war chiefs wouldn't want to risk attacking such a large, well-armed band. In the decade or so since repeating pistols had been introduced, the Indians had learned to respect them.

So if that hunting party saw them tomorrow, let the warriors go running back to their village. Jamie would keep his people moving and hope for the best.

"Mr. MacCallister?"

Jamie turned to see Philip Saunders. He had assigned the young man to the first shift of guard duty, along with Billy Bob Moore. And he had stayed awake, too, to speak with Preacher when the old mountain man got back and to help keep an eye on things.

"What is it, Saunders?"

"I saw you talking to Preacher just now. Is anything going on?"

Jamie shook his head. "He just went and did a little scouting, is all."

"Did he find anything?"

"Nothing we didn't expect."

"You mean there are Indians ahead of us."

"We've known that ever since we started," Jamie said.

Saunders sighed and said, "I know. I guess maybe I hoped that, by some miracle, we wouldn't encounter them."

"There was never any chance of that," Jamie told him. "But that doesn't mean they'll want to give us any trouble. It's not like we're a family of would-be settlers with nothing to defend ourselves except a single-shot rifle and a rusty old pistol. We're not easy pickings. They'll think twice before jumping us, I can guarantee that."

"Long enough for us to retrieve the treasure and get back to civilization?"

"That's the plan."

"I hope you're right."

"Only one way to find out," Jamie said, but that didn't seem to make Saunders feel any better.

CHAPTER 38

Jamie didn't tell Saunders or any of the other members of the expedition the details of what Preacher had reported to him the night before. It was possible they wouldn't even run into that Comanche hunting party. The men were on edge enough already; Jamie didn't want their nerves so tightly strung that they might open fire on anything out of the ordinary they saw.

So they moved on that morning under a blue, cloud-dotted sky, with Jamie and Preacher taking the lead as usual and Dog ranging out ahead of them.

When they came to the place where Preacher had seen the Comanches, the old mountain man nodded toward the far side of the Brazos. The gesture was so slight that Jamie was probably the only one who noticed it.

"That's where they were," Preacher said quietly.

"Yeah, I can see some droppings from their ponies," Jamie said. "Looks like they're long gone, though."

"Want me to ride across and see if I can tell which way they went?"

"Wouldn't change anything for us to know, would it?"

Preacher chuckled. "Nope, not really. I reckon we'll either run into 'em or we won't, whatever fate's got in mind for us. I'll keep my eyes open extra wide, though."

Jamie nodded and said, "Be a good habit for all of us to get into."

Once again, the group made good time and covered a considerable distance before stopping at midday to rest the horses and mules and eat some leftover bacon and biscuits from their predawn breakfast.

Jamie sat with Hannah and Saunders while they ate. Hannah said, "I'm surprised we've come this far without seeing any Indians other than the ones back at the fort." She paused, then added, "And I'm still sorry for the trouble I caused back there."

"Over and done with," Jamie assured her. He glanced at Saunders, who didn't say anything. Evidently, he hadn't mentioned his conversation with Jamie the night before, after Preacher returned to camp.

Jamie went on, "I reckon we'll see them soon enough. I'm happy to push on as far as we can without running into any trouble, though."

"Oh, I am, too," Hannah said. "It would be perfectly fine with me if they didn't bother us at all."

Jamie felt the same way, but he knew better than to count on it.

Angus McKittredge, Fred Herndon, Bert Attaway, and the other deserters from Fort Belknap had stopped early that morning to bury the body of the sentry who had stumbled on them in the stable. The grave they dug was shallow enough that the luckless private might wind up being unearthed by coyotes or other scavengers. That was just too bad because nobody wanted to take any more time or trouble than that.

Then they continued following their quarry. Even if they hadn't known that the expedition's route took them along the Brazos River, it wouldn't have been difficult. The horses and the wagon wheels left plenty of tracks on the ground. MacCallister and the others weren't trying to hide their trail.

McKittredge kept the men moving at a steady but deliberate pace. They didn't want to get too close to the other bunch where they might be spotted. Outnumbered as they were, they needed the element of surprise on their side, McKittredge knew.

Anyway, they might as well let MacCallister and the others retrieve that gold and silver first, and *then* kill them.

Around midday, they were riding leisurely along the bank when Herndon let out a sudden curse, pointed, and said, "Angus, look up there."

A couple of hundred yards ahead of them, five riders were emerging from the riverbed. McKittredge could tell they were Indians wearing buckskin leggings and bare from the waist up. They didn't appear to be painted for war, although the distance was a little too great to be sure.

Probably a Comanche hunting party, he thought as he held up his right hand in a signal for the others to stop. They might not be in the army anymore, but they were used to taking orders from him, so they all reined in.

"What do we do, Sarge?" Bert Attaway asked nervously.

"I'm not your sarge anymore," McKittredge snapped,

"and we're gonna sit right here and let those bucks go on about their business."

"Are you sure that's a good idea?" Herndon asked. "They'll go back to their village and tell the others about a group of white men riding up the river."

"You didn't think we'd make it to where we're going without running into any hostiles, did you?"

"I hoped we wouldn't see any this soon," Herndon said. "Look, they've stopped, too. They've seen us."

"We just need to keep our wits about us," McKittredge said. "We outnumber them almost two-to-one. In a minute, once they've thought about that, they'll either ride on to wherever they were headed or turn around and go back to where they came from. We'll just sit here and show them that we're no threat—"

He hadn't gotten any further in what he was saying when the Indians abruptly wheeled their ponies and charged toward the group of deserters, whooping at the top of their lungs.

"Blimey!" Bert Attaway yelled as he jerked his rifle to his shoulder and fired. "They're attackin'!"

The little Englishman had never been a good shot and the range was long, so McKittredge wasn't surprised when none of the Comanche warriors fell and the ponies didn't break stride.

"Hold your fire!" McKittredge roared. "Let 'em get closer!"

"But they're gonna scalp us, Sarge," Attaway said as he fumbled with his rifle, trying to reload.

"There are twice as many of us as there are of them, and they don't have any guns. We'll kill them before we're in range of their arrows. Just wait for my order."

McKittredge lifted his own rifle and nestled the butt

against his shoulder. He drew back the hammer and settled his sights on the bare chest of one of the charging warriors.

He could tell now that they were all young, not more than boys. That explained why they were hotheaded and hot-blooded enough to attack a larger, well-armed group. All they were thinking about was the glory that would be theirs if they emerged triumphant.

Youth never thought about the death that waited inevitably for everyone.

McKittredge drew in a breath, held it for a moment, and then called, "Fire!"

A ragged volley erupted from the deserters' rifles. Clouds of smoke gushed from the muzzles. That obscured McKittredge's vision for several frustrating seconds. When the air cleared enough for him to see again, he noted that two of the Indian ponies were riderless. The young warriors who had been mounted on those animals sprawled on the ground in motionless heaps.

Two out of five attackers down. That wasn't very good shooting, McKittredge thought. He should have made the men practice more with their weapons while he was in command of them.

But their accuracy was good enough that the other three Comanches yanked their ponies around and galloped away, still yipping their strident war cries. McKittredge laughed out loud at that. They might try to sound defiant, but in actuality they were running away with their tails tucked between their legs.

"They're leavin', Sarge," Attaway exclaimed. "We whipped them, the bloody red savages."

"Don't celebrate too soon, Bert," Herndon said. "Look on the other side of the river!"

McKittredge looked, and what he saw sent a chill down

his back. More mounted Indians had appeared, almost as if they had risen out of the ground by magic. He supposed they had been out of sight on the far side of the Brazos and were hurrying to investigate the gunshots. It wasn't a huge group, but he estimated that at least a dozen warriors were charging toward the river.

Which meant that the Comanches now outnumbered him and his men, instead of the other way around, and the Indians would be angrier than ever since a couple of them were dead.

The three survivors from the original party splashed across the river and met the larger group, which came to a stop. The three warriors yelled and waved their arms toward the far riverbank where McKittredge and his companions were. Furious whoops went up, easily heard in the hot air.

"They'll be after us any minute," Herndon said.

"I know, blast it," McKittredge said. His head jerked from side to side as he looked around, desperately searching for any sort of cover. The two groups were still close enough in size that he believed they could hold off the Indians if they just had a place to fort up.

Unfortunately, open and level ground stretched away from the Brazos for at least half a mile, without even any trees, just short grass that wouldn't provide any cover. Beyond that, some small hills, barely worthy of the name, rose and might offer some shelter.

McKittredge didn't think he and his men could get there before the Comanches caught them, however. The Indians were already splashing across the Brazos, their ponies' hooves throwing water high in the air. War whoops ripped from the throats of the Comanches.

All they could do was make a run for it, McKittredge

realized. "Head for those hills!" he cried as he yanked his horse around and rammed his bootheels into the animal's flanks. It took off with a frantic lunge.

In the face of the Comanche charge, several of the men hadn't waited for McKittredge's order. They were already fleeing, with Bert Attaway in the lead. McKittredge, Herndon, and the rest thundered after them.

McKittredge hadn't traveled more than twenty yards before he knew with a grim certainty that they weren't going to make it to the hills in time. Those nimble-footed Indian ponies were faster than the stolen army mounts. The war party—because that's what it was now, whether they were painted for it or not—closed the gap quickly.

A startled yell from up ahead caught his attention. He slowed his horse when he saw Bert Attaway sawing desperately at the reins, trying to bring his mount to a stop. The other deserters slowed down and halted as well. As McKittredge and the rest of the group caught up with them, the former noncom saw what hadn't been visible from a distance.

A shallow gully cut across the landscape, four feet deep and ten wide. Maybe a creek had run here at some time in the past and left this gash in the earth when it dried up. Maybe it still ran when there was enough rain.

McKittredge didn't know and didn't care. To him, right now, the gully was nothing more or less than unexpected salvation.

A chance of that, anyway.

"Get down in there!" he bellowed. "We'll make our stand right here!"

They had to force the horses to jump into the gully, but with the howling Comanches approaching rapidly, the men didn't hesitate to take desperate measures. They yelled and slapped at their horses' rumps with their hats. It was wild confusion for a moment, but men and horses wound up in the gully where they needed to be.

"One man hold the horses!" McKittredge ordered. "The rest of you, form a firing line here at the edge of the gully. We'll show those savages how real fighting men do things!"

McKittredge crouched and rested his elbows on the ground next to the gully as he aimed his rifle toward the Indians. Herndon took his place beside the former sergeant and said quietly, "You realize all they have to do is split up and send some men to attack us from the rear. We can't defend both directions at once and last very long."

"You have a better idea, Fred?"

"Well . . . no, I don't suppose I do."

McKittredge tightened his grip on the rifle. "Then get ready," he barked, "because I plan on us killing as many of those red devils as we can before they get us!"

CHAPTER 39

The men had to lift themselves up a little higher to see the charging Indians over the grass. As McKittredge drew a bead on one of the warriors, he yelled, "Open fire!"

Once again, shots roared. One attacker toppled off his horse, another of the ponies collapsed and threw its rider over its head, and a third warrior swayed and clutched at his bloody shoulder, which had been smashed by a bullet.

Too many of them were still eager to fight, though. McKittredge yanked out his Colt Dragoon and began thumbing off shots. Not all the men had revolvers, and the ones who didn't tried frantically to reload in time to get off another round before the Indians overran them.

Suddenly, one of the Comanches flew backward off his pony's back as if he'd been swatted by a giant hand. He flung his arms outward. Blood spurted from a hole in his chest. He landed on his back hard enough that he bounced slightly before coming to rest in the limp huddle of death.

McKittredge shot another of the warriors, saw the bullet

explode out the back of the man's head accompanied by a grisly pink spray, a mixture of blood, brains, and bone. He fired again and hit an Indian's elbow. The bullet shattered bone and did so much damage to flesh that the warrior's forearm hung from a single strand of muscle. The Indian screamed in agony and turned away, somehow managing to stay mounted as the pony dashed off.

Another two Comanches were down, but the ones who remained sent a swarm of arrows whistling around the deserters in the gully. One of the men cried out as an arrow lodged just below his shoulder. He fell back, pawing at the shaft.

A distant boom floated to McKittredge's ears. He recognized the sound as the report of a high-powered rifle. A warrior's head practically exploded as a heavy caliber ball struck him in the face. Even though McKittredge hadn't killed the man, he felt a perverse satisfaction at the sight of the grotesque corpse flopping to the ground.

Another booming shot knocked a warrior off his pony. McKittredge glanced toward the nearest hill. It sounded like at least two marksmen armed with Sharps buffalo guns were up there. That was the only place the shots could be coming from.

Between the long-range killing and the damage McKittredge and his companions had dished out, the Comanche war party had suddenly shrunk by at least half. That was enough for them. They yanked their ponies around and beat a hasty retreat. Several of the deserters fired after them to speed them on their way.

For a moment, McKittredge watched them go. As the Indians hustled back across the river, the former noncom turned to Herndon and asked, "Are you all right, Fred?"

Herndon sleeved sweat off his face. "Yeah. I wasn't hit. I don't think anybody was wounded except for Hodges."

That was the man with the arrow in the shoulder. A couple of his friends had propped him up against the side of the gully. He sat there grimacing as blood spread around the arrow buried in his flesh.

"What happened just now?" Herndon went on. "I thought we were dead men for sure. Then those redskins started dropping—"

"We had some help," McKittredge interrupted him. He pointed toward the nearby hill. "I'd say that's them coming now."

Three men had ridden over the crest and started down the grassy slope. McKittredge frowned as he realized just how big the man in the lead was. It was hard to judge such things when someone was on horseback, but even so, the fella looked tall as a tree and broad as a mountain to McKittredge, who was pretty good-sized himself.

A bushy black beard hung down over the giant's massive chest. One of the men with him sported a long beard, too, a sandy-colored, straggly affair that suited his scarecrow frame. At this distance, the third man was plain looking, nothing special about him.

"You say they helped us?" Herndon asked.

"You didn't hear those shots from up there? Sounded like a couple of cannons going off."

Herndon just shook his head.

"See those rifles the big fella and the one to his left are carrying across the saddle in front of them? Those are Sharps Big Fifties. Buffalo guns. Shoot a mile and not drop an inch. They blew three or four of those bucks off their ponies. That's what really made them give up, I think."

"I'm glad they're on our side, then," Herndon said dryly.

"Maybe we'd best make sure they are." McKittredge

raised his voice. "Watson, hang on to those horses. Calder, tend to Hodges. The rest of you get your rifles loaded and come with me."

McKittredge climbed out of the gully, followed by the other men. They stood waiting tensely as the three riders approached.

When the strangers were twenty feet away, they reined to a halt. McKittredge thought the black-bearded giant grinned, but in that tangle of whiskers, it was hard to be sure.

He sounded pretty jovial, though, as he said, "Looked like you soldier boys had an Injun problem."

"You could say that," McKittredge responded. "We're obliged to you for giving us a hand."

"The least we could do. I'll not ride past while white men are being slaughtered by red. Even though I ain't all that fond of the army."

"To tell you the truth, mister, neither are we."

McKittredge didn't add that they were so not fond of the army that they had left it.

Although it didn't really matter. He figured it wouldn't be a good idea to leave these three alive to carry stories of seeing a group of soldiers out here where they weren't supposed to be.

Without being invited, the giant swung down from his saddle with ease and grace surprising in such a big man. The other two remained mounted. The scrawny one with the weedy-looking beard had the air of a gunman about him. The other man was older, with a milky eye where an old scar slashed down across his face. McKittredge could tell that both of them were mean as sin, but the one striding toward him now with a hamlike hand outstretched was the real threat. Madness burned in his deep-set eyes.

McKittredge recognized that because he had seen the same thing in his own eyes from time to time when he looked in a mirror.

"Otis Lynch," the giant introduced himself.

Now that he was closer, McKittredge could tell that Lynch was several inches taller than him and weighed probably twenty or thirty pounds more. He was even bigger than Jamie MacCallister. McKittredge grasped his hand and said, "Angus McKittredge."

"Sergeant McKittredge, judging by those stripes on your sleeves."

McKittredge shrugged and said, "This far out in the middle of nowhere, rank doesn't mean a lot, does it?"

Lynch boomed a laugh. "No, sir. No, sir, I don't suppose it does."

He turned his head slowly, studying the men with McKittredge. The grin on his face widened until McKittredge could actually see it through the beard.

"Not often you come across an army patrol without an officer, a bugler, and a guidon to carry," he said. "You boys run into some trouble before now and lose some men?"

"That's none of your business, Lynch. Like I said, we're grateful to you for your help, but—"

As if he hadn't heard, Lynch broke in, "Could it be that you're not supposed to be out here? Like maybe you don't have orders to travel up the Brazos?" He lowered his voice to a conspiratorial tone. "Maybe you fellas decided to leave the army sort of . . . unofficial-like."

"Are you accusing us of being deserters?" McKittredge asked tautly.

Lynch surprised him with another of those booming laughs. "And why would I care if you are, that's what I'd like to know! I told you, we're not all that fond of the army. Just curious why you're out here, that's all."

"I could ask the same of you."

Lynch cocked his head to the side, gazed at McKittredge curiously, and said, "It couldn't be because you're trailing that bunch of fools led by Jamie MacCallister and Preacher, could it?"

That shocked an exclamation out of McKittredge. "You know about MacCallister and Preacher?"

"Why would my friends and I be riding into Comanche territory unless we were after them, too?"

"You know about the treasure?"

McKittredge saw a spark of interest gleam in Lynch's eyes and bit back a curse as he realized he had made a mistake. The other two sat forward a little in their saddles, also intrigued by what McKittredge had said. It was too late to call the words back now.

Lynch kept his right hand resting on the butt of the heavy revolver holstered at his hip, but he waved his left hand expansively and said, "Why, of course we know. Again, why else would we be riding up the Brazos into the heart of Comancheria?"

Letting that slip about Bowie's treasure had been a fool stunt, McKittredge knew, but he was still a shrewd man. Thinking swiftly, he said, "We might as well put our cards on the table, Lynch. Both of us."

"Go right ahead."

McKittredge jerked his head in a curt nod. "We left Fort Belknap to come after MacCallister and his bunch for two reasons. I've got a score to settle with that big hombre . . . and there's a chance there might be an actual payoff at the end of the trail."

"That's why we're here, too," Lynch said. "We've been trailing that group all the way from Fort Worth. Had a run-in with them about a day's ride east of the fort and lost some men. Since then, we've been staying behind them, figuring that we're outnumbered enough we couldn't afford to jump them again. But if the three of us were to throw in with you . . ."

"The odds would be closer to even," McKittredge finished.

"Seems like the smart thing to do," Lynch allowed.

McKittredge glanced at Herndon, whose face was carefully blank. The former corporal was leaving it up to him. McKittredge had no doubt that he and his men could blow these strangers to Hades if they wanted to . . . but there was no telling how many men they would lose doing it.

A monster like Otis Lynch might have to have five pounds of lead in him before he'd go down and stay down. The other two were dangerous, as well, you could tell that by looking at them.

A grin split McKittredge's rugged face. He thrust out his hand again and said, "Joining forces *does* seem to be the only smart thing to do."

Lynch's big paw enveloped his. "I couldn't agree more, Sergeant."

"Make it Angus."

Lynch nodded and waved at his companions. "The lean and hungry-looking gent is Teddy Keller. The one-eyed breed goes by Tuscarora. That's all, just Tuscarora."

"Glad to meet you men," McKittredge greeted them with a heartiness that they probably all knew was fake. He introduced Herndon but not the rest of the men.

The trooper named Calder said from the gully, "Sarge, we need to get this arrow out of Hodges. Won't be able to stop the bleedin' otherwise."

Lynch said, "My friend Tuscarora can handle that. He knows about arrow wounds, being half Indian and all."

"All right." McKittredge nodded to Tuscarora. "Be obliged to you."

Tuscarora grunted and then dismounted. He flipped his reins to Teddy Keller and climbed down into the gully to examine the wounded man. Lynch moved to the edge of the gully to look down at what was going on. Keller turned and rode to the side, leading Tuscarora's horse.

For a moment, that left McKittredge and Herndon standing somewhat apart from the others, so that Herndon was able to lean closer and say in a voice that only the former sergeant could hear, "You know that big varmint's more than likely already planning how he's going to use us and then double-cross us and kill us, don't you?"

"I'd be disappointed in him if he wasn't," McKittredge said. "Because I'm thinking the same thing about him."

CHAPTER 40

Jamie and Preacher were riding about a hundred yards ahead of the others when the sound of approaching hoofbeats made them look over their shoulders. Walt Reynolds was coming toward them with a worried expression on his face.

"Something wrong, son?" Jamie asked as Reynolds pulled alongside. None of the three men stopped, but they were moving slowly enough that they could talk easily.

"I don't know, sir. I thought I heard something a while back, and it's been nagging at me enough that I finally decided to come tell you about it."

Preacher said, "You mean them gunshots a good long ways behind us?"

Reynolds frowned at him in surprise. "You heard them, too?"

"I'm old, but my ears still work just fine."

"We heard them," Jamie said. "Whatever it was, nothing we could do about it, so it seemed like a waste of time to worry."

"I reckon that's one way to look at it," Reynolds said. "You didn't take it to mean we're being followed?"

"That could be what it means," Jamie allowed.

"And it could mean that whoever was followin' us got theirselves jumped and wiped out by the Comanch'," Preacher added.

"Or maybe killed all the Indians who attacked them," Reynolds suggested.

"Maybe. But that don't seem likely."

Jamie asked, "Has there been any talk about it among the men?"

"No, I'm not sure anybody else even heard what I did. If they did, they're keeping quiet about it. To tell you the truth, I wasn't even sure if *I'd* heard it, or just imagined the whole thing."

"You didn't imagine it. It was a good-sized fight. We heard revolvers and rifles, including what sounded like a couple of Sharps buffalo guns."

Preacher said, "The huntin' party I saw yesterday didn't have no guns, just bows and arrows."

Reynolds looked shocked again. "You saw Indians yesterday?"

"Just a huntin' party, like I said," Preacher replied with a shrug. "And it was last night, when I was doin' a little scoutin' around."

"They didn't see you?"

"Nope," Preacher said.

"Folks generally don't see Preacher if he doesn't want them to," Jamie said with a smile, then grew serious as he went on, "I'd appreciate it if you'd keep this to yourself, Walt. I don't want to spook anybody for no reason."

Reynolds grunted. "Like that Saunders gent, you mean. He must really like Miss Craigson to come out here like this, as much as he's scared of Indians."

"Well, he's figurin' on marryin' her," Preacher said. "I don't figure you'd get hitched to a gal less'n you were a mite fond of her."

"No, I don't reckon you would." Reynolds twisted around in his saddle so he could look back at the wagon and the other riders following them.

Jamie noticed that and looked, too. He had a pretty good idea what the young man was gazing at. Hannah rode on the driver's seat next to Pete Barnes, who seemed to have taken on the job of handling the team permanently. She had a wide-brimmed hat she wore sometimes to protect her head from the sun, but her head was bare at the moment and the light made her auburn hair gleam like dark fire.

Jamie had no doubt that Walt Reynolds was looking at Hannah, even after he'd been cautioned about not stirring up any romantic trouble. Young fellas usually didn't listen to advice—even good advice—where pretty gals were concerned.

"Why don't you take one man with you and drop back a ways, maybe half a mile or so, just to make sure nobody's coming up on our back trail?" Jamie said. "Get Tankersley to go with you. He seems like a good man in a fight."

"Yes, sir, he is. You, uh, think we're liable to run into a fight?"

"No, not really. But any time you're not ready for trouble out here, sure enough that's when it comes up and wallops you in the face."

"Yes, sir, I'll remember that."

Reynolds turned his horse and trotted back toward the others. Without watching him go, Preacher said, "Sooner or later, that youngster and Saunders are gonna tangle again, likely over that gal. You know that, don't you, Jamie?"

"I know it," Jamie replied. "I just hope that when it happens, it doesn't contribute to getting all of us killed."

"You want me to do what?" Ox Tankersley said when Reynolds told him what Jamie had suggested.

"We're gonna be scouts."

Ox shook his head and pointed. "Scouts go out in front, not behind."

"You can scout a back trail, too. That's what Mr. MacCallister wants us to do."

"I've heard some of the men talk about how Indians like to pick off stragglers. That's what we'll be, Walt. Stragglers." Ox frowned. "I think MacCallister's just using us as bait to try to get the Comanches to come out in the open. I'll bet he knows they're stalkin' us right now."

"No, blast it, that's not it," Reynolds argued. "Look, Mr. MacCallister suggested that I take you with me, but if you don't want to go, I'll just get Billy Bob."

"Wait a minute. Why'd MacCallister think I ought to go with you?"

"He said you were a good fighter," Reynolds explained. "And he was right about that."

"Hmmph. Sounds to me like he's expectin' we'll get jumped. But I'll go with you. Just in case there *is* any trouble, you'd be better off with me than with Billy Bob."

"That's what I've been saying all along."

The two young men slowed their horses and allowed the others to pull ahead. When the rest of the group had opened up a good gap between them, they turned and rode back the way they had come from. The leisurely flowing Brazos was on their right now, instead of their left.

"How far are we supposed to go?" Ox asked.

"Mr. MacCallister said half a mile or so."

"And you want to do everything MacCallister says, don't you?"

"What do you mean by that?" Reynolds asked.

"I mean that to hear you talk about him, you'd think Jamie MacCallister was your pa or something."

"Not hardly," Reynolds scoffed. "My pa was a drunk. I don't think I remember seeing him sober more than half a dozen times the first eight years of my life, before he went and got himself kicked in the head by a mule. Nearly took his head clean off his shoulders. Killed him in the blink of an eye."

Ox frowned. "I didn't know that. Sorry, Walt."

"It was a long time ago," Reynolds said.

And it had been. Two-thirds of his life had gone by since that day. He hadn't even thought about it for a long time or wondered if his ma was still alive and where his brothers and sisters were.

He had chosen a lonely existence for himself. Most of the time he didn't regret it, but now and then he did.

He knew who could help him not be lonely anymore—Hannah Craigson. Any fella lucky enough to have her around could never be lonely. But that wasn't for the likes of a saddle tramp like him.

Thoughts of Hannah still occupied Reynolds's mind when Ox said, "Haven't we gone half a mile yet?" He waved at the landscape in front of them. "And we haven't seen anything except miles and miles of nothing!"

Reynolds reined in and his friend did likewise. Shading his eyes with his hand, Reynolds peered into the distance, swinging his gaze back and forth. He was searching more for dust clouds that would indicate the presence of riders than anything else.

After a minute or so, he was satisfied that there was nothing to see. "Come on," he said to Ox. "We might as well head back."

They turned their horses and rode northwest, following the river.

Neither of them noticed the distant pair of figures on horseback on the other side of the Brazos, watching them go.

Walt Reynolds reported to Jamie and Preacher that there was no sign of anyone on their back trail. When the young man had rejoined the rest of the party, Preacher said, "You reckon he's right, or they just didn't see anybody?"

"That shooting we heard means that *something* was going on back there," Jamie replied, "but there's no telling who was involved in that fight."

"Or who won. Who'd be trailin' us all the way out here?" Preacher scratched at his jaw. "You know, that big varmint Lynch got away when they jumped us, and one or two of the fellas with him did, too. You don't reckon he'd be loco enough to still be comin' after us, do you?"

"From what I've seen of him, I wouldn't put a limit on just how crazy Otis Lynch can be."

"If that's what happened, I'll bet the Comanch' got 'em."

"I won't lose any sleep over it if that's how it turns out. But you know, Preacher, there could be other people traveling out here who don't have anything to do with us at all."

"In the middle of this here Comancheria? That ain't likely, Jamie."

"Well, if we just keep moving, we're liable to find out."

The rest of the day passed peacefully, as did that night. As they moved on the next morning, Preacher commented,

"You know, I don't reckon I've ever seen a river that twists around as much as this here Brazos. We go north a ways, then turn around and go right back south. If the good Lord had just straightened it out, it'd stretch a lot longer distance."

Jamie pointed. "Look up yonder. Unless I miss my guess, that's the first of the forks."

Preacher rose a little in his stirrups, peered into the distance, and said, "Durned if I don't believe you're right."

They reached the fork a short time later. Jamie and Preacher sat there on their horses and waited for the others to catch up to them. When they did, Hannah leaned forward on the driver's seat with a look of excitement on her face and said, "You see, Mr. MacCallister, my grandfather's map is right. The river splits here."

"I never doubted that, Miss Craigson," Jamie told her. "I'm not all that familiar with this part of the country, but I know enough about it to know that the Brazos forks several times, and the branches split even more upstream. Do you need to get that map of yours out and look at it to see which way we go?"

Hannah smiled and shook her head. "I've studied it so much that I know every line on it by heart." She waved toward the river's right-hand branch. "We go that way."

That agreed with what Jamie remembered from his brief look at the map. "That's easy, then. We don't have to ford the stream, just keep following it on this side."

"We will have to ford farther up. Our destination is between the last two forks on this part of the stream, although it's not far past where they come together."

"Yes, ma'am. With luck, we'll be there in a couple more days." Jamie lifted his arm and waved the expedition forward.

The afternoon was the hottest one on the journey so far. Jamie was glad when the sun finally started to slide down toward the western horizon. That didn't offer much relief, but any lessening of the heat was welcome.

A few low, flat-topped mesas had started popping up from the landscape, breaking up the flat, monotonous terrain. Preacher pointed them out to Jamie and said, "Those'd make mighty good lookout points. Wouldn't be surprised if there's been Comanch' on more than one of 'em we've passed."

"I wouldn't be, either."

"You know they're gonna hit us sooner or later, Jamie."

"I know it. The men are all alert. We're as ready as we can be."

"If I was the sort of fella to feel regrets, I might be startin' to feel that way about bringin' that girl out here."

"In the end, it didn't seem like I had the right to hold her back," Jamie said. "None of us would be here if it weren't for her."

"She don't lack for grit, I'll give her that. But it'll all be different when those savages come a-ridin' straight at us, howlin' for our hair."

"I know," Jamie said.

But what he didn't know was just how soon that was going to happen.

CHAPTER 41

They had made camp, cooked their supper, and had the fire out before night fell, the same routine they had followed for the whole trip. Jamie and Preacher didn't see any point in announcing their exact whereabouts with a fire that would be visible for miles out here.

An arch of gold and orange streaked with blue and purple lingered in the western sky, a reminder of the sun that had gone down a short time earlier. Darkness descended quickly at this time of year, but for a few precious minutes, the world was filled with a glow that softened all the sharp edges.

Jamie and Preacher were talking quietly near the picketed horses when Hannah approached them. "Jamie, would you mind taking a walk with me?" she asked as she inclined her head toward a large clump of brush about fifty yards away.

Jamie knew what she was talking about. He had made it clear to her from the start that while they would do everything possible to protect her privacy whenever she had personal business to take care of, a guard had to be close enough to reach her in a hurry if need be. She wound up asking Jamie to perform that chore most of the time, since she knew him the best and he was the second oldest member of the group, next to Preacher.

"I'd be happy to, Hannah," he told her. They were on a first-name basis now, when they weren't out on the trail.

Jamie nodded to Preacher and then walked toward the brush with Hannah. He knew that the old mountain man was planning to slip out of camp with Dog as soon as it got full dark and make a big circuit around the camp, just to make sure no threats were lurking in the vicinity.

Hannah disappeared into the brush. Jamie had gone over with her the necessity to be alert at all times, even this close to camp. In a situation like this, she needed to be especially watchful for rattlesnakes that might be hidden in the thick brush.

She had that .31 caliber pocket revolver with her at all times, and although they had been trying to avoid any shooting, she knew that if she spotted a rattler, it was all right for her to go ahead and kill it.

Jamie stood there waiting, enjoying the breeze that blew from across the Brazos. It wasn't actually cool, but after the heat of the day it felt good anyway. Somewhere not far away, a night bird let out a pleasant-sounding warble.

Jamie's back stiffened and his jaw tightened. He glanced toward Preacher and saw that the mountain man's casual attitude had deserted him just as swiftly as Jamie's had.

Another bird responded from the far side of the camp.

Jamie knew that was no bird . . .

"Hannah, we need to go," he called in a quiet but urgent voice.

"I'm almost done," her reply came from the brush. "Is something—"

The scream she suddenly let out was answer enough to the question she'd been about to pose.

Jamie charged into the brush, ignoring the way the branches clawed at his clothes and flesh. He heard Preacher shouting a warning, followed swiftly by twin blasts from the mountain man's Dragoons. A sharp popping sound came from in front of Jamie. That was Hannah's pocket pistol.

She had screamed only the one time. Now she was fighting back.

Jamie burst into a clearing and saw Hannah struggling with a Comanche warrior. Even in the fading twilight, Jamie spotted blood on the warrior's left arm and knew that Hannah's shot had winged him. But he was still able to use that arm and had it wrapped around her, pinning her arms to her sides as he lifted a knife in his other hand.

Jamie had the Walker Colt in his hand and was about to risk a shot when Hannah yanked her right arm free and jammed the muzzle of the gun she still held under the Comanche's chin. She jerked the trigger. Flesh muffled the shot, which wasn't all that loud to begin with.

The Indian's head rocked back. He seemed to still be trying to stab Hannah, but the effort was feeble and aimless. His muscles no longer followed any commands from the bullet-scrambled brain. Jamie knew the .31 round must have bounced around quite a bit inside the Comanche's skull, lacking the power to punch straight through. The warrior was dead but didn't quite know it yet. Hannah gave him a hard shove, sending his lifeless shape toppling to the ground.

Jamie called, "Hannah!"

She whirled toward him, bringing the pistol around, and he realized that in her panic-stricken state, she might try to shoot him, too. He reached out, caught hold of her wrist, and forced her arm up.

"It's me, Hannah."

"Oh! Jamie . . . what—"

Gunshots, angry shouts, and shrill war cries filled the air. Hannah shrank against Jamie's broad chest in sheer terror. He felt her trembling.

"Come on," he told her. "We've got to get back to the others."

She looked up and nodded. "Philip could be in danger—"

"We all are." Jamie got a firm grip on her upper right arm with his left hand. The Walker Colt still filled his right hand. "But we'll be safer with the others."

He led her out of the brush. When they emerged from it, he saw that most of the men had taken cover under or behind the wagon. They were firing along the riverbank in both directions. The Comanches had them pinned against the Brazos.

One member of the expedition lay facedown with a pair of arrows protruding from his back. Jamie couldn't tell who it was. He saw at least twenty more arrows stuck in the wagon's sideboards.

Shapes flitted back and forth in the shadows. Those would be the Comanche warriors, never giving the men around the wagon a good target.

Jamie didn't need as good a target as most men did. He stalked forward, pulling Hannah with him, and thumbed back the Colt's hammer as he raised it. Without even seeming to take aim, he squeezed the trigger and the heavy revolver roared and bucked. One of the attacking Indians tumbled to the ground, a fist-sized chunk of his head blown away.

Brush crackling behind him warned Jamie. He looked

over his shoulder and saw three warriors emerge from the clump he and Hannah had just left. As they charged, they whooped in anticipation of killing him and the girl, or maybe taking her prisoner.

He pushed her toward the wagon and said, "Run. Don't look around and don't stop. Just run."

He swung around to face the trio of attackers. The Colt boomed twice more. One of the Comanches went backward as a slug drove into his chest. Another stumbled, doubled over, and collapsed with a bullet in his guts.

But the third man was close enough to leave his feet in a diving tackle that carried him into Jamie, who got another shot off but didn't think he hit anything with it.

The warrior was a head or more shorter than him, but heavily built and powerful. The impact of his collision with Jamie knocked the big frontiersman back a step. The Comanche wrapped his arms around Jamie's knees and jerked his legs out from under him. Jamie went down hard on his back but managed to hang on to the Colt.

The Indian howled in triumph and scrambled up onto his knees and one hand. He raised a tomahawk with his other hand, intending to bring it smashing down into Jamie's face.

Jamie moved faster, swinging the revolver and slamming the barrel against the side of the Indian's head. He felt bone crunch and give way. The Indian dropped the tomahawk, made a strangled noise in his throat, and fell to the side, where he twitched uncontrollably for a moment and then died.

Jamie rolled over and surged to his feet again. Hannah hadn't reached the wagon yet, and two warriors were closing in on her in the dusk, almost close enough to grab her.

Before they could do so, a figure leaped out from behind the wagon, flame spouting from the muzzle of the gun in his hand. One of the Comanches fell, but the other changed course and leaped at the man who had come to Hannah's aid. They grappled and went down.

Jamie's long legs carried him swiftly in that direction. From the corner of his eye, he saw Hannah reach the wagon and slide underneath it. That was far from a safe place to be right now . . . but Jamie knew there were no safe places here in Comancheria. At least Hannah had a little cover behind one of the wagon wheels.

The two men wrestling on the ground in front of him rolled over and over, with first one having the advantage and then the other. Every time the Comanche was on top and Jamie thought he might have a shot at the attacker, they rolled again.

Jamie had assumed at first that Philip Saunders was the one who had saved Hannah from the Indians. Now, though, he saw the rescuer's long, fair hair and knew the man was Walt Reynolds. Reynolds had dropped his gun while struggling with the Comanche, but his opponent still held a knife. Reynolds leaned desperately one way and then the other as the Comanche tried to skewer his throat.

Reynolds grabbed the warrior's wrist with both hands and hung on for dear life to keep that sharp blade away from him. He twisted the Comanche's arm and threw himself on top of the man . . .

Reynolds staggered to his feet a moment later, leaving the knife buried in the chest of its owner.

Then he ducked instinctively as an arrow whipped past his head.

Jamie twisted around, spotted the warrior who had just fired that shaft, and drilled a .44 round through him as the man tried to nock another arrow.

"Reynolds, come on!" Jamie said. "Get back to the wagon. I'll cover you."

Reynolds stumbled toward the wagon while Jamie shot another of the Comanche raiders.

From somewhere in the gathering darkness came a growling and snapping, followed by a bloodcurdling scream. Dog was getting in on the action, and Jamie was willing to bet that Preacher was out there somewhere, too, gliding through the gloom like a phantom, cutting down every Comanche he found. Having Preacher on your side was about like having a whole army patrol with you, which was why Jamie wouldn't have come on this journey without him. Throw Dog into the mix, and they were close to an unstoppable force.

The old mountain man and the big cur went through the Comanches like a wind blowing through grass, leaving death in their wake. The arrows stopped flying, and a moment later, Jamie heard the swift rataplan of hoofbeats. The surviving members of the war party were getting out of here in a hurry. The price for killing these white invaders had proven to be more than they wanted to pay.

"Jamie," Preacher called from the thickening shadows.

"Here."

"Got something for you."

The curt statement told Jamie it might be something important. He glanced toward the wagon and saw that Hannah appeared to be all right. She was sitting on the ground under the wagon, leaning on one hand and breathing heavily.

He could check on the men later. For now, he stalked toward the place where he had heard Preacher's voice.

Preacher stood next to a scrubby mesquite tree. Dog was with him. A man lay on the ground at their feet, unmoving except the rise and fall of his chest as labored breathing rasped in his throat. His hands were clasped over a bare midsection dark with blood.

"Thought you might want one alive enough to talk to," Preacher drawled.

"How's your Comanche?"

"Good enough to get by, but that ain't necessary. This fella speaks white man's lingo."

Jamie hunkered next to the wounded man. The warrior didn't seem to have any fight left in him, but Jamie kept the Colt ready just in case.

"What's your name?"

The man had to struggle to answer, and something broken inside him made his voice thick. "In your tongue . . . Gray . . . Gray Cloud."

"What chief do you follow, Gray Cloud."

"Spotted . . . Dog. The one who will . . . kill all of you!"

"He didn't do a very good job of it tonight. Your side looks to have lost a lot more than we did. Why did Spotted Dog attack us? Just because we're here in Comanche territory?"

"You . . . you killed his son!"

"When? In this fight just now? That's not our fault, Spotted Dog attacked us—"

"No. Back down river. In the first fight."

Preacher said, "The one where we heard the shots. That's what he's talkin' about."

"Has to be. And it sounds like Spotted Dog came off second best in that one, too." Jamie leaned closer to the wounded man. "Listen to me, Gray Cloud. We never fought with Spotted Dog and his warriors, not until just now. It wasn't us who killed his son."

"It don't matter, Jamie," Preacher said. "This hombre ain't gonna live long enough to go back to Spotted Dog and tell him anything, and even if he did, Spotted Dog ain't likely to believe it. He's got it in for us now. He thinks we've whipped him twice *and* done for his boy. He ain't gonna rest until we're dead."

"Or until he is," Jamie said as he rose to his feet. "Is there anything to be done for this man?"

"Just this." Preacher leaned down, and with a quick slash of his knife he cut the warrior's throat. "Dog had gnawed into his guts. He'd have died long and mighty hard."

"You did the right thing, then," Jamie said with a nod. "We'd better get back to the wagon and see how much damage was done to the others."

CHAPTER 42

The man Jamie had seen with two arrows in his back turned out to be Billy Bob Moore. Walt Reynolds and Ox Tankersley stood beside his body. They had pulled out the arrows and rolled Moore onto his back.

"Sorry about your friend," Jamie said as he and Preacher joined the young men.

"He have any family?" Preacher asked.

Reynolds shook his head. "Sad to say, I don't really know. Billy Bob never talked much about where he came from or who he might have left behind. I reckon we all just sort of . . . started over out here."

Jamie nodded, understanding what the young man meant. The past meant very little on the frontier. What was important was today . . . and surviving until tomorrow.

"Did we lose anybody else?"

"A couple of men were wounded. I don't think anybody else was killed. Not sure, though."

Jamie rested a hand on Reynolds's shoulder for a

moment. "We'll lay him to rest proper, don't worry about that."

"Yes, sir, thank you."

As they headed toward the wagon, Preacher said quietly, "I reckon Dog and me will go take a look around, just to make sure none of them varmints try to double back and hit us again. I don't think they will, but you can't never tell with Injuns."

"Good idea," Jamie agreed.

"Come on, Dog," the old mountain man said. He and the big cur headed off and quickly disappeared in the shadows. Only the faintest lingering glow remained in the western sky. In a matter of minutes, it would be full dark.

Hannah had crawled out from under the wagon, as had Philip Saunders. They stood together, but Jamie sensed a certain separation between them as he walked up.

"Both of you are all right?" he asked.

"I think so," Hannah said. She rubbed her upper arm with the other hand and winced slightly. "I have a bruise here where that Indian grabbed me."

"I might've been responsible for that. I seem to recall that I was hanging on to you pretty tight while we were trying to get away from them."

Saunders reached over and stroked her hand where she held her arm, as if trying to comfort her. Without seeming overly dramatic about it, Hannah moved slightly, just enough that he was no longer touching her.

"You knew the Indians were about to attack, didn't you?" she said to Jamie. "When you told me to hurry out of the brush, you knew they were here. How?"

"I heard them signaling to each other with bird calls. So did Preacher. It's pretty common among all the tribes."

"I thought Indians wouldn't attack at night."

Jamie smiled. "Well, it wasn't full night yet. And anyway, that's just a legend. Indians will fight whenever they think the time is best suited for an attack. They care more about winning than anything else, but they want to win without losing too much at the same time. We were killing more of them than they were of us, so they decided it was time to light a shuck." When they both looked at him with puzzled expressions, he added, "They got out of here in a hurry."

"But they'll come back, won't they?" Saunders asked with a fatalistic tone in his voice.

"More than likely. Preacher and I questioned one of them before he died." Jamie didn't explain how that Comanche warrior had died. "He said Spotted Dog is the war chief that led this raid. That's not surprising. Captain Glennister back at the fort told us that Spotted Dog is the most active of the war chiefs right now. And he's got another reason for coming after us. He thinks we killed his son."

"Tonight, you mean?" Hannah asked.

"Nope. In an earlier fight."

"But there hasn't been an earlier fight," Saunders said with a puzzled frown. "This is the first time we've clashed with the hostiles."

"That's right. I don't know who they had the ruckus with, but it wasn't us. Spotted Dog doesn't know that, though, and I doubt if we could convince him it was true, even if we had the chance to talk to him. He'll want to settle that score, and we're elected as his targets."

Hannah said bitterly, "It seems as if everyone out here on the frontier has some sort of score to settle with someone else. Isn't anything motived by something other than revenge?"

"Greed comes up a lot," Jamie said. So did lust, but he didn't figure it was proper to discuss that with a young, unmarried lady. "Revenge is mighty important to a lot of folks, though."

Saunders cleared his throat and said, "I believe I'll go check on my horse."

"That's a good idea. We're lucky the Comanches didn't stampede them. The men holding and protecting them did a good job."

Saunders nodded and walked off. Jamie watched him for a second, then said to Hannah, "Things seem a mite awkward between you two. Not that it's any of my business—"

"Everything about this expedition is your business, Jamie. I've known from the start that trusting you was the only real chance of success." Hannah sighed. "Do you know where Philip was when I got back here? Hiding under the wagon. Oh, I know what you're going to say. I hid under the wagon, too. But he was lying on his belly with his arms over his head, whimpering in terror. I . . . I never knew that I'd agreed to marry such a . . . a coward."

Jamie didn't particularly like Philip Saunders, but he felt like the man deserved a fair shake.

"I don't know that he's a coward. He stepped up and fought against Lynch back in Fort Worth and when that bunch jumped us on the trail. It's just something about Indians that gets under his skin. You remember how Lynch acted so scared of Dog? And that fella's as big as a mountain! Most men have something that bothers them more than anything else."

"Not you, though," she said, looking up at him. "You're a careful, practical man who takes the necessary precautions, but you're not terrified of anything."

Jamie chuckled. "Maybe I just haven't run into whatever it is that scares me yet."

"And Preacher is the same way. You're men without fear, both of you."

"Some might say that's a failing."

Hannah looked toward the spot where Reynolds and Tankersley had gotten shovels and were digging a grave for Billy Bob Moore. Jamie could hear the shovel blades biting into the earth. He had figured they would wait until morning to do that, but if Moore's friends wanted to take care of it now, he supposed there was no reason why they shouldn't.

"Walt saved my life when those Indians almost caught me," Hannah said quietly.

"The young fella came in handy, all right." Jamie couldn't help but notice that she'd called Reynolds by his first name. "He seems like a good hand. Got a feeling he's been mixed up in some shady dealings in the past, but everybody deserves a second chance. I reckon that includes Saunders, too."

"Well, we'll see." She drew in a deep breath, and her voice trembled a little as she went on, "I don't think it's really soaked in on me yet that I . . . I killed a man tonight. That Indian I shot, he's really . . . I mean, he couldn't have . . ."

"No, he's dead," Jamie said as gently as he could. "And he was about to kill and scalp you. If you hadn't shot him, I would have about half a second later. Never feel bad about protecting your own life or the life of someone you care about."

"I'll try not to. Thank you, Jamie."

"Walt said there were some other fellas wounded. I'd better check on them. Try to get some rest."

"Right now I don't feel like I'll ever sleep again."

But she would, Jamie knew. Exhaustion would claim her.

* * *

Jamie caught a few winks himself that night, but not until after Preacher and Dog returned and the mountain man reported, "Ain't no Injuns within a couple of miles all around. Dog would've sniffed 'em out if there was."

Everyone in camp was still on edge the next morning. The two wounded men had their injuries bound up and weren't hurt seriously. The night before, Jamie had some of the men drag the bodies of the dead Comanches into the brush, but the dark stains where their life's blood had drained out were still on the ground.

The group gathered beside Billy Bob Moore's grave for a brief prayer, and then they moved out. Jamie saw Philip Saunders bring his horse alongside the wagon and speak to Hannah. She replied to him, but only briefly. Jamie didn't know what they had said, but Saunders dropped back to ride beside the others.

As he did, he scowled in the direction of Walt Reynolds.

It would be nice, Jamie mused, if people could put aside their own personal troubles and concentrate on staying alive. But it seemed to take dire circumstances to accomplish that, and he wasn't sure if he wanted anything more dire than they had encountered already.

More than likely that's what they'd wind up with, whether he wanted it or not.

But not that day. They didn't see a soul, white or Comanche. Being away from the dark and bloody ground they'd left behind, plus a day's travel without running into more trouble, lifted the party's spirits.

When they made camp that evening, they weren't exactly jovial, but at least the mood wasn't completely grim. The men were more watchful than ever, though, because they knew that Spotted Dog and his warriors could return and attack at any time.

Jamie and Preacher were probably the only ones who didn't expect that just yet. When they talked privately before turning in, Preacher said, "I reckon ol' Spotted Dog's gonna have to lick his wounds for a spell before he tries to jump us again, no matter how mad he is at us. We killed enough of 'em that he's liable to have to go back to wherever his village is and round up some more fellas who want to fight."

"I thought the same thing," Jamie said. "That small hunting party you saw was probably an offshoot from a larger party, but it wouldn't have been a big enough bunch to wage war. He's not going to forget about us, though."

"No, I don't reckon he will. But it may be a few days before he's ready to strike again, and in that time, maybe we can get where we're goin' and find out if comin' all the way out here was just a fool's errand."

"Yeah, I'm kind of curious to know that myself."

Preacher scratched his jaw. "Still, we got at least one good tussle out of the deal, and the prospect of more to come. Saw some country that ain't exactly pretty, but it's interestin' lookin', anyway. So I reckon it was worth the trip."

"Fighting and seeing new country is pretty much what you do, isn't it?"

The old mountain man grinned and said, "I been at it for a whole heap of years now, too. Ever comes a time when I can't do those things anymore, that'll be the end of the trail for me."

Jamie didn't say anything, but he wasn't sure that day would ever come for Preacher.

* * *

Not long after they started the next morning, they came to another fork in the river. Again, Tobias Craigson's map indicated that they should follow the right-hand branch.

"At the next one, we'll need to ford the river and follow the branch to the left," Hannah told Jamie. "The place that my grandfather marked won't be far beyond that. At least it doesn't look that way on the map, although it's difficult to say what scale he used when he drew it. Or if he used any scale."

"More than likely he just drew it from what Colonel Bowie told him," Jamie said. "But I think there's a good chance we'll know the place when we see it." He gazed into the distance ahead of them. "And if nothing happens to slow us down, we might get there late this afternoon."

Pete Barnes, on the other side of the driver's seat, leaned forward and said past Hannah, "You mean, if those Comanch' don't jump us again, Mr. MacCallister?"

"Lots of things can happen out here, Pete."

"Yeah, and most of 'em are bad." Pete flapped the reins. "But for some reason, I got a hunch that we're gonna make it where we're goin'."

"So do I," Jamie agreed.

Those flat-topped mesas had become more common. Jamie could see a dozen of them scattered around the landscape. Most of them had a reddish cast from the sandstone of which they were formed.

The riverbed itself was red in places, and there was a lot of bed showing because this far north, the Brazos had shrunk to a shadow of what it was downriver. Only a narrow channel writhed along the riverbed. When the time came to ford the stream, the challenge would be to avoid getting bogged down in the sand. The water in the channel was less than a foot deep.

Late in the afternoon, they came to the place where the river split for the final time. Jamie and Preacher, out ahead of the group, rode a short distance up the right-hand branch, looking for a good place to ford.

"This here's a likely place," Preacher said as he reined in. "I'll check it out. If there's any quicksand, Horse won't step in it. He's mighty good about things like that. Dog, stay here with Jamie."

Preacher rode the stallion down the gentle red clay bank and started slowly out into the riverbed. While Preacher was doing that, Jamie gazed across the stream, studying the country that lay between these two "fingers" of the Brazos. A mile or so away, a mesa rose, and as Jamie looked at it, he stiffened in the saddle. He stared a moment longer, then reached in one of his saddlebags and took out a spyglass.

He extended the glass and held it to his right eye. After squinting through the lenses, he slowly lowered the instrument and breathed, "Well, I'll be damned."

Preacher rode back across the river a few minutes later, following the same path he had taken across.

"The horses and wagon won't have no trouble," he reported. "The bottom's sandy, but solid enough." A frown suddenly creased the mountain man's forehead under the brim of his hat. "Jamie, what's wrong? You look like you done seen a ghost."

"Not a ghost," Jamie said, "but something I never expected to see out here, that's for sure."

"I reckon you'd better explain that."

Jamie lifted his hand and pointed. "See that mesa over yonder, sitting exactly between these two branches of the Brazos. That's the spot Tobias Craigson marked on the map."

"The spot where Jim Bowie's treasure is supposed to be hid?"

"That's right. I don't know if the treasure's there, but something else is."

Preacher squinted toward the mesa for a long moment, then said, "Well, I'll be hornswoggled. Is that . . ."

"It's a house," Jamie said. "A white man's house."

CHAPTER 43

Jamie handed over the spyglass so Preacher could take a look. As he peered through the glass, the mountain man said, "Appears it's made out o' adobe, like the houses over in New Mexico Territory. There are so few good-sized trees out here that a fella would have a hard time comin' up with enough lumber to build a house."

"Do you think anybody lives there, or is the place deserted?"

Preacher studied the house some more, then said, "There are some bushes out in front that look like somebody's been takin' care of 'em. Smoke comin' from the chimney, too. Yeah, somebody's there, Jamie." He lowered the spyglass. "But who in tarnation could it be? No Injun'd live in a place like that, and no white man would settle exactly in the middle o' Comanche territory!"

"You wouldn't think so," Jamie agreed. He took the spyglass that Preacher held out to him and put it away, then inclined his head toward the approaching riders and wagon and went on, "One of us needs to go take a look around before we lead that bunch in. I don't want them riding blindly into trouble."

"You can stay here with them," Preacher said without hesitation. "Me and Dog and Horse will go see what we can find out."

Jamie considered the suggestion and nodded. "That's probably the best idea. Maybe you could use a smoke signal to let us know whether to come ahead."

"Yeah, three puffs'll mean it's all right. Until you see that, just keep the pilgrims right here. If it looks bad, I'll come back and let you know in person."

"And if we haven't seen the signal in a couple of hours, or you haven't come back, I'll leave Pete in charge and go find out what happened to you."

"That'll work," Preacher said with a nod. "Come on, Dog."

The mountain man and his two trail partners crossed the stream and headed toward the mesa with the unexpected dwelling on it. Jamie rested both hands on the saddle in front of him and leaned forward to ease weary muscles as he watched them go.

A couple of minutes later, Pete Barnes pulled the mule team to a halt and the rest of the company reined in. "Is this where we're going to cross the river, Mr. MacCallister?" Hannah asked.

"Yes, ma'am, I reckon it is," Jamie said. "Preacher rode across to check it and says that we should be able to ford here without any trouble."

Hannah frowned slightly. "Where *is* Preacher?"

Jamie nodded toward the mesa and said, "He's gone to have a look around. If I'm remembering that map you have correctly, that mesa is right where your grandfather claimed the treasure is."

Hannah looked excited. "You think so? You mean we're almost there?"

"Almost there," Jamie confirmed, "but I can't guarantee we'll find the treasure. Fact of the matter is, we don't know what's up there . . . but that's what Preacher's trying to find out."

When Preacher got closer to the mesa, he couldn't see the house anymore. It was set too far back from the edge for that. But he could see a ledge winding back and forth up the side of the craggy upthrust. It was wide enough for two men on horseback and provided a trail to the top.

Preacher reined in and swung down from the saddle. He could have ridden Horse up the ledge, but it would be quieter to approach on foot. He told the stallion, "You stay here, old son. If I don't come back after a spell, you head on back to Jamie. That'll let him know I ran into trouble."

Horse bobbed his head as if he understood Preacher's words. Most of the time, the old mountain man believed that was exactly the case.

"Dog, you're comin' with me, but stay quiet."

Preacher saw faint hoofprints in the sandy soil where the trail began. They were unshod, which meant Indian ponies had made them. That came as no surprise. His horse was probably the only mount with shod hooves that had been around here for a long time. The ledge was sandstone and scuffed here and there from riders headed up or down.

So the Comanch' paid regular visits to this place, whatever it was, he thought.

Might even be some of the varmints up there now, although he hadn't seen anybody moving around when he looked through Jamie's spyglass.

Preacher and Dog made very little sound as they climbed

toward the top. The hour was late enough in the day that the mesa itself shaded them from the sun and eased the heat a little. Halfway up, Preacher stopped to listen. He didn't hear anything. A vast, echoing silence hung over this whole part of Texas.

The mesa rose about eighty feet from the ground. From what he had seen, Preacher figured the flat top of it encompassed maybe a hundred acres. That gave it a squatty appearance. The sides were ragged, covered with deep gashes carved out by the elements. In some places, whole chunks had sheered off and fallen to the ground to break up into scattered boulders. Preacher had seen plenty of geographical features such as this in his decades of wandering.

When they were almost at the top, he paused again to listen. Still hearing nothing, he said quietly to Dog, "All right, we'll go up and take a look around."

A few more steps moved them out onto the mesa. The house sat facing them, a hundred yards away. There were no windows and only a solid-looking wooden door, which led Preacher to believe it must be built in the Spanish style, around a central courtyard. The tiles that formed the roof must have been made from red sandstone, judging by their color.

Off to the side were a barn and a corral, as well as a smaller building that might be a smokehouse. Trees grew behind the house, telling Preacher that there must be a spring back there. Whoever lived here had to have some source of water other than the river. Well cared for shrubs grew along the house's front wall. In this semiarid climate, they would require careful tending to stay alive.

Preacher had his rifle ready as he walked toward the house. If any threat emerged, he could whip the weapon to his shoulder, aim, and fire in less than the blink of an eye. Dog padded along beside him, equally watchful.

Nothing happened until Preacher was about twenty feet from the door. Then, it began to swing open slowly. The wall was thick, and Preacher could see now that it was constructed of blocks of sandstone with a layer of adobe over them. A wall like that would stand up to any arrow or bullet, in addition to making the place warm in the winter and cool in the summer.

The wall's thickness also made the doorway shadowy. Preacher saw someone standing inside but couldn't make out any details. However, he heard the voice that spoke out clearly—and in English.

"Come in, friend," the man said. "Welcome to my home."

CHAPTER 44

Time seemed to pass even more slowly than usual as Jamie, Hannah, and the others waited to see whether Preacher would send them the signal to proceed across the Brazos and approach the mesa.

"After coming this far . . . surviving everything we've gone through . . . I'm not sure I could stand it if it all turns out to be for nothing," Hannah said with worry in her voice as she and Jamie stood beside the wagon. She shaded her eyes with her hand as she peered toward the mesa.

"Folks can stand more than they generally believe they can," Jamie told her. "Bad news stings for a while, but sooner or later it gets better. The Good Book says something somewhere about the sun coming up in the morning and going down in the evening, and the world keeps turning. If you look at it that way, maybe the disappointments don't seem quite as bad."

Hannah smiled at him. "Now you sound like a preacher, Jamie."

He grinned back at her and said, "Not likely."

Jamie turned and looked at the group gathered on the riverbank. The men had dismounted but not unsaddled, in case they needed to move in a hurry. They were clustered in small bunches, talking and waiting. Pete Barnes was with his brother Gil and a few more men. Walt Reynolds and Ox Tankersley stood together. They had lost their two companions during the journey and weren't close friends with anyone else.

Philip Saunders paced nervously by himself, a sullen expression on his face. The falling-out he'd had with Hannah might or might not be permanent, Jamie thought, but for now, at least, Saunders wasn't happy about it.

Jamie saw Walt Reynolds straighten suddenly from his casual attitude. At the same moment, Hannah caught hold of his arm and said, "Mr. MacCallister! Is that it?"

Jamie swung around and looked again toward the mesa. Sure enough, a puff of white smoke was rising into the air above the flat top, stark against the blue sky in the light from the lowering sun.

"Is that the first one?" Jamie asked.

"Well, it's the first one I saw, and I've been watching pretty closely because I didn't want to miss anything. It's Preacher's signal, isn't it? He's telling us to come on."

"Let's wait and see."

They stood there side by side, watching as a second puff of smoke appeared and followed the first one in a lazy ascent toward the heavens. The first ball of smoke was starting to break apart and disperse now as it reached the stronger winds high in the atmosphere.

The third one rose a moment later. "That's three!" Hannah said excitedly. "That's the signal."

That excitement was echoed in the hubbub of conversation from the men behind them.

"Wait a minute," Jamie said. He doubted if anybody could force Preacher into doing something he didn't want to do, but he also knew that if anybody tried to coerce the mountain man into drawing them into a trap, more than likely Preacher would send the wrong signal as a warning, no matter what the consequences for himself.

But no more smoke came from the mesa. It was the signal they had agreed on, all right.

"That's it," Jamie said when he was confident. He turned again to call to the men, "Mount up!"

Pete Barnes hurried over and climbed onto the seat while Jamie helped Hannah onto the wagon. Then Jamie swung up onto his horse and took the lead. He had watched closely every time Preacher crossed the river and was confident that he could retrace the mountain man's route.

"Follow close behind me," he told Pete. "The rest of you men, string out behind the wagon and don't stray from the trail it leaves."

They forded the Brazos quickly and without incident. Jamie sat on his horse on the bank and watched closely to make sure none of the men had trouble. Once everyone was across, he fell in alongside the wagon again.

"I wonder if Preacher already found the treasure," Hannah said as she beamed with happiness and leaned forward, eager to reach their destination.

"Well, I wouldn't go getting ahead of yourself," Jamie advised, "but it won't be long before we know, one way or the other."

As they approached the mesa, Jamie spotted the ledge that formed a trail to the top. He pointed it out to Pete, who said, "I'm not sure we can take the wagon up that, Mr. MacCallister. It looks like it turns back on itself a mite too sharp for that. At least from here it does."

"I agree," Jamie said.

"I don't mind walking," Hannah said. "It's really not that far."

"You can use my saddle horse if you want, Miss Hannah," Pete offered. "He's pretty steady and won't be likely to give you any trouble."

Jamie nodded. "That's a good idea, Pete."

Hannah said, "Jamie . . . I thought I saw something up there on top of this mountain. A building of some sort?"

"It's not really a mountain," Jamie said. "They call it a mesa because it's flat on top."

He had heard some of the men talking among themselves about the mysterious house. They hadn't spotted it from as far off as he and Preacher had, but once they were on this side of the Brazos, it was hard to miss.

He went on, "There's a house up there. Preacher and I saw it earlier. He went to take a closer look at it before he signaled us to come ahead."

"But Indians don't live in houses, do they?"

"Some back east do, like the Cherokee, but not the Comanches."

"And no one lives out here in this part of Texas except the Comanches, you said."

Jamie nodded. "That's right." He shrugged. "At least, that's what we thought."

"Then who . . . ?"

Hannah's voice trailed off and she left the question unfinished, as if realizing there was no way to answer it without going up onto the mesa, which they were about to do anyway.

When they reached the foot of the trail that led up the side of the mesa, Jamie said to Hannah, "You'll need to stay down here with some of the men until I've gone up and checked things out."

She shook her head and asked, "Why? Preacher's signal means that everything is all right, doesn't it?"

She had a point there.

"Besides, we wouldn't be here if it weren't for me, would we?" she went on. "I have a right to go up and see what's waiting for us."

"All right," Jamie said. He called out the names of half a dozen men, including Walt Reynolds and Ox Tankersley. "You fellas will come with Miss Craigson and me. The rest of you, wait down here for now. Pete, you're in charge of this bunch."

Pete nodded in understanding. He said, "If we hear any kind of ruckus break out up there—"

"Then come a-running as fast as you can," Jamie said.

Philip Saunders said, "Wait a minute. I'm coming along, too."

"That's not necessary—" Hannah began.

"I don't know how I can get back in your good graces, Hannah," he broke in, "but I've come this far with you, and I think *I* have a right to see what's up there, too."

Hannah glanced at Jamie, but he kept his expression blank. This was her decision to make.

Finally, she nodded and said, "All right, Philip. I suppose I understand why you feel that way."

That meant both Saunders and Reynolds would be part of the group ascending to the top of the mesa, Jamie thought. He hoped that wouldn't lead to any trouble.

"Let's get you mounted up on Pete's horse," he said to Hannah. "You'll have to ride astride."

"After coming this far, do you think I care about that?" She lifted her skirt slightly. "Let's go."

A couple of minutes later, they were on their way. Jamie took the lead and motioned for Walt Reynolds to join him.

The young man had demonstrated that he was reasonably handy with a gun if they happened to be riding into a fight.

"Hannah, you'll come next behind me and Walt," he told her. "Ride on the inside, next to the wall. Ox, you take the outside next to Miss Craigson."

"Don't worry, I won't let nothin' happen to the lady," Ox rumbled.

Saunders clearly didn't like it that he wasn't next to Hannah, but Jamie didn't care about that. He trusted Tankersley more, despite the man's background as a saddle tramp and quite possibly a shady character.

The ride up the trail wasn't difficult, but it seemed to take longer than it actually did. That was the anticipation working on them after the long, perilous journey.

Quietly, Walt Reynolds asked, "What do you think we're going to find up there, Mr. MacCallister? Will there really be a treasure?"

"Your guess is as good as mine, Walt," Jamie replied honestly.

They reached the top of the trail and emerged onto the mesa. The house sat there, impressive in the late afternoon light, and Hannah let out a little gasp when she saw it.

"That shouldn't be here," she said. "Not in a place like this."

"It's not what I expected to find," Jamie admitted. "But there it is, and there's Preacher."

The mountain man had just stepped out the open doorway. He must have been watching for them. He took his hat off, waved it over his head to let Jamie know that everything was all right, and then motioned with it for them to come on. Jamie nudged his horse into motion again and trotted across the mesa with Hannah, Reynolds, and Tankersley alongside him, forming a line. The other five men were close behind.

They reined up in front of the entrance where Preacher stood grinning with Dog beside him. Jamie knew from Preacher's casual attitude that there was no danger.

Hannah blurted out, "Did you find it? Is it here?" She looked around. "What *is* this place?"

"Before we get to that," Preacher said, "there's somebody here who wants to meet you."

He stepped aside so that a tall, spare man in sandals and loose-fitting trousers and shirt could step through the doorway into the light. A Mexican serape was draped over his shoulders.

The man's skin was tanned a deep, permanent brown that made his white hair and close-cropped beard stand out sharply. Wrinkles creased his lean face. He was old, but age didn't appear to have dimmed his surprisingly light blue eyes, which indicated that despite his dark skin and clothing, he wasn't Mexican.

"Hannah?" he said in a husky voice that didn't sound as if it were used very often.

Utterly bewildered, Hannah blinked and said, "Who . . . who . . ."

"Miss Hannah," Preacher said, "I'd like for you to meet your grandpa."

CHAPTER 45

"Grandfather?" Hannah blurted. "But that . . . how . . . that can't be . . ."

Jamie leaned forward sharply in the saddle. "Craigson?" he demanded. "Tobias Craigson?"

His mind went back almost two decades to those tense days in the Alamo with Santa Anna's army sitting half a mile away, ready to wipe out the old mission's defenders.

Sure, it had been a pretty grim situation, but there had been lighter moments, too, moments such as the one when Davy Crockett and some of the other men had taken out their fiddles and played a sprightly tune. A couple of men had gotten up to caper around in time to the music. One of them had been Tobias Craigson.

Jamie had been standing there, clapping along with the other spectators. Those memories were vivid in his mind. Was the man he looked at now the same as one of those laughing, dancing fighters? So much time had passed, it was hard to tell . . .

But Jamie recalled the way the man's light blue eyes had flashed in the lamplight that night. Tobias Craigson's hair and beard had been brown then, but the eyes were the same, Jamie realized. They hadn't changed.

"Tobias," he breathed.

"That's right," the man said. "I remember you, too, Jamie. I told my wife that she could trust you, if she ever took it in her head to try to lay hands on old Jim Bowie's treasure."

"My . . . my grandmother has passed on," Hannah said, clearly having to force the words out past the amazement she felt. "So are my parents. But I came . . ."

"My granddaughter," Craigson said. "My beautiful granddaughter." He smiled at Jamie. "And you brought her here, old friend. You brought me a greater treasure than any I might have sought elsewhere."

A feeling stirred inside Jamie, a vague sense that something wasn't right. He didn't want to press the issue at the moment, though. Not with the reunion between Craigson and Hannah going on.

She cried out softly, obviously almost overcome by emotion, and slipped down from the saddle. Craigson raised his arms under the serape and opened them. She ran into his embrace and tightly hugged the grandfather she hadn't known she still had.

After a long moment, she lifted her head, looked up at him, and asked, "How is this possible?"

"Come on inside, and I'll tell you all about it." Craigson looked at Jamie. "You come in, too, old friend, and my new friend Preacher. Your men can go around back. There's shade under the trees, and it's mighty pleasant this time of day. Cold water from the spring, too. I'll have my cook see about putting a surrounding together for everyone."

"There are still some men down below, too," Jamie said.

Craigson nodded. "Tell them to come on up. All are welcome here."

Jamie turned to Ox Tankersley and said, "You can take care of that, Ox. Tell Pete he can leave the wagon there." He lowered his voice and added, "Tell him to leave a guard at the top of the trail, too, just to keep an eye on things."

"Sure, Mr. MacCallister." Ox nodded to Reynolds, then turned his horse and rode back toward the trail.

Jamie dismounted and handed his reins to Reynolds. The young man could keep up with his horse, too.

Philip Saunders cleared his throat and said tentatively, "Hannah . . . ?"

For a second, she looked as if she were about to tell him to go with Reynolds and the others, but then she relented and said, "Of course, you can come along, Philip. We are still officially engaged, after all."

"Engaged?" Craigson repeated. He grinned and thrust out his hand toward Saunders. "To this young fella? Well, put 'er there, son! Welcome to my home."

Saunders clasped the old man's hand. Craigson herded him and Hannah through the doorway together. Jamie and Preacher brought up the rear.

"He's a mighty colorful old pelican," Preacher said under his breath.

"He's probably not much older than you are," Jamie pointed out.

"Maybe not, but clean livin' keeps me young."

Despite the heat of the day that was ending, the air inside the house was cool because of the thick walls, just as Jamie expected. His hunch as to the place's architecture was confirmed as they went along a hallway and stepped out into a stone-paved courtyard. Clumps of cactus and scattered mesquite trees decorated the area. The other three sides of the house completed the square around it.

A roughhewn table sat in the shade of a small covered area, with several chairs around it. Jamie knew it must have taken a lot of time and quite a bit of work to find enough wood to build the furniture. Not to mention constructing this impressive house in the first place.

But Tobias Craigson had had a lot of years to fill.

"Please, sit, my friends," Craigson said as he waved a hand at the table. There were four chairs, and he insisted that the guests take them while he remained standing.

A door in one of the other wings opened, and a woman emerged. She was middle-aged but sternly attractive. Her long, black hair was gathered in two braids. Jamie knew right away from her buckskin clothing and the coppery tint of her skin that she was Comanche.

But she carried a tray with a crystal pitcher and five brass goblets on it. As she placed the tray on the table, she smiled at Hannah, which relieved her grim demeanor, and said in perfect English, "Welcome, Miss Craigson."

"Thank you," Hannah said, still so nonplussed by all the unexpected developments that she probably couldn't summon up any other response.

The woman nodded to the other three men and said, "Gentlemen." She began pouring water from the pitcher into the goblets.

Craigson said, "This is Evening Star. That's what I call her, anyway. She cooks and takes care of me. Has ever since I first came to this place."

"How in the world *did* you come to this place?" Hannah asked. She seemed to be recovering somewhat from her surprise at finding her grandfather alive, but the whole situation was still pretty amazing to her.

Jamie understood that. He felt the same way.

Craigson drank from the goblet he held and then said, "Well, that's quite a story. Goes all the way back to the Alamo, as Jamie here knows. All the fellas in there figured out pretty quick-like that none of us were likely to make it out alive. And we sort of accepted that and were determined that we'd hold out against old Santa Anna as long as we could."

"I reckon I would've stayed," Jamie said, "if Colonel Travis hadn't insisted that I leave to carry dispatches to the other forces gathering in Texas."

"I would have, too, if it hadn't been for a fella from Bexar who slipped through the lines the day after you left and brought a message to Travis from some of the folks in Bexar."

Jamie leaned forward, keenly interested in what Craigson was saying. "I never heard anything about that."

"I'm not surprised," Craigson replied. "Not many people knew about it." He looked down for a moment before continuing, "And I'm the only one of 'em still alive." He had to pause again as the memories coursed through him. "You see, Santa Anna wasn't the *presidente* of Mexico because everybody loved him. They were afraid of him. Some of the folks in Bexar realized they might have a chance to get rid of him, if they worked it right. They were providing the food for the Mexican Army, or rather, Santa Anna was commandeering the provisions for his men. The fellas I'm talking about came up with a plan where they would poison the grain going to the army. Some of the soldiers would die, and the others would all get sick. Then, once they were weakened like that, a bunch of the men from town would attack from the rear, while those of us in the Alamo came out of the mission and hit Santa Anna from the front. We'd catch him between the two forces."

Jamie and Preacher looked at each other. Jamie could tell that the mountain man agreed with him—Craigson's story was plausible.

"That might have turned the trick, all right," Jamie said. "Ended the Texas Revolution right then and there."

"Colonel Travis thought so, too. That's why he sent me to slip through the lines and arrange things with the rebels in Bexar. But it was going to take several days to set everything up . . ."

"And you ran out of time," Jamie guessed.

Craigson set his goblet on the table and covered his face with both hands for a moment. He had to take a couple of deep breaths to regain his composure.

"I hadn't been in town, talking to the plotters, for more than an hour or so before they started playing the *Deguello* out at the Mexican camp. We all knew then it was too late. That was a little while after midnight on March 6th."

"March 6th, 1836," Jamie said softly.

Craigson nodded. "Yeah. The fall of the Alamo. To this day, part of me feels like I ought to have gone back anyway. There was enough time. Even with the Mexican forces on the alert and getting ready for the attack, I think I could've made it back through the lines."

Hannah said, "But you were out of danger. And it wouldn't have changed anything to go back."

"No, it wouldn't have," her grandfather replied, shaking his head solemnly. "Except for the fact that I would have been able to die fighting alongside my friends. I would have been at Colonel Bowie's bedside, holding off those soldiers who broke in there . . ."

Craigson's voice trailed off, overcome again by memories. Silence hung over the courtyard until he went on, "I didn't go back. I lit a shuck out of San Antonio. I had that map to the colonel's treasure up here"—he tapped the side of his head—"and I wanted to find out if it was true before I headed home. Figured if it was, I'd go back a rich man. So while the rest of Texas was fighting for its freedom . . . I headed up the Brazos to see what I could find."

He threw back his head and laughed. "But it wasn't here! All I found is this!" He flung his arms out to indicate their surroundings. "This mesa! It's a good place, a beautiful place in its way, but it's not the treasure I was looking for."

Saunders's face had gone pale under the tan he had acquired during the journey. "Bowie's treasure," he rasped. "It's not real?"

"I don't know, son, but if it *is* real, it's hidden somewhere else because it's not here. I spent years looking before I finally gave up for good!" Craigson shook his head. "I reckon all those stories the colonel told me, the map he had me draw, all that was because he was out of his head from the pain of his injured leg, and from the medicine he was taking."

Saunders looked stricken. He leaned back in his chair, shook his head, and muttered, "Not real. Nothing."

Jamie's eyes narrowed. He had never fully trusted Philip Saunders, and apparently with good reason. It was obvious that Saunders had been more interested in getting his hands on Jim Bowie's gold and silver than in Hannah.

Preacher said to Craigson, "So you decided to just live here, among the Comanch'? And they didn't just kill you?"

"I fully expected they would. I was prepared for that, too." Craigson's mouth twisted wryly. "It seemed like a better idea than going home empty-handed, carrying nothing with me except the shame of leaving my comrades to die in that godforsaken place."

"But you had a wife and family," Hannah said. "People would have understood."

"You overestimate the human race's capacity for forgiveness, my dear."

Preacher frowned and ran a thumbnail along his jawline as he looked at their host. He said, "I reckon I'm startin' to understand. The Comanch' didn't kill you because they figured you were harebrained. Touched by the spirits. They were afraid of you."

"Once I started building this house, they came and watched me. They always turned and rode away after a while. I could tell how puzzled they were. I was still hunting for the treasure at that point, too, so they knew I was after something. It was the house that really convinced them I'd lost my mind."

Preacher chuckled and said, "I have some experience along those lines my own self, only with Blackfeet instead of Comanch'. But they're all superstitious critters and don't like to mess with the spirits."

Craigson nodded. "After enough time had passed, one of the men who spoke some English came and talked to me. He said they would allow me to live here in peace as long as I wouldn't ask the spirits to bring any evil down on them. I gave them my word. They sent Evening Star to care for my needs. She was a widow, and her late husband had no brothers to take her into their family. So I provided her with a home."

"And taught her to speak English," Jamie said.

"It was a natural progression," Craigson replied with a fond smile.

"This is just an astounding story," Hannah said. "I don't think I've come to grips even yet with the fact that you're alive, Grandfather."

Craigson came to stand beside her and rested his hand on her shoulder. "And I never dreamed that you'd come to find me," he said. "I could barely believe it when Preacher told me who you are and why you're here. I thought I actually had lost my mind for a moment. But I'm glad you came. It's nice to know, after all these years, that I still have family. We'll have to have some nice, long talks, and you can tell me everything about your life."

She smiled up at him. "I think I'd like that—"

An urgent pounding came through the open hallway leading to the entrance. Jamie came to his feet as he heard someone shout, "Mr. MacCallister!"

"That's Walt Reynolds," Jamie snapped. Preacher was already out of his chair, too, and together they hurried through the passage. Jamie had his hand on the butt of the Walker Colt as he swung the heavy door open.

"Mr. MacCallister," Reynolds gasped as he stood there breathing hard. Dusk had thickened into almost full dark, but light spilled through the opening onto the young saddle tramp. "I was standing guard at the top of the trail, and I saw them coming. They're headed up here now!"

"Who is Walt?" Jamie asked, although he had a bad feeling that he already knew the answer.

"Comanches," Reynolds said. "At least a dozen of them. I figure it's a war party."

Tobias Craigson had come up behind Jamie and Preacher in time to hear Reynolds's report. He shook his head and said, "That's not a war party. They're friends of mine, I tell you. They always stop by for a visit around this time of the month."

"Friends, eh?" Preacher said. "One of 'em wouldn't happen to be a fella called Spotted Dog, would it?"

It was Craigson's turn to look surprised. "That's right," he said. "How do you know him?"

"I expect he's here to kill us," Jamie said.

CHAPTER 46

Craigson seemed shocked at that declaration.

"I've heard rumors that Spotted Dog has led a few raids on the white settlements back east," he said, "but what reason would he have for wanting to wipe out your group?"

"Other than us bein' white, and him bein' Comanch', and us bein' on what he considers his land?" Preacher asked.

"There's more to it than that," Jamie said. Quickly, he filled Tobias Craigson in on what had happened while they were on their way here, concluding, "Some other white men must have killed Spotted Dog's son in that earlier fight because we only tangled with them the one time."

"What other group of white men would be out here?"

"That's a good question, but I don't have the answer."

Craigson stroked his bearded chin and said, "Well, it's clear what we need to do. Have all your men come into the house here where they'll be safe. Then I'll go out and explain the situation to Spotted Dog."

Preacher said, "He's liable to be too out of his mind with grief to listen to you, Tobias. He might just kill you and attack the house."

Craigson shook his head. "He'd never do that. We're friends. Or as close to it as a white man and an Indian can ever be."

Jamie said, "We need to get all the men inside, that's for sure." He turned to Reynolds, who was still standing just inside the door. "See to that, Walt. Spread the word, fast."

"Yes, sir," Reynolds said. He hurried out.

Philip Saunders was pale and shaken. He'd suffered a double blow—another impending Indian attack, and the loss of the treasure he'd had his heart set on. Jamie wanted to get to the bottom of that, if possible, but it could wait.

"You didn't build this place to be defended, did you?" he asked Craigson.

The old man spread his hands. "I didn't believe it was necessary. When I started, I didn't really care if I lived or died, and then later, it seemed that the Comanche were no threat to me."

"Can you get on the roof?" Preacher asked.

Craigson shook his head. "Not without going up a ladder on the outside."

"We'll do the best we can," Jamie said. "Right now, the important thing is to get all the horses into your barn and all the men in here."

That was accomplished in a matter of minutes. Jamie didn't know how far away the Comanches had been when Reynolds spotted them, but they had to be getting close by now.

Sure enough, several riders appeared at the top of the

trail a few short minutes later and came toward the house. More warriors followed them. Jamie, Preacher, and Craigson stood in the open doorway watching the newcomers. The three keen-eyed frontiersmen saw the approaching ponies in the light of a low-hanging half-moon.

"That's Spotted Dog, all right," Craigson said quietly. He pulled a torch made from a mesquite branch wrapped with dried grass out of a barrel where several similar torches were kept near the entrance and lighted it from a candle in a wall sconce along the passageway. He told Jamie and Preacher, "Stay here."

Then he strode out, straight and tall, to meet the Comanche war chief.

"Spotted Dog, my friend!" Craigson called. He held the torch high in his left hand, so that a large circle of light washed out from it. He raised his right hand in greeting.

Spotted Dog reined his pony to a halt. So did the warriors with him. Scowling at Craigson, he said, "You give shelter to my enemies, Tobias. Send them out, so that I may kill them."

Craigson's chin lifted. "You're mistaken, old friend. I have visitors, white visitors, but they are certainly not your enemies."

"They killed my son! My heart cries out for vengeance! For justice!"

"They have told me of this. They told me that the only warriors of yours they killed were in battle when you attacked them, in defense of their own lives."

"They have told you lies! Why would you believe them?"

"Because they have brought my granddaughter, my own flesh and blood, to me."

Spotted Dog took a breath and leaned back a little. Clearly, he hadn't expected to hear that.

"The girl with hair like dark flame," the war chief said. "I saw her during the battle. She is your blood?"

"She is," Craigson said.

A shrewd look appeared on Spotted Dog's face. "Is she touched by the spirits as well?"

Preacher and Jamie were listening unseen in the thick shadows just inside the doorway. Preacher whispered, "Tobias is smart enough not to pass that up."

Craigson said, "She is touched by the same spirits as myself, who have given her the same message they gave me, that a great treasure can be found here."

Spotted Dog made a slashing motion with his hand and sneered. "There is no treasure here."

"I reckon that depends on what's important to you."

"What is important to me is my honor and the blood debt I am owed by the white men in your house."

Craigson shook his head. "Those were different white men, I'm telling you."

"Different white men," Spotted Dog scoffed. "What different white men?"

That was when gunfire erupted from the top of the mesa trail.

Several of the Comanche warriors cried out in pain and toppled off their suddenly skittish ponies. Others managed to stay mounted, but bullets ripped through them as well.

Spotted Dog grunted and sagged forward. As the war chief fell, Craigson dropped the torch and leaped forward. He was there to catch Spotted Dog.

"A trap!" Spotted Dog cried in a voice strained from the pain of his wound. "Kill them all!"

"This is not our doing!" Craigson told him. "I don't know—"

He stumbled as he tried to get Spotted Dog to the entrance, away from the bullets that were whipping around them. But he managed to stay on his feet as Jamie hurried out and grasped Spotted Dog's other arm.

"Let me give you a hand."

"You!" Spotted Dog gasped as he caught sight of Jamie's rugged face. "My enemy!"

Blood was welling from the hole in his shoulder, though, and he was already too weak to do anything about his mistaken assumption.

"Right now, I'm one of the fellas trying to save your life," Jamie told him.

Preacher was out in front of the house, too, with his rifle at his shoulder. The weapon boomed, but since the mountain man was simply aiming at muzzle flashes in the night, he couldn't tell if his shot hit anything. He lowered the rifle and called in the Comanche tongue, "Get inside! Get inside!"

Hearing the command in their own language must have made the surviving warriors think that Spotted Dog had given it. They leaped off their ponies and ran through the big front entrance carrying their bows. There was only a handful of them. The others were either dead or mortally wounded. The unexpected ambush had taken a deadly toll on the Comanches.

Preacher waited until Jamie, Craigson, Spotted Dog, and the others were inside before he pulled the heavy door closed. As he did, he heard bullets thud against the other side of the panel.

He waved Jamie on. "Tend to the chief. I'll guard the door."

Jamie helped Craigson half drag, half carry Spotted Dog to the courtyard. Hannah and Saunders were still there, as was Evening Star. The Comanche woman let out a shocked exclamation when she saw the wounded war chief.

Then, in a calm voice, showing that she was level-headed in an emergency, she said, "Get him onto the table."

Spotted Dog was barely conscious now as they lifted him onto the table, but he was still aware enough to reach up with his good hand and grasp Jamie's arm.

"Why . . . why would you . . . help me . . . when I want to kill you?"

"I told you; we didn't have anything to do with your son dying. We fought back when you attacked us, that's all."

Spotted Dog's eyes rolled up in their sockets and his head fell back. He was still breathing. His bare, bronzed chest rose and fell steadily. But unconsciousness had claimed him.

An alarmed shout came from Philip Saunders. "Indians!" he cried. "The Indians have gotten in!"

He jerked his pistol from its holster, but before he could raise it, Walt Reynolds was at his side, gripping his arm and forcing it down.

"Stop that," the young saddle tramp said. "Those Indians aren't our enemies right now."

As a matter of fact, three of the five Comanche warriors who hadn't been gunned down in the ambush were wounded and didn't appear to be a threat to anyone. The other two stood guard over their countrymen, bows drawn and arrows nocked, even though they were outnumbered by the group of white men clustered on the other side of the courtyard.

Jamie swung away from the table where the unconscious Spotted Dog lay and raised his voice. "Everybody, listen to me. Somebody just attacked these Comanches, and I figure it must be whoever's been trailing us. I don't know who they are, but they gunned down half a dozen men just now in cold blood. So you fellas need to stop worrying about the Comanches for now. We have bigger problems."

"Yeah, and I reckon I know who it is," Preacher said from the arched entrance where the passageway opened into the courtyard. "I could hear somebody yellin' outside. Yellin' your name, Jamie. And unless I miss my guess, it sure sounded like that blasted Otis Lynch."

CHAPTER 47

"Lynch!" Jamie exclaimed. "What the devil! I thought we were through with that monster."

"Seems like he ain't through with us," Preacher drawled. "You say he's calling for me?"

"Yeah. Says he wants to talk to you."

Tobias Craigson stepped up beside Jamie and asked, "Who is this fellow Lynch?"

"Varmint we had a run-in with back in Fort Worth," Jamie answered curtly. "And then later on the trail." He saw that Craigson was holding himself rather stiffly and remembered thinking briefly during the flurry of gunfire outside that the old-timer might have been hit. "Are you all right?"

"Fine, fine," Craigson said with a wave of his hand. Jamie didn't see any blood on the man's clothes, so he figured he'd take Craigson's word for it, for the time being. "Is it possible he's the one responsible for the death of Spotted Dog's son?"

"I'd say that's more than likely true. Judging by that ambush, he's got a good-sized group of men with him."

Craigson nodded slowly. "There's a good chance Spotted Dog would have attacked them, if he knew they were passing through Comanche territory. I think we may have solved this mystery."

"For what good it does us," Preacher put in. "We're still holed up in here with a bunch of fellas outside who want to kill us."

"I'll talk to Lynch," Jamie said. "See if I can find out what he wants."

He walked up the passage to the front door and eased it open a few inches. Through the gap, he heard a deep, booming, and all too familiar voice.

"MacCallister! Jamie MacCallister! Come outta there, you gutless—"

The shout degenerated into a slew of obscenities.

Jamie's commanding voice cut through the stream of filth. "Otis Lynch!"

Jamie couldn't see the giant or the men with him. They were hidden somewhere around the edge of the mesa, positioned to pour lead at the house any time they wanted. Jamie was ready to slam the door, just in case a storm of bullets flew at him.

Instead, what he heard was a roll of laughter, followed by, "So you are in there, MacCallister. I wasn't sure where else you could be, but it's nice to know I've finally caught up to you."

"What do you want, Lynch?"

"I want you dead, of course. You and Preacher. You set that *animal* on me back in Fort Worth. You humiliated me in front of my friends. You've got to pay for that."

Jamie frowned in surprise, even though no one was there to see it. He said, "You killed good men, chased us halfway across Texas into the heart of Comancheria, just because you got scared of a *dog?*"

Lynch's voice shook with fury now instead of the bantering tone from a moment earlier. "It's not right that a man would unleash a beast on another man. It's just not right!"

Preacher had slipped up behind Jamie so he could hear. He said quietly, "Somethin' ain't right, and it's whatever's between that demented varmint's ears. He's crazy as a coon that's been in the sour mash, Jamie."

"Yeah, I know," Jamie said. "But he's got the upper hand right now. Or at least he thinks he does." He turned to face the opening again and called, "You've got to have some demands for ending this standoff, Lynch. Let's hear them."

"This is no standoff, MacCallister. This is a siege! There's only one way down off this mesa, and my friends and I control it. We can sit right here and let all of you starve to death if we want to."

"That'll take a long time."

"I got nowhere else to be."

Preacher said, "With that spring behind the house, we won't run out of water. But I don't know how much food Tobias has on hand. Not enough to feed a big bunch for very long, I'd wager."

"Probably not," Jamie agreed. "But it's open ground between here and the edge. We can't charge them."

From outside, Lynch shouted, "But not everybody has to die! You come out here, MacCallister. You and Preacher. I got no grudge against anybody else."

Jamie knew that he and Preacher were never going to agree to surrender to Lynch, but he called back, "You'll let the others go if we do that?"

"Well . . . you got to bring two things with you. That redheaded girl . . . and Bowie's treasure!"

Preacher let out a soft sound of surprise. "How in blazes does he know about the treasure? We didn't say nothin' about it back in Fort Worth, and we sure ain't talked to that varmint since."

Jamie shook his head. Leaning closer to the gap in the doorway, he shouted, "There's no treasure! And you can't have Miss Craigson."

A new voice bellowed, "Don't lie, MacCallister! We know all about the treasure! We know you came out here to get it!"

"Who's that?" Preacher asked. "Voice is sorta familiar, but I can't place it."

"Same here," Jamie said. Through the gap, he asked, "Who are you?"

"Sergeant Angus McKittredge, US Army." A harsh laugh. "Retired."

"Well, if that don't beat all," Preacher said. "We know Lynch only had two men still with him after that fight where we licked him. He had to round up more men somewhere else."

"If that big bruiser of a sergeant is here, he must've deserted. He could have brought some men with him."

"And they threw in with Lynch somehow," Preacher guessed, "or Lynch threw in with them. Either way, they're all against us now." The mountain man did some calculating. "Based on the shootin' durin' that ambush, Lynch and McKittredge don't have any more men than we do. Fact is, we probably outnumber 'em by a mite."

"But we're bottled up in here with nowhere to go."

"That's not strictly true," Tobias Craigson said. The old-timer had come up behind them and had been listening. "There *is* another way out. Not for all of us, but a few men could make it if they were willing to risk it."

"And leave the others?" Jamie said. "Abandon your granddaughter to those men out there?"

"You ought to know better than that, Jamie. No, what I have in mind is what we might have been able to pull off at the Alamo all those years ago, if fate had been a little kinder to us."

"Some of the trail was already there, naturally formed," Craigson explained. He, Jamie, and Preacher were in a small room with a candle illuminating the table where Craigson was sketching on the wood with a piece of charcoal. He had drawn the mesa with a ragged line running horizontally across its face.

"I hacked the rest of it out of the sandstone," Craigson went on. "I know I said that when I settled here, I didn't care whether the Comanches killed me, but I guess some instinct didn't go along with that completely. Because I figured it might not be a bad idea to have another way out besides the main trail." He tapped the table with the charcoal. "This is it."

"So we can go out a back window and Lynch can't see us," Jamie said, "climb down to this makeshift trail of yours on the far side of the mesa, and then follow it back around to the main trail?"

Craigson nodded. "That's right."

"Then why couldn't we use it to get everybody out of here?" Preacher asked.

"Spotted Dog and some of his men are wounded too badly for that," Craigson said. "I won't leave them behind. Besides, this path is too dangerous for Hannah, especially in the dark. Not only that, while a handful of good men might make it without causing enough noise to alert Lynch and McKittredge, I don't believe the whole bunch could." His voice held a grim note as he added, "If they knew we were there, we'd be sitting ducks for them."

Jamie moved his finger along the route that Craigson had sketched in charcoal. "So six men, say, go this way, then head up the main trail and jump Lynch's bunch. At the same time, the men left in the house charge out and attack from the front."

"It might have worked at the Alamo. It might work here. I'm in no mood to be starved out of my own home."

"And I ain't much for sittin' and waitin', neither," Preacher said.

Jamie nodded. "It's worth a try. Who's going?"

"I'll need to," Craigson said. "I know where the trail is. I can lead the others over it."

"Sounds like my kind o' chore," Preacher said.

"And mine. We'll leave Pete Barnes in charge in here. He's a good, steady man who'll follow orders." Jamie scratched his jaw and then went on, "Walt Reynolds and his pard Tankersley. They've handled themselves well so far."

"That's five. That might be enough."

Jamie nodded. "Let's go tell the others."

Earlier, Jamie had told Otis Lynch and Angus McKittredge to wait while he and the rest of the group discussed their demands. Now, as they rejoined the others gathered in the courtyard, Reynolds said, "Lynch is hollering quite a bit again, Mr. MacCallister. I think he's getting impatient."

"He's going to have to wait a little while longer to get what's coming to him," Jamie said.

"But what he's gonna get ain't what he's hopin' for," Preacher added.

Quickly and efficiently, Jamie laid out the plan. The men perked up considerably as soon as they realized that they might not be in for a long, nerve-racking siege after all. Fighting back was possible. For frontiersmen, fighting was almost always preferable to waiting.

When Jamie had explained things, he said to Reynolds, "Walt, we'd like for you and Ox to come with us, if you're up to it."

Tankersley answered first. "We're more than up to it," he rumbled. "I want another shot at that varmint Lynch."

"I can't promise you that, but there'll be plenty of action, I expect."

Reynolds nodded. "Sounds good to me."

"I'm going, too."

That declaration made Jamie look around. Philip Saunders had stepped forward. He glared at Jamie and went on, "I'm going, and you can't stop me."

"Didn't say I was going to try to," Jamie replied.

Hannah moved up beside Saunders, though, and said, "Philip, you don't have to do this. You should leave this to men who are better suited to—"

"Better suited to do what? Fight? I can fight . . . white men." Saunders glanced toward the Comanches on the other side of the courtyard. "I just don't like having anything to do with savages."

"You can come along, Saunders," Jamie said. "But nobody will be looking out for you."

"You won't have to. I'll be fine."

Jamie wasn't completely convinced of that, but he knew there was some truth to what Saunders said. The man didn't lack for courage except in certain situations. Facing outlaws and army deserters, he might be all right.

"When are we doing this?" Saunders asked.

"Right now. No point in waiting."

"I'd like to talk to Hannah for a moment first. In private." Saunders looked at her. "If that's all right with her."

She hesitated, then nodded and said, "All right. Whatever you have to say, Philip, I'll listen."

Jamie didn't know whether that was a good idea or not, but it wasn't his place to step in, he decided. Hannah and Saunders retreated into one of the rooms off the courtyard. While they were gone, the men checked their weapons and made sure they were fully loaded.

When Hannah and Saunders returned to the courtyard, she looked shaken but still composed. Saunders put a hand on her arm and kissed her cheek. She didn't pull away, but she didn't return any gestures of affection, either.

Saunders strode over to Jamie, Preacher, Craigson, Reynolds, and Tankersley. He smiled and said, "Just thought it would be a good idea to end things officially with Hannah. I'm afraid I won't be marrying your granddaughter after all, Mr. Craigson. I've called off our engagement."

"Well . . . that was for you young folks to work out, I suppose. Right now, I'm more concerned about getting us out of this trap we're in."

"That's what we're fixin' to do," Preacher said. "Come on."

CHAPTER 48

Jamie clung tightly to a small knob jutting out from the sandstone and wondered if Ox Tankersley was having as much trouble hanging on as he was. Big fellows like them weren't exactly made for crawling along the side of a mesa like spiders.

He couldn't look back to his left to see how Ox was doing, though. He had to concentrate on the handholds and footholds he was using to follow Tobias Craigson along this precarious path fifty feet above the ground.

Craigson had gone first to show the way. The climb down from the top of the mesa had been easy enough, just a matter of the men working their way down a steep but manageable crack in the side of the formation. Once they were on what passed for a trail, though, it became much more difficult.

Jamie was second in line, watching carefully in the moonlight so that he could put his feet in the same places Craigson did and grip all the same handholds once the old-timer had moved on. Walt Reynolds came next, followed by Ox and then Philip Saunders. Preacher brought up the rear.

Dog had wanted to come with his old friend and had whined at being left behind, but Preacher had told him to come with Pete Barnes when the fight started. The big cur would be in on the action before the night was over, Preacher promised.

Time seemed to drag, but Jamie could tell by the motion of the moon and stars that the night was slipping past. Everything was quiet on top of the mesa, which in this case was good news, he supposed. Lynch, McKittredge, and their men seemed to have settled down to wait out their quarry.

The distance they had to travel wasn't actually that far, but the caution they had to use made it take quite a while. Every ordeal had an end, however, and at last Craigson reached a spot about ten feet above the wide ledge that served as the main trail. He lowered himself, hung from his hands for a second, and then dropped the rest of the way, landing without making much of a noise. Jamie and the others followed suit.

They had made it this far without any mishaps, Jamie thought. He was going to take that as a good omen.

Gunmetal whispered on leather as the men drew their revolvers and crept upward.

A short distance below the spot where the trail led out onto the mesa, Lynch's men had built a small fire in an open area where the path began to spread out. A couple of men hunkered beside the flames. Two more stood at the top, keeping an eye on the house. None of them were Lynch or McKittredge, Jamie noted; they weren't big enough. The two ringleaders had to be among the men who had spread their bedrolls near the fire to sleep.

Jamie heard horses blowing and stomping down below. The men were keeping their mounts on level ground. There was no good place to keep them up here where they would be out of sight of the defenders at the house, which would expose them to rifle fire.

Looked like a dozen men here in camp. So the odds starting out would be two-to-one against Jamie and his companions. But when Pete Barnes and the other men joined in the fray, that would tip the odds in their favor.

Walt Reynolds eased up beside Jamie and whispered, "Are we just gonna shoot those fellas who are sleeping?"

"They wouldn't hesitate to do the same to you."

"I know, but it doesn't seem right somehow."

Preacher snorted quietly. Jamie knew the old mountain man's opinion on matters such as that, but he had to admit, he kind of leaned toward what Reynolds was saying. He'd kill a man in cold blood if it was necessary to accomplish a worthwhile objective . . . but if there was another way, Jamie was willing to give that a try, too.

Of course, with a lunatic like Otis Lynch involved, Jamie didn't believe that a peaceful resolution was even remotely possible. Lynch wouldn't give up, any more than he would have spared the others in the house if Jamie and Preacher had surrendered.

"Have your guns ready," he told the others. "We'll give them a chance to surrender."

No one argued, but Preacher gave him a dubious look in the moonlight.

Jamie stepped forward, leveled the Walker Colt, and said in a loud, clear voice, "Throw down your guns and lift your hands!"

The two men beside the fire uncoiled like tightly wound springs. They came up with rifles in their hands spitting flame. Jamie heard the flat *whap!* of a bullet passing not far from his head, and then the Walker roared and bucked against his palm. One of the men flew back into the fire like he'd been slapped.

Preacher's Dragoons began their deadly chorus of gun thunder. The other four members of Jamie's party joined in as well. But the men who had followed Lynch and McKittredge here weren't going down without a fight, even the ones who'd had to claw up out of their blankets.

For a long moment, muzzle flashes lit the night brighter than day. The whipcrack of rifle shots and the duller boom of handguns going off hammered the ears. The air was thick with leaden messengers of death flying back and forth.

Then several members of Lynch's party broke and ran, darting onto the mesa. One of them was Otis Lynch himself, judging by the giant shadow he cast. Jamie knew that Lynch was fleeing directly into the teeth of the attack from the house, but he didn't care. He started after the giant.

Lynch wasn't the only one who wanted to settle a score.

Jamie had taken only a step when he heard a pained gasp behind him. He stopped and glanced over his shoulder to see Philip Saunders staggering. A dark stain was already spreading over the front of the man's white shirt.

Before Jamie could reach Saunders, Walt Reynolds was beside him, gripping his arm to hold him up. "Saunders!" Reynolds said. "How bad are you hit?"

The pistol slipped from Saunders's fingers and thudded to the ground at his feet. "Bad . . . enough," he forced out. "Tell Hannah . . . I didn't die . . . a coward—"

Then he collapsed. Reynolds lowered him gently to the trail. He looked up at Jamie and said, "I reckon he's gone."

"Sounds like it—" Jamie began, then Reynolds came up from the ground moving as fast as he'd ever seen the young man move. Reynolds's gun flashed up and blasted a shot past Jamie.

Jamie heard another shot, but when he turned, he saw that the second shot must have gone into the ground. Teddy Keller, the tall, bearded scarecrow of a man who had once ridden with Reynolds, Tankersley, and the others, had lowered his gun hand as he swayed back and forth.

"Dang it, Walt, you . . . you shot me," Keller said. "I thought we was . . . pards."

"I'm sorry, Teddy, but that was a long time ago."

The apology fell on deaf, dead ears. Keller toppled to the side like a falling tree and didn't move again.

Jamie looked around. He heard shooting and yelling up on the mesa, but the fight here was over. Preacher, Craigson, and Ox were gone, having pursued the fleeing men.

"We'd better get up there," Jamie said to Reynolds. "Sorry about your friend."

"He dealt the hand," Reynolds said.

That was true, but Jamie knew it still had to hurt to gun down a man who'd once been your partner. Now wasn't the time to think about that, though.

The two of them ran the rest of the way up the trail and came out onto the mesa. The shooting up here had just died away. Jamie spotted Preacher and Craigson and hurried over to them.

"You all right?" he asked the old mountain man.

"Yeah." Preacher sounded grim. "But Lynch and McKittredge got past Pete and his bunch. Pete thinks they made it to the house."

"That's where Miss Hannah is!" Reynolds exclaimed.

"And Evening Star," Craigson added. The strained tone of his voice told Jamie that Evening Star meant more to the old-timer than just being his cook and housekeeper.

Tankersley and Gil Barnes came up, supporting Pete between them. From the looks of him, Pete had caught a bullet in the leg, but he said, "I'm sorry, Mr. MacCallister. I never saw anybody as big as those two fellas who can move as fast—"

"That's all right, Pete," Jamie told him. "You did a good job cleaning up the rest. We'll take care of Lynch and McKittredge."

The four of them—Jamie, Preacher, Craigson, and Reynolds—walked deliberately toward the house, reloading their guns as they approached the dwelling that was so out of place here in the middle of Comanche territory.

Several figures emerged into the moonlight before they got there. Lynch and McKittredge were easy to identify because of their size. Each man held a struggling woman. Lynch's left arm was wrapped around Hannah, while McKittredge hung on tightly to Evening Star.

"You just back off now, MacCallister!" Lynch shouted. "We'll kill the girl and the squaw; I swear we will."

"Not even you're crazy enough to do that," Jamie said. "You know that if anything happens to those ladies, you'll be filled with a pound of lead about half a second later."

Lynch's face split in a grin under the bushy beard. "You want to bet the gal's life on that?" His grip on Hannah tightened enough to make her let out a soft cry of pain. "Or do you want to step aside and let Angus and me leave? We'll turn the women loose at the bottom of the trail. You got my word on that."

"We're no more threat to you, MacCallister," McKittredge said. "Just the two of us? We'll be doing good to make it out of Comancheria alive, and you know it."

Jamie did know that, but he didn't trust either of these men, especially Otis Lynch. McKittredge was brutal and driven by greed, but Lynch was downright crazy. He was perfectly capable of killing the two hostages just out of sheer meanness.

Before Jamie could say anything, someone else took a hand, or rather, a paw. Dog stalked out of the shadows toward Lynch, growling.

Lynch cried out in horror and backed away, coming up against the wall of the house next to the entrance.

"Keep that animal away from me!" he yelled. "Get it away!"

"Dog!" Preacher's voice was sharp and commanding. The big cur stopped where he was, teeth bared, the hair on his back standing up. He trembled slightly from his eagerness to tear into Lynch.

Jamie said, "It's over. Let the women go." He stepped closer.

With a sudden curse, McKittredge shoved his captive straight at Jamie. With Evening Star in the way, Jamie couldn't risk a shot, and neither could the others. Roaring defiance, McKittredge charged right after her and barreled into her and Jamie at the same time, knocking all three of them sprawling.

Jamie didn't know if Evening Star was hurt, but the impact of the collision jolted the gun out of his hand. McKittredge grabbed him, looped an arm around Jamie's neck, and started squeezing as he tried to choke the life out of his enemy.

Jamie rolled, taking McKittredge with him, and broke free. The two men came up on their knees at the same time, slugging away at each other. Jamie landed a couple of solid punches but took a couple, too.

A few yards away, the fight had distracted Lynch enough that Preacher snapped, "Now, Dog!" The big cur leaped, and Lynch was so terrified that he pushed Hannah away and started flailing at Dog instead, just as Preacher was betting that he would. Lynch tried to run, but Dog had him by the throat and bore him down to the ground.

Jamie hit McKittredge again, knocking the deserter on his back. McKittredge came up holding the Walker Jamie had dropped a moment earlier. Before he could raise the gun and fire it, a shot roared from somewhere else. McKittredge grunted and rocked back, then dropped the Colt and sagged to the ground again. Jamie looked over and saw powder smoke curling from the barrel of the gun Tobias Craigson held.

"He never should have threatened Evening Star," the old-timer said. His other arm was around the Comanche woman's shoulders. She appeared to be all right.

"I'm obliged to you," Jamie said as he climbed to his feet. Over by the wall of the house, Lynch was still thrashing around and screaming as Dog savaged him, but his cries and struggles were getting weaker. Jamie heard a squelching sound, followed by a last gurgling moan, and knew that Dog had torn out the giant's throat. The big cur backed off, blood dripping from his muzzle, as Lynch spasmed a couple of times and then lay still.

Walt Reynolds was holding Hannah. As Lynch died, she turned away and pressed her face against the young man's chest, shuddering.

"Reckon it's all over now, Miss Hannah," he told her, quietly. "You're all right. Nobody's going to hurt you." He paused, then said, "I've got a message for you, too. Saunders . . . Philip . . . he said to make sure you knew he didn't die a coward. And he sure didn't. He fought just fine."

That just made Hannah sob harder. Reynolds continued holding her, and Jamie figured that in time, the reaction would pass.

Maybe then there would be a chance for something better.

"Tobias!" The startled cry came from Evening Star. "Your side . . . There is blood—"

She lifted his serape, revealing the dark stain on his shirt. Craigson smiled and said, "Oh, that? It's nothing. Happened earlier, when Lynch and his bunch ambushed Spotted Dog. I wasn't going to let it stop me from doing what needed to be done. Now that you're safe . . ."

Craigson's knees buckled, and he started to go down. Evening Star clung to him desperately and cried for help.

CHAPTER 49

"He was . . . a gambler," Hannah said, clearly troubled by the truth she was revealing. "That was what he told me, there at the last before he left with the rest of you. He owed a great deal of money to men who had threatened to kill him. When he found out about Colonel Bowie's treasure, he thought that might be the answer for his problems. And if not . . . at least he would have a good start on running away from them."

"That's why he asked you to marry him?" Jamie said. "To get his hands on that gold and silver?"

Hannah nodded. "He'd been courting me before that, but he didn't ask for my hand in marriage until after I'd told him about my grandfather's letter and map. I should have realized what was going on, but I . . . I just didn't."

"Hard to think sometimes," Preacher said, "especially when you got your eyes full o' moonlight and stars."

Jamie grinned at him. "Why, Preacher, that sounded positively poetic."

"Comes from bein' around Audie and listenin' to him spout that there poetry around the campfire many a night, I reckon."

From the bed where he was propped up with bandages wrapped around his middle, Tobias Craigson said to Hannah, "I'm sorry, my dear. I wish things had worked out better for you."

Hannah shook her head. "I might have lost a prospective bridegroom, but I gained a grandfather." She reached over from the chair where she sat and clasped Craigson's right hand. Evening Star, sitting on the other side of the bed next to the old-timer, was already holding his left one.

It was long into the night, probably close to dawn, in fact, but no one had been to sleep yet. There had been too much work to do: patching up the wound in Craigson's side and the bullet hole in Pete Barnes's leg, gathering the bodies of the allies they had lost, including Philip Saunders, so they could be laid to rest, and tossing the corpses of their fallen enemies off the side of the mesa to be disposed of by scavengers.

As soon as the sun came up, Jamie knew, the buzzards would be circling and gradually swooping lower and lower . . .

"Will you come back home with me?" Hannah asked Craigson.

"What? This *is* my home now, sweetheart. After all these years out here in the middle of nowhere, I wouldn't be fit to live in civilization. Besides, I have everything I need here, for the time I have left." He smiled. "More treasure than Colonel Bowie ever could have hidden." The smile went away, replaced by a solemn frown. "But speaking of the colonel . . . you should take that letter and map and burn them, Hannah. Throw them in the fireplace.

They're nothing but monuments to how foolish and gullible a man can be."

"That's not true at all! They're reminders of how a man can hope and dream." Hannah shook her head. "I'll never throw them away. Someday I'll pass them down to my children as family heirlooms."

"I hope you do, darlin'. I hope you do."

Jamie knew that Walt Reynolds had already promised to make sure Hannah got back to St. Louis safely, and Ox Tankersley figured on going along to watch over both of them. He hoped the two young men could stay out of trouble. He had a hunch they would. Walt Reynolds had the look of a man ready to put his wild times behind him.

Preacher said, "There's still a little matter of us gettin' back out of Comancheria alive. There's a heap of wild country between here and Fort Worth."

"That will not be a problem," Evening Star said. "Spotted Dog knows now that you had nothing to do with the death of his son. He still hates you because you are white and because you killed some of his warriors in battle, but he says that by helping Tobias, you have earned the favor of the spirits. Before he and the others left, he promised me he will spread the word throughout Comancheria that you are to be allowed to travel safely back to where you came from." She paused, then added sternly, "But you should never come back here."

"Not any time soon, I can promise you that," Jamie said.

Later, when Jamie and Preacher stepped out of the house and joined Dog, who was waiting patiently for them, the sun was about to peek over the eastern horizon. The sky was mighty pretty at this hour, Jamie thought.

Preacher said, "You know, ol' Tobias ain't got a whole heap of time left, shot up like that. Don't hardly see how he kept goin' like he did without ever givin' a sign of it."

Jamie chuckled. "That's because he's a stubborn, leathery old coot like some others I could name."

"Yeah, I reckon so. We gonna wait here until he passes?"

"I think his granddaughter would like that. She can see him laid to rest, here at the home he made for himself, where he can watch the sun rise every morning like it's doing now." Jamie shrugged. "When you come right down to it, that's not a bad treasure for a man to find."

"No, I suppose it ain't."

The three of them stood there in quiet companionship for a moment, then Preacher said, "Jamie, are we gettin' too old to go gallivantin' around all over the country, havin' adventures and gettin' shot at? That's got to end somctime. I mean, a fella can't just live his whole life doin' that, can he?"

"I don't know, Preacher." Jamie grinned and clapped a hand on his old friend's shoulder. "But I reckon you and I still have one or two more adventures left in us!"

CHAPTER 1

"Becky, another hungry customer just walked in," Lucy Tate said. "I'm getting some more coffee for my tables. Can you wait on him? He looks like trouble." She looked at Beulah Walsh and winked, so Beulah knew she was up to some mischief.

"I was just fixing to wash up some more cups," Becky said. "We're about to run out of clean ones. Can he wait a minute?"

"I don't know," Lucy answered. "He looks like he's the impatient kind. He might make a big scene if somebody doesn't wait on him pretty quick."

"I don't want to make a customer mad," Beulah said as she aimed a mischievous grin in Lucy's direction. "Maybe I can go get him seated."

"Oh, my goodness, no," Becky said. "I'll go take care of him." She was sure there was no reason why Lucy couldn't have taken care of a new customer, instead of causing Beulah to do it. Beulah was busy enough as cook and owner.

She dried her hands on a dish towel and hurried out into the hotel dining room. Lucy and Beulah hurried right after her as far as the door, where they stopped to watch Becky's reaction.

"Perley!" Becky exclaimed joyfully and ran to meet him. Surprised by her exuberance, he staggered a couple of steps when she locked her arms around his neck. "I thought you were never coming home," she said. "You didn't say you were gonna be gone so long."

"I didn't think I would be," Perley said. "We were just supposed to deliver a small herd of horses to a ranch near Texarkana, but we ran into some things we hadn't counted on, and that held us up pretty much. I got back as quick as I could. Sonny Rice went with Possum and me, and he ain't back yet." She started to ask why, but he said, "I'll tell you all about it, if you'll get me something to eat."

"Sit down, sweetie," she said, "and I'll go get you started." He looked around quickly to see if anyone had heard what she called him, but it was too late. He saw Lucy and Beulah grinning at him from the kitchen door. Becky led him to a table right outside the kitchen door and sat him down while she went to get his coffee. "I was just washing up some cups when you came in. I must have known I needed a nice clean cup for someone special."

He was both delighted and embarrassed over the attention she gave him. And he wanted to tell her he'd prefer that she didn't do it in public, but he was afraid he might hurt her feelings if he did. Unfortunately, Lucy and Beulah were not the only witnesses to Becky's show of affection for the man she had been not so secretly in love with for a couple of years. Finding it especially entertaining, two drifters on their way to Indian Territory across the Red River spoke up when Becky came back with Perley's coffee.

"Hey, darlin'," Rafer Samson called out, "bring that coffeepot out here. Sweetie ain't the only one that wants coffee. You'd share some of that coffee, wouldn't you, sweetie?"

"Dang, Rafer," his partner joined in. "You'd best watch what you're sayin'. Ol' Sweetie might not like you callin' him that. He might send that waitress over here to take care of you."

That was as far as they got before Lucy stepped in to put a stop to it. "Listen, fellows, why don't you give it a rest? Don't you like the way I've been taking care of you? We've got a fresh pot of coffee brewing on the stove right now. I'll make sure you get the first cups poured out of it, all right?"

"I swear," Rafer said. "Does he always let you women do the talkin' for him?"

"Listen, you two boneheads," Lucy warned, "I'm trying to save you from going too far with what you might think is fun. Don't force Perley Gates into something that you don't wanna be any part of."

"Ha!" Rafer barked. "Who'd you say? Pearly somethin'?"

"It doesn't matter," Lucy said, realizing she shouldn't have spoken Perley's name. "You two look old enough to know how to behave. Don't start any trouble. Just eat your dinner, and I'll see that you get fresh coffee as soon as it's ready."

But Rafer was sure he had touched a sensitive spot the women in the dining room held for the mild-looking young man. "What did she call him, Deke? Pearly somethin'?"

"Sounded like she said Pearly Gates," Deke answered. "I swear it did."

"Pearly Gates!" Rafer blurted loud enough for everyone

in the dining room to hear. "His mama named him Pearly Gates!"

Lucy made one more try. "All right, you've had your fun. He's got an unusual name. How about dropping it now, outta respect for the rest of the folks eating their dinner in here?"

"To hell with the rest of the folks in here," he responded, seeming to take offense. "I'll say what I damn well please. It ain't up to you, no how. If he don't like it, he knows where I'm settin'."

Lucy could see she was getting nowhere. "You keep it up, and you're liable to find out a secret that only the folks in Paris, Texas, know. And you ain't gonna like it."

"Thanks for the warnin', darlin'. I surely don't want to learn his secret. Now go get us some more coffee." As soon as she walked away, he called out, "Hey, tater, is your name Pearly Gates?"

Knowing he could ignore the two no longer, Perley answered. "That's right," he said. "I was named after my grandpa. Perley was his name. It sounds like the Pearly Gates up in Heaven, but it ain't spelt the same."

"Well, you gotta be some kinda sweet little girlie boy to walk around with a name like that," Rafer declared. "Ain't that right, Deke?"

"That's right, Rafer," Deke responded like a puppet. "A real man wouldn't have a name like that."

"I know you fellows are just havin' a little fun with my name, but I'd appreciate it if you'd stop now. I don't mind it all that much, but I think it upsets my fiancée."

Perley's request caused both his antagonists to pause for a moment. "It upsets his what?" Deke asked.

"I don't know," Rafer answered, "his fi-ant-cee, whatever that is. Maybe it's a fancy French word for his behind. We upset his behind." He turned to look at the few other customers in the dining room, none of whom would meet his eye. "We upset his fancy behind."

"I'm sorry, Becky," Perley said. "I sure didn't mean to cause all this trouble. Tell Beulah I'll leave, and they oughta calm down after I'm gone."

Beulah was standing just inside the kitchen door, about ready to put an end to the disturbance, and she heard what Perley said. "You'll do no such thing," she told him. "Lucy shouldn't have told 'em your name. You sit right there and let Becky get your dinner." She walked out of the kitchen then and went to the table by the front door where the customers deposited their firearms while they ate. She picked up the two gun belts that Rafer and Deke had left there, took them outside, and dropped them on the steps. When she came back inside, she went directly to their table and informed them. "I'm gonna have to ask you to leave now, since your mamas didn't teach you how to behave in public. I put your firearms outside the door. There won't be any charge for what you ate if you get up and go right now."

"The hell you say," Rafer replied. "We'll leave when we're good and ready."

"I can't have you upsettin' my other customers," Beulah said. "So do us all the courtesy of leaving peacefully, and like I said, I won't charge you nothin' for what you ate."

"You threw our guns out the door?" Deke responded in disbelief. He thought about what she said for only a moment, then grabbed his fork and started shoveling huge forkfuls of food into his mouth as fast as he could. He washed it all down with the remainder of his coffee, wiped his mouth with his sleeve, and belched loudly. "Let's go, Rafer."

"I ain't goin' nowhere till I'm ready, and I ain't ready right now," Rafer said, and remained seated at the table. "If you're through, go out there and get our guns offa them steps."

"Lucy," Beulah said, "Step in the hotel lobby and tell David we need the sheriff."

"Why, you ol' witch!" Rafer spat. "I oughta give you somethin' to call the sheriff about!" He stood up and pushed his chair back, knocking it over in the process.

That was as far as Perley could permit it to go. He got up and walked over to face Rafer. "You heard the lady," he said. "This is her place of business, and she don't want you and your friend in here. So why don't you two just go on out like she said, and there won't be any need to call the sheriff up here."

Rafer looked at him in total disbelief. Then a sly smile spread slowly across his face. "Why don't you go outside with me?"

"What for?" Perley asked, even though he knew full well the reason for the invitation.

"Oh, I don't know. Just to see what happens, I reckon." Finding a game that amused him now, he continued. "Do you wear a gun, Perley?"

"I've got a gun on the table with the others," Perley answered. "I don't wear it in here."

"Are you fast with that gun?" When Perley reacted as if he didn't understand, Rafer said, "When you draw it outta your holster, can you draw it real fast?" Because of Perley's general air of innocence, Rafer assumed he was slow of wit as well.

"Yes," Perley answered honestly, "but I would only do so in an emergency."

"That's good," Rafer said, "because this is an emergency. You wanna know what the emergency is? When I step outside and strap my gun on, if you ain't outside with me, I'm gonna come back inside and shoot this place to pieces. That's the emergency. You see, I don't cotton to nobody tellin' me to get outta here."

"All right," Perley said. "I understand why you're upset. I'll come outside with you, and we'll talk about this like reasonable men should."

"Two minutes!" Rafer blurted. "Then if you ain't outside, I'm comin' in after you." He walked out the door with Deke right behind him.

Becky rushed to Perley's side as he went to the table to get his gun belt. "Perley, don't go out there. You're not going to let that monster draw you into a gunfight, are you?"

"I really hope not," Perley told her. "I think maybe I can talk some sense into him and his friend. But I had to get him out of here. He was gettin' too abusive. Don't worry, I'll be all right. He oughta be easier to talk to when he doesn't have an audience."

He strapped his Colt .44 on and walked outside to find Rafer and Deke waiting. Seeing the expressions of gleeful anticipation on both faces, Perley could not help a feeling of uncertainty. If he had looked behind him, he would have seen everyone in the dining room gathered at the two windows on that side of the building, that is, everyone except Becky and Beulah. All of the spectators were confident of the unassuming young man's gift of speed with a handgun. As far as Perley was concerned, his lightning-fast reactions were just that, a gift. For he never practiced with a weapon, and he honestly had no idea why his brain and body just reacted with no conscious direction from himself. Because of that, he believed it could just as easily leave him with no warning. And that was one reason why he always tried to avoid pistol duels whenever possible. He took a deep breath and hoped for the best.

"I gotta admit, I had my doubts if you had the guts to

walk out that door," Rafer said when Perley came toward them. In an aside to Deke, he said, "If this sucker beats me, shoot him." Deke nodded.

"Why do you wanna shoot me?" Perley asked him. "You've never seen me before today. I've done you no wrong. It doesn't make any sense for you and me to try to kill each other."

"The hell you ain't done me no wrong," Rafer responded. "You walked up to my table and told me to get outta there. I don't take that from any man."

"If you're honest with yourself, you have to admit that you started all the trouble when you started makin' fun of my name. I was willin' to call that just some innocent fun, and I still am. So, we could just forget this whole idea to shoot each other and get on with the things that matter. And that's just to get along with strangers on a courteous basis. I'm willing to forget the whole trouble if you are. Whaddaya say? It's not worth shootin' somebody over."

"I swear, the more I hear comin' outta your mouth, the more I feel like I gotta puke. I think I'll shoot you just like I'd shoot a dog that's gone crazy. One thing I can't stand is a man too yellow to stand up for himself. I'm gonna count to three, and you'd better be ready to draw your weapon when I say three 'cause I'm gonna cut you down."

"This doesn't make any sense at all," Perley said. "I don't have any reason to kill you."

"One!" Rafer counted.

"Don't do this," Perley pleaded and turned to walk away.

"Two!" Rafer counted.

"I'm warnin' you, don't say three."

"Three!" Rafer exclaimed defiantly, his six-gun already halfway out when he said it, and he staggered backward from the impact of the bullet in his chest. Deke, shocked by Perley's instant response, was a second slow in reacting and dropped his weapon when Perley's second shot caught him in his right shoulder. He stood, helplessly waiting for Perley's fatal shot, and almost sinking to his knees when Perley released the hammer and returned his pistol to his holster.

"There wasn't any sense to that," Perley said. "Your friend is dead because of that foolishness, and you better go see Bill Simmons about your shoulder. He's the barber, but he also does some doctorin'. We ain't got a doctor in town yet. You'd best just stand there for a minute, though, 'cause I see the sheriff runnin' this way." Deke remained where he was, his eyes still glazed with the shock of seeing Rafer cut down so swiftly. Perley walked over and picked up Deke's gun, broke the cylinder open, and extracted all the cartridges. Then he dropped it into Deke's holster.

"Perley," Paul McQueen called out as he approached. "What's the trouble? Who's that?" he asked, pointing to the body on the ground, before giving Perley time to answer his first question.

"I think I heard his friend call him Rafer," Perley said. "Is that right?" he asked Deke.

Deke nodded, then said, "Rafer Samson."

"Rafer Samson," McQueen repeated. "I'll see if I've got any paper on him, but I expect you could save me the trouble," he said to Deke. "What's your name?"

"Deke Johnson," he replied. "You ain't got no paper on me. Me and Rafer was just passin' through on the way to the Red."

"I don't expect I do," McQueen said, "at least by that name, anyway. You were just passin' through, and figured you might as well cause a little trouble while you were at it, right?" He knew without having to ask that Perley didn't cause the trouble. "How bad's that shoulder?"

Deke nodded toward Perley. “He put a bullet in it.”

“You musta gone to a helluva lot of trouble to get him to do that,” the sheriff remarked. “Perley, you wanna file any charges on him?” Perley said that he did not. “All right,” McQueen continued. “I won’t lock you up, and we can go see Bill Simmons about that shoulder. Bill’s a barber, but he also does some doctorin’, and he’s our undertaker, too. He’s doctored a lotta gunshots, so he’ll fix you up so you can ride. Then I want you out of town. Is that understood?”

“Yessir,” Deke replied humbly.

“Perley, you gonna be in town a little while?” McQueen asked. When Perley said that he was, McQueen told him he’d like to hear the whole story of the incident. “I’ll tell Bill to send Bill Jr. to pick up Mr. Samson.” He looked around him as several spectators from down the street started coming to gawk at the body. “You mind stayin’ here a while to watch that body till Bill Jr. gets here with his cart?”

“Reckon not,” Perley said.

Bill Jr. responded pretty quickly, so it was only a few minutes before Perley saw him come out of the alley beside the barbershop, pushing his handcart. Perley helped him lift Rafer’s body up on the cart. “Sheriff said he called you out,” Bill Jr. said. “They don’t never learn, do they?” Perley wasn’t sure how to answer that, so he didn’t.

CHAPTER 2

When he turned back toward the dining room again, he saw the folks inside still crowded up at the two small windows on that wall, and he thought maybe he'd just skip his dinner. But then he saw Becky standing in the open door, waiting for him to return. He truly hated for her to have seen the shooting. The incident she just witnessed was the kind of thing that happened to him quite frequently. There was no reason for it that he could explain. It was just something that had been attached to him at birth. The same as his natural reaction with a handgun, he supposed. He often wondered if when the Lord branded him with the cow pie stigma, He thought it only fair to also grant him lightning-fast reactions. He had his brother, John, to thank for the saying, "If there wasn't but one cow pie in the whole state of Texas, Perley would accidentally step in it."

Becky broke into his fit of melancholy then when she became impatient and stepped outside the door. "Perley, come on in here and eat your dinner. It's almost time to clean up the kitchen." He reluctantly responded to her call.

Inside, he kept his eyes focused on the space between Becky's shoulder blades, avoiding the open stares of the customers as he followed her to the table by the kitchen door. "Sit down," Becky said, "and I'll fix you a plate." She picked up his coffee cup. "I'll dump this and get you some fresh."

When he finally looked up from the table, it was to catch Edgar Welch's gaze focused upon him. The postmaster nodded and calmly said, "Attaboy, Perley." His remark caused a polite round of applause from most of the other tables. Instead of feeling heroic, Perley was mortified. He had just killed a man. It was certainly not his first, but it was something he was most definitely not proud of.

Becky returned from the kitchen with a heaping plate of food. She was followed by Beulah, who came to thank him for taking the trouble outside her dining room. "There ain't no tellin' how many of my customers mighta got shot if you hadn't gone out there with him. He was gonna come back in here if you hadn't. There certainly ain't gonna be no charge for your dinner. Becky, take good care of him."

"I will," Becky said and sat down at the table with him. She watched him eat for a few minutes after Beulah went back into the kitchen before she asked a question. "Before all that trouble started, when you first came in, you said you came by to tell me something. Do you remember what it was?"

"Yeah," he answered. "I came to tell you I've gotta take a little trip for a few days."

"Perley," she fussed, "you just got back from Texarkana. Where do you have to go now?"

"Rubin wants me to take a contract he signed down to a ranch somewhere south of Sulphur Springs. It's for fifty head of Hereford cattle. Him and John have been talkin' about crossbreedin' 'em with our Texas longhorns to see if they can breed a better meat cow."

"Why can't one of them go?" Becky asked.

"John and Rubin both work pretty hard to run the cattle operation for the Triple-G. I never cared much for workin' on the ranch, and there wasn't anything tyin' me down here, till I found you. So, I have always been the one to do things like takin' this contract, and takin' those horses to Texarkana." He saw the look of disappointment on her face, so he was quick to say that there would surely be a change in his part of running the Triple-G after they were married. Judging by her expression, he wasn't sure she believed him. Their discussion was interrupted at that point when Paul McQueen walked in the dining room. He came straight to their table.

"Mind if I sit down?" Paul asked.

"Not at all," Becky answered him. "I've got to get up from here and help Lucy and Beulah. Can I get you a cup of coffee?" She knew he had been in earlier to eat dinner.

"Yes, ma'am, I could use a cup of coffee," he said. When she left to fetch it, he said, "Bill's workin' on that fellow to get your bullet outta his shoulder. I asked him how it all happened, but I swear, he seemed to be confused about how it did happen. I asked him why he pulled his weapon, if it was just you and his partner in a shootout. He said he wasn't sure why he pulled it. Said maybe he thought you might shoot him and damned if you didn't. I don't think he really knows what happened, but I can pretty much guess. Anyway, I don't think you have to worry about him. I told him I wanted him outta town as soon as Bill's finished with him, and I think he's anxious to go. Bill Jr. was already back with the body before I left there."

"If you're wonderin' about that business at all, you've got plenty of eyewitnesses," Perley suggested. "Everybody you see sittin' in here now was at those two windows up front. So they can tell you better than I can. I'm a little bit like the one I shot. It happened so fast, I ain't sure I remember what happened."

"Don't get me wrong, Perley, I don't doubt you handled it any other way than you are about everything, fair and square. I just wanted the whole picture, in case the mayor asks me."

McQueen didn't have to wait long before he received the first eyewitness report. It came when Edgar Welch finished his dinner. Before leaving, he walked over to the table. "That was one helluva bit of shootin' you done today, Perley. Sheriff, you shoulda seen it." He then took them through the whole encounter. "Perley wasn't even facing that devil when he drew on him, and he still beat him."

"Maybe it ain't such a good idea to tell too many people about it, Edgar," McQueen said. "You might not be doin' Perley or the town any favors if we talk about how fast he is with that six-gun of his. We might have the kind of men showin' up in town that we don't wanna attract, like them two today."

"I see what you mean," Edgar said. "And I agree with you. We might have more drifters like those two showing up in town. Point well taken. Well, I'll be gettin' back to the post office."

The sheriff left soon after the postmaster, leaving Perley to finish up his dinner with a brief word here and there from Becky as she helped Lucy and Beulah clean up the dining room. He promised her that he would stay in town the entire day and eat supper there that night before going back to the Triple-G. She gave him a key to her room on the first floor of the hotel, right behind the kitchen, so he could wait for her to finish her chores. She would have a couple of hours before it was time to prepare the dining room for supper. He was concerned about Buck, so he took the bay gelding to the stable so he could take his saddle off and turn him loose in Walt Carver's corral.

He suspected that Possum was going to give him a goodly portion of grief for slipping out that morning without telling him where he was going. He was halfway serious when he wondered what he was going to do with Possum after he and Becky were married.

It was after two o'clock when Becky showed up at her room. They embraced briefly before she stepped away, apologizing for her sweaty condition, the result of just having cleaned up the kitchen. She seemed strangely distant, he thought, not like her usual lighthearted cheerfulness. "Maybe I ought to go on back to the ranch now," he suggested, "and let you get a little bit of rest before you have to go back to the dining room."

"I guess I'm just a little more tired than I thought," she said. "But I don't want to rush you off. I know you stayed in town because of me." She didn't want to tell him that the incident that took place right outside the dining room made a tremendous impact upon her. She had sought the council of Beulah Walsh, the closest person to a mother she had. Her own mother had passed seven years ago, leaving her father a widower living alone in Tyler. While they had worked cleaning up the kitchen, Beulah, and Lucy, too, had tried to help her understand the man she had fallen in love with.

"The thing that happened in the dining room today is not that unusual in Perley's life," Beulah had told her. "His skill with a firearm is a curse that he has to live with," she said. "To Perley's credit, he tries to avoid it, but it always finds him sooner or later. And like you saw today, even his name is a curse and an open invitation to a troublemaker. So you have to be prepared for that day when Perley's not the fastest gun."

"I know how you feel, honey," Lucy had suggested. "But why don't you wait to see if he's gonna be working full-time at the ranch before you marry him? The way it is now, him and Possum are gone who knows where most of the time. You said he's leaving tomorrow to go somewhere for a few days, and that ain't good for a marriage. You don't wanna spend your life wondering if your children's daddy is coming home or not."

Those words were still ringing in her mind now as she tried to sort out her true feelings, and she could see the confusion in Perley's eyes as they searched hers. This was the first time since she had met Perley that she wondered if she was about to make the wrong decision. In spite of her love for the man, she reluctantly decided that Lucy's advice might be best. "Perley," she finally managed to say, "you're leaving tomorrow to take that contract for the cows. Why don't we wait till you get back to talk about any plans we want to make? I must confess, that business today really got to me. And working in the kitchen afterward just seemed to drain all the energy I had. I hope you understand. I love you."

He didn't understand at all, but he said that he did. She seemed to be a Becky he had never met before. "That's a good idea," he said. "I'm gonna go now, so you can rest up before you have to go back to work tonight. We'll talk about everything when I get back. I love you, too." She stepped up to him and gave him another brief embrace, a fraction longer than the one she had greeted him with. He reached in his pocket and pulled out her door key. "Here," he said, "I don't reckon I'll be needin' this."

She stood in the door and watched him walk down the hallway to the back door. "Perley," she called after him, "be careful." He acknowledged with a wave of his hand.

"That last kiss felt more like a goodbye kiss," he told Buck as he followed the trail back to the Triple-G Ranch. "It sure didn't seem like Becky a-tall. I feel like I just got fired." Walt Carver was sure surprised when he showed up at the stable to get Buck. Perley gave him no reason for returning so soon, other than the simple fact that he changed his mind. Without pushing Buck, he arrived at the ranch in plenty of time to get supper at the cookshack, which was where he generally ate his meals. His eldest brother, Rubin, and his family lived in the original ranch headquarters. His other brother, John, had built a house for him and his family. Perley was welcome to eat at either house, but he found it more to his liking to eat with the cowhands at the cookshack. He always felt that he was imposing, even though he knew he was a favorite with his nephews and nieces. Since he had time, he decided to stop by the house and pick up the contract and the money for the Herefords from Rubin.

"Howdy, Perley," Link Drew greeted him when he rode up to the barn. Young Link had grown like a weed since Perley brought him home with him, after the brutal death of Link's mother and father in the little store they operated. Link was nine when he came to the Triple-G. Looking at him today, Perley couldn't remember if he'd had one or two birthdays since he had arrived. "You want me to take care of Buck for you?" Link asked.

"I think Buck would appreciate it," Perley replied. "If you'll do that, I'll run up and get something at the house, and I'll see you at supper." He climbed down out of the saddle and handed Link the reins. He hesitated half a minute to watch the boy lead the big bay gelding away before turning to walk up to the house. "Knock, knock," he called out as he walked in the kitchen door. In reality, the house was as much his home as it was Rubin's, but being practical, he didn't want to surprise anybody.

"Oh, hello, Perley," Lou Ann, Rubin's wife greeted him. "If you're lookin' for Rubin, he's in the study."

"Thank you, ma'am," Perley said and headed for the hallway door.

"You stayin' for supper?" Lou Ann asked. "You're welcome, you know."

"No, thank you just the same, Lou Ann. I'm just gonna pick up a paper and some money from Rubin, and I'll be outta your way." Just as Lou Ann said, he found Rubin at his desk in the study. "You got that contract and the money for those cattle?" Perley asked as he walked in.

"Thought you weren't comin' back till after supper," Rubin said as he opened a drawer and pulled out a big envelope. "What happened? Becky kick you out?" he joked. "When are you gonna bring her down here to officially meet the family?"

"I don't know," Perley answered. "Might be a while. There ain't no hurry."

"Well, you might be wise to take your time and be sure it's what you really want. You stayin' for supper?"

"Nope," Perley answered. "I just came to get this." He picked up the thick envelope and tested its weight. "You got a thousand dollars in here?"

"Plus a contract that Weber has to sign, sayin' he got the money," Rubin answered. "He wouldn't deal with anything but cash. Take Possum with you. That's a lot of money you're carrying."

Perley couldn't help chuckling when he thought of the

remote possibility of getting away without Possum. "I'll tell him you said to take him. That way, he'll feel like he has a right to complain if something doesn't suit him. We'll leave right after breakfast in the mornin'." He turned and headed for the door.

"You take care of yourself, Perley," Rubin called after him.

"I will," Perley replied and went out the front door in time to hear Ollie Dinkler banging on his iron triangle to announce supper was ready.

"Beans is ready, Perley," Ollie said when Perley walked on past him.

"Right," Perley replied. "I'll be right back, soon as I put this in the barn." He folded the thick envelope Rubin gave him, took it in the barn, and stuck it in his saddlebag. When he returned to the cookshack, he found Possum waiting for him.

"I thought you said you was gonna eat supper in town with Becky," Possum said. "What's wrong? And I know somethin' is, so tell me what happened."

"What makes you think somethin's wrong?" Perley asked. "She just had a hardworkin' day and I thought she could use a little rest. Besides, we gotta get an early start in the mornin', and I didn't wanna get back too late tonight."

"You stickin' with that story?" Possum asked.

"I reckon," Perley answered. "Let's eat while there's still some beans in the pot."

Possum followed him inside where Ollie was serving. "You think you can find that Weber Ranch?" he asked Perley.

"I expect so," Perley answered. "I wouldn't think it would be too hard." He paused to let that simmer a little while in Possum's brain until he saw him working up his argument for the wisdom of accompanying him. "Oh, and

Rubin said it might be a good idea to take you along." Possum sighed as he exhaled his argument.

"That brother of yours knows what's what," Possum said.

They carried their plates and a cup of coffee to the table and sat down across from Fred Farmer, who at forty-four was the oldest of the cowhands. Were it not for the fact that Perley's brother, John, filled the role as foreman, Fred would most likely have been the best candidate. "Did I hear Possum say you and him are ridin' down below Sulphur Springs in the mornin'?" Fred asked.

"That's a fact," Perley said. "So, it might be a little hard to keep things runnin' smooth without Possum and me," he joked.

"That's true," Fred came back. "'Course, you two are gone somewhere half the time, anyway, so we're kinda used to it. Besides, we picked up another man today."

"Is that right?" Perley asked. Fred nodded toward the door and Perley turned to look. "Well, I'll be . . ." he uttered when he saw Sonny Rice walk through the door. He looked at Possum. "Did you know?"

"Yeah, I was fixin' to tell you Sonny came back. I just ain't had a chance to," Possum said.

Sonny filled a plate and brought it and a cup of coffee to join them. Fred slid down the bench to make a place for the young man. "Howdy, Perley," Sonny greeted him.

"Sonny," Perley returned. "I swear, I never expected to see you again. Are you back for good, or just a visit?" The last time he saw Sonny was when they were on their way back from Texarkana. Sonny left him and Possum to escort pretty young Penny Denson and her brother to their farm on the Sulphur River.

"I'm back for good," Sonny answered. "You know there ain't no way I could ever be a farmer."

"The way the sparks were flyin' between you and that young girl, I thought love conquers all, even walkin' behind a plow," Perley commented. "She was hangin' on you like a new pair of curtains on the window."

"I reckon I thought so, too," Sonny confessed. "And things was lookin' pretty good there till the feller she's engaged to ran for the hills."

"Sonny, you're better off in the long run," Fred told him. "You'da missed all this good companionship you get at the Triple-G."

"The mistake you made was goin' back to that farm with her and her brother," Possum remarked. "If you was so danged struck by her, you shoulda just picked her up and run off with her."

"Now, there's some good advice," Perley declared sarcastically. "What would you do with a wife right now, any way. You're better off without the responsibility."

"I reckon that could apply to everybody settin' here," Possum said.

The remark was not lost on Perley. He knew it was aimed at him, and Possum wasn't buying the story he told him about coming back early to give Becky some rest.